Dedication

To Fin – my rock.

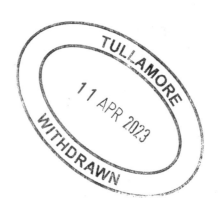

Prologue
The Brazzaville Protocol

Angolan Border July 1989

Dusk was approaching over the distant scrubland when Roy Young reported at the South African Defense Force Berayah military camp, situated along the Namibian-Angolan border. It wasn't hot and it wasn't cold. It was tepid. Across the camp's boundary a melodious, high-pitched hissing from competing crickets was overshadowed intermittently by *tu whoo* compilations from a group of resident spotted eagle owls, hidden deep inside the foliage. It was just like any other African bush land, Roy thought as he made his way through a warren of external corridors that spanned the building's perimeter. Although it may have sounded like any other African camp he had been to during his military tenure, he knew this would be the most important one.

The Berayah camp had housed a full brigade of up to 1,800 troops during the mid-1980s, when the Angolan Civil War was at its peak. Now in July 1989, it hosted fewer than three hundred people. The remaining troops were a select parachute infantry company with ground support troops, the balance of the residents mainly administration, community relations, and technical support staff.

The war was supposed to be over, but it wasn't. Roy knew it was never over until somebody surrendered, and nobody had surrendered yet. *Military Warfare 101.*

He knew nothing about the mission, only that he'd had to travel to this remote location without delay—as explained to him back at military headquarters in Pretoria. Yet he wasn't hesitant or fearful. If anything, he was unreservedly self-assured. It was in his DNA, and his training and experience had only reinforced it.

After completing the administrative check-in formalities, he traversed the final labyrinth of offices inside the camp's temporary building structure, guided by a junior liaison officer. The liaison pointed him down a final corridor occupied by several large offices—*the big brass quadrant,* Roy assumed.

The last office at the end was the biggest. Even the double doors were bigger. A brass plate on the left-hand side was embossed with the stenciled details, COLONEL JAN BREYTENBACH, COMMANDING OFFICER.

Roy knocked, heard a positive response from the other side, and pushed the door open. He stepped inside the room and saluted. The man behind the big desk eyed him, then rose. He stepped around his enormous, oak-clad workspace and studied Roy without greeting him. Roy froze in a position halfway into the office, like a mannequin on display in a shop window.

Respect, he contemplated.

Although Roy had completed his training three years earlier, he recalled the feedback he had received from his training unit leader before progressing to his first field assignment: "Roy, you are the most prominent talent to emerge from any recruit that I have seen in my entire career." Roy wondered if his training unit leader had passed the same comments on to the tanned, burly commander standing in front of him. He also pondered if Breytenbach was aware that Roy had spent the last three years on assignment in Mozambique following his graduation, leading a ground infantry company there and reaching the elevated position of captain.

If he did know, the colonel's facial expression gave nothing away. Roy waited, watching the man as he continued to study Roy's appearance.

A test, he assumed.

Roy was ready for the test. He was born ready.

Although only twenty-two years of age, Roy was already well developed physically. At six foot two and 190 pounds, there was no fat, just muscle. His chiseled face was highlighted with azure-blue eyes beneath dark, heavy eyebrows. Although he'd been born in the UK, his years in South Africa had earned him a sallow tone, allowing him to tan well—a useful attribute that complemented a military lifestyle. It also saved time and money on sunblock. His fair-haired mane had been chopped to generic army-issue number-one length. Whether in army khaki or in an Armani tuxedo, Roy looked complete and confident.

Eventually the colonel produced a relaxed smile. "Colonel Jan Breytenbach," he said, offering his hand.

Roy shook his hand. "Captain Roy Young."

"Make that Major Young."

I like this job. Accelerated career prospects, Roy thought. "Thank you, sir."

The commander guided Roy to an adjacent round table near the window. "Please, sit."

Breytenbach was a fit-looking fifty-four-year-old experienced campaigner—big round face, well-built, stocky, well over 200 pounds, with silver-black hair that was receding slightly, and a deep tan. His bio said he had served with two prior commanders before being elevated to his current senior field appointment of commanding officer, picking up a revered star along the way—a star he no doubt deserved, from all that Roy had heard. Although Roy had spent three years in Mozambique, working his way to captain, he had only spoken with his commanding officer there once. That was the way the hierarchy worked. And now he was sitting here—right in front of the colonel.

Breytenbach commenced briefing Roy on the history of enemy insurgency tactics, and the geographical preference, coverage, and skills of their aggressors—including the past and current pursuits of the Angolan Civil War. He also briefed Roy on the psychology of their role in being there. Given the diversity of nationalities and personalities involved Roy guessed the colonel was experienced enough to warrant an honorary degree in mitigation tactics for cross-cultural antagonism—and based on what Roy had seen, experienced, and read—war was about *egos*, and so-called *cross-cultural misunderstandings*—nothing else.

"Roy, we're going through the final phases of troop withdrawal right now," Breytenbach explained, "and you're being assigned to the Elite Commando Recce group—we call it 'Recce' here. Within this group we have two complementary units, the 44th Parachute Infantry Company and the 32nd Ground Support Team."

"How come we still have such extensive airborne and land-based troops, if we're supposed to be in final withdrawal phase?"

"Even though a peace accord has been signed, the combinations of competing groups to this day remain ubiquitous," Breytenbach replied without any defensive intonation in his response. "We still have the South West Africa People's Organization (SWAPO), the Popular Movement for the Liberation of Angola (MPLA), the National Front for the Liberation of Angola (FNLA), and then there's the Cubans. Not to mention the bands of Angolan deserters turned marauders, preying on their own indigenous people."

Roy moved in closer to the commander, his hands interlocked on the table. "So it's a matter of pride. No one wants to be seen to leave the place first?"

"It's a bit more than that, Roy." The colonel placed his right hand on top of a green file on the table and edged it in Roy's direction. "This is for you."

Roy glanced down at the file. The title, *Missing: Koevoet Operatives and Civilian Engineers,* was emblazoned across the front in black ink. He eyed Breytenbach again.

"Until recently, we maintained a covert Ranger unit called Koevoet," the colonel continued. "They were a light infantry counterinsurgency platoon, set up primarily to combat SWAPO rebels. The whole thing came to a head in the middle of last year. Prior to the protocol being signed, Cuba had considerably reinforced its troops in Angola, and came to the defense of the besieged Angolans. Our advance was stopped at the engagement in Cuito Cuanavale," he added somewhat defensively, almost admitting that his troops had been defeated.

Roy flipped open the file in front of him to see several documents neatly folded, separated, and referenced. He flicked through the first few dividers and pulled out an ordinance survey map titled *Calueque Region,* and opened it. He studied it briefly and then looked back up at the colonel. "What happened to the Koevoet platoon?"

"That was our biggest setback. It came in June last year, when out of nowhere the Cubans suddenly introduced a glut of MiG-23 fighters and a shitload more field troops." Breytenbach's tone became despondent. "If that wasn't bad enough, they used their expanded firepower and bombed the Calueque hydroelectric complex up in the north at Cuito." He leaned over and eyed the ordinance map, pointing at an area demarcated *Station Perimeter.* "That's a pretty strategic station that provides power for most of the surrounding regions." He tapped the coordinates that referenced the station's location. "In the air raid, they killed two Koevoet operatives and ten engineers from the hydroelectric station. Their bodies were never recovered."

"Where did the Cubans get the capital for the MiGs and the troops?"

"The Russians," the colonel pronounced. "With the death toll at Cuito, and the vulnerability we faced with a squadron of Cuban MiGs surrounding our every move, we were never going to finish the war. We had no choice but to agree to a peace accord. Our ground troops should have withdrawn from Angola in August last year before the negotiations were concluded," Breytenbach added, implying that the after-war antics could continue for some indefinite period as both sides persisted in an attempt to save face.

"So the US and the Russians are playing out the finale of the Cold War in our back yard, then?"

"You got it in one, Major."

"What about the Americans? What was their reaction when the MiGs showed up?"

Breytenbach rolled his eyes modestly. "It's the bloody CIA and their sedulous desire for Cold War success. As long as the Russians are still supporting the Cubans, they won't keep their paws out of this. They've even assigned a full-time field agent, based here to act as liaison with Langley."

Roy wrestled with the notion of why the world's most expansive intelligence agency was placing senior agents in a place like Berayah. *This place has nothing to offer, except maybe a good R&R cycle and probably better health insurance cover.* "What's his name?" Roy probed.

"Agent Clay Parker. He's supposedly an up-and-coming guy in the agency. A bit like yourself." Breytenbach chuckled.

Roy wondered why the colonel hadn't expanded on the most fundamental issue brought up so far, and he decided to ask directly. "Do you think they're still alive?"

"The crew from the power station?"

"Yes."

Breytenbach nodded slowly. "That's what I want you to find out, Roy. That's your mission."

Roy took a few more documents from the file and placed them around the desk, including several official reports with UN logos, seals, and stamps. There was also a set of elevation and plan drawings for the power station, and a list of infantry personnel and equipment. "Okay," he said, nodding. "Tell me more about what happened."

"I received a message three months ago from the UN-appointed representative handling the transition." Breytenbach drew closer to Roy, as if preparing to unveil some secret military theorem. He tapped on a second report—one of those Roy had removed. "It's completely unofficial, and no one else is aware, but he believes that the two missing Koevoet operatives and ten engineers may in fact be alive, held in captivity by a paramilitary Cuban group calling themselves Resistencia. Our Recce unit has one mission left—to find the Cuban Resistencia and investigate if these twelve men are still alive." The colonel's tone turned more prudent and lucid. "If they are, we need to get them out of there. We've searched for two and a half months and haven't found one iota of a clue."

Roy wondered why he was being exposed to such highly sensitive information. He knew from his training to be respectful, but also to engage assertively. This was how he had operated from the very beginning. After joining the defense forces, Roy had immediately been enrolled into the compulsory six-month training program at the Lohatlha military training institution in the Northern Cape. It was regarded as one of the most comprehensive training facilities around, covering almost 390 acres, with more than 2,000 students and 62 different military training programs. It wasn't WestPoint, but it was the best there was in Africa, probably the entire antipodal region. Roy guessed he was fortunate to be on the receiving end of that training. At Lohatlha he had learned a lot, inspired by the Latin motto that appeared throughout the combat center: *Si Vis Pacem Para Bellum*, translated, "If you want peace, prepare for war." Roy understood this. He had been privy to a few secrets back at base camp, too, but nothing on the level that Breytenbach was now unveiling.

"I understand the mission, Commander, and I'm excited about the challenge. I have just one question, if I may?"

"Yes, Major Young?"

"Where do I fit in?"

"I've been close friends with Louis Ferreira at Lohatlha for over twenty-seven years. I called him two days ago to say that I needed someone—

someone who excelled in reconnaissance, satellite, and radar—someone who has since gone on to show leadership and progression, elevating up the ranks since graduation. He could think of only one name—yours."

Good, so he did tell him.

"Roy, I want you to lead this mission." Breytenbach's eyes were firmly fixed on him, searching for a positive sign in his body language.

Roy didn't blink. He didn't move.

Roy had excelled in everything he had participated in at the training camp, including officer training—academic, practical, tactical, psychological, military, weaponry, and emotional. With his background, it felt like child's play. His Youth Cadet schooling, and his natural talent in military combat, had made him stand out from the others—significantly. Despite all of this, he knew Breytenbach was taking a big personal gamble here.

"Are you not concerned that I might be a bit young?" he responded.

Breytenbach shrugged. "Look at it this way: we've tried everybody else, and they've failed. We have nothing to lose. We're giving you an opportunity to show us what you're made of—in the real world, that is."

Roy nodded. "Thank you, sir." He grabbed the report authored by the UN representative and waved it gently in the air. "If these twelve people are still alive, I will do whatever I can to find them. I promise you that, sir. And I will bring them safely home to their families. Let me study this ordinance survey data for the area, and the station's elevation and plan drawings. I'll let you know if I have any questions."

"Anything else you need, I can arrange."

"When do I start?"

"Tomorrow morning. That okay?"

"Good. The sooner the better."

Roy spent the remainder of the evening back in his room, reviewing the ordinance survey reports and plans of the power station. With airborne and ground infantry troops at his service, he needed to come up with an efficient and tactical plan that would identify the location of the kidnapped victims—assuming, of course, that they were still alive.

~~~

The following morning at six sharp, Roy and the members of the Recce unit assembled at the central hanger reception. The mission to Cuito Cuanavale was about to begin. Roy turned to face Breytenbach, eying him curiously. "One question, sir, if I may?"

"Yes, Major?"

"Why would they still be keeping hostages after all this time, and not issue a ransom request?"

"Good question, major." Breytenbach shifted his weight and moved closer to Roy. "If they are alive, I can only imagine that it's a Russian tactic—perhaps the last bartering chip—and one they intend to play when they need it most."

"You mean as an instrument to lever their final negotiating position?"

"Exactly."

Roy nodded. "Well then, let's hope that's the way they're thinking."

Roy knew there and then that the task ahead was significantly more important than the lives of twelve people—if that wasn't enough pressure already. Success would probably mean a quicker end to an already extended Angolan Civil War, and would most definitely save lives. On the flip side, failure would be cause for substantial additional losses. If he understood Breytenbach correctly, this could even have an influence on the outcome of the Cold War.

With his mind still spinning Roy exited the briefing room and saw eight gleaming Aerospatiale Super Frelon heavy-lift military transport helicopters lined up in perfect parallel formation outside the maintenance and operations hangers, awaiting the Recce units. Around them, an enormous collection of intersecting linear shadows from the metallic composite rotor blades appeared across the entire width of the apron, collectively illuminated by the morning sun.

Roy shook his head in amazement. He knew these helicopters were prototypical for remote reconnaissance missions involving potential counterinsurgency combat, as he expected to encounter in Cuito. Each unit could accommodate up to thirty-eight equipped troops, including a crew of five, if required. For Cuito, each Frelon would be less than half full, but Roy needed eight units to implement his combined air and ground attack plan. Each Frelon also had surface search radar with a two-mile operating radius—plenty of capacity, along with bespoke 20mm cannons and four homing torpedoes hung under the starboard side of each fuselage—a V-20 model retrofit. If everything went according to plan today, he wouldn't need the extended firepower.

On the outside, Roy remained calm and in control, with a confident smile. On the inside, though, he was anxious. From his time at Youth Cadet, Roy had been a fast learner, and consequently he had learned a hell of a lot, drawing inspiration from this when he needed to. He needed that inspiration now. He recalled Reconnaissance Drill Days at Youth Cadet, which had taken place every Friday and put classroom learning to the test. One drill involved recovering concealed military materiel placed out in the wilderness by the fervent trainers who ran the drills. Roy had learned about the uses of ground radar surveillance, retrieving maps, and ordinances that would guide them to hidden locations. Even with the limited technology available at the school, his knowledge was enhanced enormously. In later years, as their training advanced, they had patrolled as troops and military intelligence specialists, setting up covert observation posts, which involved establishing army-issue tented Bivouacs for overnight reconnoiters. It was like hide-and-seek for big kids, with lots of techno-gadgets to help.

Now this was the real world.

Real Bivouacs.

Real radar surveillance technology.

Real Frelons.

Real hostages.

It was Real Reconnaissance Day.

Roy assembled his troops inside the number one hanger and went through a full briefing of his plan, lasting about twenty minutes. Breytenbach, who sat in on the session, nodded frequently. Roy assumed he approved.

After they finished, Roy met up with one of his captains, Leon Chamois. They had been at Youth Cadet military school together. Leon had been a few years ahead of Roy, but there was a bond. As a captain leading the first ground company, Leon boarded the same Frelon as Roy. The two sat beside one another along the side of the craft, facing a number of Leon's troops.

Roy pulled over his integrated lap-and-shoulder lanyard restraints, locking them into the central four-port clasp. "Steadfast and strong, Leon," he said to his captain on his right-hand side after a succession of clicks came to an end.

"I will follow you, my friend, wherever, whatever," Leon responded with a reverent gaze at Roy.

As the aircraft ascended, Roy's mind drifted, recalling the conversation from the night before with Breytenbach, on how the Ruacana attack had been pivotal in the perpetuation of Cold War sentiments. Although Roy wasn't aware of their exact relationship, he did know that at the center of the transition of power in Angola were two of the world's most iconic leaders: Ronald Reagan and Mikhail Gorbachev. He also knew that both superpowers were dogged by prolonged participation in a war that neither of them should have been involved in in the first place.

After hypothesizing, he plunged his head into one of the reports Breytenbach had given him.

When the summit of leaders, for the United States and the Soviet Union, was held in Moscow in May and June 1988, it was agreed that Cuban troops would be withdrawn from Angola, and the Soviet military aid would cease, just as soon as South Africa withdrew from Namibia. The New York Accords that followed to validate these decisions were concluded at the UN headquarters in December that same year. Following this, Cuba, South Africa, and the People's Republic of Angola agreed to a total Cuban troop withdrawal from Angola. This agreement, known as the Brazzaville Protocol, established the Joint

Monitoring Commission (JMC), with the United States and the Soviet Union as observers, to oversee implementation of the accords. At the same time, a tripartite agreement between Angola, Cuba, and South Africa was signed whereby South Africa agreed to hand control of Namibia to the United Nations.

Roy shook his head and looked up from the report with a sardonic smirk. *Quite a concoction of covenants to implement common sense,* he thought. At least his hypothesis was confirmed—on the one hand, an extension to the Cold War, on the other hand, a potential conclusion.

Roy returned his focus to his mission: Cuito Cuanavale, a small municipality in the Cuando Cubango province in Angola, covering an area of 22,000 square miles with an estimated population of 65,441. Roy had anticipated that the Ruacana power station would be heavily guarded, with well-equipped Angolan and Cuban troops.

He had a plan for that.

All eight Frelons made their final approach toward the Ruacana station, flying along the river Kunene at about 150 feet above sea level as they passed the town of Cuito Cuanavale. Roy looked down through the window plate hatch in the floor to see the downward thrust from the rotors initiating a surfing wave motion across the river's surface, causing the wandering and grey-headed albatrosses to disperse horizontally to the water's edge. One by one, they scurried across the river's banks, vanishing into the adjacent scrubland.

In his mind, he visualized the Angolan-Cuban opposition doing the same thing about half an hour from now.

Once the Frelons reached the river's discharge, the picturesque Ruacana Falls appeared below them. Roy glanced briefly at the natural wonder, before returning his gaze on his Recce squadron. Inside the Frelon all eyes were directed at the hydroelectric complex in the distance.

They had arrived.

Roy had read in one of the reports that Ruacana was the first power plant of its kind built in Angola, and that the landmark complex was critical in providing electricity to the adjacent areas across Angola's vast northern border. Following the Cuban air strike, the station was damaged and rendered inoperable. It was later partially repaired, and now operated on three out of its original six turbines, producing a maximum of 240 megawatts. In the Angolan War, it was a landmark site. After today, it would remain a landmark site—but for very different reasons.

"All stations, this is Major Roy Young," he announced over the radio. "Remember, we are entering an operating facility."

At three miles out, the engineer on board the lead craft turned to attract Roy's attention. An intermittent signal flashed on one of the computer screens in front of him, growing in intensity.

"Major, I'm picking up nearby electronic signatures on my on-board avionics," he said over the internal network channel.

"Probably Cuban Resistencia operating network-based communication hardware inside the station," Roy replied. "What's the frequency?"

"One hundred fifty-eight point six megahertz."

"VHF comms from plant operators, I'm guessing. Can you tune in?"

The engineer keyed in a frequency modulation routine. "They're talking about incremental turbine speeds, so looks like operators, all right."

"Picking up anything else?"

"No, that's it."

Roy knew it was time to engage the hearts and minds of his leadership cadre. "Okay, we split up into eight separate teams as planned. Four parachute teams and four ground assault teams. Each team of four to approach the power station at agreed entry points, just like we planned."

"Roger, Major," eight distinct voices responded as each captain in charge acknowledged the instructions.

Roy followed with the next sequence. "All four parachute teams move to a height of six hundred feet above sea level and proceed."

Exactly as per plan, each airborne team was dropped at a designated point along a two-mile radius, around the station: the designated safe range from a potential Cuba-Angolan mortar attack. The Frelons then traversed along the assigned two-mile radius until each one set down at agreed intervals, astride the airborne landing sites. Roy had planned for a complete border infiltration of the station site from 360 degrees. Leon led his ground team towards the rear of the station as instructed. The seven other captains took their designated posts as directed by Roy.

Each member of Roy's team was equipped with a significant catalogue of military materiel, the most notable component being an R4 assault rifle, which was standard issue for the SA forces in Angola. With a muzzle velocity of 2,700 feet per second and an effective range of up to 1,500 feet with sight adjustments, each with four replacement 35-round detachable box magazines, it was archetype for this reconnaissance mission. Roy couldn't have picked better.

As they approached the station's perimeter, Roy cradled his radio. "All teams to set R4 fire selectors to single-fire mode now," he said. "Remember munitions efficiency—this is a live plant." He eyed a group of six Resistencia in the distance. Roy estimated they were 750 feet away, well inside the R4 range. One minute the six were standing, moving around, and the next, as Roy's squadron aimed and fired, they weren't. Roy spotted two more Resistencia teams placed at the back of the station. He directed Leon and his counterpart, who led the second regiment at the rear entrance, for them to be taken.

Although it was the middle of winter, the air outside was hot and dry, maybe 79 degrees Fahrenheit Roy estimated. With the weight of the materiel, it seemed even warmer. When they entered the station, Roy immediately saw the central turbine hall straight ahead. Inside, with all that radiant heat from the turbo machinery, it felt even hotter—maybe another 4 degrees. It didn't matter. Each of Roy's units was hydrated and ready.

Around the station Roy could hear three out of the six turbine generators functioning, communally creating a harmonious Cervelat hum. Raising his hand in midair, Roy held two teams behind an imaginary line that he had marked out. Collectively, the Recce group crouched down next to an enormous cylindrical stainless steel fuel tank, adjacent to the turbines. At the west end of the hall, Roy spotted an elevated steel-structured mezzanine level with an operator center erected upon it. Roy felt confident. It was exactly as per the drawing. Everything was going according to plan, so far. Inside, he could see five civilians and two, maybe three Resistencia militias, given their attire. The operator station walls were fully glassed, allowing the plant operators full visibility of the complete turbine hall at all times. Roy knew from visiting industrial sites previously that this was standard procedure.

This was good and bad. Roy could see them, but unfortunately it gave the resident Resistencia full visibility of anyone approaching them, too. Roy had anticipated this, and on his command, a team of two Recces broke off and followed him up the underside of the steel stairwell, like Hollywood stuntmen off a *Spider-Man* set. When they reached the underside of the top grate, they traversed seamlessly to the station door and reassembled.

Roy craned his neck around the control room door and peered through the glass panel. Inside the mezzanine fishbowl, he saw operators carefully observing three panels of colorful screens, displaying the total power-generating capacity of the station. Roy could just about make out what each one said. Turbine one was running at 80 percent capacity, generating sixty-four megawatts, with turbines two and three indicating 90 percent on stream, generating seventy-two megawatts each. Any tempestuous molten carbon discharges would surely put the place up in smoke. Roy knew this, and so did his team.

On his hand signal, they stormed the operator room with lightning speed. Three R4 single rounds later, three Resistencia inside the room lay dead. All operators were told to remain on the floor, while the two Recce operatives stood guard.

Roy moved inside further and addressed the operators. "Who is the most senior person here?" he enquired slowly in Portuguese.

One little guy who lay flat on his chest tilted his head to his left, raised his hand, and spoke. "I am.

My name is Eduard Carvallio, and I'm the station superintendent."

Roy's eyes drifted to him. "Are there any underground storage areas here?" After reviewing the plans of the facility, he had anticipated that an underground area might exist. The plans had said *Future Development*. In Roy's mind, this was the most likely location for hostages to be held.

"Yes, one large one. It's at the other end of the turbine hall."

"How do I access it?"

"You have to go through the turbine outlet portal, and to the right." The superintendent spoke in his native tongue after looking around to see that the three Resistencia had been eliminated. He pointed out towards the turbines. "Access is through a large steel door at the entrance, but you will need an access code to get through."

"What is the code?" Roy asked.

"Don't know," the traumatized superintendent replied unassumingly. "We don't keep the codes for that area up here. Only the big boys keep those codes."

"And where can I find the big boys?"

"Behind the steel door—down there." Carvallio pointed again towards the access area behind the three gigantic turbines.

"Are there hostages in there being kept against their will?" Roy queried.

"Several people went in, but I haven't seen anybody come out alive," the superintendent said apologetically.

Roy jumped up from a crouching position and gestured for one of his troops to remain in the control room and the others to follow him to the underground entrance. As he moved to exit the control room with his three-man squadron beside him, a volley of shots resounded throughout the hall. Everybody dropped to the floor as shards of glass exploded from the operator center vision panel, shattering across the floor and on top of the operator station keyboards.

Roy glanced behind him. A large triangular sliver of glass was embedded in the linoleum floor an inch from Carvallio's face. Next to him, one of his operators wasn't so lucky, with a similar-sized shard buried in his head. The superintendent looked petrified. The remaining operators moaned as they shuffled for cover in the corners of the room.

More gunfire rang out, and Roy heard the ricochet of a 9mm pass over his head. It hit the mainframe computer behind him, then made its way perpendicularly towards an enclosed electrical panel. *Shit, that was close.* He fell further, his body now parallel with the deck. Spread-eagled on the parsimonious floor covering, Roy smelt the strange odors radiating from the musty, rubbery concoction beneath him. He groped for his radio and called Leon, who held a Recce group outside on watch. "Leon, enter the hall from the west end and approach on point, carefully." Still hugging the linoleum flooring, Roy called the remaining group from the fuel tank to approach in sniper mode.

Seconds later, a volley of rounds erupted from an amalgam of R4s. Roy knew Leon and his crew would arrive in a matter of seconds, and they did. With two Recce teams approaching, the Resistencia would be forced to cover themselves from both sides.

Roy rose to his knees and gawped out through the shattered operator vision panel. They had taken out half of the Resistencia forces. He watched the western Recce team dispense with the remaining Resistencia between the two turbines. He was pleased to see the turbo machinery hadn't imploded yet. If it did, they were all dead.

Roy looked down to the rear of the hall and saw a handful of well-armed Resistencia surrounding the turbine portal. He guessed they had exited from the underground bunker, having found out about the control room strike. Balanced against a steel barrier outside the operator's platform, Roy took aim with the R4, and seconds later the final Resistencia fell to the ground.

Roy noticed two Recce members had gone down in the crossfire, at the rear of the turbine hall. Incensed by the potential for loss of any members of his group, Roy launched himself from the operator platform and ran down the stairs to the other end of the hall, faster than the average Jamaican short-distance sprinter. The two bodies lay motionless in pools of blood. "Fuck," he exclaimed.

He turned the first body over. "Leon!" he cried out.

There was no pulse. He checked the private next to Leon. He, too, would not be seeing his family again. Roy grabbed his radio. "I need cover and a recovery crew here at the north end of the hall. Two men down."

After the recovery crews arrived, Roy pulled back slowly and paused for a moment. He looked around to see what was left of the Resistencia forces. None were visible. There couldn't be many left. Recce had more people, more firepower, and more intellect. In Roy's mind, there was no question as to who would come out second best.

He jumped up and launched out through the rear portal, pulling back the steel door to the bunker, now unlocked. With a team of six, leaving a further six as security detail at the bunker entrance on sentinel duty, Roy led the way with the reconnaissance team, who ascended behind him in single file.

Roy set his R4 hammer-fired trigger mechanism selector to position A: fully automatic fire mode. He switched the safety off and instructed the others to do the same. Anticipating Resistencia militias roaring up the exit gangway at any moment, his posture was prepared and his weapon suspended, ready to open fire on approaching combatants. He checked his lengthened high-strength synthetic polymer 35-round cartridge magazine: thirty-four rounds left. He approached the bottom of the stairs. The area was dark and damp. All of his senses were functioning adequately—so the military doctor had said following a medical checkup two weeks earlier. Today, though, one sensory function seemed to operate better than the rest.

His nose.

A putrid, musty smell permeated the subfloor's air. He had smelt it many times before and knew it suggested decaying tissue. He hoped he was wrong.

He approached the last step and looked left, then right. He faced forward as four Resistencia jumped out from behind either side of an orange-and-black chevron barrier. They were short, tanned, and heavily armed. Suddenly the darkness was gone, replaced by muzzle blasts as high-temperature powder gases ignited through the barrel of the R4. After the uncombusted gases evaporated, four Cubans lay twisted on the ground in front of the barrier.

He checked his selector count. The magazine was three-quarters full.

Roy's primary olfactory senses confirmed something different now. The smells of semi-combusted carbon, sulfur, and nitrates from the vaporized lead had usurped the stale, pungent cellar-like atmosphere.

Roy turned left to the first entrance room. Empty. He proceeded to the rear and found another door, this one made from some kind of structural UPVC plastic. It was locked. Determined to find the hostages alive, he nodded to his group, and in unison they fired at the handle.

The door swung open, and Roy's eyes moved from one side of the room to the other. He counted twelve desolate and anxious faces looking back at him.

"My name is Roy Young, Recce commander," he announced calmly. "I'm here to take you home. Stay close and follow me."

Roy led the way, and collectively they raced out through the bunker entrance, up the stair treads, and out the steel door. Anticipating success after they had eliminated the core Resistencia, Roy had given the instruction for the Frelons to come to the north of the station, in front of the turbine hall entrance. Frenetically they raced to the craft and began to board. After Roy had loaded the twelve hostages onto the first two Frelons, he jumped on board.

Delicately balanced about three feet off the ground as the pilot synchronized the three General Electric engines, Roy looked back from the helicopter's entrance gangway and saw a lone man come running out through the turbine hall doorway.

He stopped and stared intensely at Roy, who shook his head in response.

The man was tall, well over six feet, with medium build and dark hair almost to his shoulders. It was greased back off his forehead, but repeatedly swept across his face with the downward thrust from the Frelon's rotors. His mouth curved up at one end, extenuating his intense gaze.

He didn't look very pleased. He also didn't look very Cuban, and he certainly didn't look very Angolan.

Roy arched his R4 again, ready to fire.

The tall man continued to stare back at him. Roy could see he was unarmed. He didn't try and run, and he didn't try and hide.

Roy pulled back his weapon and stared at him.

Who the hell do you think you are?

Chapter 1
Alpha Factor

Twenty-one years later, Roy was still connected with the business of military assignments. It was in his blood. Today there was one difference—he was doing it for himself. Having left the armed forces several years earlier, after reaching the status of colonel, he was now working as a private training consultant and for-hire military operative. Despite running a series of enormously successful special ops assignments throughout Africa, the Middle East, and Russia in his final fourteen years, his skin color had predicated his hierarchical threshold. Things had changed and the opportunity to add stars to his resume in a commanding post had all but vanished. Experienced more than most, he had achieved everything he had set out to do, and things were different now—outsourcing was the new thing. He reckoned the government has received enough of his services and it was time to look after Roy.

That was what went through his mind when he decided to jump ship. Today, his mind hadn't changed.

It was November 7, 2010. It was 11:08 in the evening.

It was cold.

It wasn't Angola.

He was in Central Siberia.

Outside, the sounds of whining engines from four military-converted M998 triple cab Humvees on full revs rang out. Minutes later, the vehicles came to a standstill, and sounds of soft crunching between the tires and the snow beckoned louder, eclipsed only by the rattling of the final cadence from the 4-litre turbo-diesel drive units.

Roy sat in the front seat of the first vehicle in the convoy and looked down at the digital control panel in front of him. The GPS signal on the panel intensified, showing their destination two miles ahead.

They stopped. Before they could continue on the mission, Roy needed to intercept a similar-sized cadre of officials in four analogous black vehicles that followed closely behind them.

They waited.

The temperature had dropped to -27 degrees Fahrenheit, according to the temperature gauge next to the GPS device. Roy guessed it was correct. This was quite normal for this time of year. It would drop further in January, probably somewhere close to -60 F below.

It was an environment Roy knew, one where all of the native loons and grebes that had survived the summer seasons had flocked south already. In the distant landscape, he couldn't see a single tree. They were never included in any of the master planning for the area—they would simply not survive here.

The interior of the vehicle was warm—a second gauge indicated it was a balmy 72 F degrees.

Roy craned his neck and glanced up through the Humvee's spacious tinted glass roof. Not a single cloud concealed the sky. The prominent Polaris stood out amongst the northern stars, illuminating the tundra from its proud perch above the north celestial pole. He had never experienced anything like this before—the surrounding landscape let off an intoxicating ambiance, an eclectic fusion between something so strikingly serene, whilst at the same time frightfully eerie.

In anticipation of the arriving convoy, the Humvees sat astride the ice road, creating a temporary barricade as they waited. Roy got out of the vehicle and pulled the wool beanie down further over his head. Several strands of blonde hair slipped loose; the army cut no longer applied. He looked to his right: nothing. The road was empty. He looked left. He could see lights—lots of lights. To the average person, the land would merely look exceptionally incandescent. Roy knew, however, that in the distance eighty-two metal halide sodium flood-lamps cast out a total of 3,200 lumens and lit up the landscape for several miles. He knew because it was his job to know.

Snow had fallen for three full days now, and a powder carpet surrounded the entire vicinity. Roy could see it was not a well-traversed area. Up ahead, not a single footprint or car track was visible.

After fifteen minutes, Roy looked right again as tires crunched across the powder carpet. The second group was arriving at the Humvee barrier. Awaiting them were four black vehicles parked in chevron alignment, two abreast. It was a *W* in aerial view. In elevation, it was a roadblock. It looked like any regular security checkpoint. There were lots of them everywhere in Russia. They stopped. There were ten of them.

The awaiting squadron advanced cogently and one by one immobilized the occupants.

Before they set off again, they checked that all the vehicle engines from the immobilized group remained switched on with internal vehicular heating set to 72 degrees Fahrenheit. Now they could continue on their way.

Two miles away, within the 48,500-square-foot facility, Roy knew that 182 men were resting in their rooms. By this time of night, most would be asleep, pondering their future, or perhaps reading. Some may have just been lying awake, unable to sleep.

The recent advent of the winter solstice gave the residents only four hours of light per day. Night fell early, and morale was not good. It was never good there, anyway.

Roy was interested in only one person, a man who stood out from the rest. Roy guessed he would not be sleeping or reading. The man had done enough of that over the last seven years. Roy was sure he would be pondering his future—especially tonight.

The man's name was Mikhail Kasinov.

The problem was, Kasinov could no longer stay there.

Roy wasn't part of the problem. He was part of the solution.

Roy, however, was aware of the details of the problem. During the previous two years, Kasinov had written a succession of treatises that contained scathing revelations about government self-gratifying financial irregularities within the Russian Duma hierarchy. Whilst he wrote, Kasinov had arranged chapter by chapter to be inveigled out from his interned abode. With his network to the outside world, he had arranged for its publication once it was reassembled. His literary manuscript was praised by Western capitalist nations and many in the domestic private sector; conversely, though, as expected its publication was vilified by Russian government leadership. Several of the international media had commented that it contained some encouraging arguments for a radical change to a more socially responsible Russian state.

There were differing opinions on the book. To the average reader, it read like a fictional thriller.

In Kasinov's opinion, everything within was fact. To the Russian hierarchy, it was complete and utter tripe.

Roy wasn't interested in opinions. He had a job to do, and knew the success of the mission could define a new political and social landscape for the future Russian autocracy. Consequently, he became vaguely intrigued by Kasinov's hypothesis: A new Russian democracy, demanding a transformed Russian administration to include the Communist Party of the Russian Federation along with left-wing liberals and right-wing social-democratic coalitions.

The problem, Roy was informed, was that Kasinov's treatises had upset a lot of people within the Russian government and had caused them enormous embarrassment in international circles. They didn't like Kasinov. They wanted him eliminated. However, it would be far too obvious to the international human rights activists if he suddenly died while under the care and custody of the Kremlin.

Circumstances had changed, and now there was no alternative, no contingency—only this.

Roy's Humvee squad team, code-named *Alpha Factor*, had trained intensely over the previous six months for this day. Roy had taken his team through scrupulous planning of every minute detail of the operation; failure was not an option. They had to succeed at all costs. For this mission, strangely, his financiers had assigned him the code name *Xenop*. It was for security purposes, they said.

Alpha Factor comprised a team of fourteen in total—Roy and thirteen others.

Thirteen Russians, one non-Russian.

This included four drivers-cum-infantry support personnel, three infantry leads, four military acrobats, essentially former pole-vaulters highly trained in military tactical combat, and one systems technician. Over the previous twelve months, Roy had solicited them to participate in this secret mission. In total, Roy had considered over fifty men, but only chose those who met strict military and political qualifications. He had carefully selected each member of the team—all experts in their field.

Even for someone like Roy, this mission was unique and unlike anything he had undertaken before.

The ramifications were colossal.

Roy and the Alpha Factor team members knew how significant this event would become in Russian history in the future. This just added more pressure to their task.

The tension inside the first Humvee was heightened. Next to Roy in the front seat of the leading vehicle that approached, the fourteenth and most prominent Russian in the convoy was poised. His name was Vladimir Sakharshenko. He hadn't set foot on Russian soil for more than seven years when he had landed two hours earlier. Sakharshenko was a large, grey-haired man with a slightly receding hairline and a greasy face that had several pockmarks dotted around his elevated Slavic cheeks. He was around six foot two and slightly overweight at about 220 pounds— although when Roy had first met him, he was much heavier. Roy had put him through a personal training routine in order to get him into shape for this mission, and it had worked.

Roy had got to know Vladimir very well, and he liked him. They had spent a lot of time together. Roy had never really been friendly with his colleagues on other missions. This was different. Vladimir was different. Together they had meticulously masterminded the preparation of the mission for twelve months from their Budapest base. There was never a problem—only solutions.

Now it was showtime.

Sakharshenko looked after Russian matters for Roy, and Roy looked after everything else.

After the disposal of the trailing group, Roy sat pensively in the lead Humvee and mapped out over the radio network the succession of events set to take place within the next half hour.

This was it. There was no turning back.

He had played out this sequence of scenes so many times and thought of every possible issue that could go wrong. Then he had built that into his plan.

He figured that he had been through it enough times now. Roy's values in success were simple: rehearsal, rehearsal, rehearsal. He was ready.

Up ahead, Roy could see the Krasnokamensk penitentiary facility. Located four thousand miles east of Moscow in Central Siberia, it was a maximum-security detention center holding a diverse mix of political prisoners, KGB wastrels, cannibals, and life-serving felons. In the past one hundred years it had been the home of several elite. Roy remembered reading in the history archives on the place that Vasily Stalin had spent ten years there for embezzlement after his father's death, and several Nazi commanders spent time there after the Second World War. Apart from hosting this characteristic custodial facility, the area was also home to the site for Russia's largest uranium mine.

Not the kind of place you come to visit on holidays, he thought.

As far as the Kremlin was concerned, Krasnokamensk, as prisons go, was ideally located: 330 miles southeast of Chita in Central Siberia. It was close to the middle of nowhere, and a long way from anywhere. Ironically, though, in preparation for the mission, Roy had established that isolated regions like this became more accessible during winter, as natural ice roads traversing lake and river crossings were formed.

There was nothing new about this concept for Roy—these were the same principles used in prehistoric migration of different cultures across continents during the ice age.

Although he had witnessed modern technology advance significantly since these pioneer crossings, he calculated two restrictions, which could not be breached. First, he needed the vehicle weights to be less than four tons; anything in excess of that he knew ran the risk of cracking ice. Second, he needed to govern the speed limits on the Humvees to a maximum of thirty miles per hour. Anything in excess of this could generate wave motion beneath the surface, potentially dislodging ice from the adjacent shoreline. Any breach of this speed regulation would most certainly cause a road and subsequent vehicle collapse, resulting in hypothermia or drowning, whichever came first. Neither choice was an acceptable option to Roy.

With Sakharshenko's contacts inside the Russian Ministry of Justice, Roy knew what awaited him and his squadron. As the federal agency responsible for the execution of penal sanctions, the ministry regularly carried out improvements and upgrades to its penitentiaries. Roy established that the Krasnokamensk facility had received an investment of no less than US$180 million in state-of-the-art security throughout in 2008. He had also received the full specification of these upgrades.

One of the modifications included seven hundred new blast-proof heat-censored CCTV cameras surrounding the perimeter inside and out. Roy wasn't surprised when he read that each camera was capable of recording and storing footage from 360 degrees in both light and total darkness. He had a number of previous experiences with bypassing this type of camera—all good ones.

He also found out that a total of sixty sentry personnel ran the facility, twenty-eight of whom sat in four nodal security towers that stood one hundred feet high at each extremity of the perimeter. Each nodal sanctuary had an enclosed lookout area, encased in one-foot-thick indestructible safety Plexiglas, with each of the twelve glass interlayers bonded with polyvinyl butyral. In addition, the specifications referenced that each tower was designed to withstand ballistic attack from close- and medium-range incendiaries.

Roy spent considerable time reading the section on the central control room (CCR). He was intrigued to learn that inside the main building, beneath the lower mezzanine level, an eighteen-inch-thick reinforced concrete steel-clad structure guarded the CCR. Given that the CCR was like the central nervous system in the human body, where it basically controlled everything, he had never come across such an extravagant use of engineered products to protect and conceal the primary joysticks for the facility.

As he read further, he discovered that the CCR received feedback from all motion detection sensors, light-wave incremental change pods, and noise radars. Worse again, the activation of any of the modules within the expansive instrumentation network would automatically send the facility into complete lockdown mode, with a parallel signal to Moscow, unless overridden within thirty seconds by the chief warden.

Roy established that on this night, that responsibility was bestowed upon Igor Tishkovets. According to his bio, Tishkovets had served there for almost twelve years, initially as station warden, graduating to sergeant in 2004, and then in 2008 to the position of chief warden. He had overseen the security control system retrofit project and knew everything that needed to be known about the system.

In order to penetrate such a web of defense, Roy knew he needed to find someone who had not only intimate knowledge of the CCR, but also the supporting automation experience. When he researched further, he was astonished to learn that a company called Tegra Dynamics, identified as one of the world's leading security services companies, had carried out the security upgrade contract for the Russian Ministry of Justice. Tegra Dynamics was US headquartered.

The Cold War is dead and buried.

Tegra's brief was to oversee the complete design and installation of the upgraded system at

Krasnokamensk. Roy subsequently found out that Tegra had previously worked with several agencies within the Kremlin on other esoteric military projects and had close links with the president.

After Roy checked Tishkovets's travel records prior to the completion of the upgrade, he had discovered that the chief warden had travelled extensively to Chicago. Tegra's website showed that they had assembly facilities in twenty cities in the US, including Chicago. The chief warden had probably visited Tegra's staging center during final assembly, overseeing the testing and integration of all of the systems.

Whilst Roy was tracking Tishkovets's Atlantic crossings, Sakharshenko researched Russian regulations for the development of foreign software. He established that it was mandatory for Tegra to work through a local partner. It turned out they did. All of Tegra's design coding was reformatted at Ruscomtek, a state-controlled Russian telecommunications design institute in Moscow, before installation. This was necessary in order to comply with local standards and security protocols.

When Roy assessed all of the security enhancements, he estimated that it would have been as difficult to break in as it would be to break out.

Roy knew he was dealing with the most advanced security system in the world. It didn't frighten him. It challenged him. If he stood any chance of getting through it, he would need the most advanced systems engineer in the Russian world on his team. Roy, with the help of Sakharshenko's Russian network, engaged thirty-four year old Dmitry Dolgoruky to decode the security software. Dolgoruky's resume read well: twelve years in telecommunications systems design and one of the most promising stars at Ruscomtek.

About one mile away from the Krasnokamensk penitentiary, visibly out of sight of the control towers and certainly out of range of the motion detectors, Roy pulled Humvee 1 to a halt, and the other three vehicles pulled up beside him. He needed to complete some final preparatory work.

In the quietude of the landscape, he nodded across to the other vehicles, and the backseat doors on either side of all four vehicles opened. Three occupants from each of the Humvees exited and moved to the rear of the vehicle. In concord they removed the rear cab canopy, like pit-lane technicians on time trial testing, and one of three from each of the vehicles discreetly entered the external cab chamber. Then the canopy cover was replaced by the remaining two, who then re-entered the vehicles.

Roy looked behind him briefly, and smiled.

Ready to go. Next stop Kasinov.

Chapter 2
City Girl

A taxi came to a halt off Holborn Circus just before 3:00 p.m., and an elegantly dressed young lady hopped out. An Iveco truck driving past her momentarily aquaplaned through the fresh downpour. Melanie Bauer barely noticed. Her mind was consumed with all the things she had to accomplish for the remainder of the day, starting with her visit to the London Stock Exchange.

Melanie passed the taxi driver the £20 for a £19 fare. "Keep the change," she said.

The fare seemed a bit higher than normal from Highgate, but the inclement weather had probably caused that, she assumed.

Melanie had a distinctive fetishism in capital markets, something she had learned since completing her economics degree at Cambridge University six years earlier. She had then joined UGC Bank, a Swedish investment bank with an admirable one-hundred-year history in the market, and the last fifty of those years with a significant London presence. Now she headed up their research group.

Melanie scaled the water pool and sprinted across the road, heading straight to Costa Coffee for her habitual afternoon caffeine intake.

"May I have a medium café latte, please?" Her accent sounded more like something you would hear along the corridors of Buckingham Palace. The two Polish girls behind the counter smiled at her and made light conversation. They often practiced their English with Melanie, who had been a regular customer for the past year.

A moment later, she was carrying her drink towards Newgate Street for her 3:00 p.m. gathering at the London Stock Exchange.

The latest deal she had been working was Fastro Electronics. She had spent several months developing a model for their business, comparing it against industry peers for valuation as part of their Initial Public Offering (IPO) and subsequent listing on the London Stock Exchange FTSE 250. Eventually, after six long, intense months of due diligence and marketing, Melanie and the team at UGC had achieved the listing and set to launch on the market the following day.

Today she could relax. It was the pre-listing ceremony.

Melanie liked Fastro—they were like all good Asian techie companies, with savvy management. They had developed a niche market, operating out of Shenzhen in China, for the design and manufacture of electronics accessories for some of the larger well-established names in computer hardware. The management, along with their advisers, were due to assemble this afternoon in preparation for the bell-ringing ceremony the following day.

Melanie thought, as she made her way there, that although the ritual was very much a perfunctory gathering, secondary to all the hard work that had been completed in making the transaction a success, it was normally the event that ended up in company annual reports and newsletters. Ironically, it was the event that people remembered the most.

As Melanie approached the northern extremity of Paternoster Square opposite the historical Saint Paul's Cathedral in the heart of London, her mind was racing. It was the buzz of the place. She loved it. On top of that, today was a special day for Melanie. It was her twenty-eighth birthday, November 7, 2010.

She might have forgotten if she hadn't put it in her BlackBerry. For now, she was too busy to think about that. *Maybe later when work is all done, I'll have some fun*, she thought.

In the distance, she could see the London Stock Exchange building, a catalyst to the collegial enterprise of the London Financial District, collectively known in London circles simply as The City. She visited Paternoster Square at least once a month with some deal or other. She was reservedly proud of her association with something so successful. Who wouldn't be? After all, it was the largest exchange in Europe, with a market capitalization of over £2 trillion.

Intrigued by its origins, Melanie recalled from her history classes at Westminster College that the exchange had been founded sometime back in the early 1800s and was one of the landmark buildings in the city. Today she found inspiration in its revamped contemporary architecture, which stood incongruously with some of the other eclectic edifices sharing the same postal code, a number of them dating back several hundred years. She knew the exchange enjoyed a deep heritage, which was amplified by its own success.

Each day that she had visited there since graduating, she was amazed how its cavernous entrance invited visitors, bankers, brokers, analysts, and investors to a roller-coaster ride of money mania, where behind its exceedingly thick lime mortar walls a concoction of trading, bartering, lending, and betting ensued.

Given her Oxbridge associations and her ongoing alumni networking, Melanie was erudite whilst at the same time a serial socialite. She stopped and gazed as she caught a glimpse of her reflection in a large office window. She thought about how frequently she was complimented on her looks. She didn't pay too much attention to that, and didn't particularly appreciate how attractive she was.

Without any elevation couture, she stood at five feet ten inches, her height extenuated by her silk-like auburn hair, which reached somewhere between her twenty-third and twenty-fifth vertebrae, depending on her posture. She had perfect sallow skin, deep olive-green eyes that seemed liquid, and full lips, perfectly interposing two evident dimples.

She'd had a few boyfriends since her days at Cambridge, mostly connected with university or with her job in the city of London. But her Facebook status had recently been changed to read *In a Relationship*. Despite that, there was still one guy from her past that she couldn't forget. They had parted company in 2007, and she had never been able to figure out what happened. He had simply disappeared.

She checked her phone, expecting some more birthday messages, and there were several. Melanie was very popular and had plenty of friends. She was good to keep in contact, regularly setting up lunches, dinners, and any other social functions she could get people to come along to. She looked down through her birthday greetings, and there it was, received 2:55 p.m. She couldn't believe her eyes.

Just wanted to wish you a Happy Birthday. This is for you, in case I never get to see you again x

No contact for three years, and now this? Why now?

Melanie entered the foyer of the London Stock Exchange lost in thought about Fastro's ceremony, trying to remember all the names of the management team, and now this message— from him? Head down, she practically ran over her waiting UGC colleague as she hurried toward the reception area. "Oh!" She stumbled back. "Good morning, Paul."

Paul Coppell chuckled and reached out to steady her. "Good morning to you." Paul was head of corporate finance and had been with UGC nearly twenty years. He'd seen many companies come to the market, and a few exit from it, often unceremoniously.

"Thanks," she said as she found her balance. "Hey, well done on getting this one over the line. You must be pleased." Paul managed the different elements that went into making a listing successful and ultimately put their stamp of approval on the deal.

He shrugged. "To be honest, it was touch and go. Markets being how they've been, it's difficult to get anything to listing these days."

Melanie nodded knowingly. When deals went south, Paul and his team got the blame.

"Thanks for all your help, by the way," he added.

As a senior Analyst, Melanie's group researched company valuation, setting the overall share price for the listing. More exciting, she always thought, and a lot less pressure. She didn't know how Paul stomached taking the brunt of a deal gone bad.

"It was a true team effort," she replied, smiling. "And it's very fortunate that Fastro's fundamentals are sound."

The two grabbed their security badges from reception and ran to the lift. On the second floor they met up with the executive team from Fastro, along with a phalanx of advisers, consultants, and exchange administrators, all there and accounted for and ready to rehearse the ceremonial ringing of the bell. Fastro's name and logo were displayed brilliantly overhead in their platinum and gunmetal grey corporate colors, and also across several adjacent large LCD screens strategically placed around the room. No matter where you stood to take a photo, they were hard to miss.

Unable to control her OCD in organizational abilities, Melanie helped assemble the group on the balcony of the trading floor into a perfect bowed-shape formation. She had done this a few times before. "Right," she said, shepherding the last few into line as she took a step back from the gathering.

She looked at them, all neatly arranged and smiling generously, before joining in at the end nearest her amidst the clicks and flashes as the group of in-house photographers began to capture memorial portraits.

Another one over the line, she thought with a smile.

Chapter 3
Jettison from Siberia

Earlier that morning, Roy had arranged for Tishkovets to receive an email from the Ministry of Justice, confirmed via a telephone conversation later in the day, to expect a visit from a commission led by General Subrov. Subrov, a senior member of the Security Committee of the State Duma, would arrive late that evening with his team and would stay over and conduct a security audit on the entire system the following day. Krasnokamensk was 550 miles from the nearest airport, and any visitors to the facility would normally have this late arrival and overnight routine.

It was a bold move, but it was delivered with perfection.

Roy didn't claim to be a specialist in Arctic transportation, but he knew the vehicles needed to be uniquely customized in order to assure certainty in delivery throughout the operation. To safeguard against this, Roy ordered more modifications than a NASCAR series rally car. For combustion, the standard 6-litre General Motors D-6V Humvee engines were modified to cope with Arctic temperatures, combusting a freeze-resistant fuel mixture of low-sulfur diesel and avgas.

Heaters were added to increase fuel and coolant temperatures. For traction, the standard wheels and tires were replaced with bespoke Arctic Truck AT405 wheels with forty-inch studded snow tires. Particularly suited to these dense snow conditions, the tire design was capable of running at low pressures and a modified gearing ratio to increase tractional torque over snow.

The wheel arches and suspension were raised and extended to accommodate the larger tires. This modification extended the overall height of the Humvees to about seven feet four inches, which was necessary to incorporate the most interesting enhancement: a contraption enclosed within the rear external cab—a mechanical launch device.

Cognizant of the scale and magnitude of the undertaking ahead of him, Roy watched Sakharshenko wipe the sweat from his brow one last time before he picked up the satellite phone.

Roy nodded to Sakharshenko to proceed.

Sakharshenko selected the conference selector button and called the preprogrammed number.

The voice on the other end of the phone answered. "Tishkovets."

"This is General Nicolay Subrov," Sakharshenko announced. "We are approaching the Krasnokamensk facility and expect to be there in a matter of minutes. Please have your security patrol ready to receive us."

"Have your identification ready to show to our security team," Tishkovets replied.

As the Humvees pulled up, Roy observed nine steely-looking guards wearing thick leather coats, each hatted with genuine sheepskin ushankas, on their way to meet them. All windows in the vehicles were open for inspection. This was normal routine. Roy took a deep breath. The night air was moist, which meant heavily fogged breath. Nine guards breathing meant a lot of fog. Fog didn't aid their vision. This was good.

As they approached, Roy sensed the sullen sounds of turgid winds reflecting off the buildings and supporting structures throughout the facility. Flagpoles, shackled with steel wire rope, clanked in an alternating harmony. It was as eerie inside the fence as it was outside.

Roy monitored the sentry duty officers as they reviewed the IDs through the open windows at each of the four vehicles. The inspection would identify the occupants as members of the special Security Committee of the State Duma, with all names and documentation matching the approved list sent from the Kremlin earlier that day.

Following their review, the security ensemble looked back at the security lead at central access control station. Each gave a confirming nod of approval.

No surprises.

The gates were drawn back, and the Humvee procession passed through into a central courtyard. Roy remained in the first vehicle, and in a matter of seconds his eyes had scanned the entire perimeter: one enormous central facility with an adjacent substation and four nodal towers. *It looks just like the plans.*

At a controlled pace, the Humvees circled around in a preplanned sequence, parking symmetrically across from each other in four equidistant points around a perfect circle. When they came to a halt, the rear side of each vehicle faced one of the four nodal security towers, and each Humvee driver sat facing one of his counterparts.

They were in.

Quite an achievement, given the military firepower they were packing.

Each of the ground-based infantry leads within the vehicles was armed with a .30-calibre M1919 Browning, all fitted with military-grade night optics. Roy had selected the medium-sized M1919, which was light, quick, reliable, and had two selectors, auto and manual. Most importantly, it fitted under the seats in the Humvees. Now each Browning was back in the hands of its operator.

When he'd taken on this mission, Roy had been imparted a "Mitigation of Life" mandate from his employers. In other words, no one should be killed—just injured. Unusual, but it was what his employers wanted. It wouldn't be Roy's first time playing with rubber bullets. On the selection of ammunition, Roy had temporized for several months, and in the end, for each Browning, he'd selected a magazine of thirty batons of round rubber coated metal cylinders, each .66 inches in diameter, weighing 5 ounces.

Roy expected that the kinetic impact munitions from the batons would cause a lot of pain but not serious injury, some contusions, abrasions, and a few hematomas maybe. The injured parties would be incapacitated for several hours, and probably lethargic for another few, after they woke up. Roy had field-tested this weapon combination several years earlier in mass kidnap recovery projects in Nigeria, with great success.

As a backup, Roy arranged for each infantry lead, as well as each of the infantry reserve operatives, to carry a 19mm Walther P99, a German semiautomatic pistol, each holding nine rounds. Roy had specifically selected it because it could be held and operated in one hand quite comfortably. He'd used the same backup weapon in Nigeria to deal with the kidnappers once they were identified and separated from the hostages.

After the Humvees had assembled into their respective positions, Roy looked out the window and noticed the frozen blanket of white snow above the permafrost layer that was now laced out in an unusual design of hieroglyphically intertwined semicircles from the tire tracks. Roy then looked straight out in front of him, to the left, and to the right. Then he nodded, and three Russian infantry leads nodded back at him.

Ergo, *let's do it.*

The plan commenced with lightning speed.

Roy led the four-strong infantry squadron, alighting from the vehicles and immediately dispensing with the adjacent ten sentry personnel at the main access point. One by one, their bodies fell into the snow with graceful and compacting thuds.

Simultaneously, the driver of each vehicle pushed a button marked LAUNCH on his front dashboard panel, which jettisoned the rear canopy cover from each Humvee, unveiling four *Catalaunches* embedded within the rear chamber—best described as modern-day military human catapults. Harnessed in each of the *Catalaunches,* four vaulters were ready to launch.

From the plans, Roy had calculated the distance from the back of the launch device to the center of each tower to be 390 feet. To traverse this distance, he had each *Catalaunch* pre-loaded in tension somewhere between 1170 and 1195 pounds on a leaf spring dampened hydraulic accumulator astride the launch chamber. Given that each vaulter had a different body mass, Roy had worked out the spring tension calibration to accommodate this variance. If he got it wrong, any one of the vaulters would miss his target and most definitely fall to his death—and so, too, would the mission, and most probably everybody in the Humvees.

With a second push of the same button, the stored inertia was activated and the spring-loaded launch devices released. With the potential energy stored in each unit, each vaulter would travel the same trajectory and distance. Almost simultaneously, Roy looked up to hear a volley of resounding thuds as each of the four vaulters were thrust at a path fifteen feet above the top of the four nodal security towers, gliding through the air like human cannonballs.

Three hundred twenty years after Newton initially postulated his First Law of Motion, it was proven true once again when Roy watched the vaulters come to an abrupt state of rest, embraced by the external force of the nodal tower roof as the velocity at which they were travelling suddenly reduced from sixty-five miles per hour to zero. Each landed safely atop the center apex of the roof, just as he had planned.

Roy wiped his forehead. *Thank fuck for that.*

Despite the preferential views now afforded to the vaulters from their heightened perch, Roy knew they would not waste any time in acquainting themselves with their platform. He watched as each vaulter removed a shard device about the length of their arms from inside their Kevlar suits and anchored the device to the center of the steel section on the apex.

Roy had designed each steel shard with a built-in micro incendiary device that, after activation, heated the carbon steel insert to melting temperature and fused it to the apex. Each vaulter then removed a Venetian tarpaulin from his backpack and attached it via a central eye over the platinum shard. On release, the tarpaulin rolled out over the entire apex, down the tower for about twelve feet, and suddenly a layered plasticized sheet usurped each tower's vista.

As the view closed off, Roy watched his vaulters launch from the top of the tower like synchronized swimmers after tying their rappel devices to the shard. They reached the tower's lower-level access door, glancing briefly at the incredulous occupants on their way past. Each vaulter then sealed the singular lower-access cast iron door with a second fusion incendiary device.

Done.

Roy's eyes now turned to Dolgoruky in the rear of Humvee 1, who had his laptop open and control software launched before the four vehicles came to a standstill. He seemed unruffled by the technology barriers that awaited him. Inside the facility, according to Dolgoruky's calculations, there were four independent servers, two prime and two standby, which controlled all systems. Above the servers sat a server firewall shield controlled by Tegra's hardware and modified by Ruscomtek software protocols. Apparently this software ran a sequence that changed IP addresses that governed the host servers hourly. Dolgoruky had confirmed this. He wrote it.

Dolgoruky had assured him that his programming electronic signature would be hierarchical to the system security. "Okay, IT man," Roy said, cradling his earwig. "Let's do this—you're on."

Better still, Dolgoruky confirmed that with a single click of his keypad, he could initiate the server IP switch sequence. Once he was in, he would be able to isolate the different subsystem communications almost simultaneously. The plan to launch a scrambled Trojan into both the prime and redundant standby fiber optic cabling supplying the two primary servers, to deactivate the CCR, transferring control of the entire CCR to his laptop, was first. Then he would take over the next two servers, controlling all motion sensors and CCTV cameras. Finally he would take control of all inmate cell access control.

Roy had full confidence in his IT expert to open and close everything in his purview. However, he was interested in only one particular cell, GC-86, along with all access doors to and from it.

Roy listened intently over the encrypted mobile Tetra radio communication system that had been established after taking control of the central server.

"All electrical lighting circuits dropped out," Dolgoruky confirmed. "Prime electrical substation control system and backup generators under our control."

"Roger, IT man—copy that."

Between the combat assault on the entrance and nodal sentries, and the electronic ingresses, Roy had taken out the border and nodal guard houses in twenty seconds flat, and had gained complete access to the facility—twenty-eight out of the total sixty sentry complement were locked inside the four towers, blinded and simultaneously cut off from all communication. Along with the ten at the gate perimeter, thirty-eight were down, twenty-two to go.

Phase one complete—on schedule—on plan.

~~~

Consumed with pride over his benchmark prison, Chief Warden Igor Tishkovets nonchalantly made his way to meet his guests from inside the facility. He was ready to play host once again to what had become known in inner-Kremlin circles as the ultimate benchmark in prison security. He was running arguably the most technologically advanced penitentiary facility in the world, and was now on his third visit from the Kremlin since the new security system had been commissioned. He was well used to playing tour guide and enjoyed showing off the plethora of smart IT gadgets at his disposal. In each of the two previous visits, he had received glowing reports back from Moscow. He had nothing to worry about.

He thought one day he would sell his memoirs to some TV station and become a celebrity warden of sorts: *The Man Who Kept the Great Kasinov Under Lock and Key in Siberia.* He laughed, shaking his head. As he strolled to central access, his shuffling gait echoing inside the hollow access channel, he realized he had left his radio back at his desk within the CCR. Again, he didn't have to worry; this was just another Kremlin routine visit.

~~~

Roy cradled his Tetra earpiece once again.

"Primary circuit breaker about to be taken out," Dolgoruky's voice shouted.

Roy nodded to the ground infantry crews, then raised his hand and followed with a rotating flick of his wrist. Five night vision goggles moved from foreheads to eyes.

Dolgoruky spoke again. "Main access being released."

A loud click resounded, and Roy led the ground infantry team into the primary security center within the main facility. They moved adroitly in unison, one in front of him and two behind, with Sakharshenko next to him in a typical 2-2-1 formation.

As expected, a vehement greeting awaited them from a security convoy on entry. Roy spotted one big guy and two medium-sized guys.

Dolgoruky hadn't promised unfettered access.

Roy opened fire, followed by a continuous Browning salvo from the other 2-2-1 formations. Despite taking a few rounds, the big security lead kept running at them. Roy leaned forward to meet him, smacking him end-on in the face with the Browning, and he crunched to the floor.

Forty-six down, fourteen to go.

Roy had secured the blueprints for Krasnokamensk from a source known to Sakharshenko within the Kremlin four months earlier. By now, every member of Alpha Factor could walk the route in their sleep—they had practiced it enough times. Roy pointed to the right, nodding to Sakharshenko and two artillery leads to initiate their route to cell GC-86. Roy had something else he had to attend to.

~~~

Before Tishkovets arrived at the central access area, the power had been cut. He knew this was not a routine visit, and thought something was wrong.

He stopped.

The lockdown sequence should have started by now. There must be something wrong with the CCR server.

In darkness and alone, he made a rapid U-turn and ran back to the CCR to manually activate the shutdown procedure. Tishkovets's knowledge of the place was existential. He walked it every day. He didn't need any lights—he knew where he had to go. Frantically, he made his way to the CCR and arrived panting and shaking. Out of breath, he paused briefly and placed his hand against the access wall. Hastily, he opened the door after regaining his composure and rushed through to a concealed room at the back.

~~~

With the benefits of their night goggles, but without the aid of muzzle flash from the Browning—given the non-metallic munitions—Sakharshenko and his team cascaded their way through the cell channels in total darkness, in constant communication with Roy and Dolgoruky.

One by one, the inter cellblock steel doors opened as thuds of raw steel on steel rotating sluggishly from the wall-mounted hinges resonated along their path. The mechanical clunks from the locking devices were interspersed with invectives from the more vocal inmates. There was no riposte—no time for any conversation.

Sakharshenko approached GC-86 after exactly three minutes and thirty-two seconds. He reached to his side and checked for his Walther to make sure it was still there. It was. Next to it was a muslin cloth sack tied to his belt, which was rolled up neatly in a cylindrical shape. He pulled it out from his belt and shook it a couple of times, allowing it to open up.

GC-86 was at the western extremity of the block, and the orientation had afforded it two windows, one from within the cell and one from the access hall. A long buzzing sound, followed by a loud click, echoed in the gangway as Sakharshenko approached. The cell opened, and an illumination from the northern lights cast a silhouette onto his lower body as the prisoner approached the cell's exit. Sakharshenko rushed inside and immediately placed the satchel over the prisoner's head, tying the ends in a bow.

The inmate wore a bright orange, short-sleeved coverall with black boots—standard-issue prison apparel. Above his right breast pocket, the number 11163 was embroidered in thick black cotton thread.

"No talking—just follow me, and do what I say," Sakharshenko said, grabbing the prisoner by the arm.

They exited GC-86, turned right, and commenced their return.

The remaining security detail had valiantly assembled in the return gangway about ten cellblocks away from GC-86, and after a brief struggle, Sakharshenko and his team had no problem in using their superior vision to eliminate them—albeit temporarily.

~~~

Roy headed to the CCR. He needed to ensure that access to any of the servers or core circuits from these servers remained inaccessible to the prison IT staff. His knowledge of the facility, compared to that of Tishkovets's, was theoretical. It was knowledge learned over months of mapping out the location from the blueprints and rehearsals at their Budapest training center. He also had some empirical reference from interviews they had conducted with former inmates.

When he arrived, he saw Tishkovets seated in a room adjacent to the main CCR, panting profusely, eyes fixed on a computer monitor. Roy watched as the chief warden moved the mouse around and entered data via the keyboard faster than a zealous stenographer transcribing court proceedings.

There was a problem, a big problem.

This was not a room that was in the blueprints.

Roy cradled his right hand over the Tetra radio's wireless earwig. "Possible alternate control access from second CCR location," he said calmly. He waited and listened closely over the encrypted frequency for a response.

"I see it now, but I don't have access to it," Dolgoruky said anxiously. "Let me initiate a server ID sequence."

"We don't have time for that," Roy replied. "I'll handle it." Roy knew that every millisecond counted, and a server ID sequence check was probably going to take a lot of milliseconds. He didn't have the luxury of a lot of milliseconds.

Roy's eyes were fixed on Tishkovets. He heard the mouse furiously kneading against the desk, followed by the clicking of a button, no doubt sending a message to some microprocessor inside the hardware unit.

Shit, probably a lockdown sequence.

Roy looked down at his firearm options. He had the Browning in one hand and the Walther P99 in the other. Whatever happened, he had to stop the lockdown sequence.

Most operatives would have panicked. He didn't. He knew what he had to do.

Roy kicked open the door and approached the warden. He observed him frenetically crunching at the keyboard in front of him. "Hands up. Don't move, or you're dead!" he shouted to Tishkovets.

Frenzied with completing his code input, the chief warden made one last click and raised his hands.

~~~

Sakharshenko, the prisoner, and the ground team ran back to the central entrance area, with the exit in sight. Something was not right; the primary access guillotine steel door was closing. They raced towards it, but they would never make it on time.

Suddenly two volleyed shots were heard echoing throughout the facility.

"Shit, that's a Walther," Sakharshenko shouted. "I know that sound anywhere."

To their amazement, the closing gate stopped. There was just enough space left to fit underneath, and within seconds, the intruders were back outside the facility with the hooded inmate in custody, racing for the Humvee motorcade.

Roy followed moments later and ran to the waiting vehicles. All sixty of the prison sentinels were immobilized. He nodded to Dolgoruky. Before closing his computer, the IT man checked one more time to ensure that all communications were cut off to and from Krasnokamensk. Dolgoruky nodded back at Roy—everything was cut off—and he shut it down.

They closed the Humvee doors, drove about six hundred feet, and got out again. They boarded the awaiting Mil Mi-14 helicopter, and they were gone.

Chapter 4
Oligarchical

Roy reached forward, sticking his head into the cockpit to check the analogue altimeter on the Mil Mi-14.

It read *4,000* feet.

He pulled back, turned in his seat, and glanced at Sakharshenko, who sat in the seat behind him. Next to Sakharshenko was Kasinov, who remained hooded. Roy nodded to his Russian lieutenant, and Sakharshenko whipped off the muslin hood, saying, "*Privet,* Comrade Mikhail."

Kasinov's head darted around. He wiped his eyes, blinked a couple of times, and turned to Sakharshenko. "*Privet,* Vladimir," he said and proceeded to give Sakharshenko a big bear hug as smiles spread across their faces. The two embraced for several minutes, followed by prolonged reverential back-patting. Kasinov turned to glance through the rear riveted windows to see the Krasnokamensk facility fading into the distance.

I'm sure he'll be happy to never see the place again, Roy thought.

Kasinov peered around, doing two 180-degree loops through the Mil Mi-14 before returning to face Roy. "You must be Xenop."

"Yes, I am," Roy responded, nodding.

"Thank you," Kasinov said respectfully, reaching out his hand. "I understand that I have you to thank for everything."

Roy leaned back over the rear of his seat to shake Kasinov's hand. He looked the man straight in the eye. It was the first time he had seen him face-to-face. *Younger looking than I expected,* he thought. "No problem. You've spent enough time in that shithole. Glad you're out. You doing okay?"

"Relieved," Kasinov responded. "What's next?"

"Don't worry, Misha," Sakharshenko exclaimed, leaning over and patting Roy on the shoulder. "This man has taken care of everything."

Without Roy, they were nowhere. Roy knew that. Sakharshenko most probably knew that, too. Roy sensed, however, that Kasinov had no idea. He didn't take Kasinov as a man who was interested in detail or even understood detail. He probably had no idea as to the level of ingenuity and foresight that had gone into Alpha Factor. Nevertheless, Kasinov had a certain charm about him—for a former billionaire, anyway.

"We're heading for the China border," Roy said. "You should get some rest. You're going to need it."

Based on his calculations, with a full crew and fifteen passengers, the ferry range capacity of the Mil Mi-14 was 705 miles. He had several landing spots to choose from outside Russian territory that fell within this range, but Roy had chosen Changchun in the northwestern province of Jilin, China, as their intermediate changeover point.

Noticing Kasinov's orange boiler suit—something he had probably worn for the last seven years—Roy reached under his seat and pulled out a navy duffel bag, which he handed to Kasinov. "There's a change room at the rear behind you."

Kasinov unzipped the duffel, rummaged around inside, and cast a curious glance back in Roy's direction. He pulled out a pair of dark Armani jeans, patent-clad black shoes, and a black Hugo Boss turtleneck sweater, along with some deodorant and other incidental toiletries. At the bottom of the bag was a cashmere three-quarter length charcoal coat. He looked up at Roy again. "Thank you," he replied, nodding. "Well chosen."

After changing, Kasinov sat back into his seat. Roy could feel his gaze on the back of his head, but it didn't bother him. Many important people had gazed at the back of Roy's head before in similar rescue missions, and it hadn't bothered him then, either.

Roy was tired. He had been going now for almost twenty-four hours. He dozed for what seemed like several hours, and then woke up. He checked his watch. They had been travelling southeast for four hours and ten minutes, a journey that traversed approximately 540 miles.

Nearly there, he thought.

Up ahead in the distance, Roy could see the H-pad, and minutes later, the Mil Mi-14 Soviet anti-submarine transport helicopter touched down at Changchun airport, Jilin Province, China.

Roy undid his four-point seat and shoulder belt, and looked out the window. There was no awaiting security detail. *Good,* he thought. He watched Kasinov undo his belt with an austere grimace. *What's up with him? He should be pleased.*

Inside the craft, Roy could hear a slow whining noise as the centrifugal droning from the prime rotor on the two Klimov TV3-117MT turbo shaft engines took a full three minutes to wind down before the doors could be opened. Once it was safe to do so, all fifteen passengers dismounted whilst the crew remained inside.

Covertly and swiftly, they disembarked the craft, and Roy and Sakharshenko escorted Kasinov to a leased Airbus A-380, located a short walking distance outside an adjacent hanger. Under stealth as a diplomatic assignee, Roy had arranged for the transfer to be done seamlessly.

No need to clear Chinese customs.

No need to undergo fervent questioning from

Chinese immigration officials.

No need to draw attention.

Roy handed Kasinov a plastic folder containing cash, a phone, an itinerary, and a passport. "Mikhail, here are your papers. Everything you need is in there."

"Go well, comrade—I will leave you here," Sakharshenko added, reaching in for the hug.

Kasinov replied with a final bear hug to his comrade. He shook Roy's hand. "Thank you both. I am eternally grateful."

Kasinov turned and proceeded up the portable stairwell. Roy watched him climb the temporary structure and thought about how he would be climbing his own stairs shortly. It wouldn't be a private aircraft like Kasinov's. He was flying commercial. Didn't matter; he was glad to be returning home. He hadn't been there in two months. Roy imagined that Sakharshenko and the rest of the crew had plans, too. Probably returning home or off to some exotic island. Before departing, they walked over to the hanger, where Roy opened his laptop and proceeded to complete a series of bank transfers for their day's work. For some it had been a year's work. The bill totaled US$6 million.

Their job was done—for now, anyway.

~~~

As Kasinov approached the top of the stairwell, he was tired and felt every bit of it. He looked every bit of it, too. His eyes were bloodshot, with dark circles around them, propped up by two puffy pouch bags at the top of his cheeks. At the final step at the entrance to the A380, he could feel his eyelids drooping downwards, and forced himself to snap them wide open again to simulate a state of attentiveness.

Eventually, he made it, and was greeted by two pilots on boarding. He nodded to them as he entered the gangway without saying a word. To Kasinov, one looked Russian, the other English or American. Behind them, he noticed a cabin attendant, a very charming young lady. She looked Russian.

The young female attendant welcomed him. "If you would like to follow me, Mr. Kasinov," she said. Then she whisked him away to his first-class cabin seat, 1A in the upper deck.

Kasinov noticed her name badge. It read ANASTASIA PASKOVA. Without any fuss, he settled into his seat. The young airhostess attentively made him familiar with the functioning of the control panel and the adjacent gadgets that came with the prodigious cabin enclosure.

"Anastasia," he said, a smirk spreading across his face, "do you know what your name means?"

"It's Greek, and it means 'the resurrection,'" she replied, smiling back at him. "I was told it suited this particular flight, and I think I know why." She gave a subtle wink.

Mikhail let out a deep chuckle, his first in a long time. "Well good then, Anastasia. I look forward to flying with you."

Vladimir has thought of every detail, or maybe it was Xenop. Xenop. Quite an impressive guy. One of a kind, I imagine—but a strange handle. I think I may be using his services in the future.

He smiled.

With a capacity of 853 passengers, the leased A-380 could fly up to eighteen hours with an empty cabin and up to sixteen hours when full. That was what he heard the copilot say. Kasinov may not have been aware of the Airbus's technical specifications and capacity, but tonight he knew that he was the only passenger. Roy had mentioned to him while they were on the ground that the preflight routine would be kept to a minimum, and all safety checks would have been completed prior to boarding. Roy was right. Within ten minutes they were accelerating down Changchun's primary runway. A minute later they were airborne. Ten minutes later he heard another noise from the Tannoy speaker.

"This is your captain, John Futcher," the pilot pronounced in a lucid English accent. "We have reached our cruising altitude of thirty-five thousand feet. We will maintain a speed of about five hundred and sixty miles per hour. This should give us a flight time of approximately fourteen hours. The flight path for this route would normally only take about twelve hours, I'm afraid, but we're unable to traverse the more efficient Arctic Circle routing, understandably due to self-imposed Russian airspace restrictions. Tonight we'll be routing over Hong Kong and Southeast Asia instead. Hope you enjoy the flight."

After resting for about an hour after takeoff, Kasinov rose from his seat to retrieve his bag from the overhead compartment. From her galley, which was pretty close to his seat, he could see Anastasia looking back at him. He noticed her shy smile before she looked away. *Probably admiring my lithe physique*, he thought.

Whist in jail, Kasinov kept himself in good shape, following a conscientious training routine each day. He had plenty of time and few distractions. His body was toned, and at just under six feet, carried a sylphlike muscular frame. Determined to productively use his time, in addition to writing his book, Kasinov spent at least an hour each morning pumping iron. Every afternoon, he did yoga. This was his routine. Seven years of it. It allowed him time for peaceful reflection, or as he put it, "to stop himself from thinking about taking his own life." Not many inmates joined in the callanetics, but he was very different from the rest of them.

Prior to his incarceration, he certainly did not lack female company, yet still he remained single. It had never been one of his priorities. Obsessed with growth of his business, and a penchant for his position in the power hierarchy amongst Moscow's corporate scions, he was far too consumed with grasping every business opportunity that came his way. There had been one girl, someone he met just a year before his arrest. She had captured his imagination in a way that he had never experienced. He wouldn't admit it to himself, but he looked forward to seeing her again.

Kasinov's mind was racing. He thought about the last ten years of his life. There was a lot to think about, good and bad. He tried to close his eyes, but he couldn't. It was almost as if he had forgotten how to close them. In one way, the anticipation of what awaited him was exciting—in another way, it was daunting. He was engulfed with deep hatred for those that caused his incarceration. It had been like this for Kasinov for seven years.

Retribution will come, he thought. *Later, perhaps tomorrow, I will think more about that.*

He prepared his mind for the next twenty-four hours. That was all he could think about for now. Eventually Kasinov's impatience got the better of him. He was never going to sleep unless he cleared his mind. He got up from his first-class seat and walked around the aircraft. It was quite capacious, and felt somewhat strange to him. Perhaps it was the fact that the aircraft was 852 passengers short of full capacity. As he moved along the upper deck, all he could hear was the somewhat muted but uncanny humming from the four H64 Rolls-Royce engines positioned on either side of him.

He glanced down through the cabin's apparent infinite aisles and adjacent galleys, and for the first time, he noticed the logo FLY EMIRATES at the entrance to the galley ahead.

They must have leased this aircraft before, he thought. *Well, at least I don't have to listen to them telling me that on board the staff speak twenty-two different languages.*

He laughed. It was his second laugh in an hour. His second in seven years.

Kasinov glanced in the opposite direction, where he noticed his reflection in one of the galley mirrors. He patted his neatly cut dark hair, thinking that his looks hadn't changed that much in the last seven years. *Just a few flecks of grey,* he thought. *I think I look quite a few years younger than forty-six. I think she will like what she sees.*

Some humor with a little self-adoration, and his mind was settled. It was time to return to 1A. There, he noticed Anastasia walking away from his seat, so he hurried over to see what she had been up to. Seven years in confinement meant nobody could be trusted.

He was pleasantly surprised by what he saw. She had made up his sleeper bed. It was now horizontally suspended with a mattress cover topped by a fluffy duvet neatly folded back halfway to reveal two large Oxford pillows all dressed in brilliant white.

I think I'll sleep well tonight.

~~~

Twelve hours later, Kasinov awoke from the

best sleep he'd had in seven years. He got up from his bed, took a stroll down the aircraft, and stopped off at the first galley. After about ten steps, he was met by a distinguished gentleman that Kasinov recognized as one of the pilots that had welcomed him aboard the previous evening. He was a tall man, well over six feet, and wore black flannel trousers and a white cotton shirt with black-and-gold epaulets exhibited flamboyantly on either shoulder.

The uniformed man proffered his hand. "Mr. Kasinov," he said in a classic public school English accent. "I'm Captain John Futcher."

Kasinov looked at him for a second. *Tannoy-man.* "Good to meet you, Captain."

"Hope you had an enjoyable and relaxing flight, sir."

"Yes, thank you. It was very comfortable."

"We should be touching down in about an hour and a half or so. Now would be a good time to get yourself freshened up, if you wish." The captain pointed to a place behind Kasinov. "We have shower facilities and a pressing service for you just behind the galley here."

Kasinov looked over to where the pilot pointed, noticing that half the cabin had been converted into a series of vastly oversized bathrooms. "Thanks."

Kasinov had come from a rather modest upbringing, where the living room in his parents' house was smaller than one of these oddly shaped cubicles. Despite this, he had grown well used to five-star facilities prior to his incarceration. He smiled, glad to be embracing luxury once again.

After showering, he made his way back to his seat, which Anastasia, he assumed, had returned to the upright position. He sat, closed his eyes, and tried to think about the positive things that awaited him in his new life. His mind, however, had other ideas—it wanted to ruminate about the past.

Consumed by engagement with Communist officials during his early rise to fame, with his chemical engineering degree in hydrocarbon exploration from Mendeleev Russian University under his arm, Kasinov recalled how he had taken his talents into a lucrative government position in 1988 as national oil reserve assessor. In this role, he led a series of geological surveys for rich oil and gas reserves. It was a role that meant he had to stand back from his thriving private business, leaving his partners to run the day-to-day operations. To him, it was worth it.

Kasinov remembered how, after joining state ranks, he had contrived his way into the role of lead assessor on the well test programs, which were carried out at significant expense to the state. Although Kasinov didn't have any capital at risk in this venture, he certainly didn't let this minor detail hinder his enthusiasm. He knew he would have investment opportunities in this sector—if only in the future.

It had all started during his formative years, when the adjunct of excessive Soviet expenditure in the Cold War and state sponsorship in domestic and foreign international military campaigns, without comparative income, pushed the Soviet balance sheet close to bankruptcy. During the late 1980s, against a backdrop of overwhelming state deficits, the Soviet Union needed to boost the value of state assets in a faltering economy. Kasinov, meanwhile, continuously convinced himself that his business ventures had helped the Soviet economy.

To the astonishment of the world—although Kasinov himself was not that surprised—the Soviet Union was dissolved in December 1991, and Mikhail Gorbachev resigned. He remembered standing in Red Square when Boris Yeltsin became the first president of Russia in 1991, arriving there on the back of an armored tank. It was an office he had witnessed him serve until 1999. Kasinov was aware that, despite being an original supporter of Gorbachev and developing under the Perestroika reforms, Yeltsin emerged during the pro-development twilight zone as one of Gorbachev's most feared political adversaries, ultimately replacing him. Kasinov liked this move. It suited his plan. It suited all entrepreneurial capitalists in the new Russian Federation.

Kasinov observed how Yeltsin, like his Soviet predecessor, showed his commitment to overhauling Russia's socialist economy into a more capitalistic free market economy. Gorbachev had stopped after incremental reforms, when social anarchy resisted his changes. Kasinov knew Yeltsin had no choice now but to go all the way, and go all the way Yeltsin did. With price liberalization and privatization programs, he implemented his version of economic shock therapy, which many of his opponents and former allies called "Economic Genocide." Others like Kasinov preferred to call it "Economic Liberalization."

In the subsequent aftermath of the Soviet Union's collapse, Kasinov recalled how Yeltsin's campaign had received much criticism when the new leader led a privatization process to sell state assets—more specifically, the assets that held rich hydrocarbon resources. Fortunately for Kasinov, in the chaos that followed, Yeltsin remained resolute in his conviction, believing this to be the only solution to generate much-needed state cash reserves to fund debts and continued outgoing capital requirements. Kasinov's only criticism— beyond the Russian premier's tenacity—was that it took Yeltsin all of five years to implement his plan.

He hadn't planned on waiting that long.

Kasinov believed he would have achieved it in a much shorter time frame if he had been in charge. Some things were outside of his control back then.

During the chaotic twilight that ensued,

Kasinov continued to appear omnipresent, holding both private and government positions as he job-hopped to suit his strategic plan. After an eight-month spell as the national oil reserve assessor, he unsurprisingly ventured back into his thriving private business, in which he was the major shareholder. In 1994, at the age of thirty, Kasinov rejoined the government. This time, however, he took a more illustrious position: deputy minister of fuel and energy. During his second tenure at government, which spanned a two-year period, he became engrossed in the pending sale of rich hydrocarbon reserves. On completion of his term in 1996, he returned to the private sector. He knew he needed to be on the other side of the fence when this deal came to market.

When the privatization process of state assets eventually took place, a significant portion of the national wealth was acquired by a group of industry titans, sparking the advent of a new era in the new Russia: The Oligarchical Era.

Kasinov, in his private capacity, along with some of his minority partners—ergo, the ones he invited—participated in this acquisition process. Together they acquired several oil and gas assets throughout Central and Northern Siberia for the sum of US$250 million in 1997. That was when Kasinov joined the oligarch club, a time he would never forget. Unbeknownst to him at the time, he would become the most successful of all the oligarchs, and when he did rise above the rest, he wasn't surprised.

At the time of the acquisition, Kasinov had set up his new company, KasOil, to own the assets, and in the years that followed, he went on to run one of the largest Russian companies to emerge from the privatization process. In 2000, he listed KasOil on the London Stock Exchange, raising £1 billion in one week, which valued the company at over £20 billion.

Kasinov had developed enormous value in business, along with personal wealth. All of this had come without reproach. Back in 2002, several Russian media outlets said his ego might have lost the run of itself, but now he sat reflecting, proud of his achievements.

Before they locked me up, I was the wealthiest man in Russia, and ranked twelfth on Forbes's list of billionaires. Fuck, I used to be one of the richest people in the world.

Kasinov thought about how, back in 2002, his stated net worth was US$10 billion. The celebrity lifestyle this afforded him came to a precipitous halt when he was arrested on the 12th of May, 2003, charged with defrauding the Russian government of tax to the tune of several billions of dollars.

He didn't see it coming.

Many said he should have.

Immediately after his arrest, Kasinov became even more incensed when he learned that the Kremlin had, in Draconian fashion, frozen

KasOil's shares as financial security against the alleged liabilities. From his pendent confinement, Kasinov campaigned for a year with vocal refutation, enunciating exculpations throughout the courts at every conceivable occasion. After almost a year in detention, conviction and sentencing was bestowed. Through it all, Kasinov had remained confident. He had all the best advisers reminding him about the strength of his case.

He expected negotiation and probate.

His expectations were wrong.

On the 20th of May, 2004, he was found guilty of tax fraud and convicted to a nine-year custodial sentence in a Russian gulag. In the months that followed, Kasinov rallied with anybody who would listen to him, both locally and internationally. However, as he came to expect, he lost his battle for appeal. After having served five of his nine-year sentence, he didn't think things could get any worse.

He was wrong once again.

He was infuriated when he received further charges of embezzlement and money laundering in 2009, charges that extended his prison sentence to 2017.

What really pissed Kasinov off was how Russia's president, Yuri Koshenko, remained nonchalant throughout the trial and the aftermath, claiming rigid faith in governmental processes. In the background, Kasinov knew that he was pulling all the strings to coerce a predetermined result. Koshenko also appeared oblivious to the benefits of international cooperation on respect for human rights, and consequently paid no reverence to any European court decisions, simply dismissing their findings instead.

I was more powerful than Koshenko, and I will be more powerful than him again.

The one single thing that enraged Kasinov the most happened two days immediately after his initial sentencing. The Kremlin, which had continued its tirade against KasOil, went on to assume government control of the company. Kasinov, who was by then well-ensconced in gulag-conclave, only heard the news a week after it happened. Worse again, he heard about it in writing. He wasn't surprised.

He reached into his bag and pulled out a copy of a newspaper report he had kept from that time. It was a special supplement that appeared in *The Moscow Times* in the days that followed his imprisonment. It featured the spectacular collapse of the company's share price. He sat in 1A with his eyes glued to the story.

It was discolored now, and brittle in parts from the dampness it had endured in confinement, but the contents hadn't changed. Not a day went by that he didn't look at it, and there it was in front of him once again. Although the report was pretty scathing, today he felt more relaxed as he read.

The article dedicated an eight-page pull-out

section covering a number of well-known UK blue chip investment houses that took some pretty big hits in KasOil's demise. Understandably, all the UK fund managers interviewed were pretty pissed. The center spread of the article devoted two full pages specifically to calculations on Kasinov's wealth, more specifically predicting the evaporation of his billions. It was colorful, with copious amounts of graphs to aid interpretation, all of which pointed downwards.

He shook his head. *What a fucken disaster.*

It was the same thought he had every day he read it.

Thoughts like this didn't change.

He nodded furiously as he placed the vintage supplement back in his bag. His thoughts had shifted, now focused on setting that disaster right. *Koshenko, you bastard, you publically humiliated me in front of the London Stock Exchange.*

In his treatises from jail, Kasinov dedicated a whole chapter to Koshenko's duplicity. His theory: that his sustained imprisonment was one of the great idiocies of the decade. He felt some comfort when the world media agreed and acclaimed his story on several occasions. Despite the unnatural worship he witnessed, he cringed every time he saw the moniker with which they had dubbed him: "The Prisoner of Conscience."

Kasinov felt that he had paid the price for his actions.

He had served his time.

Now it is time for Koshenko to pay for what he has done to me.

Suddenly Kasinov's ruminations were disturbed by a series of thuds underneath the aircraft as the Airbus's wheels hit the runway. The flight from the Changchun airport was complete. He checked his watch. It was 10:00 a.m. local time. He had been travelling for over fourteen hours, as the captain confirmed.

He wasn't interested in the arrivals headlines. He was more interested in the media headlines about to hit the airwaves. *"The Prisoner of Conscience is back,"* or something along those lines, he expected. Whatever they wanted to call him, he was ready for it.

The ground team guided the aircraft to a secured parking bay with a protected air bridge close to the central arrivals center.

Everything can be arranged for the right fee.

He threw on the charcoal cashmere coat that Roy had given him, flung his bag over his shoulder, and stood at the doors, ready to leave.

When the doors opened, Kasinov disembarked the plane and walked sharply through to the airport arrivals concourse. He moved speedily, without paying any attention to other arriving passengers from other flights that shared the concourse. Likewise, they didn't seem to pay any attention to him. He wasn't bothered either way.

As he made his way through the arrivals area before customs, he suddenly stopped and looked to his left. Despite his admission into the over-forties category a number of years earlier, his vision was still twenty-twenty. He craned his head further to his left, over to where a number of arrival shops were located about eighty feet away. One shop in particular drew his attention. It was a bookshop. He went inside, picked out what he wanted, turned to the shop assistant, and handed him his selection.

"How much?" Kasinov asked.

The ardent shop assistant looked up and immediately took a step back. Kasinov assumed that he recognized him from the photo neatly positioned at the bottom right-hand corner of *Siberian Liberty*.

"That will be eleven pounds and ninety-nine pence, sir," the shop assistant said calmly before turning the book over to scan the price.

Kasinov quickly paid the shop assistant, picked up the book, and paused to look at his purchase. He smiled.

The manuscript, published in hardback, was enfolded with a dark, fitted, plasticized sheet that contained a condensed vignette map of Russia across the front cover. Within the image, the cover designer had placed an embossed aerial view of the Krasnokamensk facility. It was his first time seeing the finished article. It had been published in Russian as well as English, but Kasinov only saw the English version on display.

During his seven years in jail, Kasinov had

become fluent in both written and spoken English, and whilst obstinately self-taught, he delivered both the original and translated treatises from the privacy of his cells. Kasinov knew that whilst *Siberian Liberty* provided a vivid assembly of the journey since his imprisonment, it lacked any prophetic definition of the future.

That definition will follow. That will be the next chapter. The final chapter.

He placed the book inside his shoulder bag and set off on his way towards the passport queue. Within minutes, he reached the inspection booth, where he offered his passport for inspection. The immigration officer looked at him and then his passport studiously. He repeated this motion with a slow nodding sequence as he flicked through the fresh new passport, brushing his thumb against the clean, crisp pages. Then he handed the passport back.

"Welcome to London, Mr. Kasney."

Chapter 5
London Calling

It was 7:00 a.m., exactly the time for which Natasha Volkonski had set her alarm. She hadn't slept well the night before, apprehensive that she might sleep through the wake-up call. She woke regularly to check the time at what seemed to her like hourly intervals. Now she simply lay there scrutinizing the clock in disbelief.

She looked around her room. "Shit!" she cried.

She launched herself from under the covers. *It's okay, only 7:00 a.m.*

As a seasoned narcissist, Natasha would need at least an hour and a half to get herself ready. Because this morning was special, she had allowed herself two hours. Like every good narcissist, she was also a good planner. Today was Thursday, and in making her way out of London this morning, she had to consider peak business traffic. She had built all of this into her plan.

After showering, she gently dried herself, maneuvering leisurely from one appurtenance to another inside her bathroom. She wrapped her hair in a bath towel and sat at her dresser inside her walk-in wardrobe. She gazed into the sizeable mirror. Looking back was a pair of deep blue, playful eyes that resembled a turquoise seascape brightly illuminated by sunshine. She shook her head slowly, leering back at herself without breaking eye contact. She liked her eyes. Everybody liked them. Then she teased herself, thinking about how she might deploy them when she returned.

For later, she thought.

After drying her hair, she tied it into a ponytail and looked into the mirror once again. Her hair was dark and shiny, falling to just below her shoulder. She moved her head from side to side, something she did often in an effort to check that the ponytail bounced at the right pace. She liked that, too.

Then she got dressed.

When the morning beautification ritual had reached its conclusion, she glanced at her watch. She flushed with pride—one hour and twenty-two minutes flat. *Still plenty of time for a morning coffee.*

She strolled through the corridor of her spacious, 3,600-square-foot Covent Garden penthouse apartment, making her way to the kitchen. Inside the central aisle of the kitchen, she pushed the espresso button on her Miele coffeemaker, and after a few seconds of clicking and churning, the formidable purring sound of pure Indonesian Java beans under brew began to resonate. As she awaited her espresso, she pushed a remote control button, and a slick, electrically operated curtain blind opened on the underside of the roof, flooding the room with reflective natural light. Espresso in hand, she tugged at the bifolding glass doors, opening them just enough to lead her out to a capacious private terrace, where she lit up her first cigarette of the day.

She smiled down on Waterloo Bridge in the distance and thought about how today might unfold. *I will show him what he has been missing. I hope he likes this place.* Her apartment was quite retro when compared with most of the new buildings in some of the more urbanized areas of London, but she preferred it this way. She had lived there now for six years, loving the location, the view, the residents, and its proximity to the West End. She particularly enjoyed the nightlife, and her new job.

Interested in art from a young age, but equally interested in being around people with lots of money, Natasha had chosen to work part time at the Royal Academy of Arts, a position she had taken up a few months earlier. She didn't need the money, as she was pretty well financed, but the gallery location was ideal, right in the heart of London's West End on Piccadilly, about ten minutes from her Covent Garden residence. In her unwavering social world, she looked forward to respite in the art exhibitions she hosted. As a part-time staffer, she only worked Mondays, Wednesdays, and Fridays. Today was a day off.

As she prepared to depart, she gazed in the mirror one last time. She wore a slim-fitting white silk blouse undone down to the third button, a black pencil skirt, a full-length red cashmere overcoat, and to complete the ensemble, a pair of 4.72-inch black patent Louboutins that supported her long, well-defined, tanned legs. Her makeup was impeccable, and her striking black hair, pulled back in a comely ponytail, bounced enthusiastically from side to side. She was ready.

She left the apartment and headed into the lift that took her down six floors to reception. When the lift doors opened, Dougie the doorman looked on in amazement, the same way he did every morning when she appeared. She spotted his ogling eyes as they followed a gradual path along her course. She didn't think Dougie was extraordinarily salacious. She simply had come to accept that most men looked at her this way.

She feigned a smile in the doorman's direction. "Good morning, Dougie."

"Good morning, Miss Volkonski," Dougie replied enthusiastically. "I've brought the Range Rover around, as you requested."

Together they moved outside the building through the revolving entrance. Natasha looked back towards the penthouse, marveling anew at its wonderful Victorian façade nestled amongst a series of spectacular edifices within Saint Martin's Lane. *Not bad for over a hundred forty years old,* she chuckled. *See you later.*

She jumped into the vehicle and nodded to the enthusiastic porter. "Thanks, hon." Once inside, she set the GPS sat-nav to the postcode RH6 0RN and made off.

Twenty-five minutes later, lost in her own reverie, Natasha's mind wandered as she drove south along the M23 motorway. She thought about the last time she had been with her quiescent lover, and wondered if he would still be the same. They had only been together for less than a year. She was surprised when she received the call the day before that he was coming to London. Although they hadn't been together for a long time, it felt like they had experienced so much together.

Before her mind wandered any further, a stern, preprogrammed, monotone voice suddenly came over the quadraphonic speakers. "Please make a U-turn at the next available exit."

She looked down at her GPS and realized that she had missed the highlighted turn.

After two consecutive highway exits and entrances, Natasha eventually arrived at Gatwick Airport at ten minutes after 10:00 a.m., a bit later than she had planned. Without thinking, she drove her Range Rover straight into P3 VIP parking, reserved parking with a minimum fee of £25 for one hour, or £250 for a day. She hadn't made a booking. She didn't even know that such a lot existed. She did know, however, that she could probably inveigle her way in somehow. She was well used to inveigling her way into places. So she positioned the car in the first available VIP space she saw, switched the engine off, and jumped out to greet the approaching attendant.

Natasha delivered a partial pirouette, like a figure skater launching out of a triple axel. "Hello," she said in an overtly affable tone. "I really hope you can help me."

"Of course," the attendant replied enthusiastically. "What can I do for you?"

She placed one hand on his arm. "It's my first time this far out of London, and after getting a bit lost this morning, now I'm late for an important pickup. Do you know anywhere safe where I can leave my car while I nip inside to collect my friend?" She blinked her eyes with all the adorable helplessness of a lost puppy.

The attendant smiled. "Leave it here with me. I'll look after it."

She feigned a swoon. "Oh, that's great. Can I pay you?"

"Don't worry about that. You carry on and collect your friend. Your car will be right here when you get back." The attendant pointed to the VIP designated space she had already assumed.

Best practices in how to win friends and influence people, she thought. *Dale Carnegie needs a new chapter in his book.*

She raced into the arrivals hall, with her heels clattering feverishly against Gatwick's porcelain tiled floor. Inside, she paused and frantically looked around to see where he might be. There was no sign of him. The electronic screen display offered no indication of a noncommercial flight on the arrivals digital scroll.

She checked her phone. Nothing. Then suddenly she looked up, and there he was right in front of her.

"Hello, Natasha," he said calmly in a deep voice.

The moment her eyes met his, she felt ominously weak. It was the same way she had felt the first time they met. She looked back down again. She felt like fainting, as if too much blood had been drawn from her brain. *Deep breath*, she thought as she regained her composure. She looked up again and caught him straight on. She smiled brightly as she raised both hands to his face. "Hello, Mikhail, my darling." She hugged him tightly.

She had never really expected to see him again after his imprisonment. She had, however, kept herself in training, in case one day Mikhail Kasinov, one of the most powerful men in the world, would find his way back into her arms once again.

And there he was right in front of her.

As she embraced him, Natasha clearly recalled the day of their first meeting. It was in

Vladivostok, on the 12th of July, 2002. She had just completed her studies in English and French languages at the Far Eastern Federal University in Vladivostok, and had been engaged in some temp work with Vinehall, a national promotions company that specialized in running big corporate events. KasOil had picked Vinehall to run their new Vladivostok office complex launch. Mikhail was visiting as the corporate dignitary assigned to cut the ribbon at the ceremony. Natasha served on the reception group for the function, along with about twelve others.

She was just twenty-one then. She had been so taken with Mikhail's speech, and was so dumbfounded by his nonchalant brevity in speaking to her afterward, that the first thing she did upon returning home that evening was to search online for a new career with KasOil. There and then, she completed the application to the careers administrator, extolling great anecdotes and references to her experience in simultaneous translation. Unashamed, she amplified her polyglottal credentials, which no doubt she thought would be advantageous in international business. She finished with a glowing reference from the Far Eastern Federal University.

One month after submitting her application, she was ecstatic when she received a six-month probationary assignment at KasOil's headquarters in Moscow, then even more ecstatic when she was thrown straight into the deep end, working with the international exploration group for production sharing agreements in the Arctic region off the Yamal Peninsula. As part of this team, she found herself in constant discursive deal-making sessions with senior international oil company executives from the US, France, and Italy. It was this arrangement that would lead her into a young career working with high-level executives on a US$660 million deal that would change KasOil and Kasinov's life forever.

~~~

Kasinov held her tightly as he vividly recalled the day he became totally smitten with her. In was on one of his international business trips outside Russia. Whilst on international duty, he always travelled with his own translator, Olga Tenerav, a fifty-four-year-old professional that had served under Gorbachev towards the end of the Cold War. Kasinov could have chosen from a wealth of talent in their translation group, but he chose her. He was pleased to have her services. Unreservedly, she was known inside KasOil as the best there was. Kasinov, even with his limited knowledge of vernacular English, knew that, with the increasing international breadth of his business, he would not survive without her.

On the day Kasinov met Natasha, Olga had fallen terribly ill during the flight into London. Met with the prospect of losing face before his counterparts on this acquisition, it was KasOil's head of exploration, Surgey Yusovitch, that recommended they turn to the young Natasha to fill Olga's role.

After waiting as long as he could for his team to fetch Natasha from her purported shopping excursion in the city, Kasinov entered the boardroom on the forty-seventh floor of 25 Old Broad Street. The contesting groups looked at each other in sustained silence as they each took their seats. The American Zeron Oil executives were on one side, interposed by their CEO, Brad Dunkley, the Russians on the other. Kasinov sat poised, ready to commence battle from the furthest end of the table. He saw Yusovitch at the opposite end of the table, wiping beads of perspiration from his brow.

Suddenly the door flew open. Kasinov looked up to see a beautiful young lady come bounding into the meeting room. Oblivious to the tension in the room, she wore a broad smile, the kind that suggested she had just graduated from university with first-class honors. She wore a slim-fitting, shoulder-less, blue-and-red cocktail dress.

Hardly formal enough for the occasion, Kasinov thought. *But she is stunning.*

He watched attentively as the young lady dispensed with a selection of shopping bags, all six of them, near the cloakroom. The bags were emblazoned with Prada, Gucci, and Valentino emblems, all of Sloane Street's finest. When she had finished stashing her purchases, she made a beeline for Kasinov and stretched out her hand.

"Hello, I'm Natasha," she said unpretentiously as her smile widened. "Nice to see you again, Mikhail."

Kasinov nodded. *Where have I seen this girl before?* He was captivated by her beauty as she took the only spare seat on the Russian side of the table. *"Davayte nachnem,"* he snapped as soon as she looked ready.

"Let us begin," Natasha translated dutifully.

Game on, he thought. Kasinov thrived on cutting deals, even more so when dealing with American oil companies. To show the power he held, he began by making them wait. He did so with a great deal of rigorous tea stirring as the two sides awkwardly introduced themselves. He listened to ten minutes of platitudinous reflections on unsuccessful and aborted negotiations over the previous two days. Kasinov figured that tolerance for dealing with ambiguity was not one of his strengths—something he actually favored, as he believed it was the Russian way. He preferred his style of negotiation: beat the opposition up with histrionics.

He glanced at his watch again. *Ten minutes of bullshit; that's enough.*

He stood, raised his fist unhurriedly and clenched it tightly. "This is the deal: 25 percent share ownership in Block 46A for US six hundred sixty million. It's my final proposal. If you don't agree to this now, I will leave this meeting and call the French in, and you will not get another chance to deal. Furthermore, I'll make sure that you'll never drill another well on the Arctic shelf, let alone conduct a seismic study."

His counterparts grimaced in astonishment at his demeanor until the volley of his adopted vernacular came via translation. Four seats down, Natasha stood at the same pace as Kasinov had and began performing a perfect theatrical rendition of the KasOil CEO's disposition, her fist raised, her face now transformed in a haughty posture, and her voice calibrated with austere and stern inflection. She repeated what Kasinov assumed were the same words in English with even more energy and passion than he himself had delivered. She even maintained the same intense stare at the US executives, as he had done.

Kasinov turned to cast a rare elated glance at her.

Natasha's eyes remained focused on the Americans, who clearly didn't know at whom they should be looking. By the time she had finished, they were accepting the deal with the kind of exhausted resignation typically reserved for the tail end of a marathon negotiation session. Natasha translated the Americans' acceptance with a slower and more salacious intonation as she stared at Kasinov.

In her perfect deportment and her liquid blue eyes, Kasinov was smitten.

Now, embraced together again for the first time in seven years, the two emerged from the airport arrivals terminal and made their way towards Natasha's car. Kasinov couldn't take his eyes off her, and she couldn't take her hands off him. Kasinov thought it seemed like a fair deal.

He knew he wasn't a wanted man in the UK. He had done nothing wrong here. He had chosen London in the first place so he could avail himself of political asylum, if needed. Several other oligarchs and leading Russian businessmen, including Boris Berezovsky, Roman Abramovich, Akhmed Zakayev, Alex Litvinenko, and Alexander Goldfarb, had done as much already, enjoying the protection of the crown during the early 2000s.

Now it's my turn.

He wasn't sure if he was ready quite yet to become part of the so-called London Oligarch Circle of Russian exiles. He wasn't very good in teams and clubs and things like that. He was more individualistic. As far as he was concerned, the only benefit from joining this illustrious club was that collectively they continued to remain in the UK without seemingly any risk of repatriation—except for Litvinenko, of course. He had died. *Poisoned.*

Kasinov was most encouraged by how the British government had cooperated with the London Oligarch Circle in fighting off extradition requests from Moscow. They even went as far as exposing Russian court convictions as politically motivated. *Pretty courageous of them to tackle Koshenko like that,* he thought. *Maybe I'll join, after all.*

Kasinov felt safe here in London's primary airport hub. He had no immediate intention of travelling back to Russia—certainly not in the short-term, anyway. In fact, he had no intention of travelling anywhere in the short-term.

Hand in hand with Natasha, he approached the VIP P3 parking area to a slightly disappointed looking attendant. "Here you go, madam," the attendant muttered. "Your keys."

Natasha briefly looked up. "Thank you," she said, half-smiling back at him.

She jumped into the driver's seat of the Range Rover and started the car. Kasinov slid into the passenger seat at the same time. He contemplated the media reaction that might follow. It was Thursday morning. He expected that the tabloids would pick up the story pretty quickly, but most likely, they wouldn't be running anything until the following morning. Likewise, he assumed that *The Times* and *The Telegraph* would run a story on him in the morning.

Apprehensive that his story would already be over the airwaves, he turned on the radio. He flicked through the channels until he found BBC Four.

No news on any jailbreak story.

No news on the arrival of a new oligarch.

He was comforted.

The Kremlin will keep a lid on this as long as possible, he thought. *At least for today, until they figure out what they're going to say.* He chuckled, nodding to himself. *This is going to be a major embarrassment for them.*

Kasinov had entered the UK by stealth—as if he had just walked through the front door—and nobody noticed him. His facial expression changed from a tense grimace to a tranquil smile as he switched channels to London FM. "Freedom," by Robbie Williams blasted away. He smiled. *I've done it.*

He glanced to his right to see Natasha's eyes looking back at him. "It's amazing to see you," she said sincerely as her hand graced his knee. "Amazing to have you back. I never thought I would see the day."

Mikhail turned further to his right to assess her fully. "I'm very happy to be back with you, especially here in London."

"I loved your book, by the way." She let out a little giggle. "Nice photo of you, too."

Kasinov reached for his bag and retrieved his purchase. "Thanks. I just picked up a copy on the way through. First time I've seen the finished article. It looks pretty good."

"So what are you going to do now that you're a free man? I mean, after I've finished with you, that is." She flitted a big wink across the luxury Tata automobile.

"I'm going after those bastards, the whole top tier of the Russian government."

"What do you mean?"

"You want me to be more specific?"

"Yes, please. I would love to hear about your plans. I hope it's nothing too dangerous."

Kasinov assumed a stern gaze. "No, not really. I'm going to attack them; I'm going to expose them to the international media; I'm going to bring them to their knees for everything they have done to me; I'm going to make their lives so fucken miserable that they will wish they had never interfered with Mikhail Kasinov. Then, when I have finished with them, I'm going to become president of Russia."

Chapter 6
The Blarney

From his perch on the rooftop terrace at Natasha's apartment, Kasinov scanned the lower part of the Strand and Summerset House, where he was afforded a portal view of the Thames. The sounds of squawking seagulls circling nearby resonated as he looked back at the bloated Gherkin edifice piercing the skyline in the distance. The new Saint Mary's Axe Gherkin structure hadn't been finished when last he was in London. He tilted his head slightly and saw it there, right beside the Gherkin: the NatWest International Financial Center. It appeared to have been supplanted by its newer, phallic-like companion standing like a rocket just beside. He pondered how Natasha had amazed him that day, when he had first met her in that building as she helped close the deal with Zeron.

Interesting that, eight years later, almost to the day, we are back in London together. I'm quite lucky to have her.

He smiled. *She's lucky to have* me. *Seems like a fair deal.*

Kasinov glanced across to the furthest window on the penthouse, where he saw Natasha standing at the mirror in her dressing room. *Probably the same place she stands every day for hours, if I know her.* He watched as she slowly slid her hands back into her hair and undid her ponytail, then massaged her fingers through her long, flowing locks. She shook her head, letting her hair fall back into its natural position. Then she stripped off her clothes. One by one, each piece fell from her body like confetti off a bride. Now she stood completely naked. Her skin color, a natural sallow tan for which all Europeans longed, glistened in the semi-fogged room. At twenty-nine, and despite her general aversion to the gym, Natasha looked fit. She wasn't a big eater, Kasinov knew, instead relying on her vegan nutrition to serve as medium to her fitness. More materially, though, Kasinov guessed that her investments in cosmetic and aesthetic surgery over the last few years had surpassed any exercise. He chortled. *All good investments, I'm sure.* He nodded. *Almost time for the trophy to get to work, I guess.*

Kasinov picked up the phone from the table next to his chair, scrolled down, and found the name David St. Ledger in the contacts page. He pushed the call button.

"David St. Ledger," the voice on the other end of the phone answered.

"Good morning, David. It's Mikhail."

"Mikhail? Or should I say Michael?" St. Ledger said with a chuckle. "It's good to hear your voice."

"I called to say thanks. Everything went according to plan. Thank you for organizing the passport. I didn't get a single question about it."

"No problem."

From Kasinov's recollection, St. Ledger was well travelled. He wanted to enquire about his whereabouts, more out of courtesy than curiosity. He was sure he could hear the sound of road noise coming through the phone. "Where the hell are you, David?"

"I'm currently traversing the rural cambers of Glendalough in the Wicklow Mountains—your favorite place, Mikhail. Just back from a few days in the Middle East. Only a few kilometers from home now."

Kasinov knew the place well. He had been there many times before, to visit St. Ledger on the east coast of Ireland. He could visualize the circuitous and meandering roads that traversed the fertile landscape to St. Ledger's abode. Most probably, at this time of year, it was splayed with birches and oaks from the adjacent forests, all of them likely still glistening from the morning dew. Kasinov imagined the sense of smell that a warm spring spell might offer. It was quite different from the muggy, salty smell he sensed from where he sat.

He had really enjoyed his time in Ireland. It had been relaxing, and also quite rewarding.

"Very nice," Kasinov said.

"How did you like your new name?" St. Ledger enquired, sounding like an errant schoolboy getting away with spraying graffiti all over the headmaster's office.

"It's got a nice ring to it," Kasinov continued with reserved reverence. "Good choice, David."

"It wasn't my choice," St. Ledger responded innocently. "I went to see my old Irish schoolteacher, and got her to translate Mikhail Kasinov into Gaelic. The closest thing that she came up with was Mícheál Kasney."

"St. Ledger, you old bugger, you're full of stories. I'll give you that."

"It certainly sounds more Irish than that other handle you've got, anyway. What was it? Misha, or something like that?"

"Well, it did the business, and I must have even *looked* Irish."

"Don't push your luck," St. Ledger said with a laugh. "You'll never be as good-looking as an Irishman."

By contrast, Kasinov knew he had the face of a Calvin Klein model, while St. Ledger's was more a face for radio. He hadn't seen him in eight years, so it was with some strain that he tried to visualize him in his mind. St. Ledger was usually quite well dressed and groomed. However, on occasion, the combination of his wild, curly mane, a series of crimson veins that made his cheeks look like road maps—a dyspeptic feature from his appetite for life itself, no doubt—and his excessive travel schedule left him rather disheveled looking. *He probably doesn't even notice.*

"When are you coming back to Ireland to see us over here?" St. Ledger enquired.

Kasinov had fond memories of staying with St. Ledger at Kinlough Castle. Located at Lugnaquilla, the highest peak in the mountains of County Wicklow on the east coast of Ireland, St. Ledger's abode was almost three-quarters of a mile above sea level. He had acquired the castle back in 1990 without encumbrance when he received a seven-figure fee for delivering a project in Saudi Arabia. Kasinov knew St. Ledger was fortunate to have gotten his hands on such a prodigious piece of land, a property that represented a significant presence in the area. With it came Yoda-like status within the community.

Kasinov had visited on several of the many occasions St. Ledger threw one of his renowned open house parties. Kasinov was most often treated as the special guest. Some people took St. Ledger at face value, and some tried to take advantage of his generosity. Either way, his parties made him remarkably well known and well liked.

St. Ledger was also a shrewd man, and up for any challenge. In both his business dealings and in life itself, he demonstrated a cavalier attitude, an attitude that had made him a multimillionaire. Kasinov always assumed that St. Ledger lived his life reciting one self-created aphorism after the next. He had a saying for everything.

"Not sure," Kasinov said regarding his next visit. "I need to stay put here for a while, but I wanted to let you know that we're having a little celebration party here in London on Saturday evening. Might you make it across?"

"If I know you, there'll be nothing little about it," the Irishman responded eagerly. "And, yes, I wouldn't miss it for the world."

"Great. I'll send you the details. Natasha is arranging everything."

"Looking forward to it."

"How's security there these days?" Kasinov enquired jokingly. The only one alteration to the castle he recalled St. Ledger conniving was an old cannon, the only remaining permanent arsenal from the original fortification. He often wondered if the artillery artifact had been around since the Middle Ages, along with the castle itself. If so, it was probably about six hundred years old. St. Ledger had told him that the vintage armament was dilapidated, and that he had found it hidden in one of the external buildings. He promptly had it refurbished and returned to the westerly turret, where he figured it belonged.

"Oh, it's still up there, shining and looking out over the landscape. Keeps away the terrorists."

Kasinov laughed. "Good to hear." Then he added in a more supercilious tone, "David, one last thing."

"Yes, Mikhail. What is it?"

"I hope we don't have to look backwards on this thing," Kasinov said rhetorically. "With the passport, I mean."

"Well, if we do," St. Ledger replied in an outlandishly witty tone, "we'll just have to double-cross that bridge when we get to it."

Kasinov almost broke into hysterics, but instead just shook his head. "Goodbye, David."

With that, he laughed and placed the phone back on the table. *Putting the aristocratic moniker and the palatial habitat to one side, David St. Ledger, you're just a good old gregarious Irish rogue—a risky rogue.*

There was one thing—one big thing—that worried him about St. Ledger: the passport. Kasinov knew that he had entered the UK covertly, but not illegally. Prior to his imprisonment, his philanthropic initiatives in Ireland had been far-reaching, with several investments into the Irish Youth Art Development Society in the late 1990s. His gallant generosity had earned him an honorary doctorate from Trinity University in 1998. Following the receipt of an Irish passport, his frequent visits and ongoing investments earned him his dual citizenship in 2001.

Whilst Ireland recognized dual citizenship, Russia did not. So in order for him to avail himself of his new Irish passport, he would have to give up his Russian one. That was clearly not an option in 2001. Now Kasinov knew the choice was much easier, as Moscow held his Russian passport. He wasn't going to have much need for it, anyway—well, at least not in the short-term.

Kasinov had heard St. Ledger was single now. His wife, Martha, had died of cancer seven years earlier. He didn't want to say anything on the phone about that. *Maybe I should have.* He had heard that she had suffered a protracted battle over three years, and that St. Ledger had been by her side for all of that time, expending every conceivable medical initiative to save her. *I should have enquired about his daughter, Catherine. She's probably turned twenty-one now. I wonder if she still lives at home?*

From his terrace perch, Kasinov glanced around the perimeter of the massive apartment and recalled how St. Ledger had helped in its acquisition some time after Kasinov's imprisonment. Kasinov had arranged for funds to be sent to St. Ledger to purchase an apartment in central London. He hadn't put any conditions to it—just that he wanted Natasha to leave Russia and wanted St. Ledger to find her a discreet upmarket place in London where she could live. They had found this place in Covent Garden after six months of searching. *Her taste was different from his, I imagine. She won, I guess.* And then St. Ledger had supervised the completion of the necessary legal documents for registration. *He's been a good friend.*

His thoughts were interrupted when he heard Natasha's voice, drowned out somewhat by the sounds of flowing water inside the apartment. As Kasinov's trophy-in-waiting, Natasha had been his kept woman since she had moved to London.

He knew that Natasha knew this, too.

He rose and navigated his way to the bedroom, following the sounds. When he entered the en-suite bathroom, he saw her in the centrally positioned oval glass shower. He undressed and then slowly entered, trying not to look overly excited. His lively eyes, however, betrayed him.

Arranged symmetrically at either side of the shower door were two cloth rails. Adjacent were six high-pressure Grohe showerheads placed around the internal circumference and operated from a central valve station. The shower network had a selection switch. Left to right, it read, THERAPEUTIC OR CARNAL. *Interesting pleasure selection,* he thought. *At least it's more utilitarian than the rails.*

As he closed the door behind him, Natasha immediately began to caress and scrub his back and front in all the areas she could reach, her hands emerging intertwined with his limbs like an octopus in flight. He turned around to face her. He kissed her. He held her arms. They felt tender and soft. He took her hands and pinned her against the shower glass wall. The glass, structurally embedded in the floor, with vertical struts to distribute any force against the panels, was quite thick. Kasinov wasn't aware of the design specification. It just felt solid enough to him.

Slowly he entered her and began to gently oscillate—as if their connection point was a cam. He moved his hands to caress her breasts and held them there, pushing her back against the glass as he began to oscillate faster. He turned her around, entered her again, took her by the hair and pulled her backwards. She followed with a series of unmerciful groans.

Still embraced, they left the shower and moved into the bedroom towards Natasha's bed. It was a large, neoprene-enclosed waterbed with a two-inch Tempur layer on the surface. Water dripped from their bodies, scattering everywhere, but they didn't notice.

As she lay on her back in the center of the bed, Mikhail entered her in a missionary locus and maneuvered himself so that he was deep inside. She grabbed him with both hands and pulled him further inside her. With her eyes lost in some pseudo cosmos, Natasha's thoughts were distracted when she saw the reflection of his thrusting gluteal muscle collection, flexing and pommeling in perfect synchronization through the glass reflective ceiling in the panel above the bed. *Even better than cosmos,* she thought.

As he pounded in mid-coitus, they both wore aberrant expressions: he had the face of a wild beast about to catch his prey; her face resembled that of a gharial reptile with her eyes protruding as if ready to explode from their sockets. This time, she let out a deafening scream as she felt a gushing flow inside her, her body reverberating in a spasm as they climaxed together in an almighty roar.

When it was over, Kasinov lay beside her with a smile on his face. His seven-year ascetic hiatus from passionate copulation was finally at an end. They lay floating on her bed. Then their heads turned, their eyes locked on one another as they smiled.

Chapter 7
The Kremlin Retort

From his heightened position on the top floor of the Kremlin's Senate building, Yuri Koshenko, the president of Russia, scrutinized a twelve-strong sentinel regiment that frog-marched the perimeter of the entrance. Dressed in full-length coats, the security detail performed a ceremonial duty in place for over a hundred years. Koshenko liked to watch them every morning he visited his primary office at the northern part of the Kremlin grounds.

He pulled back from the window and contemplated his tasks for the day, his gaze still fixed on the sentinel below. Koshenko was a big, burly man with raised cheekbones. Even in his midsixties, he was well over 220 pounds. His hands were like shovels. He had silver-grey hair that he kept slicked firmly back with Brylcreem—enough to hold this position all day. His eyebrows were deep-set and black and hadn't been pared for quite a while.

He glanced at his watch. It was 7:10 a.m. That was when his phone rang. On the other end of the telephone, Valentin Sokolov, his minister of security, spoke timidly.

"Sir, I have some disturbing news."

"What is it, Sokolov?"

Whatever was on Sokolov's mind, he sounded like he didn't know how to break the news. Eventually, he spat it out. "Kasinov is gone," he croaked. "We don't know how he did it, and we don't know where he has gone. He just *disappeared.*"

Koshenko felt the fury rise in him. Turning away from the Senate frog march, he stood at his desk, his jaw visibly tightened, his fist clenched and banging against the table. "Damn you, Kasinov, you fool!" he cried out.

Sokolov said nothing.

Koshenko moved haphazardly across his office floor. He was distressed to the point of delirium. "How the hell could he have escaped?" he barked into the cordless phone. "That place was supposed to be impenetrable. Where is he gone to?"

"I have to assume he's heading for the UK," Sokolov theorized. "That's where they all seem to go these days. We're still trying to pull the CCTV footage together on what we have."

Koshenko's mouth twisted in outrage as he threw the phone across the room. It lodged itself in an eighty-year-old, wall-mounted watercolor of Vladimir Ilyich Lenin, connecting right in the head of the world's greatest Marxist proponent, causing a tear in the canvas from which a goatee and a bald head protruded on either side of the imploded handset. Koshenko didn't even notice. It was the last thing on his mind.

Demented with the news, he called an emergency meeting with Prime Minister Vasily Popov, Minister of Security Valentin Sokolov, and FSB Director Andrey Borodin—the FSB being the more contemporary version of the now defunct KGB. They gathered hastily from nearby offices within the Kremlin and assembled around Koshenko's board table in the private meeting room adjacent to his office.

"Sokolov, you sit here," the president said, motioning to him to sit directly opposite. Valentin Sokolov was former KGB. He was a big man with a rigid face, and was bursting out of his rather shiny tan suit. He looked shell-shocked. The Russian premier didn't waste any time as he stared intently at his minister of security. "Sokolov, how the hell could you let this happen? I gave you everything you asked for at that facility. What went wrong?"

"I don't know, sir, Mr. President," Sokolov responded, his face revealing the stupor of a beaten man. "I still haven't managed to speak with

Igor Tishkovets, the chief warden. We lost all comms from there around midnight. I'm running blind, and I'm still trying to find out his condition. I'm told he was flown to Moscow Central Hospital."

"Gentlemen," Koshenko said disquietly. "Kasinov is set to become a world martyr, and will make us look like fools. We have to act quickly and decisively. We have to find him, get him back into our custody, and make a fool out of *him*."

Koshenko knew he was not particularly well liked outside Russia. Inside Russia, he wasn't exactly top of the pops either. Six years earlier, he had undermined the sovereign integrity of Russia after he froze shares in KasOil, *transferring* all of the oil and gas reserves, as well as production facilities from KasOil, over to the state oil company, Rus Energy. Consequently, several of the world's leading premiers lost whatever remaining trust they had in him. He lacked credibility with the international media for the same reason. In the world media, this *transfer* was seen as pilferage by the state. The act had delivered a major reputational blow for Russia's democracy and its ability to attract international capital. Several of the emerging Russian elite also disaffiliated themselves from Koshenko's polices and left the country following the action against KasOil.

Despite his communitarian upbringing, Koshenko believed that he was a strong adherent of capitalism. His problem was that he never showed it in his policy-making decisions. Morally, he was also on the wrong side of the high ground. Over the previous six years, the Kremlin had entertained several interventions and pleas for Kasinov's release—from France, Germany, and from the US. Koshenko knew well that they had treated them all superficially.

Koshenko's trusted prime minister, Vasily Popov, glanced around the room. Nobody else had anything to say, and as the number two, he finally decided that he should speak. "Yuri, to be totally frank, the world media showed no reverence about the sincerity of our claims against his fraudulent tax evasion," Popov said. "We need to up our game. We need to let the world know that Kasinov's personal reputation has more to it than is currently known in the public domain."

Popov was scrawny, with grey, deep-set, penetrating eyes, a balding head, and an oversized charcoal suit. He looked like a weak man, but Koshenko knew better. Popov was a shrewd man, and capable of anything, so long as it suited him.

"I don't know if you guys know it," the president shouted, "but there is a major PR game about to start out there." His finger darted in the direction of the window behind his desk. "And we need to win."

"Maybe it's time we made the Vitaly Kuznetsov case visible to the international media," Popov suggested.

Kuznetsov was KasOil's former head of security, arrested in August 2009 for the murders of three people. He was currently on trial at the Moscow City Court. He would most likely receive a life sentence, if found guilty. Koshenko firmly believed that Kuznetsov worked under Kasinov's direction and instruction. Although he had no definitive proof, the Kremlin's legal fraternity had kept their version of contemporaneous records and circumstantial hypotheses on Kasinov's activities.

That was good enough for him.

Now Koshenko contemplated releasing this to the world media. He clearly did not have concern about the risk of resulting libel following the release of such anecdotal information. He felt that his arch nemesis was in no position to launch any attack on the Kremlin, in any case.

He never was and never will be.

Popov passed Koshenko a paper that summarized the three murders for which Vitaly Kuznetsov, KasOil's former head of security, stood charged—each of which, according to the Kremlin's findings, were symbiotic with development initiatives at KasOil. Koshenko pondered the details as he read. *Mikhail Kasinov, you must be involved.*

According to Kuznetsov's attached résumé, he started out with the KGB in 1987, moving on to work for the Committee for State Security, where between 1989 and 1997, he was part of the secret military operations service within the KGB. There were several hundred guys out there like him, all with the same credentials. When he left Russia's intelligence federation, he joined Kasinov's emerging empire as head of security, and transpired to take over the same position in KasOil when it became the holding company for all of Kasinov's businesses.

Koshenko's jaws tightened. He was now up on his feet, pacing around the boardroom table. He paused—his lungs almost bursting out of his suit—and took in a deep breath. "Popov!" he roared, pointing randomly in the direction of his scrawny number two. "We need to let the world know about the cash he siphoned out of here."

The others around the table didn't say anything. They just nodded in the president's general direction, offering tacit agreement.

Koshenko glanced out the window. In the distance, at the entrance to the Senate building, he could see a rambunctious media gathering outside. They had been congregating there all morning after rumor had broken of big news. It was the third time he had checked, and now at nine thirty, he could make out about forty or so media antagonists—all this despite lack of confirmation about the nature of the rumor. He had his man there in the middle of them.

Outside it was bitterly cold—-4 degrees centigrade, although it probably felt much colder. Snow was falling as the media group huddled together around their equipment. Some of them moved in circles to keep warm. All of the Russian TV stations and newspapers were there. *I can control most of them.*

He also saw CNN, CNBC, Al Jazeera, and many others with their cameras ready. Most of them had employed some sort of snow-covering protection on their equipment, suspended and ready to be whipped off at a moment's notice. *The Wall Street Journal, The Washington Post, The Times,* and *The Telegraph* all had their own representatives in Moscow. Reuters was present, ready to sell the story to everybody else in the international press who wasn't represented. The collective agitation seemed to be growing, Koshenko estimated. They had been waiting now for several hours. He guessed it wouldn't dampen their tenacity on what was set to be the story of the decade.

Andrey Borodin, the tall, well-dressed FSB chief, had been particularly quiet up to now. Borodin was shrewd, and much younger than the other triumvirate in the room. He represented a new generation of Russia. He didn't have any previous KGB affiliation. He was much too young for that. Instead, he had joined the FSB straight out of university. Ten years later, he was now the man in charge there. His taciturn demeanor expired when he threw out his suggestion. "Why don't we consider doing a deal with Kasinov?"

Koshenko anchored a stern gaze on his intelligence chief. *My ministers are worse than irritable children sometimes.* "We don't do deals with criminals," he said dismissively.

Silence fell around the table. Then, after about thirty seconds, Koshenko, thinking his dominion may lay in the balance, waved in Borodin's direction. "Go on then, Andrey. What sort of a deal are you suggesting?"

"We could give him a pardon," Borodin said, his eyes directed at Koshenko, who in turn had taken to staring at the ceiling. "Providing, of course, he agrees not to pursue any political retribution." Borodin looked around the table at his peers. Nobody had eyes for him. "That's the biggest risk to all of us. We drop the murder investigation, and he keeps his billions."

Koshenko eventually peeled his eyes from the intricate cornice design that surrounded every crevice of the room, and shot them in Borodin's direction. "You might accept that if you were in his shoes," he bawled at his young FSB chief. "But Kasinov will never accept such a proposal. He is simply not the biddable type."

Borodin shifted his shoulders.

"If he *is* in London," Koshenko said, this time in a more conciliatory tone, "and I have to assume he is, then we need to get the Brits to give him back to us. It's as simple as that. It's the only solution I want to entertain right now."

Incensed by the insanities of the morning, Koshenko retreated to his office after finishing the meeting with his ministerial assignees. There, he paced up and down his stone-clad floor like an actor practicing his lines before a scene call. It was 11:00 a.m. in Moscow, 7:00 a.m. in London. He waited one hour before picking up the telephone and calling Andrew Wood, the British prime minister, on his private cellular phone. He got his voice mail and Wood returned the call three hours later. "Andrew, this is Yuri Koshenko from Moscow. We have a situation. Mikhail Kasinov has escaped, and I believe he has taken political asylum in your country. I want him back."

"Yuri, my good friend," Wood replied arrogantly, "I've just heard of your dilemma. I have to report that it appears that your Mr. Mikhail Kasinov has entered the UK under an Irish passport bearing the name Mícheál Kasney."

Koshenko threw his eyes up to heaven. "How the hell can that happen?"

"Don't ask me. You need to direct that question to the Irish prime minister," Wood answered. "There is nothing I can do with someone who has entered the UK with a legitimate European passport. The European Community permits such exclusively, and he is entitled to stay here as long as he likes, I'm afraid."

Koshenko slammed the phone down in a rage. This time, it spared what was left of the Lenin portrait and instead reached the cradle. He knew he now had no alternative but to phone Eamonn Burke, the Irish prime minister in Dublin. Almost one hour later, after several attempts, his office assistant eventually tracked him down and transferred him through to the Russian premier.

"Eamonn Burke here."

"This is Yuri Koshenko." The Russian premier spoke in a stern tone. "President of Russia."

"Yes, Yuri," the Irishman answered in a friendly voice. "What can we do for you?"

"We have a major situation with Ireland. We understand that your government has issued a passport to a known Russian criminal, Mikhail Kasinov, and he has now taken up residence in the UK. I need you to revoke this passport so he can be returned to Russia immediately." Koshenko paid no mind to the excessive disrespect his tone showed to his Irish counterpart.

"I'm sorry, Mr. Koshenko. I have just been briefed on this, and it appears he originally received the passport back in 2001." Burke sounded confident. "Apparently he has Irish ancestors, which entitles him to receive a passport. At the time he received it, he was not a criminal. The name change to Kasney happened more recently, and I'm still getting to the bottom of that, I'm afraid."

"Irish ancestors!" Koshenko shouted in disbelief. "You've got to be kidding me."

"Yes, Yuri. They're apparently from County Wicklow."

Koshenko slammed the phone down for the third time that morning—a new personal best. He shook his head vigorously. "Bloody Irish!" he cried out as he stared up at the nineteenth-century internal ceiling architecture. A TV screen suspended from the wall inside his office interrupted his gaze. On the top right-hand corner, the image read CNBC EUROPE. More specifically, something on the TV caught his attention.

He grabbed the remote control device and pushed the volume up several notches. "Reports are being received this morning concerning hierarchical challenges at the Kremlin," the young female reporter said. "As yet, there are no details." Below her pretty face, a ticker tape scrolled across the screen, just slow enough for Koshenko to make out what it said. He saw one Russian stock after another decorated in a scarlet red, their arrows all pointing south.

"Fuck you, Kasinov! When I get my hands on you, I'm going to make you pay, you bastard."

After Koshenko calmed down, he sat back at his desk and contemplated his next steps. He knew that neither London nor Dublin was about to intervene and send Kasinov back on the next flight to Moscow. He guessed that he couldn't keep a lid on the rumor much longer. He leaned forward with his elbows on the leather insert of his desk and held his hands to his head. Then he grabbed his pen and started writing.

At around 11:00 p.m., a Russian governmental official made his way through the main corridor that led from Koshenko's office. After escaping the warren of wood-clad timeworn offices and secondary corridors, he descended the cascading stairs of the Stalin hallway inside the Kremlin and went down the escalators. He passed through the security perimeter and headed for the main entrance. Four men sat inside the guard station, but didn't look at him.

He stepped outside to face the audience of cameramen, journalists, and photographers. He wore a large grey overcoat with a matching grey sheepskin ushanka, thick black leather gloves, and black boots. He stopped short in front of the media gathering, took one step up to the microphone-infested soapbox, and listened to a barrage of questions in English and Russian.

He paused. He looked up at the crowd of media and held his gaze. The tumult began to calm and fade into the frozen stone paving along Red Square as the anticipation grew. Then he looked down at the sheet of paper in front of him. "I have prepared a statement, which I will read," he said before briefly looking up at the crowd.

Then he read. "Last night, just before midnight, Mikhail Kasinov escaped from the Krasnokamensk prison in Central Siberia. A number of Russian security personnel, along with members of the Committee of the State Duma, were severely injured in the incident. To add to the charges to which Mr. Kasinov has been sentenced, charges that include tax evasion and fraud, we will now be examining his link to three murder investigations connected with the trial of former KasOil head of security Vitaly Kuznetsov. Further, we have been made aware that Kasinov has stolen cash belonging to the Russian government, to the value of two point five billion US dollars. We will be rigorously pursuing its repatriation to Moscow, along with the perpetrator. Mr. Kasinov will be brought to justice through the international courts, through close cooperation with our international allies, and ultimately here in Moscow. We expect Great Britain and Ireland to do the sensible thing and hand Mr. Kasinov over to us. Any insidious threats to Russia's stability made by Mr. Kasinov will not be tolerated."

Then he looked up and paused. Within a few milliseconds, there was a torrent of questions thrown at him.

"Has President Koshenko spoken with the British PM about a rejection of political asylum?"

"I thought that prison was supposed to be impenetrable?"

"Do you suspect any political repercussions with Europe and the US?"

The orator's calibrated performance was exceptional, and answers to the volley of questions were not forthcoming. Instead, he stood phlegmatically, nodding through a cold grimace. "I have made the Kremlin's position very clear in the statement," the president's emissary answered flatly. "I won't be answering any questions."

Then he turned around, dismounted the soapbox, and walked away. He re-entered Stalin Hall as the second round of tumult faded away.

Chapter 8
Invitation

Roy returned back home to his villa in Florence twenty-four hours after he left Kasinov at the stairs of the Airbus. After years of relentless international hotel hopping and short-term leases in different cities around the world, he had chosen Italy as his base two years earlier. As the birthplace of the Italian Renaissance, Roy figured it was politically, economically, and culturally one of the most important cities in Europe since the fourteenth century. He loved it mostly for the deep historical heritage it offered.

Following a brief search not long after his arrival, Roy had acquired a villa in the suburban area of Porte Santé. Neatly situated in the mountainous outskirts of Florence with the most magnificent panoramic views, the villa made him feel fortunate that he wasn't resigned to one of the estates on offer today. From the platform on which the property stood, he could see a profound architectural mix embracing the horizon that spanned five separate centuries. Current contemporary designs interspersed with Romanesque, Gothic, Renaissance, and Neoclassicism masterpieces pierced the skyline from every crevice of his secluded vista.

A bit better than living in an army camp, he thought.

Seven years earlier, following a very successful career in the SA army, Roy decided that it was time to do something different. Several years in Angola followed by regular support missions to Uganda, Sierra Leone, and Sudan had become repetitive, and the enthusiasm he had held when he joined the armed forces was no longer there.

At the age of thirty-six, after reaching the distinction of commander, Royston Graham Young left the armed forces in the summer of 2003. Despite having had a number of girlfriends, he was arguably the most eligible bachelor in the force when he departed. He could never seem to turn them into longer-term relationships. Roy always assumed it had something to do with his work. He wasn't sure if he wanted to be married or not.

I would be a pretty high-risk husband, he often thought.

Despite having left all that behind him, Roy remained single.

Unenthusiastic about the need or desire for the daily routine of permanent employment within the private sector, Roy started doing some consultancy work with Securicon, a US security services firm. Securicon, like many private security service organizations, was engaged in providing a variety of outsourced intelligence services and contingency evacuation planning for clients worldwide. They needed Roy for work in Nigeria and Algeria—an area where he had a lot of experience. Roy needed them to prevent himself from becoming a professor in neo-classic Italian philosophy. Seemed like a fair deal.

After making his mark on the company, he had applied to, and remarkably was accepted into, Cambridge University, where he enjoyed some of the best years of his life en route to picking up some particularly useful skills in addition to his psychology degree.

Roy's degree, however, was the last thing on his mind as he sat on the terrace at his villa, the midday sunshine beaming down. He felt relaxed and contented as he sipped a glass of Gavi.

Perfect.

Surrounded by ten-foot high terracotta ramparts separated with pine green powder-coated iron gates, the entrance to Roy's Porte Santé residence was worthy of celebration for the villa's two-acre plot. Matching pine green shutters safeguarded each window, as if it was a fortress. Inside, the sandstone walls gave the place an earthy but comforting feel. The intruder access inhibitors within the architecture around the boundaries of the estate comforted him with the requisite solitude from his neighbors, adventurous tourists that ventured this far out of town, and any unwanted guests. Anybody that made it past these measures, Roy would just have to deal with personally.

He glanced through the portal between the arrangements of tall cypress sempervirens and olive trees to the plush Mediterranean landscape beyond. He looked forward to the quiet time Florence would afford him. With his strenuous employment assignments behind him, he knew great solicitude in visiting the incredible inspiration offered by some of the Florentine galleries and palaces. *Rebalance my philosophy calling,* he thought. *Something to look forward to, maybe next week.*

Roy finished his glass of Gavi and broke away from his propitious vista. He walked up a small flight of marble steps through the front entrance that led into a spacious foyer. He glanced to his right at the drawing room with its fresco ceiling. *My inspiration room—won't need that for a while.* Roy moved to the left, into his living area, where the kitchen and the main living room were arranged in an open plan. Here, the rooms were restfully furnished with Venetian antiques that he had picked up on his travels, interposed by a large settee with two contemporary chaise lounge couches either side. Roy had arranged them that way so they all looked straight into a flat screen television.

Behind them, a pair of French doors led out to the terrace on the other side of the room. Roy had some occasional guests that came to stay, and on the second floor, there were four large bedrooms that each had balcony terrace areas to enjoy the panoramic views. In the scheme of things, for Porte Santé, Roy felt the place was enchanting without being too extravagant.

In his limited spare time, Roy had become modestly acquainted with the marvels of Italian cuisine. He was adventurous enough to try anything, and had cut out some time before his last assignment to develop his culinary skills by participating in elementary Italian fine dining workshops. Inside the kitchen, a U-shaped island boasted a selection of modern utensils, traditional copper pot ware, and a quintessential pizza oven.

Roy spent a brief time mooching around, thinking about what to cook. After checking through a few cupboards, he decided to conjure up a bowl of tortellini ricotta. When he was finished preparing, he topped it off with a few leaves of parsley. He proudly placed the bowl in front of him, admiring his creation momentarily before tasting. He nodded, pleased with the result. As he took a bite from his ciabatta, he flipped open his MacBook to check his mail.

There were several new messages in his inbox. Surprisingly, one of them was from Mikhail Kasinov. Roy raised his eyebrows, wondering how Kasinov had obtained his email address. The man certainly had a long reach. And why was he sending an email to Roy?

Probably just thanking me again, Roy assumed.

He opened the email and read.

> *Dear Xenop,*
>
> *Thanks again for all your great work in Siberia. I know you were the mastermind, and I'm deeply indebted to you. I'm having a party in London this Saturday evening. We'll be celebrating my freedom. Hope you can make it. Details attached.*
>
> *Mikhail*

Reputation precedes him. Roy thought. *Why am I not surprised?*

Roy recalled the conversation that had gotten him involved with Kasinov's escape fourteen months earlier. Even though Alpha Factor was history, he found it difficult to erase the experience from his mind. He even remembered the prefix that appeared on the screen when the call came through. It was one he hadn't recognized. It bore a 1-202 dialing code. *Somewhere in the US,* he had thought. *Maybe a Washington number.* When he answered, the conversation was one-sided and determined.

"Roy, you don't know me," the caller began, "but my name is Clay Parker. I am the director for a special government intelligence services group here in Washington, DC. I hope you don't mind me phoning you on your mobile, but I have a business proposition that I would like to discuss with you." The voice on the other end of the line was decidedly emotionless.

Roy had thought for a moment that he recognized the name, so he paused before responding. "You CIA?"

"Not exactly. Perhaps I can explain when we meet."

"I'm sorry," Roy had said tersely. "I don't work with national intelligence agencies."

"I think you'll find this assignment to be very much within your sweet spot."

Roy's impression of the CIA was not a positive one, as he'd always believed their efforts to extend the Angolan conflict had led directly to the death of his friend, Leon Chamois. More specifically, he felt that they were the cause of the ego-inspired extension at the back end of the Cold War. Roy knew that the South Africans would have been out of there long before the advent of the Cuito Cuanavale hostage mission if it wasn't for the CIA.

"I'm sorry," he said. "I'm just not interested in working with the CIA. Thanks."

Parker continued with his solicitation, adding further inducement and explanation to the mission.

"I'm terribly sorry, Mr. Parker, but I have to go."

Then Roy had hung up the phone.

The moment Roy pushed the red button, he remembered how he knew the name Clay Parker. Parker was the CIA liaison officer in Angola back in 1989, and now he was director of some government intelligence services organization in Washington. *Breytenbach was right,* Roy had thought. *He was a high flier.*

About an hour later, Roy's phone had rung again. This time, he recognized the number and the name that came with it. Lee Carter, Securicon's CEO, was on the line. "Lee, nice to hear from you. I was expecting your call."

"I believe you hung up the phone on Clay Parker," Carter said with thinly veiled astonishment.

"Yes, I did," Roy replied. "I don't think I'll be working with those guys."

"Roy, you would be doing me a massive favor if you just went to meet this guy. You don't have to make any commitments. You just have to go and meet with him and see what he has to say."

Though he had no desire to help the CIA—or any other intelligence services group, for that matter—Roy figured that maybe this could be an opportunity to seek revenge, or even rectitude, with the American intelligence agency, and somehow undo the past. Also, Carter had been very good to him, so he didn't want to let him down. "Tell me what you know about Parker's plan."

The next day, Roy had arrived at Dulles

International Airport at 1:00 p.m. After clearing immigration, he went through customs and made his way outside into the arrivals area, where he was greeted with a colorful display of welcome signs: corporation logos, hotel carriers, and even antecedent iPad tablets with names stenciled in big bold fonts. Behind the front row of signage, Roy noticed a man with a dark suit, white shirt, dark tie, dark glasses, and a black hat. Roy thought he looked like he could have been from a *Men in Black* set, but he carried Roy's name on his welcome card.

Roy nodded at him. "That's me. I'm Roy Young."

"Welcome to Washington, Mr. Young," the man said.

They drove to a location a few miles west of Washington, along the Potomac River and into Langley. On arrival at the suburb, they turned two corners, made their way up a long approach road, and there in the distance, Roy saw what must have been Central Intelligence Agency headquarters. *He is CIA*, he had thought.

After traversing over-tight security and travelling through well-appointed halls—everything courtesy of the American taxpayer—Roy found himself standing in the doorway of a corner office occupied by the man he assumed to be Clay Parker. He was a surprisingly scrawny-looking man, balding, with distinctive dark-rimmed reading glasses that he wore down on his nose.

"Hello, Roy," the man said fervently as he ushered Roy into the office. "I'm Clay Parker. Welcome to Langley. And thank you for agreeing to see me, especially on such short notice."

Roy shook his hand and nodded taciturnly.

Inside Parker's voluminous office, Roy noticed a mahogany writing table with a matching boardroom table surrounded by eight black leather chairs with stainless steel spider legs. The artwork was modern deco, six different pieces spread around the room. Despite this, the place suggested a neo-Spartan aura, most probably due to its enormous footprint. Roy glanced out the window before taking a seat. The view, looking back down the glistening Potomac watercourse, with the city of Washington, DC, in the distance, was quite impressive. *Probably the best view in the house*, Roy estimated.

They took a seat at the big table, and after a few minutes of exchanging pleasantries, Parker cleared his throat and looked set to commence business. "Roy, you have an incredible record of success. We've done our research. Thirty-six different missions, and every one of them successful."

"Thanks for the update. I'm not keeping score."

"Even as far back as Angola, apparently you freed those hostages from the Ruacana power station when everybody else assumed they were dead. That was amazing. That's on Wikipedia. You're etched in history."

"You can't believe everything you read on that thing," Roy said. "Anyway, I left some unfinished business behind on that one, so let's say it's thirty-five out of thirty-six."

Parker nodded for such a long while that it looked like he was stuck for words, but eventually, his brain reconnected with his vocal cords. "Let me ask you, do you know the history around the Mikhail Kasinov case?"

Roy sat with a nonchalant expression. "I'm not following him on Twitter," he answered without intonation. "But last time I heard, he was still locked up in some Russian gulag somewhere."

Parker looked back at him, his hands clutched together and resting on the table. "Yes, he is, and unlawfully so. If I could just take you through the background information for a few minutes and tell you why I've asked you to come here . . ."

Roy leaned back in his chair and motioned for Parker to go on.

Parker sat up straighter in the chair and eyed Roy head-on. "I report directly to the Office of Congressional Affairs at the White House," Parker said, overtly pausing for a moment as if to let his proximity to the president of the US sink in. "What I'm about to share with you has the full backing of President Bill Peterson—although, as you can imagine, he would not like to be quoted."

Maybe he's expecting some form of a congratulatory glance in return? Roy had thought. Instead, he regarded his host without moving a muscle on his face—something he had learned in the army, not at Cambridge.

"Yes, well then," Parker said, fumbling. "As you can imagine, the CIA doesn't usually engage in tactical situations in the field—this is generally left to our boys at the US military or the Marines. However, on special occasions, when tactical troops can't be sent flying in the front door, Central Intelligence is required to oversee and sometimes engage in tactical and covert activities at the direct request of the president of the United States. We have such a particular situation, which is a very delicate one, and this requires us to look at what we call here ITOO, or Intelligence and Tactical Operations Outsourcing."

Roy knew this language, and did the translation for Parker. "You mean it's too hot to handle with your own operative agents?"

"It's not as straightforward as that. If I can take a minute to explain . . ."

Roy nodded.

"We are a complex organization, with several different groups residing here at Langley. One of those groups, which I lead, is called National Clandestine Services. We just call it NCS here. We take on the difficult stuff, the stuff the CIA can't handle. We hold national authority for the coordination, deconfliction, and evaluation of clandestine operations across the intelligence community of the United States. Generally speaking, once it's decided that we're going the

ITOO route, it comes straight to me."

Roy remained silent, waiting.

Parker shifted in his chair and cleared his throat. "Over the last two years, we've been working in close collaboration with Central Directorate of Interior Intelligence in Paris, and the Bundesnachrichtendienst in Berlin, on the Kasinov case. The intelligence agencies from the US, Germany, and France have been collectively united in our support towards an amicable resolution to this case. We have tried to work with the Kremlin, in a somewhat restrained fashion, to pursue a route of pardon for Kasinov and subsequent political asylum in the UK or wherever. However, it's been extremely disappointing. After six months of covert discussions, the Kremlin has just come out last week and publically avowed his case. Apparently, it's now classified as a matter of sovereignty. Further, the Kremlin has insisted that he is not a political prisoner. They've totally rejected the findings of the European Court of Human Rights, and now they've further extended his sentence on additional trumped-up charges."

"Sounds like the guy is in a spot of bother," Roy responded tersely.

"Well then, you may have heard that, two days ago, he was transferred to the Krasnokamensk prison in Central Siberia. Krasnokamensk is not a very pretty place. It's set in a remote Central Siberian location in close proximity with Russia's largest uranium mine and processing plant, where the outlook for radiation contamination is high. Kasinov spent his first six years of incarceration at a place called Fire Island in the Vologda region of Russia, but at Krasnokamensk, he risks radiation poisoning, along with a number of other contaminant diseases."

Roy could feel where this was going next. His nods became slower and longer, and his facial expression slightly more vacuous. "Surely this is an issue for the international and Russian courts to ensure he ultimately gets a fair trial."

Parker gathered his hands together as if repentant before rejecting the idea. "The likelihood of an objective and fair trial is low." He went on to explain Kasinov's apparently benevolent relationship with KasOil.

Roy gazed at Parker. He could feel his eyes pulling back into his sockets. "You make the guy sound like the pope. And since when did the CIA, or the NCS, or whatever you call yourself, develop an interest in the moral human rights of international political prisoners?"

"There are several sides at play here. His ill treatment is one of those."

"Several sides at play," Roy repeated. "This thing has more sides than a nonagon. What other sides are we talking about?"

"It's complicated. But believe me when I say that it's in everybody's best interests if he changes address."

Roy shook his head in frustration, stood up from his seat, and then fixed his eyes back on the intelligence chief. "We can make this a short meeting, if you want. Up to you. I need to understand the definition of complicated."

"Okay. If I may bring you into confidence here?"

Roy took his seat again. "Of course. My discretion is assured."

Parker took a moment to clear his throat once again before divulging his stealthy proposal. "We want you to lead a team, working with a select Russian group, to get Kasinov out of prison and back to the UK."

Roy looked briefly at a spot just above Parker's head. He elucidated a soliloquy in his mind as he paused. Then he looked back at Parker curiously, his forehead darting forward as his eyebrows weaved closer together. "Let me get this straight. You want me to be the lead international operative, representing not only American Clandestine Services, but also France's Directorate of Interior Intelligence and Germany's foreign intelligence agency, to work with a team of Russian mercenaries who neither you nor I have met, and I'm supposed to help them break into Russia's highest security prison somewhere in the middle of Siberia, where we'll get the most illustrious political prisoner in the world out of Russia and walk him in the front door to meet the queen. Are you serious?"

"The logistics of the operation will be handled by the Russian group," Parker said. "We need you for your tactical ingenuity, your military entrepreneurship, and most of all, your experience in delivering successful missions. Furthermore, the Russian group are not mercenaries, but carefully chosen private operatives with the requisite military and security intelligence knowledge and experience. A very credible man is leading them: Kasinov's former business partner, Vladimir Sakharshenko. We made initial contact with him about a year ago, and we have been working with him now for several months to jointly plan this."

Parker paused and waited for a reaction.

There was no reaction.

After a few moments, Parker sat up in his seat. "I'm able to offer you a substantial fee: two million dollars. Thirty percent up front and the remainder on completion, plus another four million for the rest of team to be apportioned at your disgression."

"It's not about the money. What you're asking me to do seems egregiously outrageous. The risks here are enormous." Roy spoke calmly, but not without some thespian emotion. "The Russians aren't going to make it easy to penetrate their venerated penitentiary and extract their most scorned political criminal."

"It's not going to be easy, I know, but I believe it's possible. Everything is possible if you put your mind to it, Roy."

Roy stood. "I can't give you an answer now. I need to think about it."

"Okay, I understand."

"When do you need to know?"

"Twenty-four hours."

~~~

"Better make it another double."

"Another double. Yes, sir."

From his seat at the hotel bar, the more Roy thought about the offer, the more ludicrous it sounded. *Sounds like something from one of those illusory Hollywood thrillers. Unbelievable.*

The doubles continued to flow. None of the thousands of Quakers at the hotel for some convention appeared. It was just Roy and the barman.

"Why does America want to control everything?" Roy blurted as his words began to slur.

"I don't know why, sir," the barman said. "I'm not from America."

"Where are you from?"

"Venezuela."

"Oh, okay. Any opinions then?"

"Because they can, perhaps?"

"Good answer. And please stop calling me sir."

"Yes, sir."

Roy looked around. Still no Quakers, but there were plenty more doubles. He sat there at the bar, shaking his head and thinking. How would all this look if it all went tits up? America's Clandestine Services, along with Europe's powerhouse duet, would be exposed. It would probably reinvigorate Cold War sentiments. Roy would probably wind up in the same Siberian gulag as Kasinov. The anathema would be so bad, it might even provoke international war. Either way, it looked like they would go through with it, with or without him.

Roy slammed the glass on the table. "Fuck it," he said as he got up to leave.

The barman just looked at him and nodded.

Roy stumbled from his chair.

"Would you like some help, sir?"

"No, I'm fine," Roy responded in an inebriated dialect. "I'm fine."

He moved a few steps and tried to negotiate his way around a large oval table with a glass-veneered top that seemed to be doing its best to block the entrance to the room. *What's that doing there?* he thought just before he walked straight into it and walloped his head on the side leaf.

That was the last thing he remembered.

The next morning, he awoke at nine with a sore head. He took a shower and ate some breakfast. Then he called Parker.

"I'm willing to entertain your proposal on two conditions."

"What are the conditions?"

"Firstly, this is a one-off event. No sequel."

"Okay. And the second?"

"If I'm not comfortable with any of the Russian

team, I'll make changes. I trust that will be acceptable."

"That's fair enough," Parker conceded. "Agreed."

"What next?" Roy enquired.

"Three things. Firstly, you will use the code name *Xenop* for all dealings. Secondly, you need to fly to Budapest and meet the Russian team leader, Vladimir Sakharshenko. Thirdly, until this is over, you cannot be close to anyone—you understand?"

"All sounds a bit clandestine, but I understand."

~~~

From his gorgeous Italian villa, Roy sat back after reading Kasinov's email. He smiled. That was then; this is now.

No harm in going to London for the weekend, I guess. It'll probably be the party of the year.

Chapter 9
In the City

Melanie awoke with a startle to the weekday biorhythmic buzzing that rang out from her alarm. Her bedside clock read *5:30*. After twisting and turning a few times, she unleashed a loud yawn before unraveling her slender, naked body out of the cotton sheets and shutting off the buzzer.

A deeply accented voice surprised her in response. "Good morning. It's 5:30 a.m., and this is BBC Radio Four. This is a special broadcast with breaking international news. The Kremlin reported late last night that Mikhail Kasinov, referred to in the international media as Russia's *Prisoner of Conscience*, their most famous political prisoner, escaped from the maximum security penitentiary facility in Krasnokamensk, Central Siberia yesterday. He is believed to be seeking political asylum in the United Kingdom."

Melanie jumped upright and brushed her long, auburn hair from off her face. *Oh my God, he's here in London with the rest of them!*

She eyed the radio again.

"It is believed that the Kremlin is seeking international cooperation from the UK and Interpol to intercept Mr. Kasinov," the BBC reporter continued. "In a subsequent telephonic interview late last evening with Sir Charles Browne, the British foreign secretary said that neither he nor any member of his government had received any application for Mr. Kasinov's political asylum in the UK. Further, he said that, according to the immigration records in the last twenty-four hours, there is no record of any Mikhail Kasinov entering or leaving any UK airport or sea terminal."

Melanie scampered naked across her bedroom and into the shower. Ten minutes later, she was out the door and on her way to the office via taxi. *How is the stock market going to react to this news when they open? Some good. Some bad. More good than bad, I think.*

In the taxi, Melanie recalled how, ten years earlier, KasOil had listed on the London Stock Exchange. Their IPO raised £1 billion in a single week, a staggering achievement. In that year, KasOil and Kasinov had received every possible investment award on offer: FTSE Company of the Year, CEO of the Year, Analysts' Choice of the Year—you name it and they had won it. She had heard countless anecdotes of how, during the time of the listing process, an extremely flamboyant and assertive Kasinov had wooed investors to buy into his vision.

After his arrest in May 2003, the stock markets reacted negatively, with KasOil's value plummeting by 20 percent in the three days that followed his arrest. Some of the more senior analysts that Melanie knew had said at the time that this was overkill, and that they anticipated an even greater upside would follow after an expected acquittal. Melanie thought it was unfortunate for investors who believed in the acquittal paradigm. It never happened. Instead, he was convicted and subsequently received a lengthy punitive custodial sentence one year later after his initial arrest.

Melanie was well aware of the underlying sentiment with former city shareholders in KasOil towards the Kremlin. It was not a very good one. The Russian government carried out what many investors labeled a *Draconian Raid* on KasOil's assets. Oblivious to the legitimacy of international investor claims, Koshenko had stated that his actions were totally within his rights, claiming it was a charge in lieu of the alleged unpaid taxes. Expectedly, following the Russian premier's austere actions, KasOil's £20 billion market capitalization evaporated overnight. Remarkably, it was about the same value that Koshenko's accountants had calculated was due to the state for unpaid taxes, resultant fines, and anticipated court costs.

On that day, billions of pounds of investment from UK investors vanished. The exact amount, nobody knew for sure. The city of London would never forget that day, the 20th of May, 2004.

Despite this investment catastrophe, Melanie was aware from her socializing that select members of the stock market community remained somewhat sympathetic to Kasinov, believing the political conspiracy surrounding Russia's anti-oligarch campaign to be responsible for the demise of KasOil. These optimistic investors believed that, if he were to escape, an opportunity for retribution and compensation towards the billions lost in UK shareholder funds might emerge. Investors who were stung the most believed that Kasinov was indeed complicit in the precipitous evaporation of value, and ultimately master of KasOil's—and his own—destiny of failure.

In the years that followed, and indeed until quite recently, Melanie had witnessed much market speculation that if Kasinov ever did get released or indeed escape from captivity, that this might be the catalyst for a resurgence in a new pro-democratic, pro-capitalist market in Russia. Melanie had researched a number of speculative scenarios if this were to happen.

Today, the speculation will be put to the test.

Still engrossed with the permutations and consequences of the news about the Russian oligarch, Melanie arrived at UGC's offices at 6:30 a.m., together with her café latte from Costa. She knew that today was going to be different from any other day she had seen before. She cleared her desk, took a couple swigs of her latte, gathered her thoughts, and immediately started working on a guidance note for her investor clients.

Melanie had started at UGC Bank as a junior research analyst for their domestic stock trading equities group, and following a number of very positive performance reviews, worked her way up the hierarchy to the position of senior analyst for all international equities at UGC—a position that got her involved in several city deals; a position where she could yield her knowledge, skills, and influence; and a position where she had some power. She was one of a select few of her gender to possess these attributes.

Today was going to be one of those days where she got to use that power.

Feverishly, she crunched away at the keyboard, rotating from spreadsheets to worded text and then back again. At about two minutes before 7:00 a.m., she had the research note completed. She brought up her usual template that included the email addresses of hundreds of investors. She looked through it one last time, and then pushed the send button. A second later, it was gone.

Her extracts concerning Kasinov's escape and the implications for the investment community were succinct and focused.

Oil & Gas
UGC Securities comment
9 Nov 2010
Oil & Gas Daily Note

KasOil (KO, delisted) Kasinov Escapes from Siberian Jail

The Russian government has announced this morning that Mikhail Kasinov, former major shareholder and CEO of KasOil, has escaped from his Siberian confinement

In light of this information, and consistent with its commitment to maximizing shareholder value in the event of any change in the now delisted company KO, former shareholders of KO may have new and legitimate claims against the Russian government for loss in investment and associated opportunity costs. Our initial estimate is that this could run into the order of several billion dollars based on information that was referenced in Kasinov's book and will no doubt be released by Kasinov now that he has escaped captivity.

The development could have materially positive implications for the long term acquisition of formerly inaccessible controlling interest in Russian assets for major international Oil Companies; Zeron Oil, L'Energie, and Ital Petroleum. BUY.

This development could bode well for other smaller UK-listed Russia exploration oil and gas companies with assets in Russia such as Han Oil and Alex Energy. BUY.

Melanie Bauer, Senior International Equities Analyst

melanie.bauer@ugcsecurities.com   +44   (0)   20   7612 4314

Melanie knew that the landscape for investment opportunities in Russian associated oil and gas stocks had changed significantly overnight. She also knew her knowledge was not exclusive—her interpretation, maybe. Other leading oil and gas analysts that facilitated equity trading knew this, too, and by 7:10 a.m., one by one, a glut of analyst guidance notes emerged like spam into investor email inboxes and global private and institutional fund manager screens.

They were the ones who wanted the notes.

They were the ones who could play with this opportunity.

It wasn't long to wait before the city would see what separated the boys from the men—or in this case, the boys from the girls.

By 7:45 a.m., Melanie looked through all the analyst notes she could get her hands on, only to discover that several of the more conservative analysts did not project the developments and subsequent outlook with the same material positivity as she had. Instead, they proffered more moderate HOLD ratings, guiding investors to *wait and see* outcomes, concerning implications, consequences, and reactions around Kasinov's escape. *Everyone is entitled to his or her own opinions,* she thought.

At 7:50 a.m., ten minutes before the markets opened, Melanie pondered how this event was not an everyday occurrence—more like a once-in-a-lifetime occasion. The more she thought about it, the more anxious she became. If she got it right, she would be a heroine; if she got it wrong, she probably would be out the door with a brown box of files under her arm.

When the markets opened at 8:00 a.m., there was complete pandemonium, with major demand for the positively associated oil and gas stocks connected with this development. Melanie's note was the one cited most.

It caused a rally.

It was a rally like no other rally seen before.

By 5:00 p.m., when the markets closed, Melanie sat sharing her concentration between the three screens that covered her desk. She focused on the middle one as she pulled up the dealing summaries for the day. As the application opened and she saw the numbers, her hand moved to her mouth. During the day, Melanie had moderately observed the positive trends, and was quite excited about them. Now that she was looking at the consolidated summary, she was flabbergasted.

Oh my God.

Trading in Zeron Oil, L'Energie, and Ital Petroleum was fierce, with over 122 million shares changing hands, the largest one-day trade in the history of the London Stock Exchange, with all three of Melanie's referenced major stocks ending significantly up—+25%, +22%, and +23%, respectively. The minor exploration companies, which she had identified with Russian interest, were up almost 20 percent on average for the day.

She chuckled. *Very nice to see them all sharing the same jungle green arrows.*

Excitedly, Melanie had observed during the day that the liquidity trends were positively disposed towards UGC, but she knew that it would not be until the markets closed before all the deals would be accounted for and the full liquidity could be calculated. Now she clicked on the tab that read *Trading Source* to see how the league table of city bankers had actually faired. She couldn't believe her eyes. She glanced around to see if anybody was looking at her. They weren't. Instead they were staring into their own screens. *Probably doing the same thing*, she thought. The screen in front of Melanie showed that UGC had done almost 80 percent of the trading in the London market.

We've probably earned fees for the firm in one day alone equivalent to what we would normally see in a year.

Melanie then pulled up a screen for Moscow's RTS stock exchange. Almost 1,600 miles away in the Russian capital, the picture was a very different one. She wasn't surprised to see it was a different color, too: scarlet red. Russian stocks had plummeted against the international rally, almost 10 percent down—their single biggest one-day loss in history.

Melanie's gaze into her monitor was broken when she noticed Richard Finlay, UGC's CEO, emerging from the bottom of the staircase that led to the trading and research floor. He was wearing a light navy suit, a white tailored shirt, and a matching navy tie. *Quite timely that his appearance is coincidental with the stock exchange closing,* Melanie thought. Finlay was somewhere in his late forties. He had been CEO now for almost three years, and had built up enormous credibility with the market during his tenure. Melanie had seen UGC grow quite significantly under his stewardship. She was reasonably impressed with him, but not overwhelmingly so.

Finlay began to gather the research, sales, and broking teams together around the room. Today, his confidence appeared at an all-time high as he moved graciously and cheerfully towards the central area. A few minutes later, after everyone had finished shuffling into the vacant spaces around the perimeter of the room and between the desks, the informal assembly was complete.

Finlay nodded, looking around the gathering, and after clearing his throat, he began. "One of our core values here at UGC is *Expect the Extraordinary.* We certainly achieved something extraordinary here today, and I have to say we certainly didn't expect it. Today has been a momentous success for the firm. We have traded over one billion pounds in oil and gas shares—the largest day of trading in our one-hundred-year history. I want to thank Melanie particularly for showing great foresight and leadership in anticipating the market reaction." He paused, looking over at her with admiration written all over his face.

Melanie wasn't surprised by the look. *He probably picked up a couple million for himself today,* she thought.

Everybody on the floor followed the direction of Finlay's gaze.

Finlay raised his right arm, pointing his index finger in her direction. "That piece of work today was masterfully insightful and exceptionally noteworthy," he said. "You certainly have the best crystal ball in the business. Drinks are on me tonight. Let's pack up our things; we're going to Temperance."

Finlay was not alone in his approbation for her mastery. No sooner had he finished dishing out the drinks invites than an assemblage of traders, research analysts, and brokers overwhelmed Melanie. Several of her colleagues patted her on the back with great reverence. Some even gave her big hugs. She felt a little overwhelmed with the attention, but she also knew that she deserved the kudos.

Ten minutes later, along with several of her colleagues, Melanie arrived at Temperance, a typical trader and banker hangout situated a few minutes away from Paternoster Square. Melanie liked the place, as it was one of those venues that just seemed to get exponentially louder as the night went on. By 6:30 p.m., the place was full, and with Finlay's credit card secured by the Temperance staff, the volume of trading at the bar was analogous to that on the stock floor several hours earlier. By 7:00 p.m., the pub was vibrating with energy somewhat incongruous with the venue's appellation.

There was good cause for celebration within UGC. Putting Finlay's bonus to one side, the research, sales, and broking teams at the bank had collectively earned a bonus pool of about £2 million for the day. Tonight was a night that Melanie was definitely going to celebrate. She knew she deserved it. She spent time chatting with everyone: colleagues, associates, and directors. Several of UGC's main investors had joined when word got out that Finlay was paying for the drinks. He was known as a bit of a cheapskate in city circuits, so on this historic occasion, people came from as far as the West End just to see him roll out the cash.

Although exceptionally pleased with the day's events, at around 11:30 p.m., as the party fizzled out, Melanie took a breather from the festivities. Finlay and all the other head honchos had gone home. She grabbed a seat at a quiet corner of the bar.

Now it was just her.

A forlorn expression forged across her face as she thought about the last few years of her life. She had received a text message from Roy a few days ago and hadn't replied. Still, she couldn't fathom why they had split up, or where he had gone. *He just disappeared.* It had been three years since they broke up. Unfortunately for Melanie, there seemed to be no correlation between time and healing. She wished there was. She just tried to keep herself busy, keep her mind on other things—things she enjoyed doing.

She rooted through her bag, took out her BlackBerry Gold, selected his name, and typed the text message.

Wish you could have been here, especially today, Melanie x.

She paused, looked at it, and thought about changing it.

Then she thought about sending it.

In the end, she just saved it.

She put her phone back in her bag and tried to think about the positive things in her life. She deliberated her involvement in Cambridge Phenomenon, a business cluster development group for ex-graduates. She knew it simply as "CP." Since completing her degree, Melanie had maintained a strong link with the alumni business network group and was putting her time there to good use. Despite the iconic academic status the university held, it strongly supported sustainable entrepreneurial development. As an enthusiastic fusion of converted academics and thriving entrepreneurs, CP met every second month on campus, at the Great Court of Kings College. The group was specifically designed to support former Cambridge students to develop start-up companies. By 2005, it had become the largest alumni venture capital fund in the UK. With Melanie's experience in the city, coupled with her Cambridge degree in economics, she joined CP a year after graduating, and hadn't missed a meeting since.

Although it was something that kept her busy over the last three years, it was also through this same association that she had met Roy. Well, indirectly anyway. She remembered it well. It all started at a CP gathering in February 2006. Following the meeting, meandering her way through the campus back to the car park, Melanie met up with Robert Williams, one of her old friends from her graduation year. Very kindly, Robert invited her to join him and some of his friends for the annual boat race.

Melanie enjoyed this special day, and had been to just about every Oxford-Cambridge Boat Race since her first year at Cambridge. In the university annual calendar, it was by far the premier event. It took place biorhythmically each year at the advent of the spring equinox. Rowed along the River Thames, the race of the year featured the top Oxbridge rowers, men who competed passionately for the revered prize in an eight-man format. Ironically, both teams called themselves the *Blues*, with one difference: Cambridge was adorned in light blue, whilst Oxford wore dark blue. As they went into the April 2006 race, Cambridge held the advantage, having won the race seventy-eight times compared to Oxford's seventy-two times.

On race day, the starter groped for his loudspeaker and pistol at the Putney launch platform as Melanie maneuvered her way through the crowd en route to the meeting point. From her watch, she could see she was late. As the race start-time approached, several thousand spectators, having found vantage points along the arduous serpentine route that traversed from Putney to Mortlake, had gathered to support the prestigious four-mile-long event. Melanie could see the university boat race stones that marked the finish line on the south bank at Chiswick Bridge in the distance. This was her destination.

Behind them, she noticed a series of white tarpaulin marquees that she guessed had been feverishly erected in the days before the race, exactly as they had been every year she had attended in the past. She also remembered each year how they were filled to the brim with a wealth of local young waiters and waitresses that stood guard over copious cases of Moet, Pimms, and enough beer to satiate an army.

She continued to move purposefully along the passageway as people made way for her. Robert had told her to come to the middle of the bridge, where she would find him waiting. She made her way in that direction, but found it difficult to gauge her exact position in the midst of the vast crowds. The fervent bridge-top gathering moved excitedly as the final muffled words from the race starter rang out over the Tannoy system in the distance. Melanie thought it sounded like he said the race was about to commence. Then she heard her name being called just before a loud crack reverberated in the sky. She looked around and located the direction of the sound of the voice she recognized.

Robert stood about fifteen feet away, right in the middle of the bridge.

Wow the perfect spot, she'd thought. *Exactly where he said he would be.*

~~~

In one of those little cosmic coincidences that go unnoticed among the complex interactions of daily life, whilst Melanie was reliving the moment she met Roy there on the bridge, he was relaxing at his Porte Santé villa thinking about the same moment.

He'd been dressed in a white short-sleeved T-shirt and jeans when he joined Robert with some friends, and together they'd found the perfect panorama from the center of Chiswick Bridge. Outside, the temperature was warm, and the sunshine had started to break through the sparse clouds. Summer was on the way, and everybody was smiling.

Robert moved to introduce everyone amidst the tumultuous clapping. "This is Melanie," he said. "She's my good friend from when we were undergraduates here a few years ago." Then, turning to Melanie: "Melanie, these are my really good friends David, Andrew, and Roy."

Roy noticed her straightaway. He was immediately attracted to her light, flawless skin that seemed to radiate a deep serenity in every move she made. When her smile emerged, Roy was definitely curious. His eyes shifted across to Robert and then back to Melanie.

Robert, you never mentioned that she happened to be stunningly beautiful.

He noticed Melanie looking at him, her dimples accented inside her growing smile. She was dressed casually in jeans and a light grey wool sweater with a black leather jacket adorned with fur appendages to the collar and sleeve ends.

Melanie reached out her hand, offering an introductory salutation. She passed through the first two, delivering confirmatory glances as they greeted. When she got to him, Roy offered a disarming smile as their hands touched. Then they greeted, and eventually she slowly pulled her hand away as he held her in his gaze.

"Here, slip in here in front of us so you can see," Robert said, motioning to the space he had created.

It was as if Robert had broken a magnetic field that connected them. Melanie slowly broke eye contact with him as she moved to the front. Calmly, he watched her pass, sensing a glorious combination of lavender and spice as his eyes closed involuntarily to absorb the aroma. When he opened them again, he noticed her body twitch briefly as she touched off his chest with her shoulder.

Before Melanie had time to settle, Roy could see that Oxford had already stormed into an early lead. Their club president had won the toss and elected to take the North Middlesex Station with the advantage of the first and last bends. Roy estimated this would give Cambridge the advantage of the South Surrey Station, as well as the longer middle bend. By the time they had passed Hammersmith Bridge, Team Oxford was two lengths ahead. Cambridge tried hard to catch up, but they were unable to close the gap despite increasing their stroke rate. He looked up to see the two teams approaching Barnes, only to see Oxford six strokes ahead. Cambridge continued to push. Tumultuous cheers for each crew roared out along the water's edge as both teams approached the finish line. It was too late. Oxford won by two lengths.

Unruffled in defeat, Roy glided his way confidently towards the Darwin marquee following the race. He and his pals had arranged to attend the exclusive after-party there. Reputed for having the most revelry and fun, it was the place where most people tried to get into after the race. Roy could see Melanie gazing at him as he picked through the crowd. He could see her so clearly without having to look.

Roy pulled out a bunch of Darwin entry passes and flashed them to a young waitress whose name badge read PENELOPE. She ushered them to a table outside on the west-facing area to enjoy the beautiful sunshine. Outnumbered in gender, Melanie sat perched between Roy and Robert on one side with David and Andrew on the other side of the table.

"Ah well, at least we are still six up!" David exclaimed, unleashing another illustrious platitude.

Melanie turned to Roy. "Where is your accent from? It's quite different."

Roy's eyes rotated slowly towards her until they were fixed on her pupils, before dropping to scan her lips. "It's a bit of a mixed bag, to be honest. "I was born here in the UK, but I've lived and worked in several interesting places in Africa. More recently, I've been spending a lot of time in the US."

"Oh, of course," Melanie said with such excitement it was almost as if she had just made some new breakthrough in genetic therapy. "It does sound a bit South African, now that you mention it."

"You must live somewhere close to the queen, with that accent of yours," Roy responded with a smirk.

Melanie left out a little giggle before blushing. Then she delivered a playful but forceful jolt to his shoulder with her right hand.

That was the day he fell in love with her.

Now he guessed it would have been better if they had never met.

Chapter 10
The Glamazon

It was Saturday evening in London, and the winter chill had taken the temperature to 38 degrees Fahrenheit outside. That might be cold for most Londoners, but it was pretty warm for a former Siberian inmate. It was dry now. The wet spell had passed—at least for the next four days, according to The Weather Channel.

From the rear seat of the pristine metallic silver Bentley, Mikhail Kasinov looked up to see a chauffeur raise his head towards the rearview mirror and announce they would be arriving shortly. Minutes later, they were stopped. As the hum from the Mulsanne's V8 engine began to wane, an austere-looking man with a black suit approached the vehicle and opened Natasha's door.

From the rear seat, Kasinov watched Natasha slip out her left foot first, followed by her right, where she was greeted by a profusion of clicking and flashing from the assemblage of photographers and media that had gathered outside 44 Berkeley Square. Kasinov gazed at her as she alighted. She looked particularly svelte in her Hervé Léger shrink-fit dress that emerged from under her open-seamed, navy, full-length, hybrid wool coat. As she approached the awaiting frenzy, he saw her smiling fleetingly as she flirted with the paparazzi brigade. *She hasn't changed a bit,* he thought.

Kasinov climbed from the Bentley directly behind her to repeated shouts of his first name, followed by a volley of questions about his escape and future plans. He nodded to the crowd with a pompous smile. The simultaneous questions were so voluminous and loud that they even drowned out the clicking and flashing from photographers. Kasinov wore a navy suit with slim-fitting shirt, a skinny navy tie, and a navy cashmere overcoat. He looked more like a GQ model than an escaped oligarch. He caught up with Natasha, took her by the hand, and paused. The questions continued, so he decided to choose the one he wanted to answer. Selective listening was one of his many traits.

Kasinov nodded to one of the reporters at the front of the gathering who repeated his question enthusiastically. "Mikhail, how does it feel to be a free man, and how long will you be staying here in London?"

Kasinov glanced at the reporter before looking at Natasha. "As you can see, I'm very happy to have left Siberia, and I plan to stay in London for as long as London welcomes me."

A young reporter adjacent to Natasha probed a microphone towards him and almost knocked him over. "Mikhail, will you be launching a campaign against those who you claim locked you up unfairly?"

Kasinov's gaze on his trophy girlfriend was broken as a frown forged across his face. His upper lip turned as he eyeballed the young reporter. He had thought about formal interpellation, but he knew it was not recognized in Russia. *If it were practiced, this would have been the first step in ousting government officials who kept me locked up, but as it's not, I'm just going to have to do this the hard way.* "I will be devoting all my time to achieving complete subjugation of the regime that has held me in jail illegally for seven years. I will interrogate the system until I find incontrovertible evidence that will prove my innocence."

"Does that mean you are planning on bringing down the Russian government?" the persistent young reporter followed.

It was the question he'd been hoping for. Kasinov's grimace remained stern as he pointed his index finger at the enthusiastic journalist. "I promise you, the negative impact upon the current Russian government hierarchy will be pernicious. Once the truth is uncovered, there will be very few survivors."

"Will you be entering Russian politics when this has all sorted itself out?"

Kasinov, knowing that he always had a prodigious vision of the future for Russia and the ability to personally impact it, took a deep breath as his chest bulged. "What has happened over the last seven years just debunks all of the myths of democracy invented by the Russian government. What they have now in Russia is a so-called managed democracy, where the military and security services exercise too much authority. Things will have to change for Russia to regain international confidence and credibility. I have a significant amount of international experience from my time at KasOil, and I believe I have the skills to lead Russia into a new pro-capitalist regime. I also have enormous support inside Russia."

The reporters exploded with questions once more.

"Mikhail, what about . . . "

"Natasha, any comments from you . . . "

Kasinov interrupted the questions. "Now if you will excuse us, we have a party to attend." He nodded to the enthusiastic media group before moving forward with Natasha closely clasped to his arm. "Thank you, ladies and gentlemen."

Kasinov had delivered his geopolitical homily to the media gathering. He hoped they would act as the conduit for his message to a wider international audience. More particularly, he wanted his message directed at, and delivered to, his adversaries at the Kremlin. Specifically Koshenko.

As Kasinov passed through the crowd of tepid photojournalists and media that hindered the entrance, he looked up to see the discreetly engraved ANNABEL'S NIGHTCLUB sign ahead of him. Then the door opened, and three severe-looking bouncers ushered them inside.

In the limited time available, after finding out about Mikhail's arrival in London, Natasha had frantically planned the welcoming reception for him to celebrate his escape. Mikhail approved. He enjoyed social occasions like this—especially ones where he could publically broadcast his Blighty domicile to the world.

This will piss Koshenko off no end, he thought.

Regarded as London's most salubrious nightspot, Mikhail had learned that Annabel's had attracted a number of ritzy clientele, aristocracy, and royalty, including the queen herself, Richard Nixon, Aristotle Onassis, Frank Sinatra, Lady Gaga, and Kate Moss. He liked exclusivity in these circles. Even though Annabel's owners enjoyed a reputation for being overtly ostentatious, it didn't bother him in the slightest. In fact, he thought it suited him better. Conceived by one of London's top interior designers, Nina Campbell, the place featured an extravagant interior design that on first impression was both eclectic and opulent. Although the club was over forty years old, it had benefitted from regular contemporary facelifts. As Kasinov moved through the entrance corridor, Natasha still clutched to his arm, he noticed a labyrinth of options left and right.

To the right was an obscured dining area that could seat perhaps fifty people. With its dominion interspersed by a series of radiant brass-clad pillars and columns, it looked a bit blingy to Kasinov. To the left stretched a passage that led to the veranda, its route florid with tables housing copious baroque vases of white lilies and yellow chrysanthemums. Although more than twenty feet away, he could smell the distinctive, exotic, almost therapeutic fragrance as he drew in a deep breath. Kasinov's senses were in overdrive since leaving Central Siberia three days earlier. They hadn't had this much opportunity to function in seven years.

Kasinov chose neither left nor right. Instead, with Natasha still grasped by his side, he went straight ahead into the main club area. Before him, he observed a vacant but colorful dance floor. *You won't find me on that thing.* The lounge was to the right, and the bar to the left of the illuminated floor tiles. They veered left towards an abundant number of enthusiastic guests that had gathered, standing two to three deep at the bar.

He could hear the lyrics from Usher's "Oh My God" coalesced with some will.i.am autotune vocals as hip-hop rhythms reverberated throughout the room in a cyclical trance. *These quadraphonic beats are too intense for me.* Kasinov glanced around the room, let out a deep breath, and shrugged. *I really do have an antipathy for nightclubs.*

Natasha had invited several of Mikhail's former so-called friends and colleagues. Of particular interest to Kasinov was the London Oligarch Circle. Although most were either exiled or imprisoned, London had attracted and retained quite a few. They all had one thing in common: success. However, success in these circles was relative. In his prime, Kasinov was seen by his peers as the putative Yoda in the business world of an emerging Russian economy of entrepreneurs. Now he was just an escaped criminal. In his own mind, he was much better than that, believing that he had been the most successful of them all. He was also the one who had served the longest prison sentence. He supposed there was a correlation.

Also included on the guest list were some London-based investment bankers who had continued to support him through his exile. Mikhail had given Natasha several names. The remainder of the entourage were mainly Natasha's friends or beneficial acquaintances, he guessed.

Within minutes of their arrival, crowds began to gather around the former Russian statesman. The brave ones who got to talk exclaimed great flattery

over his life achievements, his escape from
Siberia, and his vision for a future Russia. To him,
it was banal, endless, and scripted. Prior to his
incarceration, he was used to being surrounded by
sycophants. *Some things haven't changed, I can see.*

Kasinov glanced up at the bar and spotted
David St. Ledger seated and talking to two young,
attractive, tall women. *Natasha's friends, most
probably,* he guessed. He saw St. Ledger peering at
him before jumping from his seat and heading his
way with a smile. Although slightly rotund in
shape for his medium height, St. Ledger was
several pounds off his 160 pounds boxing weight.
He thought the Irishman looked a little unkempt,
and well advanced on the inebriation scale for this
early in the evening. Kasinov presumed it was
probably the side effects of profuse amounts of
Jameson dissolved during the course of the last
twenty-four hours. He knew St. Ledger's success
in life had come from using antediluvian tactics
over the last twenty-five years, and he wasn't
about to change his spots now.

St. Ledger made his way through the
ingratiating congregation, almost knocking a
young waitress off her feet as he raised his arms to
greet Kasinov. "Mikhail, you look extremely well.
I had visions of seeing you arriving here in an
orange boiler suit or something."

Kasinov knew that, regardless of his blood-
ethanol concentration, St. Ledger was a master in
the art of palavering, a skill for which everyone

loved him. Kasinov stroked his left lapel with his right hand. "Thank you, David, but I went for the navy Zegna look instead tonight. Sorry to disappoint."

St. Ledger took a step back and looked him up and down. "Very smart indeed."

Kasinov ushered St. Ledger to his right, away from the crowd. "So, David, tell me, has there been any reaction from your contacts back home? With the passport, I mean."

St. Ledger nodded. "I've spoken to a few people here and there, and I think it'll be fine," he said. "I don't expect any reaction from the Irish government. They'll want to keep a low profile on this, I can assure you."

Kasinov looked askew at his friend. "But this is being built up to be a major international incident, and the Irish government looks like it's complicit in a crime. Things could get very messy indeed."

"Nobody knows how you acquired the passport, except you, me, and one other person, and as long as you have it, you're safe. You'll be grand; don't worry!"

Kasinov shook his head. "You're not a very intellectual person, are you?"

"Definitely not. And I'm proud of it."

Fortunately St. Ledger's teenage truancy had never hindered his ability to spot opportunities or to get deals done. His convoluted communication style, though, continuously challenged Kasinov's tolerance for dealing with ambiguity. The Russian was known for his candor, which frequently insulted people not close to him. He couldn't insult St. Ledger, though. No matter what he said, it was like water off a duck's back.

"What if somebody finds out?" Kasinov asked cantankerously.

"I wouldn't worry about it. That's just another pothole on the road to Damascus."

Kasinov threw his eyes to heaven. When they settled, he noticed two of his oligarch comrades at the bar. "I hope we don't need to have this conversation again," he said. Then he patted his colleague on the shoulder and walked away.

Kasinov glided his way along the bar, bypassing adoring guests with his eyes firmly fixed in the direction of his Russian comrades. When they saw him coming, they jumped out of their seats. They zealously exchanged hugs with him, followed by a series of cheek kisses.

Shots were poured and waiting. "*Nazdarovya!*" they cried out in unison as three glasses of Stolichnaya premium vodka were hailed and then downed by the Russian troika. Together next to the bar, they huddled like the front row of a scrum, exchanging strident opinions in their native Russian. The two former Russian prodigies had lived in London now for several years, and had not experienced any risk of extradition during that time. Their presence and continued residence in the UK reassured Kasinov that London was the right place to be.

Halfway through the bottle of Stolichnaya, Kasinov glanced behind the bar to see six fashionably dressed mixologists combining consortiums of cocktails for the enthusiastic guests. Panu Alexanderson was the celebrity mixologist Natasha had brought in for the evening. Instantly recognizable to those who watched his TV show on BBC, *Celebrity Mix,* he was well known in London circles as the best in the country, if not all of Europe.

Kasinov studied the electronic dashboard menus that flashed at either end of the bar. They bore the celebrity mixologist's recommendations for the evening. They said things like Porn Star Martinis, Pisco Sours, Passion Fruit Mojitos, Kamikazes, Screaming Orgasms, and something he assumed was included just for laughs: a Kremlin Colonel. *I'm not laughing.* Then he studied Panu. He seemed to be a popular guy—blonde, about six feet five, twenty-nine years old, and definitely of Scandinavian origin. He was a big hit with everyone, especially the ladies. Kasinov shook his head. *Someone better tell him this is my show, not his.*

After spending at least an hour with the Russians, Kasinov went on a walkabout. It wasn't really in his character, but he felt he should be seen doing the host thing. Ahead of him at one of the illuminated pod tables, he could see a number of CEOs from London's top investment banks, each man among them from a long line of UK banking scions. He knew each of them from the KasOil IPO in 2000.

Richard Finlay from UGC spotted him first. He greeted Kasinov with an ardent grasp. "Welcome back, Mikhail. Great to see you."

"Thank you, Richard. And thank you for that analyst note you put out yesterday. It was very complimentary and extremely positive. Your head of research there—that girl—what's her name? She seems quite a clever young lady."

"Melanie Bauer. She's our new head of research, a very intelligent young lady. The markets reacted particularly well indeed. We ended up trading enormously well, I must say." He grinned smugly. "Best day in my life, in fact."

"She certainly seems a lot smarter than most of the city analysts."

"Indeed she is. In fact, you might see her here tonight. She comes in quite regularly with her boyfriend, Lord Jeremy Ashburton-Jones. Several of the aristocracy get life memberships here. He's one of the *chosen ones*—quite zealous in his social exploits. Annabel's owners seem to love the publicity he generates for the club, I guess."

Kasinov said nothing.

"Have you been busy since you arrived?" Finlay enquired.

"Yeah," Kasinov replied proudly. "In fact, I've received quite a few calls from city bankers."

"Watch out, Mikhail. The city is full of these little emerging boutique banking firms claiming all sorts of specialties. At UGC, we remain focused on servicing our larger clients, and look forward to seeing your next project. We've grown our team significantly in the city, especially in corporate finance."

Again, Kasinov did not speak.

"Well, you know what they say. There's never a bad time to make a good investment. We're right here if you need us."

Kasinov tapped Finlay on the shoulder. "Watch the space, Richard. Just watch the space." With that, he moved away from the pod table, which had changed color from bright pink to orange.

He noticed that the revelry at the bar had escalated as several of Natasha's friends gathered in the frenzy zone. Entertained by the tall blonde Scandinavian and his entourage of mixologists, the Amazons cheered them on, crying out their orders. Some just cried out the barmen's names that appeared on the name badges.

Kasinov shook his head.

Collectively, the Amazon gang boasted an average height of just over six feet, he estimated— probably much taller than the average female at Annabel's or any other London night club. Kasinov laughed as he observed them, all robed in the latest fashion, some more garish than others. He could hear the flamboyant laughter from the throng of young women resonating against the collection of crystal optics as each one of Natasha's rather tall friends tried to outperform the next. As absorbed as they were in the cocktail show, and judging by the noise they were making, Kasinov guessed each of them had consumed at least one of each of the special recommendation cocktails.

He glanced behind to see what he guessed was the only temptation to compete with mixologists: the vibrant amethyst-lit dance floor next to the bar. The place was coming to life, as it did most nights. Kasinov looked at his watch. *I hate nightclubs.*

Annabel's was known for attracting flagrantly coquettish women, and Natasha's friends certainly didn't let this longstanding reputation suffer. If anything, they probably intensified it. St. Ledger was fixated on a few of the young women in the group out there in the middle of it all. Untroubled by personal reputation erosion, St. Ledger lived his life vicariously and with great regularity through the memory of himself as a twenty-one-year-old. However, when it came to dancing, by his own admission, he was built for power and not for speed.

Kasinov, on the other hand, didn't enjoy dancing. He didn't see the point of it at all. Instead, he remained po-faced at the bar, intermittently pontificating with the two other oligarchs who had rejoined him. Since his escape, Kasinov suffered from the side effects of megalomania, unable to differentiate his former eminence with his current status. He laughed to himself at the thought of how he was going to regain his former power and come back with an even greater authoritative platform.

The highest platform.

The presidency.

Kasinov's desire grew daily to destroy those who had conjured evidence against him for tax liabilities and fraudulent business practices. *They will be punished.*

The sounds from "Nothing on You" by B.o.B. and Bruno Mars rang out as Kasinov shifted his gaze across at Natasha on the dance floor. Infatuated with dancing, Natasha was unfortunately a bit of a klutz when it came to the delivery, and tonight her awkwardness was exacerbated by the combination of the Louboutin heels and the consumption of several Jägerbombs. She was dancing with a super-Amazon in the middle of the dance floor. The girl was wearing a luminous pink top that could be seen from all corners of the club. Attracted by the luminosity that must have acted as a homing beacon, St. Ledger made his way over to join them, and after a short while, Kasinov saw Natasha slip away. St. Ledger and the Amazon lady danced and cavorted together for quite a while. Then they left for what Kasinov assumed must be a tryst. *The old dog still has life in him.* He tutted in disapproval as the two escaped through the lily-chrysanthemum jungle.

Mikhail eyed Natasha with amusement as she bounced around the dance floor. When she sidled up to a good-looking man and embraced him, his anger flared. *Who the hell is that guy?* He watched as the two chatted and repeatedly erupted in laughter. It seemed to Mikhail that Natasha rather conspicuously and regularly leaned in close as the man spoke into her ear. Mikhail tried to catch her eye, but she didn't seem to notice.

His phone vibrated in his pocket, alerting him to a message. The number on the screen surprised him. He drew the device closer and read the text. When he looked up, Natasha stood in front of him, her arm interlocked with her friend from the dance floor.

She flashed him a broad smile. "Mikhail, this is Jonathon Princeton," she said. "He's one of my best exhibition customers at the Royal Academy of Arts."

Mikhail managed a stiff smile. *The way she's looking at him, you'd think he'd just been awarded a Nobel laureate.*

"Jonathon, this is Mikhail, my—" Natasha hesitated "—my boyfriend."

Princeton extended his hand. "Nice to meet you, sir."

Mikhail cringed inwardly at the boy's feigned humility. "Good to meet you, too," he said. "Sorry to rush off, but I've got to attend to something." He brushed his way past, vaguely noting Natasha's disbelieving gaze.

As Kasinov moved towards the terrace exit, he bumped into the back of a tall blonde man who turned around to face him.

"Xenop," Kasinov said with surprise as he shook Roy's hand fervently.

Roy raised his hand dismissively. "Now that the mission's over, please call me Roy. Xenop was just to satisfy the US intelligence guys."

"Where did the name come from, anyway?"

"Parker at the CIA. Said it was something to do with Russia's xenophobia towards foreign investment in its own vast resources. Anyway, that deal is done now, and I'm not working for them anymore."

"How did you do it?" Kasinov enquired.

"Do what?"

Kasinov raised both hands. "The training, the research, penetrating the IT, the team, the helicopters, the plane. *Everything.*"

"Mikhail, you're good at finding oil in the ground and turning it into billons. I specialize in reconnaissance. Just different skill sets."

"Okay, mystery man. I just wanted to thank you for all your great work."

"No problem. That's my job."

"I may have some other assignments, if you're interested, that is . . ."

"I have a busy schedule. Your last project took up a lot of my time."

"Okay," Kasinov replied, rubbing three of his fingers together. "Well, I'm sure I can make it worthwhile for you."

"I pick the assignments that suit me, not the ones that pay the most."

"Well, let's see if I can find something that will suit you then." Kasinov nodded and made his way towards the terrace.

~~~

Roy moved to the bar. On the way, a stunningly beautiful young woman approached him curiously.

"Roy, is that you?" she said in a surprised tone. "It is! It's really you, isn't it? Oh my God, what are you doing here?"

Roy smiled as his eyes adjusted to the low light. "Hello, Melanie," he said, opening his arms to embrace her. "So nice to see you. It's been a long time."

They embraced for several seconds. *Most probably several seconds too long*, Roy thought.

She took a step back to eyeball him. His tall, muscular frame overshadowed most people, and in the club's neon troposphere, his blonde hair and blue eyes distinguished him further. He was hard to miss. His skin was tanned and firm, with a soft flush, but with visible bristle that shadowed a contoured shaving line.

"You haven't changed much," she said. "You look in great shape."

Roy guessed from the look on her face that she was very pleased but surprised to see him. He felt his eyes drawn to her hazel green corneas. They seemed to glisten in reflection from the neon lights that surrounded the perimeter of the dance floor. With the illumination behind her, there was a radiant nimbus glowing around her face. He smiled at her. *As beautiful as always, maybe even more beautiful.*

"What?" she probed.

Roy was about to offer some flattering observations on Melanie's look and physique when a man approached with two drinks in hand. He was a well-groomed young man, about six feet two, chiseled face, and maybe 180 pounds. He wore a navy polo T-shirt with the collar turned up and dark beige chinos. Roy estimated he was at least ten years younger than he was—midthirties maybe. His hair was perfectly cut. Not a single strand was out of place.

"What have we got here then?" the metrosexual man uttered as he cocked his head as if to suggest that they should leave.

"Roy, this is Jeremy, my boyfriend." She extended a hand in Roy's direction. "This is Roy. We, ah . . . we spent time together at university."

"Very nice to meet you, Roy," Jeremy said, proffering his hand after dispensing with the mojito that had occupied it. "Can I get you a drink?"

"No, it's okay. I was just headed to the bar myself, in fact."

"Nonsense. Let me get you one. You must try one of these passion fruit mojitos." He pitched the idea like a salesman running a special promotion for the stuff. "Here, take this one." He placed the second drink into Roy's hand and made his way back to the bar.

Melanie watched her boyfriend move far enough away before her eyes shifted back to Roy. "What are you doing here in London?"

"I'm here to attend this party of the year." Roy's eyes scanned the room for the prototypical oligarch. "Mikhail's party. You know, the guy who escaped from the Russian prison?"

Melanie's grimace tightened at Roy's reply. "Oh, how do you know him?"

"It's a long story, but let's just say I've done some work for him."

"Must have been way back before 2003. You never mentioned that before."

"Actually, it was very recent."

Melanie paused, squinted, and turned her head. "Don't tell me you had something to do with his escape from Siberia."

Roy looked down. "I don't want to involve you in any danger."

"I want to know what's going on, Roy!" she snapped.

He sighed. "I know I can trust you implicitly. But are you sure you really want to know about this?"

"Yes, I want to know. Are you in some kind of trouble with the Russians?"

Roy took a sip of the Passion Fruit Mojito, followed by a look around the room to make sure there was no other accidental or unintended audience. "No, I'm not in any trouble with them," he said calmly. "I was part of the rescue team that went into Siberia earlier this week and broke him out of there. Simple as that."

Melanie frowned, and after what seemed like a very long pause asked, "Why did you do that?"

"Payback time with the CIA."

Melanie, who had already gulped back her mojito, looked around as if seeking a top-up. It hadn't arrived yet. Her incredulity was palpable. Her mouth was open, and her eyes turned feral. She slowly shook her head. "You could have been hurt," she mumbled. "You could have been killed even."

"I'm fine," Roy insisted. "Relax. I'm perfectly fine."

"So what are you up to now?"

"Time off for a while. No plans."

"Where are you living now?"

"Florence. I love it there."

"Florence. Very nice. I didn't know. We lost touch. You just disappeared. What happened?"

Roy saw the question coming a mile away. "I'm sorry, Melanie. I should have called before. I should have explained. I shouldn't have just left like that."

She stared back at him with her glaring hazel eyes. "You hurt me. I don't see you for three years, and now you just turn up here out of the blue."

"My life became very complicated," Roy replied. "It was better that I wasn't in a relationship." He paused. "I'm sorry, Melanie." He realized in that moment just how much he meant it.

Jeremy approached them, carrying a fresh round of mojitos. "Here we go," he said, handing them off and turning to Roy. "Sorry for what, old boy?"

Roy's eyes darted nervously from Melanie to Jeremy. "Sorry for this chilling weather I seem to have brought to London," he offered. Not very smooth, but it seemed to do the trick. Roy could sense Jeremy's interest in the tension between him and Melanie.

As soon as the metro man started chatting with some royal enthusiasts that had gathered next to them, Melanie looked back up at Roy. "I've been doing a lot of research on your new best friend, Mikhail Kasinov," she said. "You know, at UGC. Remember the bank where I work?"

"Of course. So you know what he has been up to, then?" Roy asked with surprise.

"My research has been focused primarily on the consequences for oil and gas companies operating in the vast Russian hydrocarbon reserves. There has been quite a lot of movement in the stock market since he escaped, you know."

"That's good for you then, I imagine?"

"Well, it's funny . . . I was going to message you yesterday."

"Okay," Roy said, keeping his elation under control.

Melanie's face lit up. "I had a big day at the office," she said with clear excitement.

"Tell me about it. I would love to hear."

"Oh, it was nothing." She sounded suddenly diffident.

"Oh, okay then. Not sure if you got it or not, but I did send you a message a few days ago, just before I left for Siberia. Just to say hello, in case I didn't come back, I mean."

"Yes, thanks. I received it."

~~~

Kasinov stood on the terrace with an unaddressed envelope in his right hand as he gazed at the exit corridor through the open frame. He checked his phone and read the message again. It had three parts:

Envelope left on terrace table for you. Please go and collect. I will be watching to make sure it is you who collects.

Then he looked back through the window and rotated 360 degrees, but no one was there. He folded the envelope in two, placed it inside the breast pocket of his jacket, and re-entered the club.

~~~

Following an elongated crescendo of R&B fusion from the house DJ at around 2:00 a.m., the festivities eventually came to a halt, and the remaining crowd that had soldiered until the end exited the club. As the final gathering poured outside, they were greeted by a pretentious anthology of Maybachs, DiMoras, Maserati, and Ferraris. The lucky ones got into them. The rest got taxis.

Kasinov headed for the Bentley with Natasha under his arm. As he opened the door, he noticed a few of the intractable paparazzi, tenaciously still waiting to catch opportunistic snaps of some of the celebrity guests as they departed. Their lenses were focused on the Bentley and some of the other flashy automobiles.

Kasinov nodded back to them with a wry smile, visibly resolute to implacably eradicate those who had orchestrated his captivity in 2003.

Chapter 11
The Trinity

The following morning, Kasinov sat outside on Natasha's penthouse terrace. *No seagulls circling today,* he thought. He had heard on the radio that a high-pressure front was approaching. *Probably keeps them back at their nests.* Instead, he heard the clattering and shuffling of busy feet from the streets below, streets filled with cosmopolitan shoppers and tourists wearing down the cobbled warrens.

Natasha was at the art gallery. He was alone. It suited him.

With his arms folded, he smiled and nodded, thinking about the Glamazon exhibition from the previous evening. He was pleased with how it all went. He had delivered his message. He announced his vision to the media, and he assumed they would publish it just like he had delivered it. If they didn't, he would have to deal with it a different way.

He was a bit surprised by the unexpected delivery he had received. He knew it was coming, just not last night, not at Annabel's. He had read the contents and understood it well. After he read it, he placed the contents back inside the envelope and filed it away in his room.

He shuffled his body and sat back in his seat. With his hands interlocked behind his head, he stared down over the Thames, deep into the south of London. He pictured his former business partners Vladimir Sakharshenko and Alexander Zolotov. Together they had been a unique trinity. Now they were a disjointed trinity.

Kasinov had brought Sakharshenko into his first two business ventures in computers and diamonds. He hired him as the nuts and bolts man, which meant Sakharshenko travelled extensively to resource locations throughout Africa and Asia, cutting supply chain deals with vendors and factories and arranging logistics routings through to Moscow and some of the more challenging areas throughout the Urals, Volga, and Siberian regions. Sakharshenko was a few years older than Kasinov, and after seeing him for the first time in seven years, Kasinov thought his former business partner looked every bit of it. Maybe more, even.

Some people age better than others. He pursed his lips. *I have aged better than others. Better than most, I would say.*

To his close friends, Sakharshenko went by the nickname *Vova,* a name Kasinov bestowed on him early in their business ventures. Kasinov recalled that Vova was in Shanghai the week of the arrest. He had sent him there. He didn't expect him to return to Russia after that, and he didn't. Instead, he moved to London and spent a number of years there before relocating to Budapest, where he settled.

Sakharshenko had acquired a 3 percent shareholding in KasOil from Kasinov in 1998, giving him an individual net worth in the order of £600 million in 2000 at the time of the IPO. Kasinov paused and wondered about Vova's current net worth. He had no idea.

Kasinov hadn't seen his other partner, his financial man, Zolotov, in seven years. He had gone into hiding after Kasinov's arrest. His presence remained unknown for almost six years, until Kasinov read about his mysterious reappearance in Amsterdam in 2009. Kasinov had made contact with him, and he became his covert literary agent for *Siberian Liberty.* Kasinov didn't believe Zolotov had any particular skills in the area, but he trusted him, and he did a pretty good job.

Kasinov and Zolotov had studied together during the same years at Mendeleev. Zolotov completed a degree in accounting and finance, and since then, the two shared a rich alumni bond that kept them connected in business and friendship for many years. The image of his former bagman was clearly engrained in his mind. Zolotov was a tall, severe man, at least six feet one, and looked rather like a gangster—one of the reasons Kasinov hired him. *Good for the difficult assignments. He scared people.*

Although quite a reserved man, Zolotov always struck Kasinov as efficient in taking care of domestic financial, commercial, and political arrangements for the emerging businesses. What Kasinov liked about him the most was that he understood authority and followed instructions from his leader diligently.

Zolotov, too, had acquired a 3 percent shareholding in KasOil. Previous net worth: £600 million. Current net worth: unknown.

~~~

Visibly fatigued after twelve intense months of preparation and the eventual execution of Operation Alpha Factor, Vladimir Sakharshenko was back at his Budapest base with his girlfriend of seven years, Nikoletta Lukas. The planning and preparation had occupied his mind for as long as he could remember. He had returned several days earlier after completing the Siberian Houdini act, but in Sakharshenko's mind, the gravity of the coup was only beginning to sink in now.

It was Monday morning. He was relaxed. Alpha Factor was over, disbanded, no loose ends. Everything went exactly as planned.

He observed Nikoletta running around the house, looking for a pair of shoes, trying to get ready whilst he sat patiently in the lounge, his coat and shoes on, ready to go. He was reading a book, an 1878 Russian classic written by Fyodor Dostoyevsky, *The Brothers Karamazov.* He had started it before Alpha Factor commenced and was now about halfway through.

"Just another four hundred and eighty pages to go," he mumbled.

Nikoletta, originally from Budapest, was thirty years old and archetypal Hungarian. Hers was a medium height, a slender physique, strikingly natural fair hair, dark blue eyes surrounded by brilliant white sclera, and ruby pink lips that rarely smiled. She dressed in black most days. It was her favorite color. She looked very good in black.

Sakharshenko's mind often wrestled with the thought of one day returning to Russia. He never ventured an imprudent return following the events in 2003. Instead, he spent four years in London. In 2005, they moved to Budapest.

Although it was not part of his motivation to move, when Sakharshenko took on the task to rescue his comrade years later, he was pleased that Hungary's position in the Carpathian Basin in Central Europe met with Roy's approval as the central location from which to run the preparation phase of the mission. The Sholnosk property was pretty utilitarian. It possessed a separate accommodation block with nine rooms, providing all the space Alpha Factor needed for training during the preparation phase. These rooms were all vacant now.

In London, they had lived in a three-bedroom Knightsbridge penthouse suite overlooking Harrods along Brompton Road. Now they lived on a smallholding of land with twelve bedrooms that overlooked a big, empty field about ten miles south of Budapest in a town called Sholnosk.

A few minutes later, Nikoletta was standing in front of him. "Right, I'm ready."

Sakharshenko replaced his bookmark. "Only four hundred seventy-eight pages left now," he said. "Let's go then."

He had worked hard for his US$2 million fee for freeing Kasinov, and needed every cent of it. He had lost everything in 2002, regrettably retaining his entire net worth in KasOil shares. Today they were taking the train from Sholnosk to Keleti Railway Station in Central Budapest, a journey that they had both taken with abundant constancy. They were going to sign some paperwork at the main branch of Hungarian National Bank to transfer the funds received.

~~~

As they departed, a diminutive-looking character peered back at them from the front seat of a metallic silver Toyota Land Cruiser. He observed them both, but more to the point, he leered in Nikoletta's direction. He was short, quite rotund, just over five foot and about 180 pounds.

He had a cherubic face. The vehicle's privacy glass, along with his distance from the property, obscured suspicion of his presence. As he waited, he sat up in his seat—a seat cushioned sufficient to provide a colossus feeling—and watched them leave the estate with a pair of Kahles binoculars glued to his eyes.

Composed and prepared, the cherub-faced observer drove up to the house and parked his jeep away from the main entrance. From the floor of the Toyota, he grabbed a small black bag and headed to the front of the house. As he approached the portico, he removed a small sledgehammer from the bag and proceeded to smash open the double-glazed side window panel next to the front door. He cleared away the loose shards of glass with the butt of his hammer, then reached inside and opened the lock.

Once inside, he immediately immobilized the alarm, having acquired the access code from the security company during his visit to their offices in Central Budapest the afternoon before. With the help of a 9mm Glock, he had enticed one of their service agents, who succumbed to breach a number of security protocols.

The cherub toured the interior. The house was palatial. It had high ceilings and extremely large rooms with ornate appendages on the walls and ceilings. Cautiously he made his way through the Italian tiled reception area and started up the slalom staircase to the right. Once upstairs, he advanced to the last room on the right-hand side. He entered the room and turned immediately to his left to the walk-in wardrobe. The room must have been eighteen feet wide by the same deep. The attiring area led through into an en-suite bathroom at the other end.

He placed his bag on the floor and reached inside a second time. He pulled out a rolled-up scroll, removed the elastic band wrap, and opened an A3-sized plasticized sheet. The sheet bore a drawing depicting a plan view of a safe within the floor inside the middle wardrobe on the right-hand side. He opened the wardrobe, reached down, and searched for a removable floor panel. Exactly per the drawing, it was there. Inside the panel was a grey, zinc, powder-coated safe with a numeric panel on its face. Pleased with himself, the cherub proceeded to punch in the nine-digit code highlighted on the drawing. He pulled open the door, ready to retrieve the contents.

"Fuck!" he said, shaking his head in disbelief.

It was empty.

~~~

Twenty minutes after they departed from Sholnosk, Sakharshenko and Nikoletta arrived at Keleti Station. They disembarked and walked towards the foyer at the center of the station before strolling along the platform. They smiled at each other, pleased that they were returning to a routine life.

As they approached the exit of the station, Nikoletta noticed a young couple briefly cut between them. Then a tall man wearing a black coat and a grey balaclava ski mask seemed to maneuver his way through a parabolic twist to avoid an obvious collision with the young couple. After realizing she had moved a few steps ahead, Nikoletta stopped, paused, and turned around to see a small crowd gathering. Her head darted from side to side to see where her partner was. When she couldn't see him, she ran back, pushing her way through the arriving onlookers. Then she fell to her knees.

Vladimir was on the floor. His eyes weren't open. She noticed a hole in his forehead, from which a small amount of blood seeped.

She checked his pulse.

There was none.

Then she screamed.

~~~

After carrying out an exhaustive search at the house, the cherub was livid. He eventually left empty-handed. He made his way to Budapest's international airport, dropping off the Land Cruiser at the rental parking before continuing to the check-in area.

There, his collaborator was waiting for him. He was a tall man with a black coat. He checked his watch. "You're late," he said.

"I had a problem," the cherub responded with an agitated expression.

The tall man grimaced. "I have delivered my end of the bargain. Please tell me that you have retrieved the package."

"There was nothing there. I found the safe and opened it, but it was empty, I swear. I searched the whole place. I turned it upside down—nothing."

"Then you can phone him and tell him!"

"I will, but not now, not today. Let's check in and get the hell out of here."

Chapter 12
Russian Roulette

Melanie picked up a copy of *The Telegraph* as she entered King's Cross tube station en-route to the office. As she boarded the tube, her attention was immediately drawn to the article on the front page.

Russian Roulette?

Melanie pulled the paper close. The article headlined with a report on the murder by professional assassin of Vladimir Sakharshenko the previous day. It had happened at close range inside Keleti Railway Station in Central Budapest. "Oh my God!" she cried as other tube passengers stared in her direction in surprise.

After the initial shock, she read on. The article referenced the linked history between Kasinov and Sakharshenko and their prior business cooperation in Russia. It commented on how ironic this was, given that Kasinov himself had just escaped from prison not five days earlier. The article went on to quote Kasinov's remarks outside Annabel's on Saturday evening past, where he gave the press clear indications of his intention to not only challenge the current Russian administration by entering the political race, but to supplant the incumbent president, Yuri Koshenko. It also quoted the views expressed by the Kremlin, linking Kasinov to a triple murder investigation along with Vitaly Kuznetsov, former head of security at KasOil, coupled with additional money laundering charges. They finished with the quintessential hostile Moscow warning: *Any insidious threats to Russia's stability made by Mr. Kasinov will not be tolerated.* The only positive message referenced in the article was the apparent plateau reached in Moscow's stock market, following the precipitous fall in earlier days.

Melanie placed the paper down on her lap and shook her head. *The whole thing sounds like a plot from a spy novel.*

Invigorated by what she had read, Melanie arrived at UGC's offices at 8:25 a.m., and eagerly made her way to the second floor for a scheduled meeting with Richard Finlay and Paul Coppell. On the way, she noticed several marketing posters that UGC regularly published and displayed for staff and customers. She recalled that when she joined UGC, they were rated number three in the world by independent sources. However, by UGC's own presentation materials exhibited in front of her, they had selectively arranged the data to show that they were number one in just about everything they did.

She shrugged with a little chuckle. *According to their own estimations, all the banks seem to be number one these days.*

Then reality hit her when she recalled how the investment banking community was not a very modest place. She had one last chuckle before getting down to business.

Straight-faced, Melanie entered the meeting room. Finlay and Coppell were already there, pouring coffee. "Have you seen this Russian Roulette piece in *The Telegraph* this morning?" she enquired as she tossed the paper on the table.

The men turned to look down at the front page as three photo faces stared back up at them: Kasinov, Koshenko, and Sakharshenko, in that order.

Finlay's gaze moved from the paper, back to Melanie, and then down at the paper again. "Yes, I've read it. The stories referenced in this article are all over the wires and tabloids this morning."

"Yes," Melanie interrupted, "but no one else is using the nexus of three incidents in the same interconnected conjecture as *The Telegraph* seems to have done."

"We'll have to wait to see the market reaction to this latest news," Finlay said sheepishly. "It probably won't be good."

Melanie looked over at her boss, who was moving to the other side of the table. "I'd say it's more about opportunity," she argued. "At the end of the day, we aren't dealing with reality, Richard; we're dealing with people's perceptions of what reality might be. And history in capital markets has shown us time and time again that greed drives everything. The more unstable the Russian government is, the more opportunity there is for marginal stocks connected with the instability."

Finlay uttered something in return. Melanie didn't hear exactly what he said, but it appeared to be confirmatory, judging by his nod.

~~~

Roy had returned home to his villa in Florence a couple days earlier after his brief but intriguing visit to London to attend the Glamazon spectacle. Although he probably wouldn't say it to his face, he was quietly pleased to see Kasinov enjoying his deserved freedom. The truth was that his mind was more consumed by the fact that he had run into Melanie Bauer—and with a boyfriend. *Shit,* he thought. He felt a little green about it. He guessed he had never really gotten over her.

Got to move on, he told himself.

He cleared his mind and opened his MacBook to check his emails. There was another message from Kasinov.

Dear Roy,

Thanks for coming to the party. Good to chat this weekend. I need you to come back and see me in London ASAP. Vladimir Sakharshenko was murdered yesterday, and I need your help. I don't know where you are in the world. I'm enclosing a voucher for British Airways made in your name. It enables you to fly from anywhere to here. Please come ASAP.
Mikhail

Roy drew back when he fully comprehended what he had just read. "Fuck!" he cried out. *Vladimir was a good man. He didn't deserve this. Who the hell could have done this?*

He had worked with Vladimir for twelve months, and the two had built up a working relationship. In fact, it had been a good friendship.

I'm going to find these bastards and make them pay, he thought.

Roy contemplated what taking up this challenge would mean. He knew that getting involved with Kasinov again probably meant getting involved with the Russian FSB and probably ex-Chechen rebels—lots of egos, big egos, and lots of muscle, too. He had come across a few of them during Alpha Factor.

He had no choice. He knew what he had to do.

Roy knew how to protect himself, though. He also knew how to calibrate egos. He had been doing it for a long time, and was ready to do it again if necessary. His mind shifted back to Vladimir. It was time to find out what happened to him, and most probably, it was time to calibrate a few egos along the way.

Chapter 13
Polonium

Kasinov paced up and down the apartment's main living area, moving like an exposition concert pianist as the elevator doors opened to a sonorous chiming double drone. He stopped and turned to see Natasha emerge from the lift and walk into the reception area, where she proceeded to unload several large shopping bags from a number of different haute-couture designer outlets. After she placed the bags in the entrance hall, she approached him.

Mikhail moved forward and stopped her, pushing one hand out and placing it on her right shoulder. His excessively covetous personality couldn't reconcile what he had been ruminating on for several days. "Who was that guy you were flirting with at the club on Saturday evening?"

"Which guy are you talking about?" Natasha innocently enquired.

"The guy you were dancing with at the end of the evening. The one you brought over to me under your arm. You two looked far too friendly."

"Are you talking about the guy I was dancing with for a few minutes just before we left Annabel's? The guy I introduced to you and you just ignored him? As I told you on Saturday, he's one of my best art customers, and his name is Jonathon Princeton."

"I don't want you to see him or talk with him again," Kasinov said abruptly. He stared at her coldly before bringing his arm up so he could glance at his watch. "I have to go to a meeting." He turned to grab his jacket.

He pushed the elevator button and silently waited there for a few seconds. The silence was interrupted by the lift's double chime. He glanced back at Natasha as the doors closed between them. The last he saw of her, she was standing in shock, her mouth hanging open.

I think she got the message.

~~~

Following Kasinov's invitation, Roy arrived at London Heathrow Terminal Five at 3:00 p.m. on the scheduled BA flight from Rome. The Boeing 777 short-hall routing arrived after only two hours and twenty minutes, ten minutes ahead of schedule. Roy quickly made his way through customs and jumped into a cab. The taxi driver, enclosed in his own Perspex cabin, threaded his way through the M4, winding down the connecting roads along Cromwell Drive before navigating his way through the final stretch of Covent Garden's warren of side streets until he reached The Strand.

Roy arrived early at The Savoy Hotel. He strolled around the reception area for a few moments before making his way over to the lobby seating area. Amidst the tooth-shaped stools and mini totem pole tables, candles lit the surroundings. He relaxed into a large, concave settee opposite the reception area. One of the magazines on the table in front of him illuminated an evening photograph of the London Eye. He smiled to himself, thinking of all the wonderful things he had done in London back in his days at Cambridge. Most of them, he had done with Melanie.

He wondered what she was up to now.

Most probably out with her male-model boyfriend.

He wanted to make contact with her, but was apprehensive about it. He wanted to meet with her to explain what happened. He wasn't sure she would ever agree to meet, but he took out his phone and began to write a message, all the same.

Hi, Mel. I know it's a bit short notice, but I'm back in London for a few days and was hoping we could meet up, if you're here and have some time? Roy.

Before he even put the phone back in his pocket, he heard the tinkling sound indicating a new message.

Hello, Roy. It's so nice to hear from you. What a surprise! Again! I am quite busy, but I'm sure we can find some time.

Roy boldly texted back.

What about an early supper tonight?

He was certain she would be shaking her head in disbelief at his cheeky suggestion. He waited for nearly a minute before the tinkling sound returned.

I'll be done at the office around 6 p.m. Let's meet at our favorite restaurant then. See you there just after 6. Looking forward to it.

~ ~ ~

Roy's eyes were focused on the revolving door when he saw Mikhail Kasinov march self-assuredly into the lobby of The Savoy Hotel. He moved with a confident stride, his suit jacket tied by the top button. His crisp, white shirt collar fit perfectly around his neck. His patent leather shoes beat a discerning path forward. He moved calmly and distinctively through the lobby before stopping and casting a series of slow, calculated glances in several directions—as if he owned the place.

Although technically the two had shared an iconic four-hour journey together across Siberia and into China, Roy didn't know Mikhail Kasinov very well. He only knew him by reputation, and there were two different sides to that reputation. There was the CIA version, which portrayed Kasinov as an altruistic, morally upstanding, and hard-done-by capitalist tripped up by an envious Kremlin abhorrence. And then there was another version, Roy's version of the terse, cold personality he had met face-to-face. *The reality remains to be seen*, Roy thought, but he was normally pretty good at reading people—even before he went to Cambridge.

Roy rose and went over to greet him. Distinguished in character, both men held remarkable presence. However, Roy felt Kasinov's imperious demeanor was somewhat more humbled on this occasion.

"Thank you for coming to see me at short notice," Kasinov said as he gently rolled his right palm to an open position, indicating that they should both take a seat.

As they landed on the settee, Kasinov took a fretful glance to either side as if to ensure that the private rendezvous remained exclusively private.

"As I said in my email to you yesterday," Kasinov began, his face conjuring a look of desperation, "Vladimir Sakharshenko was murdered in cold blood two days ago as he exited Budapest's central train station. This atrocity must be revenged. I need you to find his killer."

Roy ran his hand pensively through his blonde hair. "This is not my kind of work," he explained inoffensively. "I'm planning to spend most of my time now on private security training with larger US multinationals."

"After Krasnokamensk, Vladimir said that you were the most experienced military operative he has ever come across." Kasinov's tone was uncharacteristically sycophantic. "He said you're capable of anything you put your mind to."

"Thanks, Mikhail," Roy responded. "But the Krasnokamensk deal was a one-off performance."

Kasinov moved forward in his seat. "Look, Vladimir was a comrade, a great man, a fearless leader, and he has been taken out in cold blood. We must find revenge for him."

Roy looked at Kasinov blankly, trying to seem supportive but disinterested at the same time. He didn't respond.

Kasinov opened his arms and raised them, embracing Roy's carriage. "I'm willing to pay you a handsome fee for this," he said. "Let's say half the fee as the last time from Parker, but this time, it will be less than a quarter of the work."

Roy didn't need the money. However, after having worked with Vladimir for a year, he had built up enormous respect for him. He knew him as an extremely honorable individual. If he were doing this, it would be for Vladimir, for his legacy, and not for money. "Any idea who might have wanted him killed?" Roy asked after a few seconds of silence.

"Lots of people," Kasinov responded flippantly. "May I suggest you start with sources connected with the Kremlin? They're probably after me next. I'm sure they'll want to silence me now that I'm outside their grasp."

Roy pulled back without showing his feelings of skepticism. "Hold on a second. I can't just walk through Red Square and into the Kremlin, asking them if they know who killed Vladimir Sakharshenko."

"I've seen this happen before many times—the deceitful tactics they used, especially here in London." Kasinov seemed suddenly alarmed. "You know, a few years ago, they killed a defected KGB agent named Alex Litvinenko."

"I remember the Litvinenko story. Everybody does, in fact. I think sushi sales in London dropped through the floor for several months following the revelations." Roy moved forward in his seat and placed his hands in front of him on the table, engaging the Russian. "But what has this got to do with Vladimir? Or you, for that matter?"

"Litvinenko was once an officer of the Russian Federal Security Service, and a KGB separatist," Kasinov recited. "The Russians claimed he was a spy working for MI-Five, and arrested him. Whilst he was on trial in Moscow, he fled from Russia and received political asylum here in the UK. The oligarch community helped him while he was here, and supported him in a campaign against the Kremlin." Kasinov paused, leaning back in his seat.

"I'm still waiting to hear the connection, Mikhail," Roy probed.

"Litvinenko spent most of his time here as a journalist. Unfortunately, he had a lot of negative energy that he channeled through a Chechen separatist publication called the *Chechen Press*. Most of his articles were pretty vocal in undermining the Russian so-called democracy. He also wrote a few books connecting Kremlin terrorist activities and the power crusade of the current hierarchy. The Russian government did not like this one bit."

Sounds a lot like you, Mikhail, Roy felt like saying. Instead he blurted out, "Probably not a good idea for him to be undermining his former employer. I'm still listening."

Kasinov did another quick scan around the hotel with his deep-set eyes before refocusing on Roy. "Sometime around the beginning of November 2006, he ate lunch at the Itsu restaurant on Piccadilly. He was meeting with an old acquaintance, and was apparently overheard making some serious allegations regarding KGB terrorist activities. A few days later, he became desperately ill. Within the first few days after his trip to Itsu, Litvinenko suffered from nausea, diarrhea, and vomiting." Kasinov held up both hands.

Roy thought he was emulating Rio's *Christ the Redeemer.*

"After two weeks, his condition became significantly worse," Kasinov added. "He continuously drifted in and out of consciousness, and by the end of November, he was dead."

Uninterested by the melodramatic exchanges, Roy lowered his head and eyed him. "Did they determine what it was that killed him?"

"The autopsy report highlighted significant amounts of the radionuclide, polonium-210, or Po-210 as it's known in the medical fraternity," Kasinov replied. "Scotland Yard and CIA scientists alike said they had never come across the use of Po-210 as a poison before Litvinenko's death. Even with all the medical professionals and investigating professors engaged during his sickness, they couldn't detect a single picocurie or an alpha particle of the stuff in his body."

"How come?"

"The polonium isotope, or any variation of it, is like some amorphous non-gamma-ray emitting object." Kasinov cupped his hands and moved his body like a misshapen creature. "It's quite unlike any other radioactive substances. The polonium-210 radiation poison produces alpha particles not powerful enough to penetrate the epidermis, making it extremely difficult to detect. This only appeared in the media weeks after it was discovered. The final report concluded that he was given about two hundred times the lethal dose of the stuff."

"How did they administer the poison?"

"Apparently the poison was placed in Litvinenko's teacup. It turns out that alpha-emitting material can only cause substantial harm when put in direct contact with living cells."

"You seem to know a lot about the details of his murder."

"I have plenty of contacts, Roy."

"So it would seem."

Kasinov looked back at Roy with a sarcastic grin across his face. "You don't have to commit murder to write about it, my friend."

"Did anybody ever connect this murder back to the Kremlin?" Roy asked calmly.

"Not exactly. But the deputy of the State Duma of the Russian Federation, a guy called Alexei Lugovoy, went public in December 2008, saying that 'anyone harming Russia should be exterminated.' He's wanted for questioning by the police in Britain. He's the number one suspect. Russia has, as you can well imagine, rejected the request for his extradition."

"Where is Lugovoy now?" Roy queried.

"Number One Red Square," Kasinov said, shaking his head furiously in condemnation. "He's still in Russian politics, alive and kicking. Bastard should be locked away—for good."

"Any idea what they used to kill Sakharshenko?" Roy asked.

"Initial ballistic examinations from Sakharshenko's postmortem confirmed that he was killed from close range, probably less than three feet, with a nine millimeter Yarygin PY pistol. This is the successor weapon to Russia's most famous Makarov pistol." Kasinov shrugged. "Two guesses where that came from."

"You're saying he was killed by a fellow countryman?"

"Maybe he was; maybe he wasn't," Kasinov replied in a haughty tone. "But it certainly looks that way."

Roy began to feel some personal risk now, as the Kremlin might have already connected him somehow with Kasinov's escape from Siberia. Coupled with that, Roy found Kasinov difficult to read. He had the opacity of a reinforced concrete wall. He looked Kasinov straight between the eyes. "What you're asking me to take on is a suicide mission."

Kasinov glanced above Roy's head momentarily before looking back at him. "One last thing, Roy."

Roy was starting to think that Kasinov was the kind of guy who always had to have the final say—a desire to maintain the limelight, like an orchestra conductor. He could feel the charm he had initially felt from Kasinov's personality starting to wane. "What would that be?"

"Before Litvinenko died, he made a number of allegations and accusations that the Russian president was behind his malaise. The claims resulted in an international media furor. Since then, the relationship between the UK and the Russian governments has not recovered. With my escape, relationships between the two powers have reached a new level of distrust. That's why I've got to get to them before they get to me. I need your help."

Roy looked back at him blankly. "If I'm going to find out who killed Vladimir, it'll be to revenge his legacy—not for anything else."

Chapter 14
Reunion

Roy arrived early at Yakatori to a rapturous welcome reception from Watanabe Yakatori, the restaurant's owner. After the greeting ceremony concluded, Roy took a seat with reassuring aplomb, as he always had, in the same seat where he always sat. He thought about his earlier meeting with Kasinov and tried to reflect on what was really going on in the Russian political underworld. He felt a distinct obligation to help his deceased friend Vladimir, but he was not convinced about Kasinov's integrity. Even so, he always loved a challenge.

This assignment is pushing the envelope a bit too far, he thought. Then he reminded himself that such things were best left for tomorrow. Tonight was the reunion dinner—a dinner over their shared proclivity for sushi and Pinot Grigio.

Minutes later, Roy felt a brief chill rush in from outside. He looked up and there she was, her silhouette entering the foyer as Yakatori-san, the maître d' for the evening, greeted her with a respectful salvo of short bows. As Yakatori-san took her navy coat from her, Roy watched her flick her glistening auburn hair briefly from her face. Then her eyes scanned the restaurant for him.

Roy stood and smiled in her direction. Her eyes gleamed when she saw him. Enthusiastically she made her way through a maze of rope-clad chairs and gazed back at him with a glowing smile. She stopped and eyed him head to toe. Roy didn't feel he was overdressed for the evening. *Smart casual,* he reckoned. He wore a simple pair of slightly faded blue jeans, which wrapped him fittingly, black leather shoes, which looked new, and a black, long-sleeved cotton shirt with the top button opened. As she took him in, he could feel the attraction again.

He gracefully moved forward to greet her. "Hello," he said, holding out his arms. They embraced cozily, holding onto each other for several seconds. Intuitively, Roy noticed her eyes close in what looked like adoration. He sensed the aromas from her body.

Neither of them wanted to let go.

Roy eventually broke from the hug, but kept his hand on her shoulder for quite some time after. He looked at her admiringly. He guessed she didn't have any time to go and change and was still wearing what she wore to work that morning.

She chose well, he thought. Her colorful, slim-fitting, silk Pucci dress amplified all the wonderful characteristics of her frame: her wide shoulders, her profound collarbones, her elegantly long, thin arms, and her tall, slender physique.

He stepped back and motioned to the table.

Her eyes twinkled as she took a seat. "Nice to see you."

"Nice to see you, too," he said. "You look amazing."

"So, Roy," she said with some degree of apprehension in her voice, "tell me what you're doing back here in London so quickly."

"Sorry for the surprise call and the short notice," he replied. "I only discovered yesterday that I had to come back here again."

Melanie moved forward in her chair as if preparing to ask him a question. She was interrupted as a short Asian waiter approached the table. "Are you ready to order something?" he said courteously. "Drinks? Food?"

Roy pulled the menu closer. "Shall I order for us?"

Melanie rubbed her hands together and smiled all over, revealing her perfectly straight and manicured white teeth. "Yes please," she replied. "As long as it includes sushi."

As Roy looked through the menu, Melanie brimmed with anticipation. "Who are you meeting with in London?"

Roy remained focused on the menu card. "Can we have some prawn sushi negiri, tuna sashimi, and a spicy roll for two?" he ordered, glancing over at Melanie for tacit approval.

She nodded with a sincere smile.

"Russian business," he said in answer to her question.

Melanie looked startled. "Again?"

"Can we also have some mixed tempura and some of your teppanyaki beef with some fried rice?" Roy concluded as he handed the menu to the waiter.

Melanie glanced up at the waiter. "Can we also have a bottle of Garganega Pinot Grigio?"

"Of course, madam," the waiter said with a bow before slinking away.

Melanie sat pensively with her head slightly tilted. "Well?"

After a brief pause, Roy leaned forward and lowered his voice. "Mikhail Kasinov asked to meet me. He said that he had a proposal for me to consider."

"Sounds interesting. So when are you meeting with him?"

"I already met with him this afternoon."

"That was quick going!"

"Yeah, straight off the plane from Florence."

"So what does he want you to do, bump off the Russian president or something?" Melanie said jokingly.

"Not exactly, but I wouldn't put it past him. He wants me to go to Moscow to find Vladimir Sakharshenko's killer, as if I'm to be some sort of a covert emissary on his behalf."

"I heard about Sakharshenko. He was an ex-partner of Kasinov's. And after you've done that?"

"That was it."

Roy dipped his hand into the complimentary edamame. He knew that wasn't it. There was more. *Lots* more. Even though Roy pulled *Mission Impossible* to get Kasinov out of Siberia, he was having mixed feelings about the guy. The CIA had painted Kasinov as someone that had been dealt a great injustice. Maybe he had, but Roy didn't see any humility or remorse. Vladimir had said very little, if anything, about his former partner. He had just said he owed him everything—as if he idolized him. Everything he achieved, he did because of Kasinov, he had remarked. He certainly never commented on his personality. "Yeah, that's it," he added as if convincing himself.

The waiter arrived with the wine and poured two glasses. When he finished pouring, Roy nodded to him, and then a second time—restaurant code for, "Thanks. Now please go away. We're trying to have a conversation here."

Roy, unsure about how much to pry about her work—and at the same time not wanting to make their dinner meeting come across like a formal inquisition into UGC's research of the Russian oligarch's business affairs—reached in for a second time. "Melanie, there's something I wanted to ask you about," he said reservedly.

Melanie looked back at him with anticipation. "Go on."

"You mentioned that you've been doing some research on Kasinov," Roy said in an open-ended way, hoping she might accentuate the key features of what she had been working on. He wasn't sure what kind of research she was doing.

"As I said to you at Annabel's, I know the story," Melanie offered. "It's been all over the media here since he arrived last week. Several years ago, he went through a significantly oversubscribed IPO with KasOil before he went to prison. A lot of people were stung after it collapsed, but for some reason, investors still like him. I've been primarily looking at the potential around the so-called what-if scenarios."

"And what scenarios might those be?"

"What if Kasinov gets back into the oil and gas market in Russia? And how might that open up opportunities for several oil-related companies—particularly in exploration, development, and services, and especially the American companies? They're the ones most bullish about Russian oil. And what if he gets a political mandate and usurps Koshenko and his cronies?"

"From your research, what are your thoughts on Kasinov?" Roy asked frankly. "As an individual, I mean?"

Melanie gulped back the rest of her Pinot Grigio in one go. "I'm not sure about him and his motives," she replied. "He's a bit of a shifty character. I guess you probably need to be if you want to be that successful. He's marmite-like; you either love him or hate him. I will say one thing, though: his imperial aspirations are a bit outlandish for this day and age, don't you think?"

Roy chuckled. "My own thinking exactly!"

"You should read his book," Melanie said.

"Have you read it?"

"Yes I have. It's quite a story. Apparently he smuggled a series of treatises out from his Siberian cell. They went out for publication a few months before you jettisoned him out of there. It's just hit the bookstores now. I imagine he saw it as his opportunity to share with the world his views of a very distinctive and morbid underworld from his time in the gulag."

"I'll have to get a copy," Roy said with a nod. "I was just thinking, to help your research, I have a good friend named Alistair Dunwoody. He spent several years in Moscow. We worked together in Angola and lots of other lovely places. He was like our intelligence chief back then. Really great guy. He's a Kiwi by birth."

Melanie laughed as she brushed her hair from her face. "That would be magnificent. You can never get enough contacts in this business. Every little bit helps. And hey, you never know; he might have something powerfully insightful on the guy."

"I'll send you on his details."

"Thanks." She paused for a moment as if considering how she might switch tacks. "So what's next?"

"I need to let him know tomorrow if I'm going to take on this new assignment."

"What are you thinking?"

"I'm thinking a bit like you, in fact," Roy said. "Something isn't right with the guy."

"What do you mean?"

Before he could answer, the food arrived and the waiter fussed about with the juggling and shuffling of all the condiments, glasses, and plates until everything eventually fit onto the table. Roy glanced down at the fusion repast. He thought it was probably enough for four people—no different from any other time they had been to Yakatori. But like on previous occasions, there was no doubt they would devour it.

Roy's mind quickly shifted from Asian culinary delights to research in Russian psychology. His education at Cambridge had taught him to be somewhat agnostic when listening to people he didn't really know that well, especially powerful people. "Something from his body language wasn't right."

"Go on," Melanie urged.

"After I asked him if he was sending me on a suicide mission, I looked him straight in the eye. I wanted to draw out his true emotion. He looked above my forehead as he started his response, and to be honest, he looked somewhat disingenuous."

"How could you tell?"

"Kinesics."

"Kinesics?" Melanie repeated.

"Better known as body language. Fifty percent of people who aren't telling the truth can't make straight eye contact. The other fifty percent are generally introverted, suffering from an anxiety disorder, are taciturn or shy, and find it hard to make eye contact. Kasinov is none of the latter. Throughout the meeting, he seemed a very direct guy and made good eye contact. This momentary slip was a sign that he wasn't being open with me."

"Maybe he was just being pensive," Melanie said with a chortling but cherishing laugh. "Perhaps he was looking upwards momentarily, hoping to find some inspiration as to what to say to attract the great Roy Young to join his latest covert mission."

Roy's concentration remained focused. "These kinds of nonverbal clues are telling."

"I'm sure they are, Roy," she said, smiling broadly. "I'm only kidding."

"In the Russian value system, personal space is culturally fluid. He's a collectivist kind of guy—a hugger type—but he was a bit distant with me.

Also, during that suicide mission conversation, his hands kept touching his face. This generally represents deceit, or the withholding of information. I just don't trust the guy."

"But he barely knows you," Melanie said, chortling again, this time more gently. "He's hardly going to go around hugging you. After all, it was only your first date!"

Roy smiled.

"I, on the other hand, am someone who *does* know you. I don't know everything, of course." Her expression softened. "For instance, what happened to us, Roy? Why did we lose contact?"

Roy knew she had asked the same question at Annabel's. Now he assumed that it slipped out again because she found his previous answer unsatisfactory. Roy eyed her squarely. "Let's just say I didn't make contact because I felt it was for your own good. My work sometimes doesn't allow me to get close to people, Mel. You understand that."

Melanie nodded. "Yeah . . . I understand," she answered in an auspicious tone. Her eyes were suggesting something otherwise. "But what I don't understand was how you just vanished and never made contact."

"I thought it was better that we didn't speak. I felt our relationship was getting too strong, and that it was better to finish it before we went too far." Roy felt awkward, as if his words were a front for some other reason—a reason he didn't want to disclose.

Melanie shook her head in disbelief, not wanting to get into a fight with him over something that happened three years ago. "So you're still single then?"

Roy looked at her with an adoring smile. "Yeah, still just me. Whereas you, on the other hand . . . I see the perfect man has come and whisked you off your feet." He tried to sound unperturbed by Melanie's new, younger, royal, model-like boyfriend.

Melanie looked hesitant in answering. "Jeremy is a nice guy," she snapped. "He's very British and very royal."

"Fantastic. So when's the wedding, then?"

Melanie clenched her jaw. "Don't worry; you'll be waiting a long time for that."

An uncomfortable silence fell between them as they picked at their food. Just when it grew unbearable, it was Melanie who spoke first.

"Do you remember back in Cambridge," she said in a jovial tone, "the night after the pub crawl on Trinity Street, when we ran down to Quayside and exchanged tops?"

"Yeah, I remember it well. I think you looked much better in my polo shirt than I ever did."

"Sure I did," she said, beaming. "That Ralph Polo guy had you in mind when he made that shirt. Anyway, *camisole* took on a whole new meaning that night—you stretched my shoulder straps!"

"Ralph *Lauren*, actually. And you shouldn't have taken it off, should you? Still have the photo—one of my favorites, I have to say."

They both laughed as they stared at each other. Her alluring eyes took him in, swinging his thoughts back to the first time he went to her flat, when she had invited him for dinner and they had made love for the first time. He pictured her standing in the kitchen, cutting up fresh salmon into neat, bite-size pieces. He pictured himself holding her from behind and caressing her shoulders. Then he remembered his realities—remembered how his job made him anything but relationship material.

"So why would you do it?" she asked.

"Do what?" he asked, snapping out of his reverie.

"Help Kasinov."

"I wouldn't do it to help him. If I do it, it will be for Vladimir. He has a family and friends who care for him. They at least deserve to know the truth."

"I'll help you as much as I can." Her eyes brightened. "In fact, if you're going to be in Moscow, you could try and look up a guy called Oleg Greshenko. He was KasOil's chief financial officer around the time of the IPO road show in London. The city really liked the guy. He was well-spoken and always engaged well with investors, but for some reason, he bailed shortly after the raise and before Kasinov got arrested."

~~~

After finishing at Yakatori, they stood along Farrington Road, all wrapped up and ready to embrace London's winter chill. Roy hailed a taxi and helped Melanie inside. "Thanks for a lovely evening," he said, kissing her on the cheek. "Call you tomorrow."

I missed you. That's what she wanted to say to him, but by the time it processed through her mind, it had changed. "Goodbye," she lip-synced back at him.

As the taxi pulled away, she waved.

He waved back.

She turned around and thought about the way he looked. It didn't really matter what he wore; there was an inner self-confidence he portrayed that made her feel this way about him.

Melanie arrived home to her Highgate flat, took off her coat, put her handbag on the table, and removed her contact lenses. As she looked in the mirror, she felt quite excited that she had spent some time with him. She had been hankering over him since seeing him at Annabel's. To break the eerie silence, she switched on the radio and poured herself a glass of water. The Jimmy Ruffin classic "Hold On To My Love," was playing with perfect enunciation.

What happened to us, Roy? Why did you just leave? Suddenly she could feel pressure building up in her tear ducts. Her eyes began to water. As Ruffin sang, "I'm nothing, and I can't get along without you," she couldn't hold them in any longer. She let the tears flow.

Why have you come back again? Why couldn't you have just stayed away?

She grabbed a tissue, wiped her eyes, finished off her water, and went to bed. An hour later, she was still staring at the ceiling. *I'm nothing, and I can't get along without you.* She couldn't get the chorus out of her head.

Chapter 15
Muscovite

A sober air chilled each of the five expansive floors of the Kremlin Senate building. On the fifth floor, however, inside the Senate room itself, the austerity was decorated with melodrama as Koshenko turned in anger and slammed his phone into its cradle.

"Don't you have any manners?" he grunted at the person standing in the doorway.

"You said you wanted to see us at nine, and it's one minute after nine now, sir," the man in the doorway replied humbly.

Koshenko looked up to see a triumvirate of senior ministers standing in his doorway: Prime Minister Vasily Popov, head of the FSB Andrey Borodin, and Minister of Security Valentin Sokolov. "Come in, gentlemen," he said with a distinctly less strident intonation. As the men took seats, Koshenko pulled his chair back and joined them. "Tell me what is happening in the media on our adversary."

Popov, who was sitting opposite, directed his grey, penetrating eyes at his two colleagues and then at Koshenko. "It's not looking good for us. The UK's *Telegraph* is running the story daily, and they're trying to connect all sorts of dots. They issued a conspiracy theory article this morning that links everything from Chernobyl to vicissitudes in ballet dancing steps. The story adds a new angle."

Popov picked up the newspaper, held it aloft, and pointed to an article on the front page.

Koshenko nodded impatiently. "What are you waiting for? Carry on, then."

After clearing his throat, Popov began to read. "Sources have now confirmed that there may be a symbiotic relationship between Kasinov's escape from Siberia, the Vitaly Kuznetsov murder investigation that is ongoing here in Moscow, Sakharshenko's assassination in Budapest, and Alex Litvinenko's radiation poisoning case from London." Popov recited the article as if he was performing the role of a TV anchor man. He looked up at Koshenko once his recital was complete. "That's it."

Koshenko remained taciturn, an angry look on his face.

Borodin interjected before Koshenko could blow a gasket. "It's Kasinov fuelling the fire here. He's going around telling everyone about his futuristic democratic vision of Russia. And he's cost the country billions in lost value in our stock market."

Koshenko shook his head vigorously. "I simply cannot afford to have him meddling in Russian government affairs," he said in an intensely contemptuous tone. Then he turned to face his prime minister. "Popov, I want you to call the Russian embassy in London. Tell our overpaid ambassador to Great Britain, Mr. Igor Pushkin, that it's time he earns that handsome salary I've been sending him. Tell him to invite Kasinov over for dinner, and let's see if we can cut a deal with him."

He noticed Popov looking back at him incredulously. He supposed it was owed to his uncharacteristic magnanimousness.

"Yes, sir," Popov replied. "Will do right away."

"And Popov," Koshenko said, raising his finger at his prime minister, his strident disposition returning. "Once it's set up, you should fly to London, as you will be there for that dinner."

Popov looked stupefied. "Why should I go there?"

"Well, if you don't do a deal with Kasinov," Koshenko shouted, "then you better be prepared to stay back and do a deal with Charles Browne."

"Charles Browne? The British foreign secretary?"

"No, Charles Browne the painter. Of course Charles Browne the foreign secretary, you fucking idiot." Koshenko turned to face Sokolov. "In tandem with this plan," he said, his finger raised and now firmly pointing at Russia's minister of security, "I want you to craft up a nefarious plot to bring Kasinov to his knees."

"Yes, sir. I will get working on it." Sokolov fidgeted with his thumbs. "Any particular agents you want involved or not involved, sir?"

"Where is Alexei Lugovoy currently?"

"He's here in the building," Sokolov said smugly.

Koshenko's eyes darkened. "Then bring him in."

Chapter 16
In Pursuit

Cognizant that time was of the essence, Roy arrived at Moscow's Domodedovo International Airport at 6:00 p.m. the next day. He chose Domodedovo over Sheremetyevo—or more to the point, BA over Aeroflot. From his experience, BA was the safer bet. Also from his experience, 80 percent of murder cases were determined within the first week of the act being committed. If the Kremlin were involved, they would most probably still be covering their tracks, he guessed. On Kasinov's recommendation, Roy booked himself a room at the Lotte Hotel at a staggering 18,200 rubles per night. Kasinov was footing the bill. Moscow's premium five-star hotel was located in the salubrious New Arbat area, right in the hub of the financial district, but also within walking distance of Red Square. Roy anticipated that he would be spending quite a bit of time around that area. *Good location*, he thought.

Before boarding, Roy had picked up a copy of *Siberian Liberty* and read a couple chapters on the plane. He was quite moved after reading Kasinov's thesis, and was starting to find some sympathy for the guy after learning what he had been through. Roy thought it gave an eerily vivid representation of the torture he endured at trial, and subsequently during his custodial sentence in jail. It also provided details about the "mysterious circumstances," as Kasinov referred to them, behind his arrest. The circumstances revolved around the sabotage of information to wrongfully convict Kasinov of a series of what he referred to as, "concocted mistruths."

After making his way past immigration and the throng of taxi drivers offering him a ride at discounted rates, he connected with his pickup, a Lotte chauffeur that guided him toward the exit. On his way out, Roy noticed a fellow traveller from the flight hustling his way through the crowd, looking like he was in a hurry to get somewhere. He ran with long strides right up until the moment he reached the exit. As he stepped onto the iced path just outside the building, the zealous traveller lost his balance, one foot flying into the air, followed closely by the second. He was on the ground on his backside in a millisecond. Roy exited more cautiously. As he passed the fallen passenger, he proffered his hand in assistance. *First time in Moscow's winter,* he assumed. The passenger took it and gave his appreciation with a grunt and a nod.

Once Roy was safely inside the car, he took out his phone and began to type.

Mel, you began to tell me about what happened at your work last week. I would like to know about it. Roy

Almost an hour later, the black Volkswagen Passat bearing Roy pulled up outside the Lotte, where a chirpy attendant wrapped in wool garments greeted its passenger. Roy nodded and went straight inside, where he made his way to the concierge. He was ravenous, having not eaten on the plane. "I'm just about to check in," he said. "What restaurants do you have here at the hotel?"

"We do have the best restaurant in Moscow right here in our hotel, Les Menus," the man at the desk replied. His name badge read, IVAN; CHIEF CONCIERGE. "It's our French restaurant run by three-star Michelin chef Pierre Gagnaire."

"Anything else?" Roy retorted.

The concierge looked surprised by Roy's response. "If you prefer Asian fusion cuisine, we have MEGU. You could try our chef's degustation menu there and sample a bit of everything."

Roy thought about the sushi he had the previous evening at Yakatori. "I'll go with the French."

"How many will be in your party?"

"Just me."

While Ivan went off to book a table, Roy checked his phone. There was a message.

It's nothing. I can tell you about it when I see you next. Thanks for dinner last night. Mx

Roy studied the message and wondered why she was being so evasive over something that was apparently so potentially flattering. He clicked the reply button and started typing.

Can you send me your research note? I would like to read it.

Roy put his phone away and headed to reception. "Roy Young," he said, nodding to the check-in assistant.

"Welcome, Mr. Young," the charming young lady at the desk replied in impeccable English. "Thank you for choosing the Lotte. We've been expecting you."

Roy nodded.

"I would just like to make you aware that you have access to our luxurious Mandara Spa, our club lounge, and our atrium garden for afternoon tea."

"Lovely," he replied. *I can't imagine I'm going to get to use any of that.*

Roy grabbed his key, offloaded his black leather

shoulder bag to the bellboy, and proceeded to check out Moscow's number one restaurant. As he passed Ivan's desk, he received a thumbs-up that a table had been secured.

He studied the menu board framed on the wall outside the restaurant before entering, only to learn that Les Menus had a reputation for bold and experimental cuisine with Chef Pierre Gagnaire hailed as one of the most innovative and artistic chefs in his field. Reportedly, his culinary artistry brought a modern twist to classic French cuisine.

Here in Moscow?

Roy proceeded inside, perused the menu, and ordered steak au poivre with a bottle of 1986 Château Margaux. After a meticulous decanting process, the sommelier presented Roy with a glass of the refined mixture. On caressing it for a little while, Roy felt his palate splayed with a rich and warm bouquet. He enjoyed a good vintage red wine. It gave him inspiration. After devouring his meal and polishing off the remains of the Margaux from the decanter, he retired for the evening.

He awoke the next morning to the sound of his 8:00 a.m. alarm. He switched it off and turned over in bed. *Nothing will be open this early,* he thought.

At 10:00 a.m., Roy finally rose and made his way to the Kremlin. Once outside, he felt the extremities of the weather differential. It was 17 degrees Fahrenheit, and although he hadn't been to Moscow for nearly five years, he distinctly remembered how cold it could get here. Despite the fact that he had been to Central Siberia only days before, where the numbers read a further 12 degrees negative, the chill from Red Square's non-entropic bricked surface made it seem even colder. Roy was well cocooned for this, wearing a mixed-wool, three-quarter length Brioni Crombie and cashmere scarf with a tight-fitting navy woolen cap.

When he arrived at the main Kremlin entrance, he passed the unmanned security booth perched on the roadside entrance mote and made his way over Troitsky Bridge and through the perimeter of Red Square. When he reached the other side, he gazed up at the bricked ramparts that stood proud from Troitskaya Tower. He cogitated on the antiquities contained therein, and also on the collection of diverse leaders that had occupied the central fortified complex—Lenin, Stalin, Khrushchev, Brezhnev, Gorbachev, and significantly, Yeltsin. Roy recalled from CNN footage back around 1991 how Yeltsin arrived at the very spot he was now standing, rolling in on the back of an armored tank to quell a brewing rebellion.

Behind the bricked expanse to Moscow's citadel, he saw the Kremlin Palace of Congress shrouded in white marble with tinted windows, the images from swarms of gathering tourists reflecting back at him. He moved adroitly towards the northern part of the Kremlin grounds and approached the Senate building, where, according to Kasinov's intel, Lugovoy's office was situated. Although it wasn't his first time here, Roy was impressed once again by the Senate's residence. Dubbed by classical architects as "the Russian Pantheon," it was delivered in a neoclassical design and built in the unusual shape of an isosceles triangle. In the middle of the main façade was an enormous domed passage fashioned like a triumphal arch that led to the inner courtyard. He went straight through, expecting to receive a taciturn greeting.

As he approached, several guards awaited him, but only one spoke. "What do you want?" he said. His was the sternest look, and he spoke in a deep and unfriendly accent.

"I'm here to see Alexei Lugovoy," Roy answered, trying to give the impression that he and Alexei had been the best of buddies since somewhere back in their childhood.

"Do you have an appointment?" the guard enquired.

"Not exactly," Roy responded self-assuredly. "But Alexei will be pleased to see me, I'm sure."

"What's your name?"

"Tell him it's Roy Young. I just want to chat with him to clear up this whole London polonium mess. It shouldn't take more than five minutes."

The security guard spoke in Russian on the

phone, occasionally casting short, suspicious glances in Roy's direction. Roy gazed upwards, admiring the curvaceous fifteenth-century Greek and Italian inspired artistry that splayed the ceilings of the entrance area. The view was interspersed with irregular columns the size of 200-year-old tree trunks. Shadows cast in all directions throughout the circular hall from the ornate chandeliers perched at the upper extremity of each adjoining arc that reached the ceiling. *I would love to get an official tour, but something tells me it won't be today.*

The security guard put the phone down. "I'm afraid he is not contactable."

"I'm in town for a couple days and keen to catch up with him. I'm sure he's keen to see me. Any chance you have his mobile number or home address?"

"We don't give out personal information."

Roy didn't anticipate a result from his first approach. Before he even arrived, he had already reconciled that Plan B was probably the only plan, as Plan A never really had much of a chance of success.

He left Red Square and returned several hours later. Invigorated after assembling the pieces of his Plan B, he sat on a small wall on the northwestern extremity of the square, a perch that provided him a perfect view of the exit from the Kremlin. By now, temperatures outside had jumped up to 28 degrees Fahrenheit. He got himself a hamburger from a reputable-looking local café situated close to where he had settled. *A new meaning to alfresco dining*, he thought.

Roy could hear a collection of spirited acoustics from a balalaika trio resonating from across the other side of the square. Whilst its silvery plucking melody might have been persistent and infectious, it didn't distract Roy's mind. He remained focused on one thing only: Lugovoy.

It was now 3:00 p.m. He pulled out a photo of Lugovoy that he had downloaded from a nearby Internet café. Following the Litvinenko case and the subsequent bombastic proclamations from the Kremlin's representative, Lugovoy's mug shot went viral. Roy had managed to download a few different snapshots to gain a few assorted profiles. He analyzed the face in detail to make sure he would recognize him. Lugovoy had a rugged, round face. He was clean-shaven with elevated and protruding cheekbones, and black hair cut tight at the back of his head with a fringe at the front. He had deep-set grey eyes with bushy eyebrows. Roy estimated that he was in his late forties. He wasn't smiling in any of the photos.

Not exactly a pretty-boy, but at least he's discernible.

At around 6:20 p.m., Roy spotted in the distance a man resembling Lugovoy exiting the main building. He verified by comparing two of the photos with the man he saw. He was sure it was Lugovoy, and he was sure he was alone.

Roy watched him approach Red Square and

then take a left turn into Prospekt Marksa. He placed the photos back in his bag, jumped up from his resting post, and followed from a distance. He finessed his way through the crowd gathered around Lenin's granite-encased mausoleum, staying about ninety feet behind his target. He observed his target travelling towards the Moscow River. Roy glanced behind him to find the Bolshoi Theatre and get his bearings. He knew where he was. The Kremlinite walked for fifteen minutes, exiting the 700-year-old fortresses and crossing over Kropotkinskaya Street and then onto Ostozhenka Street. Despite the latter street being reportedly one of the most affluent sections in the capital—home to many of local artistic elite and the playground for nouveau riche Russians— Roy was surprised when an old beggar stopped him as if he owned the place.

Roy gave the guy a handful of kopecks from his pocket, not wanting to stay and argue with the old man. "Here, take this."

"Spaceeba Bolshoi."

Roy crossed onto Ostozhenka. Suddenly the usual grumbling from Moscow's floods of cars was gone. All around, he could hear nothing except the sweet twitters of blackbirds flitting in and out through the foliage that covered the street up ahead. The landscape transformed before him into a bright crescendo of breathtaking classical creations. He noticed there were no more drab grey concrete monolithically draped facades.

Instead, to Roy's astonishment, the architecture boasted a bizarre mix of prerevolutionary and art nouveau structures, along with several neo-Gothic apartment buildings.

Roy inhaled deeply as he maintained a firm eye on his target ahead. He noticed that this place smelt different from the rest of Moscow, too. The air gave a pleasant aroma like a heterogeneous concoction of maple and elm. Along the pathways, columns of root-infiltrated trees provided a somewhat tousled combination of secret warrens throughout the opulent district. Roy passed a number of young, well-dressed couples bouncing out onto the pavement from trendy after-work bars. All the while, he kept his focus on his target.

Disbelief came to Roy as he recalled the article he had read on the plane about how Ostozhenka was referred to as "Moscow's Golden Mile." He thought it was no wonder that it was considered one of the most expensive places in the world to live, with an average price of US$4,000 per square foot. *What's more amazing*, he thought, *is how a deputy minister can afford to live in a place along here.* Roy shrugged.

Up ahead, the Kremlinite continued for another six hundred feet and then turned off to what Roy assumed must have been his residence. Outside the house, Roy noticed a line of flashy new German cars—Mercedeses, BMWs, and Audis— each one bigger than the last. Between them stood an incongruously placed Lada.

The target swiftly entered the building and closed the door behind him.

Roy arrived at the door, finding it locked. *Okay, let's make this swift and silent.* Twenty seconds later, the door was open, compliments of Lohatlha's covert entry techniques training module. Roy gently closed the door behind him and emerged through a large entrance area that protruded at an obtuse angle. He looked around briefly to take in a lavish interior. Then, straight ahead, he watched the man take off his coat and place his briefcase down in the hall. Ten feet away, the target stood. The man looked back to see Roy's tall silhouette positioned in the hallway.

"Good evening, Alexei," Roy said calmly.

"Who the hell are you?" the man said.

Roy looked around the surprisingly opulent interior that boasted a vast collection of what looked like pre-Renaissance artwork before returning his gaze to his target. "I didn't realize the ministry had re-baselined their pay grades," Roy said, gesturing to the paintings. "Very nice pad you have here, Alexei."

"What do you want?"

"Apologies for the intrusion. I tried to see you at your office today, but they said you were not contactable."

"You've got some balls coming in here," Lugovoy said in clear disbelief. "How did you get in here? How do you know where I live?"

"Let's just say I used some basic sensory surveillance and intervention skills," Roy said cheekily as he followed Lugovoy, who had started to move slowly towards a rear reception hall.

"Who are you?"

"My name is Roy Young. I just need to ask you a few questions, if I may, and then I'll be on my way."

As they spoke, the Kremlinite shuffled slowly over an enormous Persian rug. Roy followed him, keeping the same ten-foot boundary between them. He glanced down at the floor covering molded to the floor. *Like a magic carpet*, he thought. It was almost the size of the room. *Probably imported from Iran.*

"Whom do you work for?" Lugovoy asked tersely.

"Mikhail Kasinov," Roy answered in an equally terse fashion. He didn't figure that now was the time to lie. Besides, he wanted to gauge Lugovoy's reaction at the mention of the former oligarch's name.

Lugovoy's mouth curled. "He's a criminal. He's got some cheek sending you here."

It was the reaction Roy expected. "Have you travelled to Budapest in the last week?"

Lugovoy shrugged. "What are you talking about?"

"What can you tell me about Vladimir Sakharshenko's death?" He could tell that Lugovoy was confused—and alarmed, most probably.

"Nothing," Lugovoy said, holding out his hands in disbelief. "I don't know what you're talking about!"

"Okay then. Tell me about polonium-210. I understand you're an expert in these chemical compounds."

"Those matters are completely extraneous," Lugovoy said, his expression one of great offence. "I find your question totally irrelevant."

Roy simply waited as if giving him a second chance to answer. Then he eyed Lugovoy suspiciously. He knew he had something to say. He just needed to make it easy for him to say it.

Lugovoy reached into his top inside pocket and pulled out a gun, placing it on the table next to an old gold samovar. The table sat in the center of the magic carpet. Lugovoy and Roy stood at either side of the table. The gun was an Italian-made Mateba auto revolver, a hybrid semiautomatic. Small, compact, each press of the trigger fired a cartridge. Although Roy knew this was much faster than a generic double-action revolver, he didn't feel any threat, for as long as he remained in close proximity to Lugovoy, he would be able to disarm him before he could fire the first cartridge, if it came to that.

Unarmed, Roy remained completely calm. He reached into his inside pocket and pulled out an old Parker pen, which he placed gently on the table on the other side of the samovar. Then he returned his right hand to the side pocket of his Crombie jacket.

Lugovoy eyed him. "You don't stop asking stupid questions, you go to the jail!"

"Look," Roy said calmly but confidently. "I'm not going to harm you as long as you cooperate."

"Harm me?" Lugovoy uttered, pointing down at the table. "I've got a gun. You've got a stupid little pen."

"It's not a stupid little pen; it's a very clever one."

"Looks like a stupid pen to me."

"It may look like an ordinary pen. It even writes like an ordinary pen. However, it has one minor modification. It's loaded with compressed carbon monoxide. In my pocket, I have a transponder device that, when activated, can send a signal to activate a release valve at the top of that pen."

Lugovoy was taciturn.

He looked at Roy and then the pen, and then he looked at Roy again. Then he glanced at the gun.

"Alexei, being the chemical guru that you are, I'm sure you know that carbon monoxide is a bit different from other poisonous gases."

Another reticent pause followed from Lugovoy.

"You see, if I push the button on this little switch in my pocket, you won't even know. In case you're not familiar with its biochemical characteristics, carbon monoxide is not just deadly, it's also colorless, odorless, and tasteless. It's even more deadly when it's compressed to one hundred times its volume." Roy pointed to the table with his opposite hand. "So in there, in that stupid little pen, there is enough gas to fill this room and every other room in this place faster than you can get off this magic carpet."

Roy paused and watched Lugovoy's fretful eyes darting about in all directions. "Now there are two things you don't know," he added calmly. "Firstly, you don't know whether I'll push this button, and secondly, you're not going to smell or even taste a thing, even if I do push it. Me, on the other hand, I will know, because I'll be the one activating the transponder. So I'll be able to hold my breath and watch you enter a state of drowsiness followed by unconsciousness. In minutes, it will lead to respiratory failure when your body becomes saturated with carbon monoxide. Your choice, Alexei."

Roy could hold his breath for three minutes. More if he needed to. Weekly aqua training drills as a young army cadet had taught him that. He didn't think he needed to pass this onto Lugovoy, but either way, the Russian remained speechless.

"So are you ready to answer my questions?" Roy asked after a brief pause.

Lugovoy's gaze drifted from the pen to Roy's eyes. He swallowed hard. "What do you want to know?" Lugovoy eventually said.

Roy breathed a silent sigh of relief without giving away a thing with his expression. "Did you or any of your associates travel to Budapest in the last three days?"

"No."

Roy glanced at the gun. "Are you planning to terminate Mikhail Kasinov?"

"No," Lugovoy said. "But I would like to."

"Did you poison your fellow countryman, Alexander Litvinenko at Itsu, in Piccadilly?"

"Not personally," he replied with a smirk.

"Did you arrange for him to be poisoned?"

"Yes."

"Why?"

Lugovoy folded his arms across his chest. "Because I was told to."

Roy approached the table with his eyes still fixed on the Russian. He slowly picked up his Parker pen, reached into his pocket and took out a card, placing it on the table. His eyes shifted to the card as he wrote his mobile number on the back, and then placed the pen back inside his pocket. Then he looked directly into Lugovoy's eyes. "I think we can help each other." He turned and headed for the door. "I'm in town for a couple days. Call me if you think of anything you may have missed."

Chapter 17
Riverdance

It was 9:50 p.m. on Friday, and David St. Ledger was balanced awkwardly on a stool at Molly's bar, his local pub in the town of Glendalough. One foot was resting on the stool's lower stainless steel rim and the other on the floor. He had one hand on his knee and the other socketed under his chin, supported by his elbow, which rested on the bar counter. He wore a forlorn look on his face as he stared vacuously at a selection of whiskey optics erected vertically and equidistantly behind the bar.

Molly's owner, Paddy McHugh, was on duty at the bar, serving customers and traversing up and down the twelve-foot-long serving area, keeping collective pints of Guinness, Harp, and Heineken flowing. Friday night was Ceili Night, and Molly's was full to the brim of its fifty-persons capacity. In olden times in rural Ireland, a Ceili evening was arranged to facilitate courting and prospects of marriage, but today in most towns, they had been appropriated by neon-illuminated nightclubs. There were no neon lights and no nightclubs in Glendalough—only Molly's Ceili Dance. For many, including St. Ledger, it was the main event in the weekly social calendar.

In the corner, a sonorous Gaelic group of four began to plangently capture the attention of the on-looking drink-laden punters. The harmonic mix of sounds from John on fiddle and flute, Mick on tin whistle and accordion, Sheila on the bodhrán, and Eamonn on acoustic guitar began to resonate throughout the pub. Adjacent to McHugh's worktop, with the music gaining momentum in the background, a congregation of enthusiastic dancers had assembled in formation for the Siege of Ennis rendition—a traditional humdrum dance dating back to the days of Cromwell and the exodus of several locals from a prison in the rural town of Ennis in 1686.

St. Ledger's long-time friend Sean O'Connor was there, holding up the bar with him. "What's up with you?" O'Connor said candidly. "You have a worried face on you, like a pig heading for the abattoir."

"Sorry, Sean," St. Ledger replied awkwardly. "I've got a lot going on in my mind at the moment."

"Is it business or pleasure?" O' Connor probed. "Or lack of both?"

St. Ledger nodded as he stared at the bottle of
Jameson behind the bar. "I may have bitten off
more than I can chew this time, Sean."

"Would you stop acting like a big girl's blouse
there and get up and dance?"

St. Ledger patted O'Connor on the shoulder.
"No, I'm grand. Up you go yourself. I'll be
grand." There was something in his eyes that said
otherwise.

Not needing much encouragement, O'Connor
was on his feet with a fresh creamy pint of
Guinness in one hand and his girlfriend Martina
fastened to the other. Dressed in traditional steel-
tipped brogues, he began his entrée with a torrent
of riveting Irish dance steps.

"One more there, Paddy," St. Ledger bid. "And
then I'll be off."

O'Connor took one large gulp and delicately
placed his pint of Guinness back on the bar top as
if he was replacing the Holy Grail back into its
casket. He then moved to take up his place in the
center of the troupe and waited for the exact
moment within the jig sequence. The group raised
its arms with joined hands, each with their right
foot drawn forward, toes pointed directly
outwards, and as the note hit out, they launched
into a giant leap.

"You're looking a bit down, Mr. Celebrity,"
McHugh said from behind the bar.

"Ah, just a bit tired, Paddy, that's all."

St. Ledger was the local superstar. He was a multimillionaire, and despite that, everybody loved him. He was a generous and genuinely altruistic person, and he always showed it in the humblest of ways. He had done much to support the social and civic development of the Glendalough community and the surrounding areas, along with several programs for advancement of the town's youth. Above all, his character was jovial, friendly, and full of energy. He was the one normally first up there, ahead of O'Connor, bouncing the brogues off the floor. He just wasn't in the mood tonight, primarily because the gravity of this whole Kasinov affair was playing on his mind.

St. Ledger downed his last Jameson and slipped away to the door with all the grace of an ice skater leaving the rink, tipping his cap to Sheila on the way out as she pummeled away at the bodhrán. She looked up in amazement, as if to say, "Why is the greatest rogue in town leaving the party before it even started?"

Preoccupied, St. Ledger made his way home through the neighboring escarpments. After a ten-minute drive to Kinlough Castle, he jumped out of his BMW X5. By then, beads of sweat ran down his forehead. Kasinov was certainly making a name for himself in the world's media, and St. Ledger didn't need to be connected with the entire hullabaloo.

He began to think about what might happen if the truth around the illicit passport acquisition came out. He would most probably get into some serious trouble with the law. He would have to leave Ireland and the castle. After alighting from the car, he thought as he wiped the sweat from his brow, *I don't think I'll be able to beg for forgiveness on this one.*

Chapter 18
Fabrique

Roy left the affluent Ostozhenka area after the Q&A session with Lugovoy and headed for Tverskaya Street, home to Moscow's acclaimed nightlife. *A fifteen-minute walk*, he estimated. He made his way to the current top spot in town, Fabrique Bar and Club—at least that's what it said in the booklet Ivan had given him.

On arrival, he modestly joined the compulsory pre-entrance face control routine, which included a series of platitudinous questions at the door. He passed the test and paid the five-hundred-ruble entrance fee. Roy figured that was the way things were done around there, and wasn't going to argue. He had no desire to get into a fracas in Moscow and raise his profile with the authorities, especially after the Siberian mission.

On entering Fabrique, he was welcomed by a lively, lurid crowd dancing frenetically to excessively loud music. Most were scantily robed, displaying more flesh than clothes. He made his way to the heated terrace in the rear, where he could hear himself think.

"Adin Baltika, *pazhalsta*," he ordered from the bar.

Once he settled, he regarded the crowd, his eyes drawn to the young Russian eye candy. There was lots of it. He also attentively scanned for any suspicious Russian males on the lookout for him. Both Plan A and Plan B had downsides. They each attracted attention. Although Roy had spent a significant part of his life in southern Africa, his antipodean traits were well balanced with his global experience. As a foreigner in a Moscow club, he would most likely attract attention anyway. Now he tried to decipher if anybody was there specifically to meet him.

Roy noticed one shifty-looking individual that maintained a haughty gaze on him from the bar opposite where he sat. He recalled seeing him arrive at the club right after he had. He was stocky, maybe 180 pounds, and medium height. He looked like typical ex-KGB, most probably FSB. He had a tightly knit number one haircut and wore an equally tightly knit, blue, round-neck pullover with no shirt.

After Roy finished his second beer, he thought it was time to head back to the hotel. He bid farewell to the two young ladies that had come to his table to talk with him. When he emerged outside, he shuddered at the cold and wrapped his

Crombie tightly against his body. The wind chill had brought the temperature down to 4 degrees F below zero. That wasn't the only thing that awaited him, though. Roy looked up to see he had a welcoming reception outside the club. There were four of them. The leader was a tall man with a reddened complexion and well in excess of 200 pounds. He had a fully shaven head and a bridge-shaped nose that had been broken in a few places. He put his index finger to the side of his forehead, mimicking firing a gun, as if to indicate that Roy was a dead man.

Roy laughed to himself at the performance, but in fairness, he had seen a lot worse. He noticed that the leader bore a symbol emblazoned on his long black leather jacket. It was a gold, two-headed eagle that rose up on open wings, shrouded with a quadrangular, red heraldic shield. On the eagle sat two crowns and a third larger one above them. The eagle held an orb and a scepter in either hand.

The second guy was a bit shorter and had a deeper center of gravity. His engorged forehead shadowed his unkempt goatee and unveiled a crew cut that revealed the true size of his extra-large wing-nut ears. He looked like he was carrying a heavy limp as he moved closer—probably a prosthetic limb on his right-hand side. He was bursting out of his black sheepskin jacket.

The third guy was a short, stocky, rotund bruiser with a granite face and plenty of extra pounds. He carried a knife in his right hand.

The leader held a pistol. From what Roy could see, it looked like an early generation Glock 17 semiautomatic. He was waving it around like a machete cutting confetti strips as he reviled Roy in Russian. Roy translated the words in his mind, finding them less than complimentary.

The fourth guy was a carbon copy of the leader. *Probably his brother doing some sort of imitation routine,* Roy thought.

Most people would have tried to make a run for it. Roy didn't. He knew what he had to do.

Suddenly a fifth attacker grabbed Roy from behind in a bear hug. Roy looked down and recognized the molded, spray-on blue pullover from inside Fabrique. They struggled momentarily as the blue pullover guy tried to pull off what felt like some form of hybrid Heimlich maneuver.

Roy could easily take out three guys. Four required planning and preparation. Five required luck. Even so, Roy didn't feel threatened. If anything, he felt humbled. *They must hold me in high regard, sending a five-man squad.*

He escaped the bear hug by grabbing the inside of his attacker's wrists and twisting both arms clockwise until he heard one of the bones snap. His attacker roared and fell to his knees like a deflating air bag. Roy immediately swung around and landed the perfect bicycle kick on the leader's head. The leader fell forward, clutching his crown and dropping the Glock. Roy caught it as it bounced off the iced cobblestone. He turned and thrust its handle into the guy with the knife, landing a blow to his solar plexus. His attacker fell, slashing the knife across in a concave contour that caught Roy's right sartorius muscle, just above the knee, ripping some flesh. Roy saw blood emerging from the underside of his Crombie. Still he wasted little time in addressing the chubby one with a knee to the ribs and a smash over the head from the Glock. The chubby one was down in a second, molded to the ice-clad floor.

The forth attacker came at Roy with a right hook aimed perfectly at his upper chin. He saw it coming and swerved to avoid. A second connected, and Roy felt a rib crack. "Shit!" he cried out.

Roy grabbed his attacker by the larynx and choked him. He continued with a blow to the chest, but it was like hitting a thick chunk of neoprene. Roy then followed with a volley of blows to his attacker's face, pulverizing him into the ground.

One by one, they had fallen like limp autumn leaves.

The final attacker, the imitator, froze.

Roy nodded in the direction behind. "Best thing you can do is turn around and walk away—unless you want me to break something for you."

The imitator turned around and walked away.

Roy paused to make sure there was no one brave enough to make a second attempt.

There wasn't.

Expectedly, a crowd had gathered to watch the exhibition. The bouncers watched, too, in clear disbelief. Over the chatter of the spectators, Roy could hear muffled cries pouring up from the ground as he walked away.

I didn't get a chance to warn them.

Roy brushed himself off, looked over at the crowd, and took a little bow.

The crowd responded with a slow applause that transformed to a loud crescendo as he moved away. He smiled to himself and raised one hand.

At least they have a sense of humor over here in Tverskaya.

Roy didn't fancy having to explain to the Russian militias how this happened—too much paperwork, too much hassle, too many Makarovs. He had a choice to make. He could take a stroll down through Tverskaya Street, or he could wait around and risk getting a Makarov in the cranium.

He chose the Tverskaya option.

He stopped at the nearby waste bin, wiped the Glock clean, and dropped it inside.

~~~

When Roy awoke the next morning, he felt stiff with the buildup of lactic acid around his wounds. He pulled off the temporary strapping he had applied the previous evening and gazed at his ripped flesh. The bleeding had held, but he needed to get something to seal the wound.

He exited the hotel after getting instructions from Ivan's day-shift counterpart on where to pick up some medical supplies. Next door at the local Apteka, he found what he needed: Neosporin skin stitch spray and a bandage roll, something he had used many times before.

He spotted a mirror and whipped off his jacket, shirt, and jeans, right there in the middle of the store. He applied the gel and wrapped several feet of twelve-inch bandage around his chest and knee to keep his rib from shifting and his wound intact. When he had finished, he examined his handiwork. *As good as new.* He grinned.

The two young female sales assistants looked on with their mouths open and their eyes bulging.

Roy put his clothes back on and turned to the two. "Spaceeba Bolshoi," he said, nodding.

He left the Apteka and headed back to the Lotte lobby. Ivan's stand-in directed him to the business center. He made his way in, settled in his chair, fired up the hard drive and monitor, and typed in the word sequence, "Eagle—red heraldic shield—orb—scepter."

It came straight up in images. It was the national coat of arms of the Russian Federation, the official state symbol. The article with the image said that, in 2000, the State Duma had passed a constitutional bill that was later approved

by the Federation Council and signed into law by
the Russian president.

*The Fabrique reception committee are from the Russian
government. No big surprise there.*

Roy checked out of the Lotte. Following
Melanie's introduction, he had made contact with
Oleg Greshenko, KasOil's former CFO. On
Greshenko's recommendation, the two arranged
to meet later that morning at Moscow's legendary
Café Pushkin, off Tverskaya.

When Roy arrived, he saw a lone bespectacled
man sitting in the corner of the restaurant. He
wore an oversized grey flannel suit, a white shirt
with a collar that looked two sizes too big, and a
matching grey tie. He seemed to have a nervous
disposition as his eyes darted around the room
before settling on Roy.

Definitely the accountant, Roy thought.

Before him rested a file bulging with papers and
held together by an enormous elastic band. He
cradled the file with his arms as if guarding it with
his life.

At least he's come prepared.

Roy went over and greeted him. The two spoke
for ten minutes. More specifically, Greshenko
spoke and Roy listened. He explained that he was
now the general director of a Russian financial
services institution and had been away from the
world of KasOil for almost nine years. Greshenko
shared some background information with Roy,
flashing reports, organization charts, and company

annual reports from the file. He explained how KasOil was started, how all the different people had joined at different stages, how people got along inside the company, the journey to success, the practices inside the company, and all that kind of soft, fuzzy stuff.

Roy looked a bit bemused as he sifted through for the real story. He interrupted Greshenko in midsentence concerning the culture of the company. "Did Kasinov have a fair trial?"

Greshenko paused. Roy guessed he had to think about his response. *Probably wasn't a question he expected me to ask.*

Greshenko took a sip of his coffee and delicately placed his mug back on the table. "Kasinov claimed all along that his trials and sentencing were all politically motivated, and that the entire legislative process was prehistoric," the former KasOil CFO said. Greshenko's hands started to shift nervously onto one of the file of papers he had. "There were several Western leaders who shared his view, but despite years of entreaties through a labyrinth of the legal structures within the Russian legislature, Kasinov and the lawyers never made any progress in achieving justice. They lodged numerous claims, pursuing reparation for infringement of his human rights by the Russian government. They were all supported by the US, France, and the European Court of Human Rights. Unfortunately, though, it was all without conclusion."

Roy had heard a similar version of this story before. "How did he do the deals? How did he become so entrenched in Russia's oil and gas market?"

Greshenko took another sip of his coffee. This time, Roy could see his hand was trembling. "Kasinov was well-educated and experienced in the chemistry of oil. That made him smarter than the rest of the oligarchs when it came to interrogating oil reservoir data. So he picked the Siberian reserves wisely. Each field he bid for was rich in hydrocarbons and easily accessible whether inland onshore or deep-water offshore enclosures. He seemed to hit the jackpot every time. From the time he was a young oil assessor in the government, he knew exactly the most efficient and likely the most profitable fields. From his time in the ministerial hierarchy, he knew how the deals were done. At the time of the sale, he had the perfect balance of technical, commercial, and political. He had every angle covered."

"And what about after the big deal? What happened then?"

"I'm not sure if I'm following you. To what are you referring?"

"I mean what about his relationship with Koshenko?"

Greshenko looked even more uncomfortable at the mention of Koshenko's name. He glanced around the room and then leaned closer to Roy. "After he became Russia's most successful oligarch, Kasinov relished being venerated in entrepreneurial circles throughout Russia," he whispered. "He particularly enjoyed being out in the limelight on TV shows, attending celebrity events, flying all over the world, and being seen with G-Seven national presidents and premiers. Kasinov knew this probably pissed off the Russian government, especially our president. This was the way he played the game."

"Who knew?"

"What do you mean?"

"I mean did anybody on the leadership team not tell him he was stepping on his dick?"

"No one had the balls to," Greshenko replied, putting his hands up in submission. "I tried, but I just kept getting shot down. In fact, Vladimir was the only one to speak out and challenge him. Believe it or not, they fought all the time. Sakharshenko's vocal flogging on several of Kasinov's media appearances and his aggressive tax schemes was folklore in the KasOil boardroom."

"And what about outside the boardroom?"

"Vladimir actually had a lot of respect for Mikhail, but I think Mikhail didn't like to be challenged, especially in front of others. Vladimir kept telling him he needed to show Koshenko some respect, but he wouldn't listen."

"Who else was aware of the rift between Kasinov and Koshenko?"

"Everybody knew. Kasinov stubbornly challenged Koshenko regularly. He even went as far as publically criticizing the president's venal practices. Once he even did it on national television."

"What about Kasinov's former head of security?" Roy enquired.

"What about Kuznetsov?"

"The charges against him."

"Yeah," Greshenko replied, his head tilting downwards. "That was when things started going wrong at KasOil."

"You have any details?"

Greshenko shuffled around inside his folder, moving reports to the side and down on the seat next to him. Then he picked out a file wrapped in a plasticized blue cover and nervously handed it to Roy. "Here you go," he said apprehensively. "This was the subpoena we received. The front page is a summary document from our barristers."

Roy took the file from Greshenko and studied the front sheet, which listed the charges against Kuznetsov. The three murders for which he stood charged were summarized.

January 2001. Klaus Muller, a director and senior executive of Munich-based AMV Petroleum GmbH. He had initiated a number of legal suits against KasOil, claiming he had acquired rights to develop the Krapivinskoye oil field from KasOil for US$200 million and wanted *his capital returned after KasOil executives failed to deliver on all their responsibilities in the joint venture.*

May 2002. Olga Corneyeva, a Vladivostok property owner who apparently "over-negotiated" the sale of her property when KasOil attempted to acquire it in 1998.

September 2002. Vlada Morozov, mayor of Komsomolsk, who had opportunistically requested that KasOil should pay increased taxes in the province.

Roy shuffled through the report, flicking from one page to the next. "I don't see any opinion from KasOil's counsel," he said. "I just see a statement of claim from the opposing counsel."

"That's everything I have," Greshenko replied.

"Interesting." Roy tore off the front page and handed back the file to Greshenko. "You don't mind if I hang onto this?"

Greshenko nodded.

"Thanks," Roy stood to move away. "Just one last thing before I go."

Greshenko looked back at him sheepishly from under his dark-rimmed glasses.

"What happened to Kasinov's billions?"

"Nobody knows. All I know is that he made a lot more money than Koshenko, and didn't share any of it."

Roy left the restaurant, jumped into the Lotte limousine, and nodded to the driver to go. "Domodedovo Airport."

In the car, he began to reflect on everything Greshenko had confided in him. He was beginning to think that the picture of Mikhail Kasinov as the quintessential humanitarian might be a bit of a stretch.

Chapter 19
Gloom

It was 7:30 a.m. when Margaret Mooney closed her cottage door and made her way to the rear entrance to Kinlough Castle. She had worked there as St. Ledger's housekeeper for almost ten years. She loved living at Kinlough, and thoroughly enjoyed working for David. He was the best boss one could have. Her light frame inclined forward ever so slightly from a back operation ten years prior. Despite this, and at the spritely age of sixty-four, she was in the best of health. At six-foot-even she was a tall woman, a feature that came in pretty handy with her job. Today, her long silver hair was tied up.

As she entered the castle, she began with her normal business of the day. First up was to let Homer, St. Ledger's ten-year-old setter, out for a run, followed by the preparation of breakfast, and then the cleaning. She went to the back room off the kitchen, where Homer slept, and called him out to the garden. There was no response. She hadn't seen him on her way across to the castle from her cottage.

"Maybe David has taken him for an early morning walk again," she mumbled. "He seems to be doing that a lot lately."

Just then, Catherine St. Ledger, her employer's daughter, strolled into the kitchen. She wore retro Victoria's Secret pajamas and flip-flops. Her hair looked ruffled. She didn't start lectures at Trinity until 10:00 a.m., so she had plenty of time for breakfast and a shower before having to set off on her day. She was quite a mature young lady for her years. Hanging around with a dad like David had taught her lots about life and how to enjoy it while it lasts.

"Good morning, Margaret."

"Good morning, dear. Have you seen your father yet?"

Catherine climbed onto the kitchen stool, extending her arms to their extremities as she let out a loud yawn. "Haven't seen him," she said. "It's nice and warm in here this morning."

"Yes, it is."

Catherine craned her neck over the kitchen counter to find a view of the parking area out the front. "Is his car still there?"

"Yes, it is, dear. I saw it on my way in."

After downing a glass of orange juice, Catherine went out the back through the rear kitchen exit to light up a cigarette. She shook her head as she let out a few casual expletives over the rogue of a dad she had. As she took a drag, she noticed something alongside the collection of mature rose bushes nearby, and walked over to investigate. As soon as she saw it, her mouth started quivering uncontrollably. She let out a scream. It was Homer. His throat had been slashed and his body lay there lifeless. She dropped the cigarette and ran back inside the house. Visibly trembling from the shock, with tears rolling down her face, she cried out for Margaret.

Inside the castle, she feared for her father. She moved at a slow pace across the main reception area, pausing for a moment when she thought she heard a sound. There was something creaking. It was like the sound of an unoiled seesaw at a kid's playground. She looked around, rotating unhurriedly as her eyes scanned the enormous reception area and adjoining rooms. There was nothing—just that sound.

Eventually she looked up. Her eyes widened with astonishment. "Jesus, Mary, and Joseph!" she cried out with an enormous screech.

Her father was dangling from the central joist inside the castle's main reception hall. His neckline was chafed from the wire rope and the taught halter that embraced his neck. His head lay delicately balanced to his right-hand side. His flaccid body swayed slowly.

~~~

By midmorning, following the news that the local hero was dead, the gloom had already spread through Glendalough. "He hung himself from a girder inside Kinlough Castle," was the word going around.

The whole town went into shutdown mode for a day of mourning. Only Catherine refused to believe the official ruling of suicide.

Chapter 20
Photo Finish

Following his two-day speculative visit to Moscow, Roy touched down at Ferenc Liszt International Airport in Budapest on Transaero flight 201. It was at midday. The approach into Ferenc wasn't pretty, thanks predominantly to the deep, turbulent pockets of towering cumulus cloud formations that lined Budapest's skyline. He thought the Transaero pilot had handled it well— better than most. He hoped the trip here would be worth it. He knew that if he was going to find Sakharshenko's killer, he needed to start back at the beginning. In order to make sense of what was happening in Moscow, he first had to find out what happened in Budapest.

After clearing the airport formalities, Roy emerged outside to an unusually darkened troposphere with distinctly moist air. He took in a deep breath. He could feel the rain coming as he jumped into a taxi and passed the address card to the driver. Once outside the airport road network, the taxi headed southwest. They arrived at the destination Sholnosk fifteen minutes later.

Roy had spent a good portion of his time on and off here in Sholnosk over the past twelve months as he prepared for Alpha Factor. Now he was back here once again, sooner than he had imagined. In fact, he didn't imagine himself ever having to come back here.

He saw Nikoletta Lukas waiting for him at the house. Roy eyed her briefly before he emerged from the car. Today was not a black day for Nikoletta. Instead, she wore a flamboyant batik blouse with black trouser slacks and her hair tied back off her face. Roy thought she looked elegant as he closed the door of the taxi and approached her.

"Nikoletta," he said pleasantly as he stretched out his arms to offer his greeting.

With the sound of the taxi's accelerating tires against the gravel in the background, she approached him with her arms opened. "Thank you for coming."

"No, thank you for seeing me," Roy said gratefully. "I'm so sorry about what happened to Vladimir. He was a great man."

Suddenly a roar of thunder resonated through the skyline, followed milliseconds later by an almighty crack that lit up the horizon for miles. It was even louder than the thunderstorms Roy had experienced in Natal, South Africa. Deep clouds had gathered.

"Can we go and sit down somewhere—preferably somewhere dry?"

Nikoletta motioned ahead. "We better get inside."

Roy followed her through the outside portico into the waiting vestibule, where he paused to take off his coat. She took it from him and placed it on a stand just inside the doorway. Although he had spent many months in the adjacent training facility and accommodation unit, he had never set foot inside the main house. Vladimir always had it that way. Roy found it was vast and Spartanly furnished—different from what he had imagined. They walked towards the main lounge area, where Nikoletta moved her hand again to indicate that Roy should take a seat. He found the sofa, and Nikoletta sat down next to him.

Roy sat forward with his elbows on his knees and his hands clutched together. "As you can imagine, when we worked together, Vladimir and I never really talked about our personal lives too much. I suppose we never really got to know each other that well."

"I apologize if this may sound rude," Nikoletta replied, "but Vova never really said much about Alpha Factor, so how do I know if I can trust you?"

"You shouldn't. You don't really know me. What I can tell you is that I want to find Vladimir's killer."

"Is this another lavishly paid assignment?" she asked sardonically.

"I want to be completely honest with you. I was offered a fee to find the killer, but I don't give a shit about the money. It was one of my conditions of taking it on: that I don't get paid."

"Who offered to pay you?"

"Mikhail Kasinov."

Nikoletta's appearance turned fractious. Roy could see she was fuming. "Fuck him!" she yelled. "He was the cause of all this upheaval for the last year, getting him out of Siberia. If he had just stayed where he was, then Vladimir would still be alive today. He devoted his life for the last two years to saving that man, and look what good it did him."

"I'm sorry for that, Nikoletta. And yes, I'm sure that is the case, but I'm also sure you want to find out what happened."

Nikoletta paused. She looked down at her lap and then at Roy. "They came here looking for something."

Roy moved closer to her. "Who came here?"

"Don't know who they were. It was at the same time we went to Keleti Railway Station in Central Budapest—the same time I imagine Vova was murdered."

"Any idea what they were looking for?"

"When I came back home, the place had been pillaged. Nothing was taken, from what I could see. Vova had several documents with him when we were in Budapest." Nikoletta turned to the table next to her and picked up a translucent green plastic folder, which she handed to Roy. "Maybe there is something in this."

Roy opened the folder and began to page through the contents just as Nikoletta's cell phone rang.

She jumped up and raced off to the adjacent room. "Just give me a minute. Sorry."

Roy continued perusing the file. There were several pages with lists of names, along with what looked like account or transfer numbers and corresponding amounts beside them. All the names were one word, almost like nicknames or code names.

Roy stood up and moved over to the window. Outside, he could hear the wind whistling around the building in a revolving crescendo. Rain was beating against the double-glazed panes like a relentless blitzkrieg. Its collective harmony only reinforced Roy's concentration. He thought that the circumstances surrounding Sakharshenko's death appeared strange—his relationship with Kasinov, his murder, the break-in, this list . . .

His mind shifted to initial CCTV footage from the prison escape. *Perhaps the Russians had picked up on this and are now retaliating.* In that case, he thought he might be in trouble. *We wore balaclavas, so it shouldn't have been possible to identify us—unless they found some DNA.* He thought this would be extremely unlikely.

He placed the list down on a side table next to the window, where he found a photo of Vladimir Sakharshenko with Mikhail Kasinov staring back at him. The two were heavily sodden with ski apparel and accessories. Considering the lavish surroundings, the photo looked like it had been taken somewhere on the slopes of one of the more salubrious parts of Siberia. *Sochi maybe*, Roy thought. Judging by the youthful appearances in the photo, it looked like it had been taken about ten years earlier.

There was a third guy in the photo. He looked like he was from a similar vintage as the others. He was slightly taller. Roy tapped the third face as if it had some allegory reference. It was a familiar face, but his mind couldn't place him. He moved on to the few other photos on the table.

~~~

Back in London, a mobile phone rang. Kasinov answered.

"Mr. Kasinov?"

"Yes."

"This is Catherine St. Ledger, David's daughter."

"Yes, Catherine. What can I do for you? Is everything all right?"

"I know that the two of you were very close, so I wanted to phone you and let you know before you read it in the newspaper," she said, pausing after her voice began to crack. "My dad is dead." Kasinov could hear her weeping on the other end of the line. "The police are saying it was suicide, but I don't believe it—not for a minute."

Kasinov thought Catherine St. Ledger had spoken bravely as she delivered a précis on the events over the past twelve hours at Kinlough Castle. "That's unbelievable," Kasinov said when she had finished. "David would never take his own life. What the hell? I can't believe it. Catherine, I am so sorry."

"Thank you. I appreciate that."

"When is the funeral?"

"It's the day after tomorrow."

"What did the police say?"

"They don't believe there's any evidence of wrongdoing."

"Catherine, if there is anything I can do—anything at all—let me know."

"Thank you. I will."

Mikhail, feeling quite emotional, put the phone down and turned to Natasha. "You won't believe this, but David St. Ledger died last night."

~ ~ ~

Roy went back and held the first picture frame in his hand again. He sensed that he knew the face from somewhere, but couldn't exactly place him. He tapped the frame again, his finger bouncing off the third face. *Where do I know you from?*

He heard footsteps and looked up to see Nikoletta re-enter the room.

"Apologies. That was my mother," she said, rolling her eyes. "She calls me every day—twice a day, since Vladimir is gone."

Roy moved towards her with the picture frame in his hand. He pointed at the tall man in the photo. "Who is the third person in this photo, and where and when was it taken?"

She studied the photo carefully. "To be honest, I'm not sure exactly where and when this was taken. I wasn't with Vladimir back then. The third guy, though, is Alexander Zolotov. The three of them go back a long way—well before KasOil started. They were all good friends before the dollars started to flow."

"What is Zolotov doing now?"

"No idea. I haven't seen him in years."

Chapter 21
Esoterically Russian

It was early evening when Roy awoke from a brief sleep as the Boeing 737 touched down at London's Heathrow Airport. He made his way through the airport terminal and jumped onto the Heathrow Express train to Paddington Station.

As he lunged down into an empty seat on board the high-speed train, he spotted a copy of the late edition of *The Times* lying on the seat next to him. He picked it up and flicked through it. On the second page, he noticed an article titled *St. Ledger Suicide*.

Famous Irish celebrity and serial entrepreneur David St. Ledger was found dead at his home south of Dublin yesterday. The Dublin police attended St. Ledger's body after it was found hanging from a beam inside his home at Kinlough Castle at around 9:00 a.m. Although not yet confirmed, it appears that the successful businessman committed suicide. In addition to his success in business, St. Ledger was one of Ireland's foremost philanthropists. As former chairman of the Irish Youth Art Development Society, he invested almost €50 million over a period of five years with former KasOil chief and now escaped prisoner Mikhail Kasinov. He is survived by his only daughter, Catherine, who found him dead at their home.

Shit, he was a great guy, Roy thought. *That doesn't make any sense.*

Roy recalled meeting St. Ledger at Annabel's like it was yesterday.

How are all these things connected? The poisoning of Alex Litvinenko in London, Vladimir Sakharshenko's cold-blooded murder in Budapest, and now St. Ledger? Roy always felt uneasy with the mysteries surrounding the esoteric Russian network. Now he was beginning to feel that the whole thing was completely arcane.

As the train emerged from an intermediate tunnel, Roy's phone buzzed. He read the text quickly.

Roy, you don't know me, but you know my dad. He was killed yesterday. He spoke to me a few days ago, and said if anything strange happened to him, I should call you. I tried your phone, but I couldn't get through. Please call me when you can. Catherine St. Ledger.

Strange, Roy thought. *I only met him once.* He told himself to call her later. For now, having committed to downloading the feedback from his short international expedition, he had arranged to meet with Kasinov.

Roy thought through the meeting he was about to have and decided he wasn't going to tell the Russian quite everything. He was beginning to have concerns about Kasinov's motives for asking him to visit Moscow in the first place. *He only asked me to see Lugovoy. I'll tell him about that. He'll probably be pissed at me for going to Budapest. That wasn't part of the brief. Fuck it, I'll tell him about that, too. I want to see his reaction when he hears about the information I found. He might be able to enlighten me on what Sakharshenko's killers were after.*

Roy picked up the list Nikoletta had given him and studied it again. He tapped the names on the sheet.

Random names.

Random numbers.

Roy thought about his meeting with Greshenko. *I don't think I'll tell him about that. That would probably send him over the edge.*

Roy had agreed to meet Kasinov at the same place near Covent Garden as last time. When he arrived, he immediately offered his condolences.

"Very sorry to hear about your Irish friend David St. Ledger," Roy said with humility.

Kasinov shook his head sadly. "I know. It's tragic. I knew David very well, and I can't believe he's dead. He was a great man. I spoke with the family earlier and offered all the assistance I can."

After a few moments of collective reverence for the Irishman, Roy was about to enquire about St. Ledger's background when Kasinov interrupted with his desire to get on with Roy's findings.

Roy didn't waste any time in providing the former oligarch with a succinct summary of events. He told him how Lugovoy had been initially elusive and unwelcoming, but after a little coercion, was more talkative. He explained how Lugovoy was unabated about his lack of involvement in the death of Vladimir, as well as the welcome reception he had received from the national coat of arms brigade.

Kasinov's response was not what Roy had expected. The Russian launched into a full-scale political invective against the Kremlin's hierarchy. Roy only picked up a little more than half of what he said—he was still coming to terms with the former CEO's parlance. Anyway, he got the underlying message: hatred.

After Kasinov calmed, Roy sat up and eyed the Russian. "I'm not convinced there's a link, Mikhail."

"What makes you say that?"

"I don't believe Lugovoy was in Budapest."

"How do you know?"

"Because he said so."

Kasinov sat across from him, his fingers drumming the table. "And you believed him?"

"I'm convinced he was telling the truth."

"Oh, and now you can tell when people are telling the truth and when they are lying, Mr. Young?"

"Yes, I can."

Kasinov paused and turned his head to one side as if caught in a trance.

"I also went to visit Sakharshenko's girlfriend," Roy added. "You may know her: Nikoletta Lukas."

"What?" Kasinov roared. "You went to Budapest? That wasn't part of the plan."

Roy didn't appreciate the frequent admonitions. He realized now that Kasinov was a rude and irascible man, and someone who clearly didn't seem to value innovation in any shape or form. For now, though, he decided to continue to play ball with him. *The golden rule*, he thought. *The man with the gold makes the rules. Well, for the moment he does.*

"Nikoletta told me that someone broke into their home," Roy said. "Apparently it happened at the same time they were visiting Budapest—the same time Vladimir was murdered. They went there searching for something."

"What were they looking for?"

Roy reached into his bag and pulled out the folder he had received from Nikoletta. He handed it to Kasinov. "Not one hundred percent sure, but she gave me this."

Kasinov's eyes were fixed on the list as he turned from one page to the next.

"Do you know what this is?" Roy asked.

"Looks like a list of names and numbers to me," Kasinov remarked without moving his eyes off the sheet. "Did she give you an electronic copy?"

"Yes, on a stick," Roy replied. "Was the only copy, she said."

Kasinov cast a brief glance in Roy's direction. "It would make it easier to conduct a search if I could have that."

Roy handed across the memory stick that Nikoletta had given him. "No problem."

Kasinov stood to leave. "Leave this with me," he uttered. "I think I might be able to find out what they mean."

As Kasinov walked away, he turned back to Roy with a grin. "Hey, Roy. I'm going to watch football tomorrow. Arsenal against Chelsea—you want to come along?"

"That's very generous of you," Roy replied. "Sure, I would love to."

"How many tickets you need?"

"Two?"

"Sure. Just head to the VIP Club entrance at Emirates Stadium. It's level three. Enter after the gate marked *P*. I'll leave the tickets at reception for you. Here, let me write that down. Save you having to phone me to confirm if you get lost. Most people somehow get a little lost in that labyrinth—so Natasha tells me."

Mikhail took out a pen and paper and slowly scribbled out the instructions.

Roy took the paper from him. "Thanks. Look forward to it."

Chapter 22
Forensics

Dublin's chief forensic pathologist, Harry Longford, glanced at the entrance wall in the basement of Dublin's central morgue to see a large, white-faced temperature gauge with a red dial that pointed to 46 degrees Fahrenheit. It needed to be that cold—otherwise it would be an extremely objectionable place to work. Beside him, his assistant Martha Rooney checked through a series of charts, clipped in a file on a wood-backed frame.

Despite the temperature, Longford could still sense the inevitable waft of putrefaction that radiated from a mix of decedent decompositions. The smells, generated from a volatile growth of bacteria, resembled a mixture of fetid cheeses and bad breath. St. Ledger's body lay flat and completely naked, facing upwards on the cadaver dissection table. Untroubled by the companionship and the aromas, the two doctors prepared conscientiously to undertake the procedure.

At Catherine St. Ledger's insistence, and with her financing, an autopsy was to be conducted on her father's body. Whilst the investigating officer did not necessarily agree with the need for such an extravagant evisceration process, Detective John Blake was willing to go along with it as long as it wasn't coming out of his budget. Whilst he had dismissed Catherine's assertions that her father had been murdered, and consequently had not instigated any investigation, he felt, however, that this procedure would set the girl's mind to rest once and for all. A forensic autopsy of this nature would at least determine the cause of death.

Longford would focus on the internal bodily organs whilst Martha examined the limbs and brain. This was the way they normally worked. The internal examination began with a large, deep, Y-shaped incision from St. Ledger's shoulders through his breastbone, extending down to the pubic bone. Longford didn't anticipate any bleeding from the cuts in the upper extremity, due to lack of cardiac functionality, but equally due to the postmortem lividity caused by the gravitational pull in the lower extremity of the body, as would be typical in a suspended cadaver. "Aorta and ventricles extremely dilated," Longford remarked as he commenced his examination.

At the same time, Martha made her way up

both tibia and commented, "Right and left patella appear to have significant hematomas, both discolored," she recited. "The petechiae seem pretty regular and consistent—like two little twins, in fact."

Longford rummaged through a few more organs and took a step back. "His pericardial sac looks totally enlarged—quite unusual for this form of death." Dublin's chief forensic pathologist held up a shriveled liver mass in his right palm, gazing at it curiously. "Looks like he was a bit fond of the whiskey, too, judging by the condition of this liver."

Martha paused as her eyes emerged from underneath her illuminated head torch. "Mary, mother of Joseph!" she cried out. "It's hard to believe he was still alive, looking at the size of that thing. That thing should be donated to medical research."

"Hand me over that ultraviolet light," Longford told his young assistant. "I just want to have a look at something here." He held the torch over St. Ledger's hands. "Hmm. That's strange."

"What?"

"The nails are different."

Martha wasn't paying too much attention to her boss, her attention diverted to initiating the skullcap extraction, and her mind fixated with inserting a fine stainless steel blade into a slot on the hand-held saw. "Okay, here we go," she said as she donned a face visor. She pushed the green button marked *1,* and the electric saw buzzed loudly. As she broke through the outer tissue, bits of shattered brittle bone covered in cold flesh sprinkled from either side of the blade onto several layers of loosely woven cotton surgical gauze that Martha had placed around the head.

Minutes later, the skull was capped and removed under some strain. Typically a modicum of energy in the removal process was sufficient to overcome the natural vacuum, but on this occasion, Martha had needed to apply a lot more force. "It was extremely swollen. I thought I would never get that skull cap off." She placed it delicately on the table next to her, and then focused back on what remained of St. Ledger's head. Looking back at her was his fully exposed brain.

She examined the cerebral matter carefully. "There is certainly some evidence of trauma there," she said. "Something happened before he was killed—something that induced a severe state of shock."

Longford shuffled a few steps closer, probing the posterior aspect of St. Ledger's cranial matter. "Hmm," he said with a sigh. "That might explain the excess subdural bleeding here on the underside of the brain. You're right, Martha. Something's not right here."

Chapter 23
Gunners

Roy made his way along Hampstead Lane to meet up with Melanie at her Highgate flat. He had called her the previous evening, enquiring if she would like to come to watch football at Kasinov's private box. He guessed that if she were doing research on this guy, she would want to come. He was right. She had accepted.

Minutes later, Roy pushed a buzzer, initiating a resounding purring noise that echoed for several seconds before it was interrupted by a clear, distinct voice. "Hello?" the voice said.

Roy bent down and leaned in to the buzzer's receiver. "Hi there. It's me."

"I'm opening the door now."

Roy entered and made his way to Melanie's flat, where he found her standing in the door. "Hello there," he said, eyeing her from head to toe.

She had her hair tied up and off her face and wore tightly fitted Citizen Jeans and a cream cashmere sweater that swathed her body, clearly highlighting the definition of her breasts. "I love it when girls wear baggy jeans," he said with a wry smirk.

Melanie let out a laugh and smacked him playfully on the shoulder. "Come in here, you," she said, waving him inside.

He entered and gave her a big hug that almost lifted her off her feet.

Standing in the reception room, Roy paused for a moment and examined her curvaceous couture. "You do look amazing. What have you done?"

Melanie's hands lifted in surrender as she looked down at herself. "Ah, it's called casual wear, Roy. We're going to watch the footy right?"

"Yes, we are. You just look different—fantastic, in fact!"

No doubt captivated by her life in the stock markets, Roy always found that Melanie was too busy to think about her appearance to others. *Although you wouldn't think that by looking at her,* he thought. Having grown up in the town of Hanover in Germany, with a German father and Scottish mother, she likely had a disciplined upbringing. He recalled her telling him that she was quite shy as a young girl, and that she only began to flourish after moving with her family to Blighty when she was fifteen.

"Nothing's changed," she said. "It's still me. Would you like some tea?"

"Sure," he said, emerging from an ogling trance.

"I'm just back from grocery shopping, as you can see," Melanie said, pointing to a couple bags on her countertop. "I just need to pack this stuff away before we head." Then she quivered in suspense. "But please tell me all about Moscow."

As Roy downloaded all the events over his previous few days, he watched with great alacrity her movements around her kitchen. She put stuff away like she was a basketball small forward. Fortunately, her kitchen was quite a utilitarian one, with most cupboards and fixtures accessible from a central point.

He told her about the visit to the Kremlin and Lugovoy's residence, his trip to Budapest to see Nikoletta Lukas, the message from Catherine St. Ledger, and the follow-up meeting with Kasinov after he arrived back in London. Roy paused, looking for some reaction. Melanie was listening with her mouth partially open. It looked like she was trying to say something, but nothing passed her lips.

"It's all a bit esoteric, I'm afraid," he said, shaking his head. "I haven't managed to figure out how—or if, in fact—these things are all connected."

Melanie gathered her emotions and eventually found her tongue. "Yeah, maybe—but I can think of one thing that connects them all."

"And that would be?"

Melanie rubbed her thumb and index finger together. "Greed," she said.

"The source of all evil," he replied.

Given their mutual penchant for football, they excitedly left the flat and made their way down to a nearby bus stop, moving together in perfect unison, like a regimental military training ensemble. It was just a few minutes' walk.

She grabbed his arm, holding it tightly as she zestfully gamboled next to him. "I love going to watch footy," she said. "Thanks for taking me."

"Don't thank me—thank Mikhail," Roy said as he turned to give her a big hug. "You're quite risible today."

"So who are we supporting?" Melanie asked.

"Well, I'm not from London, so technically I'm not supporting either. You, on the other hand, live here, so you have to be supporting one of these teams."

"I like the Arsenal boys best. They have nicer legs than those Chelsea fellows."

"Love your logic!"

Intermingled amongst a passionate and vocal crowd of fans, the two arrived at Emirates Stadium at about 2:30 p.m., plenty of time ahead of the 3:00 p.m. kick-off. Industriously they moved through to the club floor level after receiving several reverential glances along the way from stewards as they enquired for directions.

Once inside, Roy stopped and looked out through the wall-length windows that bound the entire floor. The view from the east side of the stadium offered the most spectacular panorama of the four-tiered arena, where sixty-two thousand scarlet red seats looked down onto a perfectly manicured, verdant, carpet-like pitch. Its flawless surface resembled an amalgam of seamlessly woven fibers on a brand new snooker tablecloth. Roy imagined if a spirit level were placed on the playing surface, it would probably show the perfectly balanced bubble from everywhere. Looking up, he noticed the architecturally finished roof structure surrounding the skyline with Perspex panels encased in white tubular steelwork visibly illuminating the ground. Perched at either end of the stadium were two enormous video screens ready to relay the highlights of the game for those that missed the live action or wanted to see instant replays of key moments in the game.

When they arrived at Mikhail's private box, they peeped inside to find that Kasinov and several of his friends were already there. Roy nodded in reverence.

Melanie, who had been to the stadium's affluent levels before, couldn't help comparing. "Wow, this seems extraordinarily large—maybe double the size of a normal box. He's probably bought two adjoining suites and knocked down the wall between."

Natasha introduced herself and greeted them, playing the perfect hostess as they arrived. Roy guessed she was well seasoned in cheek kissing. He had met her briefly at Annabel's, but Natasha and Melanie had not met before. Roy introduced his guest and explained their adventurous journey on the bus across London's central landscape from Highgate High Street to Holloway Road. Natasha clearly wasn't familiar with bus routes.

After the introductions were over, Roy made his way through the box and approached Kasinov. Melanie stayed chatting with Natasha.

"Mikhail, thanks so much for the invite," Roy said.

"You're welcome," he said. "But you must tell me . . . who is that beautiful young lady here with you?" He looked salaciously in Melanie's direction.

Roy glanced back at her. "That's Melanie Bauer."

Kasinov stared in amazement. *"That's* Melanie Bauer?" he said loudly.

On hearing her name, Melanie looked around. In fact, everybody in the box stopped what they were doing and looked quizzically in Melanie's direction. Then they looked in the direction of their host. The Russian turned toward the enormous window that interposed the ground and the private box as if one of the players or management staff on the pitch had caught his attention.

Roy moved to face him. "You know Melanie?"

"Not personally, no. But I have heard her name." Kasinov's tone reverted down several decibels. "I have read her recent research notes, and to tell you the truth, I was very impressed with her vision and foresight in capital market perceptions. She pitched it perfectly, and made a lot of money for a lot of people. She is quite famous, your Melanie."

Roy stared at him for a moment before looking over at Melanie. *So that's what she wanted to talk with me about.* "Thanks for that."

"I just imagined she would be a bit older—a bit more, um, non-beautiful." Kasinov appeared flustered.

"She's a special young lady, all right," Roy said proudly.

"I know her boss at UGC quite well," Kasinov added, trying to sound more professional despite his obvious difficulty in avoiding looking back at her.

~~~

Melanie glanced around the lavish interior before directing her attention back to Natasha. "You must be an Arsenal fan, given you have this box—or should I say this mini palace—situated right in the middle of the stadium."

"Yes," Natasha replied. "They are Mikhail's team, so I guess they must be my team, too. There are a few Russian connections at the club. If truth be known, Mikhail would love to buy them and transform them into the best club in the world."

As Natasha spoke, a loud roar reverberated over the ground. Melanie and Natasha turned together and looked down to see the two teams arriving onto the field ahead of the kick-off.

Natasha spun around on one foot. "Excuse me for a minute," she said. Then, one by one, she ushered everyone to their designated seats.

~~~

Roy took a seat at the back row's exit, and Kasinov sat down next to him. Then, following a short warm-up preceded by a presentation to some loyal fans that had supported the club for sixty years, the game commenced.

It wasn't long before the chanting and singing of the clubs' anthems and songs followed from around the ground. Roy glanced around the upper echelon on the club floor to observe a pretty taciturn bunch. Roy guessed that they felt they were exempt from joining the intonation.

With his arms folded and eyes fixed on the match, Kasinov angled towards him. "I had a look through that list you gave me, and it was nothing much," the Russian said dismissively. "It appears to be just a list of investments that Vladimir made. The referenced names are probably other shareholders in the same funds or schemes that he invested in. I never really discussed personal investment stuff with him."

Roy, not wishing to initiate a shameless attack on Kasinov's credibility in front of his Russian posse, nodded and pursed his lips. "Okay." He knew it was definitely not a shareholder register.

A discussion for another day, I think.

Suddenly the ball roared into the back of the net, almost penetrating the thousands of cotton fibers holding the webbed enclosure together. Roy sat back in his seat after he saw Melanie jump up two seats in front of him. She let out a loud roar and raised her fists in the air. "Yes! Van Persie! What a shot! What a goal!"

The crowd went wild as Arsenal took a 1-0 lead after nineteen minutes. Everyone in the box joined in the celebration with raised hands. The roar across the ground went on for several minutes after the Dutch forward scored his twelfth goal of the season.

Once the crowds settled and play recommenced, Kasinov leaned over to Roy again. "You've got to get back to Moscow," he said imperiously. "I need you to see what more you can dig up on Alexei Lugovoy. I'm convinced they'll be sending him here to get me."

Roy craned his neck to his left and looked at him in surprise. He wondered since when did his assignment include looking out for Kasinov's health and safety. He decided to go along and humor him anyway. "I don't think he'll be coming here to London. He's not much welcome here."

"Well, maybe not him. Maybe somebody else." Kasinov's tone was submissive, quite inharmonious with his regularly self-assured demeanor. "But he'll be directing operations from the Kremlin. I'm sure of it. This is his area of specialization."

Roy looked at him smugly. "You may have a point. He told me he did the job on Litvinenko."

"What?"

"He admitted he arranged Litvinenko's poisoning."

Kasinov shifted closer—too close for comfort, in Roy's estimation. "See I told you," the Russian scoffed. "How did you get Lugovoy to cough that up?"

Roy nonchalantly pulled out his ten-year-old Parker pen from his pocket and showed it to the Russian. "This little pen."

"What about it?"

"I told him it was full of carbon monoxide, and I was going to let it off in his face unless he answered my questions."

"Was it?" he enquired anxiously. "Is it?"

"Don't worry, Mikhail. There's nothing in there except Parker's finest oils, dyes, and solvents. I'm afraid you and your friend Alexei have been watching too much of that MI-Six fictional stuff."

Kasinov's blank look was interrupted by his phone. He slid the ringing mobile from his pocket, answered it, and then disappeared out of the box.

~ ~ ~

Two seats down, Melanie and Natasha were huddled together like two old friends that hadn't seen each other in a decade. "Thank you for inviting us along. We both love footy!" Melanie said, still hopping about in her seat and clapping her hands in excitement. "I can't believe we're here."

"You and Roy look great together," Natasha said enthusiastically. "From what I hear, your boyfriend is one hell of a guy."

Melanie glanced two rows behind her in Roy's direction. "Thanks," she replied. "I agree; he is amazing. One of a kind, I would say. But he's not my boyfriend."

Natasha's mouth fell open. "My apologies. You two looked like you were a couple." There was a momentary pause before Natasha eyed her again. "And what do you do in London?"

"I work in the city," Melanie responded appreciatively. "At one of the larger investment banks."

"Which one?"

"UGC. I'm head of research there."

"Honestly? Wow, that's amazing. It's great to see a woman doing so well in a city full of men."

Melanie let out a laugh. "I think you're more famous than I'll ever be," she replied. "So what's it like being with Mikhail?"

"What do you mean?"

"I mean being with someone who's all over the newspapers every day?"

"Never a dull moment. I'm sure it'll all settle down one of these days. Well, I hope it does, anyway."

"How are you enjoying London?"

"I love it here!" Natasha exclaimed. "I've got a nice place on Saint Martin's Lane in Covent Garden. It's so close to everything I need. I work part time at an art gallery close by."

"Covent Garden is such a lovely area."

"You should come around some time."

Melanie smiled back at her. "Thanks. I might take you up on that offer."

An enormous roar from the crowd reverberated throughout the stadium as the whistle blew to signify the commencement of the second half. The capacity sixty-two thousand fans watched pensively for twenty minutes as Arsenal battled to keep their slim lead against a barrage of Chelsea attacks. One after another, they came. Eventually, after fifty-three minutes, they capitulated.

"Oh no," Melanie shouted. "Drogba's after equalizing. That's rubbish!"

The other guests in the box simultaneously showed their displeasure.

The remainder of the game played out in a cautious manner, neither team wanting to risk defeat. Eventually the encounter finished in a 1-1 draw.

After the game and the post-match pleasantries, Roy and Melanie left Kasinov's private box and found themselves chaperoned by a battalion of horseback police attendants in amongst throngs of supporters being ushered to a selection of three adjacent underground tube stations. They made their way from the ground through the crowds of tepid fans and walked for quite a distance before finding an accessible, uncongested portal at Holloway Road Station.

"That was a great day today," Melanie said. "Thanks, Roy. Sorry to say your friend Mikhail seems like a bit of a weirdo."

"Yeah, he's a bit special. I have to give you that."

"Natasha is nice, though. She's a real sweetie. She invited me around to her apartment."

"Good for you."

Minutes later, the tube came to a halt at Holborn Station, and the train's doors opened sharply to the prerecorded announcement, "Mind the gap."

Melanie glanced up and down at Roy's body. "I have to go now. Thanks for today. Bye-bye." She gave him a quick kiss on the cheek before departing.

Roy watched her as she walked away. He remained silent.

She didn't look back.

Chapter 24
KasOil Cleanup

It was 5:30 p.m. on Monday evening. Kasinov held the TV remote aloft, frantically pushing buttons and flicking his way through the news channel segment. One by one, he scoured CNN, Fox, NBC, CNBC, and Sky News. They were all covering his story. He watched penetratingly as each in turn postulated his connection to David St. Ledger's recent demise. When he pushed one more button, the screen went blank and the remote went somersaulting across the room like a one-way boomerang.

He sat back into his Charles Eames recliner with his feet suspended in a perfect cantilever, his fingers drumming the side of the chair as he looked away from the TV. In one way, he regretted not being able to make it to the funeral. It made him feel somewhat disengaged. In another way, he was glad he didn't have to go. Either way, he was confined to the UK for now and wasn't going to risk travel of any kind.

Back home, the Kremlin-controlled media had expectedly turned against him, vilifying his actions. He knew the Kremlin's esoteric factions were the cause.

My turn to act, he thought. He looked back at the blank TV. *I need a better PR campaign.*

Incensed with the media's suppositions, he exhaled an enraged sigh. He had seen enough of the global coverage of the trials and tribulations of his life. He got up and strolled around the apartment. It was his first time taking it all in since he had arrived in London. Natasha hadn't offered any tour, so he decided to go on his own.

He counted five bedrooms, all fitted with beautifully modern Tisettanta wardrobes and en-suite Italian white marble-clad bathrooms. *No doubt she handpicked the marble*, he thought. He knew after acquiring the place for her that she had it refurbished in contemporary designs, the kinds of finishes that left all of her visitors awestruck, no doubt. Even Kasinov himself was impressed.

A significant amount of exposed limestone masonry gave a balance to the other contemporary finishes. Throughout the apartment, all the windows were new, triple-glazed sash with shutters. *Easy for her to open and close. They look good, too.* Adjacent to the kitchen was an impressive entrance and brushed oak staircase lit by LED's that led to a mezzanine floor with an open plan living area. This was the quiet zone at the uppermost elevation. Throughout, all floors were heated and covered with flush, wide-plank, darkened oak. It made it nice and warm. He recalled how she liked to walk around barefoot.

There were piles of things she had bought for the flat: volumes of books, all sorts of amorphously shaped mirrors, art-deco accessories, feature chairs, opulent lamps, and the one that got him the most, a jukebox. You name it, she had it. He contemplated how Natasha had become significantly more profligate since her exodus from Khabarovsk.

Money. He sighed again, shaking his head.

Kasinov's frugal upbringing remained in his genes, despite his excessively high net worth.

His thoughts were interrupted when he heard the lift's double chime. The doors opened and Natasha entered. He studied her, but she didn't seem to notice him standing there. Then he moved his weight onto his other foot and placed his hands on his hips. She still didn't notice him. She took off her coat and hung it up. Underneath, she wore a sleeveless camisole top, from which her soft, delicate arms protruded with a defined muscular tone.

Eventually she noticed him standing there.

They looked at each other.

She smiled.

He tried to smile. "Hello, my darling."

"Hello," she replied, glancing in the direction of her bedroom. "I'm going to grab a quick shower before we head out."

~~~

Fatigued after her day at the gallery, Natasha entered the bedroom and made her way to the walk-in wardrobe, where she began undressing. She peeled off her clothes. First her silk camisole floated off her soft, supple skin. Everything else followed just as easily.

She thought about his grimace. *Something's bugging him again.*

She spent a long time in the shower. It made her feel somewhat refreshed. After she finished, she covered her body in Coco Chanel Mademoiselle. Then she got dressed.

"Ready to face the beast," she muttered under her breath.

As she passed the dresser adjacent to the wardrobe, she noticed a file of papers that she didn't think had been there earlier that morning before she left for the gallery. Atop the file, she noticed one sheet, and beneath it, a white envelope. Both the paper and the envelope bore a mark down the center. She assumed they must have been folded that way.

Not thinking anything of it, she picked them up and studied the cover envelope. It was without any written or embossed rubric. Behind it, on the sheet, in an illustrated typeface, were the names "Sakharshenko" and "St. Ledger" with Kasinov's name beneath. Under the first two names were geometric coordinates making reference to two

"Home locations." One was titled "Budapest Train Station," and the other "Irish Publican Establishment." Under Kasinov's name, there was nothing.

That's very strange, she thought. *What are these names and places for?*

She looked again and noticed the first two names were encircled in red pen. Next, she studied the handwriting. *It looks like Mikhail's writing,* she thought. The notes in the same red pen started with the words "Tel Conversation," followed by two different dates—one against Sakharshenko's name and the other against St. Ledger's. The dates were one day apart. The notes of the conversation were pretty illegible. *Misha's handwriting was never very good,* she thought. Her eyes progressed to the top of the page, where she saw the words "KasOil Cleanup" in the same font. It was highlighted in inverted commas.

Natasha sensed a sudden inert pang that went through her whole body. Her stomach began to turn inside out with a feeling of abject anxiety. *KasOil Cleanup?* She didn't know what its context was or what it meant. Several questions entered her mind instantly. Was it something to do with the Russian contingent that seemed to occupy every minute of his mind? What did they have to do with the deaths of St. Ledger and Sakharshenko? Then she heard Mikhail call out from the lounge area less than twenty feet away.

"Natasha, are you coming?"

"Be right there," she responded, followed by two nervous pants. "Just closing up my makeup bag."

~~~

Roy pressed the call button and imagined her mobile phone ringing aloud to a cacophony of rah-rah-ah-ah-ahs from her Lady Gaga's "Bad Romance" ringtone.

"Hello, this is Melanie," came the answer.

"Hello, Mel. This is Roy."

"Yes, Roy, what is it?" Melanie snapped in a cooler tone than usual.

"I'm just about to board a flight back to Florence, but I wanted to talk with you first," he said in an unassuming way.

"I'm listening," she replied in an inquisitive tone.

"It's about Kasinov."

"Okay, what about him?"

"Something doesn't stack up with the guy," Roy said with a degree of skepticism in his voice. "He spoke to me when we were at the footy, saying that the list of names or titles and numbers that I retrieved from my visit to Nikoletta Lukas was nothing. He tried to palm it off, saying it was just some random investment paper that Sakharshenko had taken a position in."

"And what makes you think that it isn't just that?" Melanie replied tersely.

Roy pretended not to notice her chilly deportment. "Well, Mel, if there's one thing I learned from you and all your stock exchange anecdotes, it's what a shareholder register looks like. This one didn't have a schedule showing the percentage ownership in the investment."

"Not all shareholder registers have a percentage column, you know," Melanie pointed out.

"Maybe not, but after I handed him the list, he finished our meeting swiftly, after which he made a phone call. He seemed a bit rankled by the revelation of the document."

"Okay. So?"

Roy guessed she was giving off this terse approach to convey a deeper set of feelings—perhaps even ill feelings. He decided not to mention it. "Well, at the Emirates, he received a call from someone. And judging by the look on his face, it was someone he wasn't expecting to hear from."

"He was also quite rude the way he called out my name just like that," she said irritably. "Anyway, do you know who it was that contacted him?"

"I did manage to see the name that came up on the phone, yes. It wasn't a name, actually; it was a bit strange."

"What did it say?"

"It said KCU."

"What does that stand for?"

"No idea. Another thing, Mel; I don't think all is well in the camp between the two of them."

"The two of whom?"

"Mikhail and Natasha."

"How so?"

"Call it a hunch. I think she might be able to help us figure out what's going on." He expected to be rebuffed sharply, but he asked regardless. "Perhaps you could meet with her? Maybe have a chat to see if you can uncover anything?"

"Well, I suppose she did invite me to come and see her," Melanie replied.

Roy was beside himself with surprise.

~~~

Sullen in both appearance and demeanor, Mikhail and Natasha left the apartment and walked to a nearby exclusive Asian fusion restaurant just off Long Acre Street. Kasinov had booked it after his new security flock audited the place earlier in the day. He had mandated the security lead to investigate the food supply chain, food preparation procedures, and also to check out the chefs. All had come up okay, and the security lead had given it the all clear.

At the restaurant, Kasinov sat there ominously, his jaws tensed as he picked off lumps from the bread rolls. One by one, he placed them in his mouth, masticating the barley and maize concoction like a football manager suffering from dementia. Each time he picked a sliver, he glanced around the restaurant suspiciously.

Natasha remained silent as she nibbled at one of the rolls. She looked like she had lost her appetite. Kasinov had no idea she had discovered the envelope and its suspicious contents.

Crazed with interminable animosity, Kasinov turned to her and launched into acerbic criticism of the Kremlin, directing all his emotion at his dinner date as if she was holding proxy on Koshenko's behalf. It was unremitting. All Natasha could do was listen and nod. He knew he was acting like a petulant child, but she wouldn't dare tell him what she was really thinking.

She placed her hand on his arm. "Mikhail, I'm sure everything will be okay," she encouraged.

Kasinov had created a self-infused fear of polonium ingestion, and as the food arrived, he looked even more demented. The images of a balding Alex Litvinenko frothing from the mouth and lying on his deathbed were imprinted in his mind. Despite the fact that his earlier audit team had given him some comfort, he sat pushing a concoction of sizzling beef around the plate with his fork, sniffing it repeatedly in search of suspicious odors. Eventually he just pushed the plate away and stood with a scowl. "Let's get the hell out of here," he barked.

Natasha stared at him expressionlessly, as if completely addled by his behavior. She didn't have any words for him, English or Russian.

Chapter 25
Girl talk

Melanie approached the front entrance to Natasha's apartment building and paused. She thought about her conversation with Roy. "Perhaps you could meet with her? Maybe have a chat to see if you can uncover anything?" he had said.

This thing can go tremendously well or horribly wrong, she thought. *I just need to choose my words carefully.* She took a step forward and pushed the button that said PENTHOUSE.

Seconds later, Natasha pulled back the steel-lined door and greeted Melanie with a warm smile. "Great to see you again," she said. "I was so pleased to get your message." She motioned her guest inside. "Come in, come in."

Together they entered the lift. Natasha pressed the button for the fifth floor.

As the electric winch pulling the lift whined, she held up a round blue disc, showing it to Melanie.

"Sorry, it's a bit complicated. I had to come down and get you because you need one of these things to get past the door. Normally the doorman is here." Natasha shrugged. "But he must be on a break somewhere."

When the lift opened and they walked inside, Melanie was overwhelmed. Her eyes swept the vast entrance lobby and staircase. She held back a squeal of surprise as she took it all in. Natasha, appearing not to notice Melanie's expression, moved to take her coat, and after hanging it in the hall cupboard, she ushered her guest into the kitchen.

Melanie's eyes widened again when she saw the gleaming Westhal stainless steel units covering the walls of the kitchen. She shook her head in amazement. She knew from looking at the celebrity chef shows on TV that these were ranges more usually found in professional kitchens. "Wow," she said breathlessly.

Natasha smiled. Melanie guessed she probably got a kick from people's reactions when they first visited her home.

"I just threw something together for lunch," Natasha said, trying to distract Melanie from her incredulous trance.

Melanie looked across the lavish spread of salads, cold meats, cheeses, and salmon dolloped with ridiculous mounds of caviar. "Wow," she said again. "It looks delicious, Natasha. Who else is joining us? There's enough here to feed an army." She strained to extract a heavy, overstuffed leather stool from under the granite worktop.

"Oh, it's just us," Natasha replied. She motioned to the floor-to-ceiling sliding doors that framed a spectacular view of Covent Garden, the Strand, and in the near distance, the Thames. "I thought we would sit out on the terrace. It's such a beautiful day. We can grab something here and take it outside."

Although touched by the unexpected solicitude, Melanie felt somewhat off guard. She was usually the confident woman in the room. There was something about being around such extravagance that unnerved her. Maybe it was her imagination. Natasha had obviously gone to a lot of effort, and she had really liked her when they had first met at the football. In both business and social contexts, Melanie usually had very good instincts about people. It was one of her differentiators on the testosterone-laden city trading floor. She had a good feeling about Natasha. Maybe she was feeling guilty—after all, she was here covertly to ask Natasha a favor, and she wasn't entirely sure it was the right thing to do. But Roy had sounded eager, and although she didn't like to admit it to herself, she would do anything for him.

"How long have you lived here?" Melanie asked, looking for a way to break the ice and steer the conversation in the right direction.

"Four years," Natasha replied as she produced a bottle of white wine from the fridge.

Melanie's head bounced around as she glanced at the perimeter of the place. "It's a great area. Really convenient."

"Here, this is for you," Natasha said, passing her guest a glass of chilled wine without invitation. "Hope you like Pinot Grigio. But yes, I like it here. I have so many things so close."

"Yes, thanks. You really have a beautiful home here. It's amazing."

"I'm very lucky."

Natasha started to shuffle through the salad bowl with two large paddles. Famished with the display, Melanie selected from the buffet, being careful to match Natasha's own modest portion. After the two Waterford Wedgwood plates were declared replete, they moved to the balcony and sat across from each other on a table that would comfortably host twelve.

Melanie wondered about Natasha. She thought that, despite all the trappings of wealth, she would not like to be in her position. There was something about Mikhail—she felt he was probably quite intimidating. Melanie was also pretty certain that he was a man with limited patience. "It must be fantastic to have Mikhail home again. When did you two first meet?"

"We met just after I graduated from university. I took a job with KasOil and was recruited into the translation team because I spoke English pretty well." Natasha paused briefly to take a sip of wine. "I guess I was quite fortunate, really. I received a number of exciting opportunities to work on the international side of KasOil's growing business. That's how I ended up working alongside the executive management team on a number of high profile deals. It's also how I first came to London."

"Yeah, I guess we all get a lucky break now and again." Melanie pondered about what lucky breaks she had recently. None came to mind immediately.

Natasha put her glass down, craned her neck to the right, and pointed to the NatWest International Financial Center in the distance. "I got mine right over there."

"It must have been very exciting," Melanie replied with great fervor.

Natasha looked down, prodding gracefully at her food. "It was at the time, I guess," she said with a wistful expression. "It seems strange now, looking back. I was very young and very naive back then."

Melanie, seeing the opportunity, sat up and thought about how to engage with Natasha's passionate side. "I can't imagine what the last few years have been like for you, not knowing if Mikhail would be released or not."

"It hasn't been easy," Natasha replied. "To be honest, I didn't think I would ever see him again."

Melanie studied her face and couldn't tell if her expression was one of joy or of disappointment.

"But, tell me more about you, Melanie," Natasha enquired. "Mikhail said he has you to thank for raising his cause with the city markets again."

Melanie placed a slice of smoked salmon delicately onto a fresh piece of brown bread. "He's too generous. It was nothing. I've actually been following the stock and the story for a while. It was natural that following his—" Melanie paused, looking briefly to the sky before choosing her words carefully "—rescue, that there would be interest again."

"There's always interest in Mikhail," Natasha said abruptly. "The difficulty is finding the people who are genuine, the people you can trust." She looked directly at Melanie, almost daring her to blink.

Melanie broke eye contact to look down, as if inspecting the intricate lace platinum Vera Wang design on the Wedgwood plate.

"Can I trust you, Melanie?" Natasha asked in a low tone.

Melanie thought for a second that maybe she had misheard. "Of course you can."

Natasha paused for a few seconds as she rubbed her forehead. "I was pregnant with Mikhail's child when he was sent to prison. Fifteen weeks."

Melanie nodded slowly, trying to take in the sudden trust in confidence.

"I never told him," Natasha added. "I had a termination a couple of weeks later, at a private clinic in Switzerland. It was the worst day of my life."

"Natasha, I'm so sorry. Why didn't you feel you could keep it?"

"It had to be done," Natasha replied tersely. "Mikhail would never have forgiven me. I'm his trophy, but he wouldn't want to marry me or start a family. Anyway, it doesn't matter now."

"What do you mean?" Melanie probed. "You both look very much in love. Surely things have changed?"

"Oh, I don't know," Natasha said in a forlorn manner. "Mikhail is always crafting some deal or another. I don't think this is the last we've seen of his vision to bring about a new Russian democracy. He puts too much pressure on himself. He won't stop until he gets to the top."

Melanie figured this was the perfect segue. "I had that impression. Roy said he was helping Mikhail with some investigative work."

Natasha looked up suddenly, alert but taciturn, and nodded slowly, encouraging Melanie to continue.

Melanie could see this was news to her. "I mean, I don't really know the details." She tried not to sound too flustered. "It was just that Roy was checking out some background information. He has a lot of contacts from his time in the forces."

Natasha's face remained expressionless. "He must have. Mikhail is lucky to have an ally in him. Roy seems like one of the good guys. A keeper— isn't that what you say in English?" She offered a thin smile. "And isn't that what *you* would say, as well?"

Melanie shook her head. "It's not like that."

"Of course it is," Natasha urged. "You only have to look at the two of you together. The way you glance around the room just to check that the other one is there. Roy is always finding a reason to touch your arm or bring the conversation round to how great you are."

Melanie flushed slightly and looked down at her food again.

"Why don't you make the first move?" Natasha suggested. "I can tell you now, it would be reciprocated."

"I guess I haven't had much experience in relationships." Melanie shrugged. "Anyway, I already have a boyfriend."

"You are gorgeous, Melanie. Any man would be lucky to have you."

Not very good at accepting compliments, Melanie remained silent. She wondered how lunch had become so intimate so quickly. She also wasn't used to confiding her feelings to people, let alone a brand new girlfriend. Not that she had ever been that close to anyone in particular. In fact, Roy had probably been the person that she had felt closest to in all her life. "Actually, I did have a reason for getting in contact."

"Oh yes?"

Melanie's confidence picked up. She was getting back on track. "I was wondering if you could help me with something—actually, help Roy with something."

"For sure. If I can."

"It's just that Roy is keen to make a good impression." Melanie paused, *Oh dear, that doesn't sound like Roy at all.* "Well actually, he's a bit embarrassed." *Oh shit, this isn't going very well. He's never embarrassed.* "You see, Mikhail gave him some data on a disk to review." Melanie paused and looked at Natasha to see whether she had gone too far.

Natasha looked attentive, but not uncomfortable.

"He put it through the wash," Melanie said, thinking on her toes.

A smile spread across Natasha's face. "Oh dear," she replied with warmth in her eyes.

"Do you think," Melanie said, pausing briefly, "there is any way you could help? You would be doing me a huge favor."

"What can I do?"

Melanie made for her bag. "I have it here on a piece of paper, the name of the file that Roy told me. I just wondered, if at all possible, whether you would be able to make another copy—a secret one, that is?"

Natasha remained silent, but her expression was warm.

"You would be doing me a huge favor," Melanie repeated. "And you would save Roy's embarrassment. He wants to do a good job for Mikhail." She paused briefly. "Of course, if it's not possible . . ."

Natasha leapt from her chair. "Consider it done," she said as she picked up her plate and started to clear up.

Melanie looked at the plate in Natasha's hand. It was still full of food. Then she caught a glimpse of Natasha's figure, her white jeans hugging her body perfectly. It looked like she was seeing her in 3D: one view in front of her, the other her reflection in the glass doors as she passed. *No wonder she's that skinny; she can't even make a dent in a vegan platter.*

Melanie got up from the table to follow her inside. "Really? Thank you, Natasha." She grabbed the two wine glasses as she moved. In her haste, Melanie caught her toe on the lip of the step, and in one dreadful, slow moment, she tripped forward and let the crystal flutes slide out of her hands and smash across the floor. "Oh my goodness," Melanie yelped. "I am so sorry." Inside, she was dying. *What an idiot, Bauer!* She looked up helplessly. "Natasha, I am so sorry."

"Don't think about it," the hostess said casually. "We have plenty more glasses. Be careful, there. Don't cut yourself. Come through to the living room. I'll just ring Dougie and ask him to come and clear it away."

She has a Dougie?

Melanie could feel her cheeks burning crimson. "Please, may I use your bathroom for a minute?" she asked awkwardly.

"Of course. It's through here."

Embarrassed and feeling helpless, Melanie pushed the door and walked into a guest loo. She glanced around, impressed by both its tranquility and magnitude. It was about the same size as her living room. She locked the door behind her, leaned against the marble top, and let out a long sigh. *I'm sure she was very impressed with that move! Oh my God, I hope she'll still help me without telling Mikhail. I need to get out of here fast.*

Melanie splashed a little cold water across her face and dabbed it dry with a perfectly fluffed towel. She tried her best to straighten it back on the rail before heading out to the hallway. "I am so sorry again," she said. "It has been such a wonderful lunch. I hope I can return your hospitality."

Natasha leaned in and gave her a brief but tight hug. "I am pleased you called. It was good to spend some time together. I feel like I can trust you, Melanie."

Melanie felt better for it. Although some way out of her usual comfort zone, today was turning out to be full of surprises. "Thank you again for lunch, and for helping me out with ... you know."

"For sure. Of course. Don't forget to give me the name of the file you need copied. I'll see what I can do. Perhaps we could meet for lunch one day next week. I should have the opportunity to copy it for you before then—without letting Mikhail know, of course."

Melanie reached into her handbag, plucked out a piece of paper, and handed it to her. Natasha took it, smiled briefly, and folded it twice. Then she slipped it into the back pocket of her J Brands.

"Consider it done," Natasha said.

~~~

Natasha wandered into the living room and slowly paced the length of the settee. Her mind was still absorbed with what she had found on the dresser. *What does it mean?*

"Okay, Miss Volkonski, all done," Dougie said as he passed.

"Thanks, Dougie."

Natasha ran back to her bedroom, retrieved her calfskin Hermes Birkin bag from her dresser, and ran her hand along the surface. She smiled. Then she checked for her car keys, purse, and mobile— all there and accounted for. She made her way to the lift. While waiting, she checked her watch.

Still time before Mikhail is due home.

As the wood-clad Kone cage descended to the ground floor, Natasha thought about Melanie's request. She reached into her pocket, pulled out the note, and unfolded it. As she looked down, her eyes almost jumped out of their sockets. Grabbing the handrail inside the lift to stop herself from falling, she looked at her reflection in the lift mirror. Her face was ashen. As the lift door opened, she ran outside the building, took a large gulp of air, pulled out the piece of paper, and looked at it once again, hoping that she had misread what she saw.

She hadn't. On it, written in pencil, were the letters KCU.

She thought about what she had seen on the paper.

KCU: KasOil Cleanup.

She reached into her bag, quickly lit up a cigarette, and took a long drag. As the nicotine suspension hit the bottom of her lungs, she felt a soothing relaxation. A few seconds later, the feeling was gone, replaced by a deep sense of anxiety. Something was happening, and she didn't know what it was. Something in which Mikhail was involved. *Is someone trying to take his life?* she thought. Then she shook her head. *I shouldn't really be surprised. This is Russian politics. It's different from British politics.* She took another drag.

I'm sure as hell going to try and find out.

~~~

After the lift descended, the noise from the shaft echoed momentarily around the lobby of the apartment, and then there was silence. Several seconds passed, and Mikhail slipped out from the rear reception room adjacent to the kitchen. His eyes were narrowed with an enraged grimace. His right hand was pressed against the countertop, his fingers drumming its marbled surface. The ladies' lunch had revealed a lot more than he had anticipated.

What the hell is that bitch Melanie Bauer up to?

Chapter 26
Ambassadorial

Settled in the rear seat of his Bentley, Kasinov's mood was sullen and his mind preoccupied as he made his way to Igor Pushkin's Saint John's Wood residence. After receiving a dinner invitation from the Russian ambassador to Great Britain, Kasinov accepted. Initially reticent, he became more enthusiastic about the dinner after he discovered later that the invite had come from a directive issued by Russia's prime minister, Vasily Popov. He was intrigued that Popov had travelled all the way from Moscow in order to cohost the dinner. He knew they were plotting something, but he had no idea what it was. He would soon find out.

Kasinov had researched Pushkin's track record. He found nothing special, and certainly no fireworks. From what he had learned, Pushkin had performed his functionary role for just over two years. During that time, he had enjoyed what could be classified as pretty much an uneventful tenure. Kasinov thought about how that was more than likely about to change.

Glancing out the Bentley's side rear window, Kasinov reflected on his notions about acquiring property in Saint John's Wood many years earlier before deciding against it. Whilst the established architecture and a living standard known only to a limited few of London's most affluent attracted him to the place, he wasn't exactly ready to swap the city life for a cocooned suburban lifestyle nestled inside half a square mile—at least not just yet. Plus, he didn't want to be living within ten square miles of someone like Pushkin, let alone half a square mile.

Despite the grand opulent architectural distractions that surrounded the Bentley as it meandered through the distinguished conservation areas within London's most affluent borough, Kasinov's ruminations were firmly captured in the events that led to the dinner invitation. Not even the sight of Lord's landmark cricket ground and the large detached neo-Georgian and Edwardian mansion blocks along Wellington, Circus, and Abbey Roads could break his deep trance. His mind was preoccupied with permutations of surreptitious stratagems that Popov and Pushkin were most likely planning, along with optional retorts he could employ.

The Bentley stopped outside 23 Abbey Road. Two towering stone-clad walls separated by a characteristic cast-steel gate painted in metallic black greeted him. At either side of the gate were two equally black-clad security guards, the one to the right embracing his radio mouthpiece. Kasinov figured it was to announce his arrival. The second guard approached the vehicle, and following a brief inspection, the Bentley was allowed passage into a parking sanctuary that interposed Pushkin's residence and the boundary ramparts. The Bentley fitted neatly between a spanking new red Porsche 911 and a giant, classic, black Rolls Royce. Kasinov guessed that it meant the remainder of the exclusive guest list had already arrived.

As he disembarked the vehicle, Kasinov thought, *Just remember; I am more powerful than Koshenko.*

Pushkin's primary function as head of the Russian embassy in London was to maintain a balance in relationships between the UK and Russia, as well as to oversee the voluminous administrative matters for Russian citizens living in London or planning to visit London to see family or take up employment across a number of sectors. The majority of applications referenced work in the entertainment segment.

Kasinov imagined Pushkin preparing to host the Kremlin's principal adversary, and was pretty certain that this current line of work suited him. The entertainment industry generally meant more fees, which meant bigger expense budgets for him and his embassy cohorts. Kasinov imagined, though, that Pushkin probably wasn't psychologically equipped for the onslaught from someone of the caliber of Mikhail Kasinov. That was never part of his training. The Kremlin didn't have a course for this.

As Kasinov approached the main entrance to the property, his thoughts moved to the conversation he had overheard earlier between Melanie Bauer and Natasha. He was surprised that a near random stranger like Melanie, who Natasha had barely met for five minutes, was now suddenly hanging out in the apartment like they were best friends. He was even more surprised that she was enquiring on Roy's behalf about some information that he had lost. He didn't recall giving any information or files to Roy, except one email to invite him to London. Everything else was verbal. *Either Miss Bauer is doing a solo run, or she and Roy are up to something. I need to find out what's written on that piece of paper.*

Kasinov was even more surprised to hear about the termination. *She never said anything. Bitch.* His trust in Natasha was dwindling, and his suspicion levels of her and the German super-analyst were growing.

That was a job Kasinov moved to his list for tomorrow. Tonight, his list had just one item: the Popov and Pushkin Muppet Show.

As he traversed the limestone-clad stairwell at the main entrance to the property, he looked up.

Bring it on, he thought. *Bring it on.* Then he walked confidently through the front portico like he was about to give a presidential acceptance speech.

Kasinov didn't waste any time going straight through the awaiting entourage of security and into the main dining area, nodding as he walked. Inside, he saw that the British ambassador to Russia, Jeffrey Winthrop, was there. So too was Pushkin, and Vasily Popov didn't dare miss the occasion after being given clear instructions from his president. Pushkin introduced himself politely. He was midfifties and had pitted and abnormally white skin with a fusion of wild black-and-grey hair. He was an irregular-shaped man—tall, but slightly angled to one side. He was well dressed in a navy suit with a striped shirt and a red tie. His face looked flush, matching the tie.

Popov, from behind an oversized dark suit, nodded to Kasinov from the opposite side of the dining room. Kasinov barely nodded back. *Popov, you skinny, ignorant bastard,* his mind snarled. He knew Popov from 2001, before his incarceration. He held a junior ministerial post back then—very junior, Kasinov recalled.

Winthrop, who looked well into his sixties, was a dapperly dressed man in a double-breasted charcoal grey suit with yellow stripes. He approached Kasinov fervently and shook his hand. "Jeffrey Winthrop. Good to meet you again, Mikhail."

Kasinov didn't recall meeting him before, but he had heard his name. *Porsche 911 guy, definitely.*

The food was already at the table, and after formal greetings were exchanged, Pushkin ushered everyone to take their seats.

Kasinov was ravenous. He hadn't eaten a decent meal in days. The starter was soup. Kasinov thought it looked like some unusual chicken, zucchini, and artichoke amalgam. He immediately grabbed his appurtenances and started eating. As he took his first spoon, he winced when the taste papillae at the edge of his tongue suddenly turned piquant. He could taste something distinctly acrid. He spat back into the bowl. Then he grabbed a glass of water, washed his mouth out, and spat that back into the bowl, too.

Pushkin, Popov, and Winthrop looked across scornfully at him.

Kasinov was staring into the bowl. Not noticing the reaction from the others, his eyes remained fixed on the soup concoction, expecting some concealed pathogen to jump out and raise its hands. It didn't. Then he paused and thought, *If they have invited me here to poison me, it's probably the easiest place for them to pull it off.*

Suddenly he didn't feel hungry anymore. He looked up, and the others looked away. For everybody else, the starters evaporated faster than the platitudes, and Pushkin's cue arrived sooner than he had anticipated. Kasinov glanced across at him to see him clearing his throat.

"Mikhail," Pushkin said with some degree of trepidation, "we don't believe that it's in the greater interests of Russia, or in the interests of ongoing relations between Great Britain and Russia, that you continue with your rancorous tirade against the current Kremlin regime. These tactics are creating an unnecessary discord."

Kasinov pulled back in his seat with a disbelieving gaze. "The best interests of the country? Are you kidding me? What about the billions of dollars that get evaporated each year in bribery and corruption? What about the opportunities lost in the middle classes? What about transparency, world competitiveness, and sustainability?"

"Let's not get sucked into the details of different perceptions of reality," Pushkin replied with a deep, slow voice, speaking as if he had a genuine olive branch in his back pocket. "We have asked you to join us here this evening as we would like to make a proposal to you."

Kasinov guessed that Pushkin may well have had an olive branch, but he knew he had no authority to pull it out—not while Popov was in the room, anyway. *Hierarchical respect: Russian value number one.* Kasinov placed his napkin back on the table, folded his arms defensively, and assumed a grimace that resembled that of a tempestuous teenager. "I'm listening."

Pushkin looked in Popov's direction, and then across to Kasinov. "We would like you to return to Moscow, where it is proposed you will receive a presidential pardon for your wrongdoings. There are conditions, of course."

Everybody looked to Kasinov, who remained completely taciturn and emotionless, his arms tightly folded across his chest. Pushkin, expecting a response, looked apprehensive. No response was forthcoming, so he decided to continue. "The conditions being that you agree to concede all current political affiliations and refrain from venturing into any future political campaign within Russia."

Kasinov's jaw was just about protruding from his lower cheeks. "Absolutely no way," he replied in an apoplectic manner. "You have to be kidding me. There is absolutely no currency in that whatsoever. If that's your idea of amicable atonement after what I've been through for the last seven years, well then I must say I have seriously overestimated your intellectual capacity. I can't believe you brought me all the way here to tell me that."

Winthrop, who had been moving his spoon around in his soup for a while, eventually interjected. "Mikhail, if I may say, I feel tension building between our two great nations here." The lifelong diplomat delivered his stereotypical rhetoric with great lucidity. "It's not just at this table, but between the Kremlin and

Westminster—a tension that could pass its threshold very soon unless we come to some amicable agreement here."

Kasinov remained calm. "I appreciate your concerns, Jeffrey, but I'm not going to hide in a cave for the rest of my life." The former oligarch replied with simulated humility. "I've done that for seven years without choice. Now I have a choice, and I have decided I want to make a difference."

Pushkin's face had turned ashen. "But, Mikhail, we have to do something. We can't just sit back and watch you push the self-destruct button."

Kasinov's eyes narrowed, looking like they were gathering momentum to a confrontational ultimatum. "Let me tell you this, Igor," he exclaimed, pointing his finger at Popov whilst maintaining a severe regard at Pushkin. "It is you, and that guy sitting next to you, who will be pushing the self-destruct button if you try and stop me." After a brief pause, he raised his hand, showing all his fingers. "I have the moral, political, and cultural support of the people inside and outside Russia." He counted off his fingers one at a time as he spoke. "All parties will follow me. I have the Communist Youth; I have the media; I have the banks; and most of all, I have international credibility. I have everyone, and you better believe that."

Popov, who had been sitting in complete serenity—as if he was attending his first rendition of Swan Lake at the Bolshoi Theatre—suddenly leaned forward in his chair, his face lit with a derisive smile. "That is mere metaphysical presupposition and speculation on your part, Mikhail," Popov interjected strongly. "You have no grounds to make such statements."

Kasinov eyed Popov as he sat diagonally opposite. He felt that when Russia's prime minister communicated, there was something amoral about his style. Kasinov knew Popov had not risen to the top of the State Duma by making too many friends along the way. He had seen lots like him before, and knew there was only one way to handle his kind: head-on. "That's absolute rubbish, and you know it," Kasinov barked. "I spent years eradicating venal practices out of the system and culture in our country, and you guys spend all your time either directly or indirectly promoting their reinstatement."

Popov appeared unruffled by the assault on the integrity of his administration. "That is totally untrue. Corruption has no place in the future of our government. We have visibly promoted the eradication of all such practices."

Kasinov interrupted the Russian prime minister with an explosion of laughter. "That's bullshit. Yeah, you've audibly said this, but your actions don't correspond with the words, and people see through that. Everyone sees through the circus you're running."

Popov fixed his elbows into the table as he eyed Kasinov. "Mikhail," he said with deep intonation, "I'm not sure when was the last time you had a good look in the mirror?"

Kasinov stared at Popov and pointed at himself, his other hand raised. "I look in the mirror every day, and I see the same thing every time I look: integrity."

"Well, let me remind you that you are far from the paragon of virtue you set yourself out to be," Popov responded sardonically. "There are ongoing murder investigations with which you and other former KasOil executives are inextricably linked. From our records, you've siphoned more cash out of Russia than Bonnie and Clyde could have stolen in their lifetimes."

Kasinov was so livid he was ready to jump across the table and punch the Russian prime minister's lights out. "That's all complete rubbish, and you know it," the oligarch retorted. "It's just one fabricated untruth after the next. I played by the rules. Everything I earned, I did so fair and square. My auditors approved all my financial statements. There were no irregularities. It's not my problem if you and your government keep changing the laws retrospectively. Every time I came up with some innovation to blossom our resources, your regime responded with interdiction to kill it."

"In order to maintain some amity around this situation," Popov said arrogantly, "we should look at this very simply. We can drop the charges, or we can go after you. It's as simple as that. We're trying to make it easy for you."

Sitting to Popov's left, Pushkin looked like he was about to do a backflip off the chair. He raised his hands to his face after hearing Popov's ultimatum. From Pushkin's reaction, Kasinov assumed that the ambassador believed his prime minister had pushed too hard, too fast, and should have proposed an option that would have been more attractive. Kasinov wondered why they hadn't proposed an option where he didn't have to return to Moscow. *I might have considered that.* Kasinov guessed Popov was not interested in pursuing a soft approach. Kasinov also guessed that Pushkin knew he wouldn't accede to such conditions. *It's like he wants me to challenge Koshenko all the way.*

Kasinov didn't tolerate mediocrity very well. In fact, he was proud of his caprices. He was not shy of confrontation when the opportunity presented itself. If history was anything to go by, he was liable to start smashing his fist against the table and unleash abuse at everyone present. Instead, he placed his hands firmly on the table on either side of the untouched soup creation. Tonight he felt self-control would display a stronger disposition.

"Gentlemen," he said calmly but distinctly before wiping his linen napkin against his lips. "I can discern no difference between your offer and hell." Then he pushed his chair back and stood.

Judging by the expressions looking back at him, he was right. The three that remained around the dinner table looked back at him disbelievingly.

"I believe this meeting is over," he said, turning and making his way to the front door and out to his awaiting Bentley.

Big mistake, Koshenko, he thought. *You should have sent the A-team—not this bunch of clowns.*

Chapter 27
Retort

Koshenko awoke the next morning with great expectations. He pondered how his prime minister and his senior diplomat in the London embassy had handled Kasinov the previous evening. It was two against one, and he assumed they had delivered on their assignment. Failure was not an option. He waited anxiously for Popov's call to confirm Kasinov was going to be on the next flight back to Moscow.

At five minutes past nine—five minutes later than scheduled—his phone rang. It was Popov. He smiled to himself and sat back in his office chair. "Well, Vasily, have you done a deal?"

"Not exactly," Popov said.

Koshenko scoffed. "What do you mean, not exactly?"

"He was extremely arrogant. He flatly refused our proposal and just walked out of the dinner. He didn't even eat his starter."

Suddenly Koshenko sat up in his chair, his jaws protruding from either side of his face. "You fucken idiot, Popov. You let him walk out?"

"I made him a very lucrative offer. He just flat refused to negotiate."

Koshenko sat back in his chair again and deliberated. "Vasily, let me tell you one thing," he growled. "We threw in the towel on the Cold War far too early for my liking. There is no towel now. Not on my watch. We're going all the way on this one."

"What do you suggest I do next?"

Koshenko was coming to terms with the fact that it was not looking particularly positive on Popov's mission to neuter the feral oligarch. All the scenarios that he plotted portended disaster. Apprehensively, he knew that Kasinov had the temerity to pull off the challenges and the threats that Koshenko feared most. *Kasinov may have thrown a tantrum at dinner, but now it's my turn*, Koshenko thought. "Popov," the president snapped, "I want you to call Charles Browne, the British foreign secretary, and set up a meeting with him today. More particularly, I want you to challenge him with finding a solution."

"Okay. Will do."

Koshenko grabbed the phone tighter and drew it closer to his mouth. "And if you don't get any sense from him," he yelled, "*you* better get on a plane to Dublin."

~~~

Browne agreed to meet with Popov. The pair, not wanting to attract any unnecessary media attention, arranged to meet at Popov's Berkeley Square hotel in a private meeting room that Popov had booked.

It was 11:30 a.m., and Browne's state-supplied, long-wheelbase, silver S350 Mercedes pulled up outside the Berkeley to a welcoming reception of two porters dressed in illustrious attire. Charles Browne was an experienced, robust politician that had served in the previous government in the capacity of secretary of state for Northern Ireland. Under prime minister Andrew Wood's administration for the last three years, he had been the most senior representative of the government representing Great Britain within the international arena—and at forty-five, he was reputed as the heir apparent in Wood's team. He had a lot going for him: an international and culturally enlightening childhood with his father's diplomatic assignments in Central and East Asia, an Oxford education, seasoned parliamentary experience across a number of portfolios, and he also looked particularly sharp in his fine navy, Chester Barrie bespoke, pin-striped Savile Row suit.

After climbing from the vehicle, Browne discreetly made his way to the Berkeley's entrance with distinguished gentility. His head and pout were visibly more pronounced than those around him as he made his way through to the meeting rooms on the first floor. Apprehensive of Popov's request for the meeting, he entered the lobby deep in rumination. He moved without any exchange of pleasantries with the welcoming staff, and found the room on the first floor marked THAMES SUITE.

Inside, Vasily Popov was seated and gazing anxiously at his mobile. He looked up when Browne entered. "Thanks for meeting with me, Charles," Popov said, sounding weary as he stood to greet his guest.

"Not a problem, Vasily," Browne replied with some degree of reverence to the Russian prime minister. He took a seat opposite Popov with an indiscriminate regard on his face. "On the phone, you said that this was an emergency, so I cancelled some other appointments to come and see you."

"The situation with Kasinov has become untenable. I met with him last night, and he's resolute in his decision to continue his crusade against Koshenko. He has already cost our nation billions of dollars in stock market losses, and now he's trying to initiate anarchy in Russia. I have to stop him."

"I understand that such a crusade isn't good for Russia right now. What can I do to help?" Browne offered prejudiced support in his intonation.

"It's very simple," Popov said succinctly. "I want him extradited back to Moscow."

"That's going to be very difficult to swing, Vasily. He's not here as a Russian national; he's here as a legitimate Irish citizen named Mícheál Kasney. As long as he has a harp on the front of his passport, I'm afraid I have no authority to extradite him into your care. I wish it was different, but that's the reality."

"That's bullshit," Popov scoffed. "We both know he's no more Irish than Nelson Mandela. He's a f—" Popov stopped before adding the expletives at the tip of his tongue.

"Why don't you ask the Irish to withdraw his passport?" Browne queried.

"We've spoken with Irish prime minister Eamonn Burke, but he's got his head in the sand." Popov reached closer to Browne. "Charles, I don't need to tell you that this could get very messy if we don't find a solution." This time, there was a degree of hostility in his tone and his body language.

"I'm not sure if I'm following you," Browne said innocently.

"Koshenko's livid with your prime minister's benevolence to ex-KGB defectors, oligarchy residency, and now the harboring of escaped criminals," Popov said, his fist bouncing delicately off the table as he spoke. "We have an opportunity to bring this to an end quickly, or alternatively, we can watch it escalate into an international pissing contest between Russia and Britain, a contest where Kasinov will gain unwarranted publicity, and one that will drive a wedge between our two great nations—a big wedge."

~~~

After no immediate resolution with Browne, Vasily Popov travelled to Dublin that afternoon to meet with Irish prime minister Eamonn Burke at the Department of the Taoiseach in Dublin. It was a meeting that Popov had set up on extremely short notice through the British, Irish, and Russian ambassadors that day. "You better get on a plane to Dublin," Koshenko had said.

Popov arrived in Dublin around 4:00 p.m. He was met at the air bridge tunnel by an apprehensive looking Maxim Sechinov, head of the Russian consulate in Dublin. Sechinov was midthirties, clean-shaven, well dressed, with brown spiky hair. Back at the office, everybody called him Max. Today, he was Maxim. The pair was escorted briskly past arrivals proceedings before they set off en route to the government buildings on Merrion Street.

Travelling in the center vehicle, cocooned amidst an ensemble of five state-black Mercedes cars—their wing tops shrouded with Irish flags and their drivers humbly attentive in repute of their foreign guest—Popov thought about how he was going to strong-arm the Irish premier into withdrawing Kasinov's license for nationality. He had heard that the Irish were pretty resilient, immune to strong-arming in the past from several mighty nations. Two hundred years of history were there, for any empirical reference.

After a twenty-minute journey from the airport, the troupe of vehicles arrived at Dáil Éireann to be met by a throng of journalists and photographers, mostly local, but there was some international representation.

A secret meeting, I thought I said to Burke, he thought. *Some secret now.*

Popov was whisked expeditiously through a wall of state guards that had formed a channel from his vehicle to the building's entrance. Two steps behind him, Max looked on anxiously at the press that had gathered. Popov glanced behind. He could see that his aide wasn't used to dealing with situations like this. Popov guessed he was more comfortable processing visas for the Irish travelling to Russia. Popov shook his head in anger. In his estimation, Maxim was about as much use to him as Rasputin had been to the Romanov monarchy one hundred years earlier. But he was summonsed to come along, and he did.

Eamonn Burke stood outside the entranceway and proffered a big handshake, together with a warm Irish smile. Following the official greeting, the Irish head of state led his guests to an adjacent meeting room, where the three would be alone.

"Coffee, tea, vodka perhaps?" Burke enquired humorously after the escorting sentinel had closed the door behind them.

Popov shook his head. "No," he replied
soberly. "If you don't mind, let's get started. I'm
on a tight timeline here."

Although Burke had been fully briefed by his
diplomatic liaison team only moments earlier, he
played dumb. "Yes, Mr. Flopov," the Irish
premier said innocently. "What is it that you
wanted to see me about so urgently?"

Popov's face reddened. Inside, his temperature
was hitting fever levels. He thought about
answering with, "It's not Flopov; it's Popov, you
fucken idiot," but instead, he said, "Our president
has spoken with you on this matter of Mikhail
Kasinov already." Popov nodded sternly in
Burke's direction. "As you can understand, this is
an extremely critical matter to our nation."

Burke glanced at Maxim and then back at
Popov as if to say, "And Max knows all about it."
The Russian consulate had lodged a barrage of
calls with Burke's office over the last number of
days to speak with him about Kasinov's passport,
only to get rhetorical feedback from one of
Burke's high-ranking foreign affairs diplomats.

"Yes, I spoke with him on the phone, and as I
told him then and confirm to you now, we have
no record of a Mikhail Kasinov on our database.
We do, however, have a Mícheál Kasney passport
in issue currently."

Maxim said nothing.

Popov moved in closer to Burke with his
elbows socketed on his knees. "I need you to

withdraw the passport issued to Mikhail Kasinov or Mícheál Kasney or whatever you want to call him."

"I'm afraid I can't do that," Burke replied. "We don't currently have any irregularities surrounding that passport issuance."

Chapter 28
Manicure

Thirty miles away from this first and potentially historic meeting between the Irish and Russian prime ministers, Roy's Toyota Avensis rental turned up a small, graveled thoroughfare. Through the heavy drizzle, he spotted the sign KINLOUGH CASTLE ½ KILOMETER. Although he had experienced some passenger congestion at Dublin's Terminal Two earlier in the day, Roy had no idea that Vasily Popov was in Dublin at the same time. It didn't make a difference either way—he had something important to attend.

As Roy entered the grounds of Kinlough Castle, he looked up to take in the natural serenity of the place. It was typical of fortified structures built by European nobility in Europe and the Middle East during the Middle Ages, encapsulating opulence, serenity, and security. Its structure dominated an enormous earthen mote and was faced with chiseled stone and feudal mortar. He noticed how the strikingly historical exterior was captured through the gatehouse, corner towers, arrow-slits, turrets, crenulation walls, and machicolations, which projected out across the perimeter's profile. Its combined Romanesque and medieval architecture supported in the company of brave flying buttresses, carrying on their backs the distribution weight of the roof and solid walls with regimented structural columns and lintels providing foundation. *What magnificent medieval splendor*, Roy thought.

Roy enjoyed connecting with the beautiful and vast landscape of the Wicklow Mountains surrounding the castle. It reminded him of his early childhood years in the north of England. The area around the castle was densely covered in large granite stones and surrounded by a rich quartzite envelope. He remembered reading somewhere that the stonework that accessorized these ancient estates had been pushed and dragged up there during the Caledonian Orogeny and placed on top of its curvaceous topography. *Probably been there since the last ice age.*

Roy stopped and gazed out through the Avensis's front window, past the oscillating window wipers waving from side to side. He thought how the deepened valleys with their beautiful corrie and ribbon lakes interspersed throughout the range provided arguably one of the most beautiful panoramas in the world. The setting was simply stunning, and one where you could definitely get lost in your own reverie. Roy nodded understanding the meaning of the saying: "There are only two kinds of people in the world, the Irish and those who wish they were Irish." Right now though he had a job to do. He had no idea if it would add any value, but it had to be done.

The front door of the castle was large and stately with two chunky, darkened oak panels resting on six large iron-studded hinges on either side. It was arched on top. He lifted and released the brass-on-brass doorknocker, and a loud knocking sound resonated for some distance.

Seconds later, the door opened slowly. *Understandable,* Roy thought, *with all of those appurtenances holding it together.* As it opened, its hinges let off a shivering screech that seemed to last forever. Just as the creaking reached a crescendo, a young lady appeared on the other side. Roy stood at the door and nodded to her. The young lady tilted her head as she regarded him, almost as if tranquilized. Maybe it was his tall, tanned appearance with his blonde hair that surprised her. He guessed his appearance was probably a bit different from the average Glendalough farmer.

"You must be Catherine," he said, offering his hand. "I'm Roy Young."

The young lady looked back up at him, her eyes riveted in his. She didn't move. It was as though her whole body was cast in some quick-setting plaster.

"You are Catherine, right?"

The young lady eventually blinked and broke her gaze. "Yes, I'm sorry," she replied. "Thank you for coming—and so quickly."

Roy noticed her blushing. "You're welcome. Least I could do."

Catherine wrapped her hands onto the outer oak plank and pulled the door open a bit wider to the sound of more creaking. She motioned for Roy to enter. They moved through the archway, down five steps to the atrium reception.

As they walked inside, Roy moved ahead and scanned the citadel's vast Gothic entrance. He noticed how the atrium reception lit up the cavernous vaulting, along with the surrounding tapestries, gargoyles, and architraves. Across the center atrium, about twelve feet up, he saw a steel beam as wide and deep as a medium-sized travel suitcase. It traversed the entire circumference of the atrium, suspended from joist and struts from within the castle's perimeter walls. Roy could see several reception rooms, kitchen areas, studies, an entertainment-cum-banqueting hall that could probably accommodate about a hundred people, and no doubt countless guest rooms upstairs. He contemplated that this was the kind of space you needed to host St. Ledger's Gatsby-like revelries. "Nice castle, by the way," he remarked.

Catherine stopped when he did.

"I'm very sorry for what happened to your dad," he said compassionately.

She nodded.

"Catherine," he said in a gentle but assuring tone, "I only met David once, and that was recently, so I can't say I knew him all that well. When I received your call, I came here as soon as I could." Roy placed his hands on her shoulders. "Anything I can do to help get to the bottom of what happened to him that night, I will. I promise you that."

"Thank you," she said. "Here, let me take your jacket."

Roy crossed his hands around his body to signify cold. "If you don't mind, I'll hang on to it. It's a bit chilly in here."

Catherine rubbed her hands together and then wrapped her arms around her shoulders the same way. "You're right. It's bloody cold in here."

Suddenly an old lady appeared, her eyes rolling up to heaven. "Yeah, it's that geotherm thingy that has tripped again."

"Roy, this is Margaret Mooney," Catherine said. "Margaret has worked with my dad since he acquired Kinlough Castle."

Roy offered his hand. "Nice to meet you."

Catherine glanced at Margaret. "That's the second time this month!"

Margaret threw her hands up in submission. "Don't look at me. I don't know what's going on inside that plant room. I couldn't tell the difference between the water tank and the diesel tank."

"We don't have a diesel tank, Margaret. It's all piped gas now, and that geothermal thingy, as you call it, doesn't use gas either. And it never seems to work."

"I'll call that eejit of a plumber again," Margaret answered, turning away and heading in the direction of an antique phone.

Roy nodded to Catherine. "Any developments since we spoke?"

"I had a call from Detective John Blake yesterday," Catherine said, looking up at him and feigning a smile. "He told me he had some information for me about my father."

"Sounds positive."

"He said he visited the state pathologist. It appears Dad underwent some severe trauma just before he died."

"Was that all?"

"He asked me if my father was left- or right-handed."

"Why did he ask that?"

"Something about one of his nails being filed down." Catherine sighed. "Ever since I received that call from Detective Blake, I've been trying to visualize the events of that evening. I visited Molly's, our local pub where Dad went earlier in the evening before he was murdered. I met Paddy McHugh, the owner. I also received a visit from Sean O'Connor the day after the funeral. They confirmed that Dad was definitely not himself, and that he was heavily burdened by something that was going on in his business world."

"Any ideas what that was?"

"Unfortunately it's a world that nobody at home knows very much about, except that it earned him millions."

Wrapped in three layers of clothing to keep warm, Catherine took Roy through her reconstruction sequence—firstly, outside the castle, where David St. Ledger had parked his BMW. Roy didn't see anything inspiring. Then they made their way through to the main reception vestibule. Roy stopped on the way to look through the coat stand and the storage space at the entrance. He found nothing of note.

Together they paced from room to room inside Kinlough Castle, attempting to perform a reenactment of the events on the evening of the death of her father.

Again, nothing.

As they turned back on themselves, Catherine guided Roy into the main reception room. "During the police investigation, they found a button from his shirt," she said, pointing to the floor around them. "Maybe there was a struggle. Maybe he was wrestled around the floor here before they killed him."

Roy got down on all fours and scoured the floor to see if there were any clues the police had somehow missed. He moved around like a gymnast launching into a floor routine as he carefully examined the vast granite floor throughout the main reception room. Then Roy moved up to the second reception room.

"This looks strange," he commented. On the floor slab was an engraved symbol. "Looks like a chalk mark on the floor. Something small. A scribe embedded into the granite stone floor maybe. It looks like a letter—like a *G,* I would guess." He looked back at Catherine. "Here, have a look at this," he said, pointing to the mark. "Mean anything to you?"

Catherine jumped down next to him and eyed the symbol. "No," she replied, shaking her head.

Roy moved into a position directly underneath the central atrium beam and continued his search. Several minutes later, he came across another chalked scribe. It was a *U.* "Here, Catherine. Look at this."

Catherine suddenly lifted her head from the granite floor, still kneeling with her hands now resting on her knees. "Well, that might explain his left index nail!" she cried out. "I knew it wasn't an attempted manicure!"

"Perhaps you might expand on what Blake told you," Roy said.

"When Detective Blake came, he said that, during the autopsy examination, they found Dad's left index nail severely chafed."

"Sounds like he was trying to tell us something. We should keep searching."

Roy and Catherine continued scouring the floor, but there was nothing else. They went into the kitchen, where Roy pulled out a pad and a pen from his pocket. He wrote down what they had found.

Catherine peered around his shoulder. "UG means nothing to me," she said with a sigh.

Roy reordered it to GU and looked at Catherine again.

"Means nothing," Catherine replied, looking back up at Roy for inspiration.

"UG could be short for underground, right?" Roy enquired. "Is there a cellar here maybe? A silo? Something?"

Catherine shook her head. "Nothing like that."

A few seconds of silence followed, and then Catherine leapt off the stool and gave Roy a big hug and a kiss on the cheek. "Underground!" she exclaimed with a shriek of excitement. "That's the name of one of Dad's foundations. He set it up years ago for homeless kids."

Roy looked at her, perplexed.

"C'mon, let's go!" she cried out as she hopped out of the kitchen and off into the main reception room. She grabbed her keys along the way as she ran out of the house towards her car.

He followed closely behind, trying to keep up. "Where are we going?" he asked as soon as he reached the passenger door of her car.

"John Saville's office. Underground was one of the funds Dad set up to support national charities for orphaned and deprived children." Catherine started the car. "Dad used a local solicitor named John Saville to administer this fund, just like he did for several of his charitable trusts."

~~~

An hour later, they were back in the kitchen again. The visit to Saville's office didn't provide Roy with anything that would help them understand what happened to St. Ledger. Roy, whose tenacity had a pretty substantial bandwidth, paced up and down the kitchen.

"There's something missing," he said, rubbing his chin.

Catherine was sitting at the kitchen counter, taciturn and expressionless, looking more desolate than when they had left. Her chin and cheeks were firmly embraced in the palms of her hands with her elbows supported from the kitchen counter. Then suddenly the rear door opened and Margaret Mooney entered.

Margaret glanced at Catherine and then Roy. Then she made her way over to the kettle. "Cup of tea, my darling?"

"Yes, please," Roy answered.

"Not you. *Her.*"

"No thanks, Margaret," Catherine said. "I'm fine."

Margaret looked back at Roy. "Okay I'll get one for you, then." Then she looked at Catherine. "Why the long face, my dear?"

"Oh, I thought we had found something about Dad."

"You're still holding onto the theory he was murdered?"

"Of course I am!" she cried out. "There's no way he would take his own life—absolutely no way."

"You're right. I have to agree with you. Tell me, what did you find?"

Roy pulled out the piece of paper with the letter combination that concluded with *UG*, unfolded it, and placed it firmly on the kitchen counter. "We found these two symbols scribed out on the main reception floor. I'm convinced there was some form of a struggle." Roy motioned in the direction of the central reception room. "Right over there on the floor."

"The police didn't find these scribes, for some reason," Catherine said. "All they found was a button from his shirt in the same area."

"What's the difference between now and the time of David's death?" Roy probed.

"Six days?"

"Yes, I understand, but there must be something else."

Margaret and Catherine looked at each other and then back at Roy. Catherine shrugged.

"It's bloody freezing in here!" Roy exclaimed, not wanting to sound rude, but he needed to emphasize the unusual thermal characteristics he was experiencing. "Is it always this cold?"

"No, it's not normal," Margaret interjected. "It's because the geotherm floor heating is out of action again."

Catherine looked at Margaret. "Yeah, Margaret called the plumber!"

Margaret glanced out the window to see if there was any sign of him. "That plumber fella should be here any minute."

"It doesn't matter about the plumber," Roy said, trying to explain. "It matters, but for different reasons—for entropic reasons."

"Why is that?" Catherine asked.

"The morning David was found murdered, was the house warm?"

"Yeah, it was very warm," Catherine answered, sounding even more inquisitive. "Why?"

"That's very interesting," Roy commented with his hand placed beneath his bristled chin.

"What's interesting?" Catherine enquired.

"There are a few things that happen to surfaces when heat is applied and when heat is withdrawn. It's all about the conductivity. Firstly, the conductivity of the heating material has a lot to do with how quickly heat is dissipated. In this case, we're interested in how it escaped. Granite has a very low coefficient of conductivity. Heat is lost rapidly when compared with most contemporary flooring materials. Secondly, when heat is lost rapidly, it causes surface moisture to form— temporarily, that is, for a few hours. That moisture can unveil some markings that would not normally be seen in a steady state environment." Roy smiled. He was glad he had studied thermodynamics at Army Cadets.

Catherine jumped up and gave Roy his second big hug of the day. "That explains the sudden appearance of the marks," she said excitedly. "That's why we can only see Dad's nail markings now."

"And did you go and see John Saville about the Underground project?" Margaret enquired.

"Yes, we did," Catherine said. "We went straight there after we found this. He said that Underground was abandoned two years ago, and that they set up a new fund offshore somewhere—Malta or Jersey, I think he said."

Roy interjected. "There's something missing. Maybe it wasn't Underground or UG, then."

Margaret looked puzzled. "Funny, I saw a light marking this morning on the floor when I was cleaning the front vestibule."

"What? Where? Show me!" Catherine screamed anxiously as she jumped off the stool and grabbed Margaret by the arm.

"No, dear. It's not there anymore."

"Where is it?"

"Oh, I cleaned it off. It was a terrible looking thing—a light chalk mark on the granite between the two rooms."

"What was the letter?" Roy asked calmly.

"Ah, I think it looked like an *M*. No, it wasn't. It was an *N*. I'm sure. I remember it was *N* for

Noel, David's middle name. That's what I remember when I was cleaning it off." Margaret looked to the ceiling and shook her head. "Little signs of him left all over the place."

Catherine grabbed Margaret and gave her a big kiss on the cheek. "Thank you."

Roy took over the letter puzzle again, trying different combinations. He wrote as he thought.

NUG

NGU

UNG

UGN

GNU

"Gun!" Roy cried out. "Did David have a gun?"

Catherine looked puzzled. "He doesn't have a gun."

"Is there a gun room in the castle?" Roy said with his hands raised. "You know, where they stored their artillery and ammunitions back in the Middle Ages when they built this place?"

"No, there isn't."

"What else, then?" Roy probed.

There was silence followed by lots of nodding. Roy looked back and forth at them, urging them on.

Suddenly Catherine looked up and pointed towards the outer perimeter castle walls. "I think I know what it is!" she cried out. "It's his cannon! His favorite place in the castle! He was always sitting up at that turret, looking out."

The trio stared at each other.

"Where is it?" Roy asked.

Catherine nodded her head to the side. "This way. Follow me."

Collectively they turned and hurried towards the westerly turret, four rooms down from the central atrium. Catherine guided them up an old metal spiral staircase hidden within the turret's old stone-cased interior. Catherine stepped onto the limestone tread first, closely followed by Roy, with Margaret at least ten or so paces behind. They reached the top of the turret, and there they found a piece of historical armory glistening back at them. Roy could almost see his own reflection along its reinforced chase. It was in pristine condition, looking like it had been recently cleaned and painted in Gothic black. Its pitted cast iron finish sparkled in the sunlight, its neck rested on a solid plinth that surrounded the weapon and its muzzle standing slightly proud of the crenulation wall.

Roy and Catherine paused to catch their breath. "I definitely need to do more exercise," Catherine panted as her hands rested on her knees.

"You should join the army; you'll get plenty there, I promise you." Roy gave her a little wink. He reached out his muscular arm to her. "Here, hold onto me."

Catherine smiled at him and grabbed his hand.

"Okay," Roy said. "Climb up here and put your right foot into that trunnion there, and your left one over that side." He pointed to the two trunnion pillars either side of the cannon's chase.

Roy guided her into a position to facilitate the most effective ingress to the weapon's inner bore. Catherine was now on top of the main chase with her feet pinned against the protruding trunnion, Roy's hands wrapped around her calf muscles.

"Now reach in and get your hand back inside as far up to the muzzle face as you can," Roy said. "I'll hold you. Don't worry."

Composed and determined, Catherine elegantly reached in through the muzzle face and shuffled through some loose debris that had gathered there. She pulled out the rubble and threw it onto the turret floor. "Nothing in that lot." She inserted her arm once again, closer to the muzzle chamber this time, and shuffled around. She could feel her hand touching against the smooth face of the bore. Her face contorted in an unusual grimace as she tried to reach further inside. "I think I might have something. I can feel plastic. I can't seem to grab hold of it. It's in too far." She groped further inside the muzzle, her right arm now almost fully concealed.

A new wave of panting ensued when Margaret reached the turret landing. She was holding her chest with both hands as if she was about to go into cardiac arrest. "Find . . . anything?" she said between one deep gasp.

Catherine looked up at Roy and then down at the bore again. "I think so, but I can't seem to reach it."

Roy regarded Margaret's panting. As she bent down to draw in some air, he noticed the pincer hair accessory holding her silver locks together. "Margaret?" Roy pointed with his head as he maintained a firm grip around Catherine's slender torso with both arms. "Reach behind your head and undo that metal claw thing in your hair."

Margaret looked up at him, then nodded, undid it, and handed it to Roy. "Give it to Catherine," he said, motioning up the barrel with his head. "Try that," he said to Catherine.

Catherine grabbed the clip from Margaret and placed her thumb and index finger firmly on either side of the claw's rear lever. She inserted her arm again, and with the extension device in place, was able to reach the plastic sleeve she had felt earlier. "Got it!" she cried out as she delicately extracted her arm from the cannon's inner bore.

Roy helped her back to her feet, not letting her go until she had firmly landed and stopped wobbling. "You okay?"

"Fine, thanks," Catherine said as she handed her catch to Roy, who pulled it from Margaret's magical hairclip. It was a light, clear, A4-sized, plasticized sleeve with the top section taped closed to maintain a water seal. Inside, there were two sheets of paper. Roy unsealed the sleeve and pulled out the contents.

They were two email records. Both had David St. Ledger's name in the correspondence section. One was from 2000, and one was dated 2010. Kasinov's name littered both of them.

Suddenly a strange feeling came over Roy, right up his spine and into his cranium. *Maybe I should have left the bastard behind bars in Siberia.*

Chapter 29
Xenophobia

Captivated by the imagery under presentation, Yuri Koshenko hovered in suspense beneath an enormous LCD screen inside one of the Kremlin's expansive boardrooms. His eyes were glued to video footage assembled by the FSB over the last week and presented by their director, Andrey Borodin. On one side of Koshenko was Vasily Popov, who had just returned from Ireland. On the other side sat Valentin Sokolov, minister of security. Alexei Lugovoy from the State Duma was also present, seated on a chair away from the main table.

Borodin had prepared the video footage in two parts. The first part was a clip showing the armed squad that had jettisoned Kasinov out of prison. The clip focused particularly on the group that exited the Humvees and turned on the reception security perimeter immediately after they had entered Krasnokamensk. The second clip was a scene from the room to the rear of the central control room, which was taken inside the facility whilst it was under attack.

After the first run-through of the clip, Borodin looked back towards Koshenko. "Given that the primary server had been disarmed once the facility was penetrated, the initial entry attack is the only footage we have to review from the main facility server. However, the footage from inside the room to the rear of the CCR was hosted on a different server. We have extended footage from this."

"What is he doing?" Koshenko shouted.

Nobody answered.

"Why is he shooting at Tishkovets's feet?" Koshenko added, watching the video footage in disbelief.

"I don't believe he's shooting at his feet, sir," Sokolov responded succinctly.

"What the hell is he shooting at, then?"

"I imagine he's shooting at the cables under the terminal," Sokolov clarified.

"What cables?"

"I'm not an IT expert, but I would imagine it's the power and fiber optic cables."

"Why is he shooting at them?"

"My guess is he did this in order to stop power and communications access to something inside the prison," Sokolov said confidently. "The power packs for the reserve CCR are all there in that room, separate from the main substation," he added, expanding his hypothesis.

"We have something else, sir, if I may?" Borodin interjected.

Koshenko waved, indicating to Borodin that he should proceed. Borodin closed the first file and opened up a second. On the screen, there appeared CCTV footage that the FSB had assembled of Roy Young entering the Kremlin fifteen days earlier. "I believe this is the same person," Borodin said. "He has the same build, same walk, same determination."

Koshenko stood, derisively pointing at the screen. "Pause that!" he shouted. Then he stared into the image. "Who is that man with blonde hair?"

Silence fell.

"With the billions I spend on intelligence each year," he said with a scoff, "is someone going to tell me who the hell this guy is?" He was particularly upset with Popov after he failed to convince Kasinov to return to the Motherland. Popov hadn't said a word since the president had given him an almighty haranguing when he returned to the Kremlin. Koshenko stamped his fist on the table. "This is totally unacceptable. A complete stranger is allowed to wander in the front doors of our most venerated establishments?"

Borodin and Sokolov exchanged vacuous glances at one another. Popov wasn't glancing at anybody. He just sat there with his head down.

Suddenly a voice from behind cried out. "His name is Roy Young!" Lugovoy said. He said it as if he had known the guy for years. "Former commander with the South African Armed Forces, doctor in social psychology, and now spends most of his time with a US-based security and intelligence service company called Securicon. They are one of the CIA's favorite outsource services companies."

Koshenko rotated in his seat to face Lugovoy. "How do you know who this is?"

"It's my job to know these things, sir."

Koshenko pursed his lips, tightened his jaws, and looked upwards. "So," he said contemptuously as he looked at his ministers one by one, "we have outsourced CIA operatives infiltrating our facilities randomly." After a vigorous headshake and a muttering of expletives, he craned his neck back towards Lugovoy. "Track him down, Alexei, and find out what he knows. Then I'll leave you to deal with Commander Young your own way."

Chapter 30
Young DOM

Mikhail looked up to see Natasha standing anxiously in the middle of the living room with her hands placed on her hips. She was wearing slim-fitting cigarette pants and a cream silk blouse, which apart from her bare feet was far more than she would usually be wearing at this time on a Saturday morning.

Her eyes drew down on him. "Darling," she began as her lips curled into an alluring closed-lipped smile.

"Yes, my love," he replied, thrusting his head back into the *Financial Times*. He wasn't reading. He was deliberating. More to the point, he was incensed, and had been ever since he overheard Natasha's conversation with Melanie several days earlier. *Who was that girl? And why was she cuddling up to Natasha, asking questions about me? Clumsy bitch.* His tolerance for ambiguity was being stretched once again. He didn't like feeling this way. It unsettled him and made him lose concentration. Nevertheless, he despised betrayal. She had betrayed him. *Now she must suffer.*

Natasha reached forward with her right hand, gently drawing the paper down from his gaze. "My sister called yesterday," she said timidly. "She's unwell. I need to take a trip to see her."

Mikhail lowered the paper and tried to put on a look of calm concern. "Your sister?" he enquired, trying to hide the surprise on his face. *She has a sister?*

"Yes. Veronika."

Come to think about it, I do have a vague memory of Natasha taking a week off back in 2002 to go and visit her sister in Cyprus. He recalled it not because of any family empathy for Natasha, but because it had been an absolute nightmare when she was away from the office that week. There was no one whose translation skills came close to hers, and he had felt unusually tetchy that week without the presence of her easy grace. He also missed the wafts of Coco Chanel Mademoiselle. "What's wrong with her?"

Natasha turned her head quizzically. "Do you really want to know, darling?"

"Of course," he declared, nodding intensely.

"It's female problems," Natasha answered, adroitly shifting the conversation into an area she hoped he would not venture.

Instead, Kasinov jumped off the sofa and stood next to her. He took her arms in his grip, a grip that was slightly too tight. Natasha grimaced. *Relax, Mikhail,* he thought, allowing his hands to loosen and stroke her wrists. "Of course I want to know. I want to take care of you." He spoke in a soft, almost sincere tone. "And that means your family, too."

Kasinov didn't naturally possess any characteristics of filial affection, something he had observed and learned from his own upbringing. However, based on the expression on her face, Kasinov assumed that this wasn't the response she expected or sought. Natasha looked uncertain how to respond. Mikhail continued to stare at her, waiting for her to break the uncomfortable silence, but fortunately, a smiling Dougie did that when he entered the hallway.

"Hello, Miss Volkonski," the friendly porter said. "Shall I take your bag down?"

Natasha turned and pointed to where she had placed her suitcase next to the lift door. "Thanks, Dougie. It's right there."

Kasinov yanked at her, turning her back to face him. "I'll come with you. Give me ten minutes, and I'll throw something in a bag."

"I don't think it's a good idea for you to be leaving the country at the moment, Misha," Natasha said, reinforcing her point with some male logic—something that resonated more clearly with Kasinov. "You might not get back in, my darling. It's too risky."

"I'll drop you at the airport, then," Kasinov said.

"It's okay. I've booked a car to take me." Natasha moved her arms back, carefully taking Mikhail's hands and placing them down by his side. "I'm booked on a flight to Cyprus. You stay here and relax."

Kasinov's expression changed, adopting a childish look of abandonment. "Okay. Have it your way."

Natasha planted a slow, lingering kiss on his lips and then pulled back fleetingly. "It's only for a few days. I'll call you when I land." Then she pushed the tip of her tongue into his mouth and circled his lips gently. "I'll miss you," she said softly as she pulled away.

Kasinov regarded her coldly. There was something in her eyes that seemed to suggest otherwise.

Natasha turned, slipped into her Jimmy Choo pumps, and scooped up her handbag. "Bye-bye, darling," she said without glancing back as she skipped out through the apartment reception and into the lift.

As soon as the lift door closed, Kasinov paced the perimeter of the living room for several minutes like he was a land surveyor setting out a site. He stopped by the doors to the outside terrace, impatiently stroking his chin with his right hand. After several moments of looking at his reflection in the glass, he opened the patio door,

stepped outside, and made a call. When the voice
on the other end answered, Kasinov looked out
towards the Thames.

"Alexei, this is Mikhail. I need you to do
something for me. It's that girl, Melanie Bauer."

~~~

Natasha's flight arrived into Larnaca as planned
at 6:20 p.m. Energized and ready to face the task
ahead, she was surprised to see a number of
flights had landed ahead of hers. The passport
queue was both lengthy and noisy. She didn't like
long queues and screaming kids. Instinctively, she
looked for ways to bypass all the holidaymakers
that embossed the floors of the reception room.
She quickly assessed her options, and then did a
typical sideways maneuver through two adjacent
queues with an apologetic pout smeared across
her face, both hands raised in midair as if she were
under arrest. Holidaymakers with screaming kids
can get a bit angry when glamorous Russian
women are seen jumping the line.

She arrived cheekily at the empty DIPLOMATIC
AND CREW line and proceeded to the desk. She
placed her large Prada bag neatly on the counter
and started rummaging. "Hello there," she said
zestfully. Then she gazed at the man whose name
badge read STAVROS ANTONOPOULOS.

The attendant smiled. "Yes, madam."

Natasha pursed her lips with melodramatic
sadness. "I'm sorry, but I'm not a diplomat, and
I'm not crew, either, but I did go out with a

diplomat once when I was younger. He was no fun." She recited the line with controlled humor in her voice as she flashed her turquoise eyes at the passport official. "And I applied for a job once with Aeroflot—they said that I wasn't pretty enough. Broke my heart."

"Well, madam, after that life of misery, you'd better show me your passport," Stavros said, matching her humorous tone.

Stravos inserted the passport face down into the compact scanning device in front of him. "Business or pleasure?"

"A little bit of both, I hope," Natasha replied with great excitement.

"Well then," he said, handing back the passport. "Enjoy your stay with us, Miss Volkonski."

The electronic sliding doors leading outside opened and Natasha emerged. Following her inveiglement at immigration, her efficient exit continued when her bag was first off the carousel, allowing her an early exit out to the arrivals area. Veronika, her younger sister of two years, looked on disbelievingly as she ran to meet her, threw her arms around her in a big, warm hug, and kissed her several times on both cheeks. "Hello, big sis. It's so nice to see you."

Youthful and full of energy, Natasha's younger sibling had come to work in Nicosia back in 2002 to represent a Russian investment fund called Dynge, a name that translated as "money." They had grown fifteen-fold since setting up in Cyprus back in 2000.

"Hello, little sis. You look amazing!"

Veronika was slightly taller than her sister, with straight blonde hair that came to just above her waistline. She had sea-blue eyes and two cute dimples guarding her curvaceous mouth. She was as attractive and beautiful as her elder sibling.

"Thanks." Veronika pulled back and cast a prodigious glance up and down her older sister's body. "You look amazing, too."

After the greeting, the two made their way out to the car park, arms clutched together as they chatted and laughed, oblivious to the attention they had gathered from the array of intrigued onlookers in and around the arrivals hall. Cyprus was full of semi-beautiful people, but two playful knockouts together? This was special.

When they arrived at Veronika's Jeep, they loaded Natasha's bag in the back and were on their way. "It's Saturday evening," Veronika said with a playful wink. "What would you like to do?"

"Well, I've sort of set up a meeting with this banker guy—you know, the guy who does all the account management for all of Mikhail's holdings?" Natasha replied earnestly. "We met him briefly the last time I was here with you. You remember?"

"You mean the younger version of the dirty old man?" Veronika teased. "Young DOM!"

"You're hilarious." Natasha broke into convulsions of laughter. "Yes, I think we're talking about the same guy. His name is Tony Wright."

"And why are you meeting Mr. Wright tonight? I thought your real Mr. Long-Term-Right just came back into your life."

Natasha paused with an uneasy look. "Veronika, there's something funny going on with Mikhail. He's been acting really strange since he got out of prison. He spends most of his time wandering around thinking people are trying to poison him. His whole personality has changed. He's suspicious, irascible, jealous, incorrigible— and that's when he's actually talking to me."

"Wow that's a long list of wrongs for Mr. So-Called-Right!"

Natasha sat in the front seat, looking straight out the window, her hands raised in surrender. "Honestly, I can't seem to get him to take his finger off the self-destruct button. He's being completely impudent. He's supposed to come from a country where the cultural DNA possesses a high degree of dealing with bullshit."

Veronika tapped her sister on the knee encouragingly. "Natasha," she began. "The problem is that, once you think you're at the top, then there's very little respect for hierarchy up the line. Mikhail still thinks he's up there frolicking around somewhere on cirrostratus, and nobody's got the balls to tell him otherwise."

"You're right." Natasha shrugged. "But there's more to it. I discovered something the other day:

a document. It referenced several names, including Mikhail's and two people that have been murdered. I don't know if Mikhail is in some trouble, or if this is just some coincidence."

"You know it's not the first time his name and murder have come up in the same sentence."

"I know." Natasha sighed. "You're right. You're always right, Veronika. That's why I've come to you for help with Mr. Wright."

"So what about Mr. Wright?"

"He may be able to help with some information that might put some sense around what's going on—you know, with Mikhail's financial affairs. Like, where have all the billions gone? How much money does he have? And what is he doing with it?"

"How does Mikhail have his money invested?"

"I'm not really sure, but I have it here somewhere," Natasha replied as she opened her briefcase-sized Prada bag and shuffled through some papers she kept in a plasticized folder. "Here it is," she uttered as she wiggled in her seat. "It says that the investment rationale is a mixture of value growth, strategic dividend, and income, midcap, and special situations. Oh, and opportunity plus structured products, whatever all that means." She raised the paper in the air and shrugged in confusion.

"Ah, that's just all mumbo-jumbo for different types of funds." Veronika chortled. "It's what they might call a balanced portfolio." After a brief pause, she glanced across at her sister. "Why would Mikhail want you muddling around in his financial affairs?"

Natasha's eye's remained focused on the front windshield. "He doesn't."

"Oh, so what does he think you're doing here in Cyprus?"

"Seeing you." Natasha's shot a glance at her sister. "You're sick. Girl problems."

Veronika chuckled. "Very well. But what's the real reason? Apart from doing some undercover fund work with Mr. Wright."

"I just needed to get away for a little while."

"Fair enough."

"Honestly, it's like being caught inside a revolving door with no passage. You are my passage, Veronika. Thank you."

"I presume he doesn't know you're meeting this Tony guy then."

"He has no idea."

"And what makes you think this Young DOM will share Mikhail's personal financial information with you?"

"Because, as you say, he's a Young DOM," Natasha replied with a smile.

"I see," Veronika countered playfully. "It's going to be one of *those* nights."

Natasha laughed. She hadn't laughed so much in a long time.

Chapter 31
Reflection

Roy sat outside in his Porte Santé patio, gazing through an arrangement of cypress sempervirens that shadowed the distant neoclassic-inspired panoramic landscape as he tried to recollect each piece of the oligarch jigsaw puzzle. He had arrived back to Florence earlier that evening after his informative trip to Ireland. Now he had to reflect and make sense of it all.

He had a fair idea how to fix the symptom, but he still needed to find the source of the problem. The poisoning of Alex Litvinenko in London, Melanie's stock market assessments of Russian-associated oil and gas positions, Vladimir Sakharshenko's cold-blooded murder in Budapest, the raid on Vladimir's house, St. Ledger's mysterious murder in Ireland—and now the revelations found at St. Ledger's Castle.

The trip to Ireland had revealed more than he had anticipated. What Catherine had found planted in the muzzle of St. Ledger's canon was a clear trail of connectivity to the provenance of Kasinov's Irish passport acquisition. It also provided details around the name change of the passport. Both email chains highlighted breach of diplomatic protocols in their development.

But how the hell are all these things connected? What am I missing?

Chapter 32
Nicosia

Natasha and Veronika arrived a few minutes after 8:00 p.m. at Blinkers Restaurant and Club in Nicosia, where they were to meet with Tony Wright and his colleague Giovanni Tardelli, an Italian investment banker who had just moved to Nicosia to work in the financial district.

Adorned in a tight-fitting, nude-color cocktail dress that revealed and complemented her well-defined and sallow arms and legs, Natasha confidently glided through the restaurant's entrance. Every customer at the reception bar rubbernecked in her direction faster than heads revolving at Wimbledon Center Court. Veronika, not to be outdone, was dressed in a Christian Dior creation, a slim-fitting, off the shoulder black number that came to just above the knee.

As they approached the bar, Natasha paused when she saw him sitting there. Her lips pouted with one hand at her side. Although she hadn't seen him in almost seven years, she could remember him quite well. Tony was late twenties, average height, and had a slim face, which seemed to stand out from the rest of his body as disproportionately smaller. She flashed her lively eyes and approached.

Dressed in a navy Savile Row replica suit, Tony jumped out of his seat as soon as he saw her.

"Hello, Tony," she said in an exceptionally seductive tone.

The whole bar paused to watch Tony approach her. Tony's mouth hung open, his lower jaw practically halfway down his chest, his eyes still watching Wimbledon. When they eventually settled, they magnetized in the direction of her breasts.

Yes, Tony, she thought. *No silicone additives. One hundred percent Russian.*

His head moved back to its upright position as he greeted her with a long embrace. "Hello, Natasha," he said, just barely managing to inhale enough air into his lungs to allow him to string a few words together. "Wow, you look amazing."

Her eyes twinkled. "Thank you, Tony."

In the time Tony Wright had moved there after graduating from Oxford, Cyprus had become one of the more attractive geographies to attract big money, offering competitive tax-zoned status, free trade portals, and a stable Euro-based currency subject to some degree of divergence from time to time, depending on the breadth of accounting frolics from Cyprus's adopted parent across the Mediterranean Sea. Regardless, offshore investors such as Kasinov continued to flock there, as money could be moved freely in and out.

"Natasha, say hello to Giovanni," Tony said after he withdrew from the overindulgent hug and turned to introduce his friend and colleague.

"Nice to meet you," Natasha replied politely. "This is Veronika—my sister. You might remember you met her briefly last time I was here."

"Yes, of course," Tony said. "Nice to see you again. Are you still here in Cyprus?"

"Yes. Now don't laugh." Veronika pointed at the two of them, waving her finger humorously. "I'm here with the Russian investment fund Dynge."

"Yeah, I've heard of them, all right. Hope it's better working there than it sounds."

"It is." Veronika grinned, displaying a perfect set of white, sparkling teeth. "I've been trying to help them with some rebranding here and internationally. Not getting very far, I'm afraid."

"Amazing we haven't bumped into each other," Tony said, shrugging.

"It's a big city for such a small place," Veronika said as she moved closer to Giovanni and slipped into the conversational Italian she had picked up from a summer spent in Rome.

Natasha shuffled in close to Tony as they took a seat at the bar. Facing each other, Tony ordered four fresh mojitos. Visibly excited at seeing him—or so it appeared, anyway—Natasha alternated the placing of her left hand between his shoulder and biceps as they spoke. Although it was not particularly loud around the bar area, when she addressed him, she moved in close to talk into his ear, placing her right hand on his opposite cheek. She knew Tony was not exactly James Bond in his quest to meet and be with women, and if he had been suffering from any intimacy deficiency over the recent months, she was certainly making amends for that now.

After spending a couple hours chatting and cavorting at Blinkers, Natasha piped up with a mischievous smile. "So are we going dancing?"

Tony looked at Giovanni, who nodded eagerly with an enormous beam dialed across his face. "I think we should."

Clearly surprised by the offer, Tony jumped from his stool, nodded to the bar attendant, and made an imaginary scribble with his right hand to signal for the bill.

"Let's go to Locca," Giovanni suggested.

After Tony had jotted out his signature, they grabbed a taxi outside. Tony sat perched in the back, calculatingly placed between Natasha and Veronika, with Giovanni in the front. The Italian looked back at his colleague enviously. After a ten-minute journey, they arrived at Locca.

More mojitos followed. Then the four of them hit the dance floor. Natasha had all the moves, falling into Tony's arms at every opportunity, twisting and twirling her way through every song. She was at her flirtatious best, and Tony clearly loved every moment of it.

After a frenzy of energy-sapping moves, Natasha emerged from the dance floor with Tony two steps behind. Veronika came out to meet them, giving her sister a big hug. "Sofa, nine o'clock, you and Young DOM," she whispered in her ear.

Amused by her sister's ingenuity, Natasha spun around, grabbed Tony's hand, and steered him over to a lavish sofa normally reserved for VIP guests. They lunged down into the settee and almost disappeared in amongst the copious quantity of geometric patterned cushions. Natasha admired them. She loved such appendages.

Now she needed to do what she had to do. She paused, gathered her thoughts, and looked up at him. "Tony, you are so clever," she said, flashing a pair of puppy dog eyes at him. "You know so much."

"Don't be silly, Natasha, you, you," he replied in his semi-inebriated, garbled voice, "are a, a very intelligent young lady." He punctuated his sentence completion with a nod.

"I don't know anything about money," Natasha pleaded with her hands in submission, "and the stock markets and that sort of thing."

"It's pretty straightforward really. Money in, money out—profit whisked away. That sort of thing."

"Would you mind teaching me a few things?"

"Of course."

"Maybe I could just ask a few questions?"

Delighted with the prospect of talking about his favorite subject, Tony sat up and gathered himself. "Okay, shoot," he said as a broad smile forged across his face.

Natasha began inquisitively. "Okay, tell me, what's the difference between value growth, strategic dividend, and income investments?"

"Well, value growth is about the long-term. Every year, you want to see something around six to nine percent growth in value. Whereas strategic dividend and income is more about investing into companies that may not grow as much, but they are rich in cash generation and pay handsome dividends twice a year. Oh yeah, and there are bonds, too, but they're pretty low returns at the moment." Tony had regained a little sobriety in his voice, Natasha noted.

"Oh, that sort of makes sense," she said, even though she didn't fully comprehend the response. She cared only that her question had been the perfect segue to allow her to ask what she wanted to ask in the first place. Her eyes made contact with Tony's again. "Is that how Mikhail's funds are invested?"

"Yes. In fact, most of his money is in those two portfolios. The rest in is direct equities—mainly medium and large cap companies."

"And what about the tax?"

"We have specialists who handle all of that. We run everything by them. They have more schemes to mitigate taxation to practically zero than they have employees."

"Your job sounds really interesting, handling all that money," Natasha asserted excitedly. "I'm sure Mikhail is just a little part of your business here."

"Little!" Tony's eyes almost hopped out of his sockets. "He's our single biggest client, and that's globally."

"Oh. How much does he have invested with you?"

"It's public knowledge that he personally made ten billion US dollars out of KasOil. It's market rumor that he lost a good chunk of that when the company was taken over by the government. What's not public knowledge or rumored is that, during the period from 2000 to 2002, nine billion US—give or take a billion—was invested by us here in Cyprus. We didn't invest any of the cash here onshore, though. It's a bit risky with some of the local banks."

"So let me get this straight, Tony; Mikhail made ten billion dollars from KasOil. The Kremlin think they got their hands on most of it when they arrested him, but in reality, he siphoned out about nine billion of that over a period of three years—

all managed by you and the tax specialists here in Cyprus?"

"Yep," Tony said with a proud smile.

"But how did he manage to appropriate that much cash? How the hell did he get it out from under Russia's microscopic treasury lens?"

"It was all perfectly legal. It was his money, and he extracted it through legitimate means. The auditors signed everything off on his taxes. I'm telling you, Natasha, he's clean."

Surprised by Mikhail's apparent authenticity, or maybe his brilliance, Natasha's grimace looked vacuous. It was a cross between ecstatically pleased and extremely perplexed. Either way, she wasn't going to show it. She cast a nauseated glance towards him, and then moved her eyes down into her Prada bag, as if there was something much more interesting inside. The bag was pretty empty, except for a passport, a little cash, a cell phone, a packet of cigarettes, and some makeup accessories. She smiled at him. "Excuse me," she said as she stood. "I'll be right back."

As she entered the ladies' room, she felt totally flushed from a combination of the drink, the dancing, and the revelations. She immediately splashed some cold water on her face and stared into her reflection in the bathroom mirror. She shook her head and then looked down. *I need air.* She ran back out and escaped through the rear entrance of the club.

She lit a cigarette. It helped her relax.

Maybe I'm just imagining it all, she thought. *Maybe Misha is clean and one hundred percent honest—at least as much as a Russian oligarch can be.*

Overwhelmed with ambiguity regarding her allegiance for Mikhail, she returned to Tony and sat down again, closer this time. With her financial future in the balance—secured, she hoped, by some concealed promissory note—she wanted to have one final Q&A session. She was cognizant that the conversation, as well as the whole evening, was way outside any client privilege boundaries, for him and for her, but she was determined to find the truth and prepared to push even further. She knew the risks, and she certainly knew the rewards. If Mikhail knew what she was up to, she would be in big trouble. If he knew what Tony was up to, he would probably be dead.

She took a deep breath and stroked her right hand against her forehead, moving the hair off her face. "So you're saying that it's all okay and above board, his business transactions."

"Yes, all the transactions stack up."

"Everything? There's nothing untoward whatsoever? Not one single dodgy transaction?" Her voiced strained, her eyes almost liquid. "Surely the auditors must have missed something that you, with your advanced IQ, would have found?"

"Well, there was one that they may have missed, actually, come to mention it," Tony responded.

"It may be nothing, but in my view, I thought the auditors would have looked into it a bit deeper. It was a payment to this one company. Three payments, in fact."

"See, I knew you are the cleverest guy in the world. To who was the payment made?"

"It was a Chechen guy called Pavel Belayev, the son of a former field commander of the Chechen Rebels."

"And you're sure that the source of the funds definitely came from Mikhail's account?"

"One hundred percent."

Visibly washed with emotion, she knew she had taken him through a series of coquettish tangents and had extracted whatever he had to give. Her job was done. What it meant remained to be seen.

Chapter 33
When in Rome

They sat outside under the morning sunshine at Café Lito on Piazza della Repubblica. It was 11:00 a.m. on Sunday, their final day in the Eternal City of Rome. It was supposed to be a reunion weekend for Melanie and Jeremy, and for the most part, it had been. Since their arrival two days earlier, they had enjoyed visiting Michelangelo's Basilica, the Gardens of the Villa Borghese, the Pantheon, and the Sistine Chapel, shopping along Via Condotti—and they even squeezed in a visit to the Coliseum. Despite this, there was still some tension in their relationship—particularly over the last two weeks. Fatigued by his hectic social engagement schedule with family functions and friends, Jeremy had been away quite a lot from London. Preoccupied with her work and her new covert investigative role in the mystery surrounding the escaped oligarch, Melanie's mind was no longer consumed with her illustrious boyfriend.

Sitting out at Café Lito, they had nothing else to worry about except checking in on time for their 7:00 p.m. flight back to London. Melanie looked across at her royal boyfriend, wondering, *Is he the one?* It was something she thought of quite often, especially recently. Her thoughts were interrupted when the waiter arrived with their order of antipasto, and at the same time, a muffled volley of rah-rah-ah-ah-ahs, courtesy of Lady Gaga howled out. Melanie reached for her bag and shuffled through it as frantically as if she was looking for a winning lottery ticket. As she got closer to the source, the melody became louder.

Jeremy glanced around the adjacent tables, wondering where the music was coming from. "Sounds like a cheap radio set somewhere close by," he profoundly pronounced.

His hypothesis was invalidated, however, when Melanie eventually plucked the culprit from her handbag. "Hello," she answered.

"Hi, Melanie. This is Roy. Hope I'm not bothering you."

Melanie's face lit up as she stroked her left hand through her hair. "Hello, there. Not at all. This is a pleasant surprise getting a call from you on a Sunday morning." She leaned back in the chair, unconsciously creating a perception of distance between her and her boyfriend.

"I went to Ireland to see Catherine St. Ledger," Roy said tersely, for it was Sunday morning and he didn't want to hold her up. "She asked me to help her find out what really happened with her father."

Melanie began to wiggle in her chair, interested as she was to hear what happened. "What did you find out?"

"She was quite distressed. She said she couldn't believe that her father would ever commit suicide—that it simply wasn't in him; that he loved life every day; and that, despite the challenges he encountered, he always looked on the positive side of things. Anyway, after a little research, we found something hidden in the muzzle chamber of her father's old cannon. It was a copy of two carefully concealed emails: one confirming the transfer of funds to an Irish passport official for twenty thousand euros back in 2001 to secure a passport for Kasinov, and a second email confirming the process used to change the name on the passport."

"Oh my God!" she cried. "You know what that means?"

"Yes. It means he's a criminal—maybe not a major one, but he bribed someone to get that passport. This could put a completely different angle on the whole premise for Kasinov's residence. It also means David St. Ledger didn't commit suicide."

"Do you want me to come there and meet you?" Melanie spoke in a soft and friendly tone.

"No, it's a long way for you to come just to

look through a couple of emails."

Melanie glanced around as if he could be in her line of vision. "I'm not far away at all," she murmured mischievously.

"Oh, where are you?"

Melanie let out a chuckle. "I'm in Rome, actually."

"In that case, that would be very nice."

Melanie caught a quick glimpse of Jeremy sitting opposite her, looking somewhat peeved by her frivolity on the phone. He eyed her suspiciously, his gaze inwardly contorted, his head slightly angled as he made a motion as if to enquire to whom she was speaking. Melanie remained engrossed in her conversation, pretending not to see his gestures. "Okay, hon. I'll see what I can do. Just need to check the train schedule." Then Melanie pulled the phone from her ear and switched off.

She looked back up at Jeremy, who was now on the edge of his seat and trying to keep his disbelief concealed.

"Who was that?" the forlorn metro man asked.

"That was Roy—Roy Young," she said as she delicately placed her phone in her bag. "You know; the guy we met at Annabel's a few weeks back?"

"Yes, lovely fellow. What is he up to?"

Melanie sat up, all excited. "He's in Florence. He's picked up some vital clues about a case he's working on."

"Sounds intriguing," he said cynically. "You two sounded incredibly friendly on the phone, I must say. It was like listening to Mulder and Scully from *The X-Files*."

"It's nothing," Melanie said dismissively. "We're just good friends. I'm just helping him out a bit with this whole Mikhail Kasinov thing."

"I gather from your conversation that you want to go to Florence to meet with him."

"Well," Melanie paused, "I am only an hour away."

"Sure," Jeremy threw his arms into a flying motion. "I can fly back to London on my own. No problem."

"Ah," she said, smiling at him. "You're such a sweetie."

Jeremy shook his head. "This oligarch thing seems to have taken over your life."

"It's just business, Jeremy. You know what it's like."

"Where will you stay?" he asked searchingly.

"I'll figure that out when I get there. I'll just shack up somewhere. At worst, I'm sure Roy has a spare room. He can put me up."

"Oh! And you think that's okay?"

"What do you mean?"

"To go and stay with an ex-boyfriend!"

"Jeremy!" she exclaimed, lifting her hands in a mock surrender. "We are just friends. That's all."

The two of them stared at each other in sustained silence. Jeremy had a look of suspicion;

Melanie, one of confusion.

Jeremy shook his head, clearly outraged with what he had heard. "Fine," he snapped. "Off to Florence with you."

In response, Melanie remained taciturn, looking down vacantly into her plate of untouched antipasto.

Jeremy stood. "Take care of yourself, Melanie," he said sternly. "Don't bother coming back." Then he walked away.

Melanie didn't know what to think or what to feel. They had only been together for five months. They were the perfect match, everyone said. On paper, they might have been. However, if you take away the cellulose fibers and the ink, perhaps they weren't.

Is he the one? I think that answers that one.

~~~

Roy was running behind schedule. His concern over Kasinov's demeanor was growing. He was preoccupied trying to establish the connection between the former Russian billionaire and the three murder charges that had landed KasOil's former head of security Vitaly Kuznetsov in custody. *There must be a connection. Of course there's a connection. But where's the proof?*

As he made his way to the front door, he opened the hallway closet and grabbed a warm, petrol-blue bomber top. Before he reached the door, he stopped to check inside his pockets for keys. Wriggling his hands inside, he pulled out two tickets from the Arsenal. The last time he had worn it was when he went to Emirates Stadium. He laughed, recalling that day and how Melanie had reacted to Kasinov's countenance. *She's a bit sensitive sometimes.* He threw the tickets onto the hall table, and in the middle of them, a piece of paper folded in several layers slid out. He felt something inside him drawn to the semi-concealed note. He unfolded and studied it. It was the instructions Kasinov had given him regarding the box location. *We didn't even need them.*

Roy held the note aloft, studying it. Compelled by some abstract sense of familiarity, he studied the handwriting on the paper and pondered. It hadn't dawned on him at the time Kasinov handed him the directions, but he thought that he had seen similar handwriting before—not from someone he knew, but from something he studied during his time at Cambridge.

On the sheet, a number of words stood out in a distinctive scribe: *Emirates VIP Club entrance, level 3—enter after gate marked P!*

Intrigued by his recollection, he rushed back to his office and pushed open the door. Inside, the room was Spartanly furnished with four oak-clad chairs spread symmetrically around a circular table. Against the wall was a double row of shelving that housed an accumulation of all sorts of books: academia, fictional novels, some retro classics, and a few archetypal Italian cookbooks. The latter was the most recent to join the assortment.

Under pressure for time to collect Melanie at the train station, Roy desperately leafed through the academic section, searching a series of his Cambridge psychology textbooks. Eventually he tugged at one, pulling it out—*Graphology Psychoanalysis,* by Fritz Schulze. He tapped the author's name and thought, *This is the one.* He placed the book on the table and paged through it feverishly, searching to see if he could find the analogous writing style that he had come across before.

After the initial frenetic momentum elapsed, he started to flick through each page more stolidly, and eventually there it was. He knew he had seen it before. It was the same small lettering, the same definitive short pen strokes, the same angular orientation, and the same primary letter stroke tails. The writing analysis that he was studying was not that of Mikhail Kasinov; it belonged to Peter William Sutcliffe, the famous British serial killer dubbed "The Yorkshire Ripper." Although Roy wasn't around at the time, he recalled how Sutcliffe was convicted of murdering thirteen women in 1981, and was currently serving twenty sentences of life imprisonment in Broadmoor Hospital. Roy wondered if it was a coincidence that Kasinov's writing style matched so closely with that of Sutcliffe's. *Is this Kasinov's real writing style? Or perhaps it's a new one he has adopted for some clandestine reason?* Whichever it was, Roy wouldn't put it past him.

Energized by his discovery, Roy scrolled down the page to where it highlighted a number of examples with similar text that came from a collection of convicted serial killers. Each killer had been in long-term custodial residence, and each one directed through a program of surreptitious psychometric testing. It was a program that included an analysis of, among other things, writing styles. According to Schulze, distinct characteristics common to this grouping were found to exist.

Roy looked at his watch. Then he read on:

Serial killers like Sutcliffe typically possess some ideological motivation defined with the characteristics of their handwriting. Typically, their brains are extremely organized, with well-structured planning skills to continuously repeat crime after crime, as well as covering up their actions. These serial killers share a common ground: particular handwriting characteristics, possession of a high level of intelligence, and most probably have endured prolonged separation or abandonment in their lives, either from their parents or later in life.

Although up to 80 percent are schizoids characterized generally by emotional aloofness, 20 percent are enigmatic and melodramatic. The writing style of this smaller group is generally characterized by a slow, methodical process, the same manner in which they plan their crimes. Regardless of their external personality, the typical graphic signs of the writing of a killer include:

Vigilant and tense handwriting

Extremely strong pressure

Narrowness

Emphasized upper zone

Left of upright slant

High upper zone

Peculiarities and exaggeration

Large or extreme height differentials

Abundance of punctuation marks or lack of them

Such writers can expect to be any combination of psychopathic, schizophrenic, and delusional.

Roy closed the book and tapped on Schulze's embossed name at the bottom of the glossy covering. *Of course there's a connection,* he thought. *But where is the proof?*

Chapter 34
Florential

Excited about her unexpected adventure to Florence, Melanie arrived at the Santa Maria Novella railway station on Sunday at 5:00 p.m. Fortuitously for her, the scheduled service from Rome arrived early due to the cancellation of an earlier carriage. Melanie checked her watch as her mind shifted to Jeremy. She estimated that he would be on his way to the airport by now. Despite having concluded their final conversation on a psychological win, she guessed he was probably quite angry with her. *I'm doing the right thing. I have to see Roy. If anyone is the one, it's him.*

Mildly apprehensive about her venture into Tuscany, Melanie arrived at the platform arrivals area and stopped to scan the voluminous atrium-lit hall. Unaware that Roy had been sidetracked by a journey back through psychological academia, she couldn't see any sign of him.

I hope he hasn't forgotten.

She wasn't perturbed as she took a seat at a café under the central atrium just near the exit. *He'll be here.* She climbed onto an unoccupied stool and took out her phone. She had a few things to keep her occupied.

~~~

Ten minutes later, Roy rushed into the station platform at pace, his leather shoes sliding along the old marble tiles as he tried to bring himself to a halt. He stopped perfectly, right in the center of the hall. Several people noticed his spectacular entrance and nodded in amazement. Melanie wasn't one of those. Roy scanned the area and saw her straightaway. She looked graceful, dressed in a floral summer dress under a light coat with more colors than a fully blossomed oriental poppy. She was sitting on a stool in the corner café with her head buried in her BlackBerry, her fingers moving faster over its diminutive console than a Liberace concerto.

As Roy moved closer to her, he wondered how long it would take before she would notice him. He paused and smiled. For the first time, he noticed how her bespectacled appearance amplified her beatific sexuality. He could feel himself falling for her again.

Can't let that happen, Roy.

Eventually, after crunching the keypad on the BlackBerry for about a minute longer, she glanced up. When she saw him, she jumped out of her stool, ran over to him, and wrapped her arms around him.

"Hello there," he said, beaming down at her.

"How long have you been here?"

"Long enough to watch you wear a layer off that keypad of yours," he said, motioning to the phone. "Sorry I was a bit late. I got sidetracked."

"No problem," she replied, placing the phone back inside her handbag. "I was just catching up on a few emails."

"Very good," Roy said, holding up his hands and twisting his body in the direction of the station's main entranceway. "Welcome to Florence."

Melanie jumped up and down with excitement. "I'm so glad to be here," she pronounced with a clap of her hands.

She was visibly happy to see him, and it was difficult for her not to show it. Roy knew she wasn't very good with holding back feelings. That was what worried him.

They made their way out of the station and over to Roy's Jeep. As they got into the car, Roy glanced across at her in the passenger seat to see the refracted sunlight cut across her shoulders at a low angle, reflecting a softer beauty in her than he had ever before seen.

"Amazing," he said, shaking his head from side to side.

"What's amazing?" she asked.

Roy glanced away to insert his seat belt clip. "You are," he said. Then he returned his gaze at her, looking straight into her hazel eyes. "You look amazing."

Melanie wriggled in the seat with a degree of mischievousness written across her face. "Oh. Thanks."

"You hungry?" he asked, his eyes now focused on the profusion of traffic along Via Valfonda. "I thought we could go and get something to eat."

"That would be very nice," Melanie replied.

"A quick change first?"

"Sounds good."

"I've booked you a room at the hotel near my place. It's really quaint. They only have five rooms in total, so you're privileged. The owners are really lovely people."

"Oh, okay. That's lovely, thank you."

Unfailingly inspired by Florence's history and natural beauty, Roy gave her a brief history tour of the area, chatting and laughing as they meandered their way through the landscaped hills and cambers of the country roads to Porte Santé until they arrived at the boutique country hotel. He dropped her off and agreed to pick her up for dinner at about 7:30 p.m. Roy thought that would give her enough time to have a rest and a change after her short journey from Rome.

He had something else he had to do.

Back at his villa, his mind was doing somersaults after revisiting his Cambridge graphology textbook. Years of doing what he did made him question everything. Now he was beginning to question the CIA's so-called *humanitarian motives* to jailbreak Kasinov. He knew from experience that everything was done for a reason. Now he didn't believe the reason he was given.

Who stands the most to gain? Who will get access to Russian oil when Kasinov assumes power?

He fired up his MacBook Air and pulled up an email that Melanie had sent him from a few days earlier. It was the research note that she had issued the day after Kasinov's escape. He studied it. He read it a second time, and then a third. Then he launched his web browser and typed: *Major oil and gas stock trends.*

More than two thousand responses came up, referencing an overabundance of reports from banks, institutions, stockbrokers, the FT, and anybody else that had an interest in writing about oil and gas. He eyed the keyboard again and modified his search. "Major oil and gas stock movements in last two weeks since Mikhail Kasinov's release—Russian development focus."

The first return referenced an almost identical title to the one Roy had inputted. He opened the PDF attachment and studied the executive summary. It headlined with a chart highlighting the share price performance of all the major oil and gas development entities since Kasinov's departure from Siberia. He studied the chart, and one name stood out from the rest. One stock price exceeded all others in terms of volume and growth in the last twelve days: Zeron Oil.

He picked up the phone and scrolled down until he found Lee Carter's number in Washington. He checked his watch: 5:45 p.m. *That's 11:45 a.m. in Washington.* He pushed the call button, and Carter answered on the first ring.

"Lee, I need your insight on something."

"Sure, what's up?"

"What's the history between Zeron Oil's CEO, Brad Dunkley, and your illustrious president, Bill Peterson?"

Pause. "Why do you ask?"

"Call it a hunch."

"A hunch about what?"

"A hunch about the real reason I spent a year getting Kasinov out of Siberia."

"In that case, there is some history between them."

"Go on."

"It's not that well known, but Dunkley and Peterson go back a long way. They're both Texans. In fact, they're both Houstonians. I think they even schooled together. I understand that they were good friends growing up."

"And since then?"

"When they finished high school, they went their separate ways, attending different universities and following separate careers. Dunkley did chemistry at Texas A&M, and Peterson studied law at Harvard, if I recall correctly."

"Okay, thanks Lee."

Roy switched the off button on his mobile and pondered. He wondered about the CIA's intervention with Kasinov. The humanitarian rationale was wearing thin. He guessed it was more about Peterson trying to help Dunkley—more specifically, USA Inc. helping Zeron Oil.

Chapter 35
Zafferano

Thirty-five miles away, a white Bombardier Challenger private jet 300 landed at Aeroporto di Firenze, and a small, cherub-faced, rotund man wearing dark glasses and a light suit emerged. As he strolled along the airport's runway with two robustly built Russians in dark suits and dark glasses two steps behind him, he thought about the phone call he had received from his superior before getting on the plane.

From our information, the target is now in Florence.

He wondered what the target was doing in Florence. Then he stopped thinking, realizing he wasn't paid to think—just act. Alexei's orders were quite clear: "Find them and find out what they know. Then deal with them."

He took out his phone and dialed the number he had saved. "Okay, we're in Firenze," the cherub said. "Calling in, as requested."

"Proceed to track the target down," the voice

on the other end said.

"And what do we do then?"

"Depending on how good their answers are, I'll decide what to do next."

"But what if I can't contact you?"

"You won't have to. I'm here in Florence. I'll be there to make sure we do this right."

~~~

Showered, changed, and most importantly, punctual, Roy sat in the diminutive reception area of Melanie's boutique hotel. He flicked through a copy of *Firenze Spettacolo* as he waited. He was smartly attired in blue jeans, a palatinate blue shirt that propelled the blueness of his eyes, and a navy V-necked sweater with a light navy jacket. Moments later, Melanie emerged from the brass-clad lift door. Roy jumped up from the art deco couch just in time to receive a hug and a kiss on the cheek.

"I see you're still using that Chanel stuff," she said.

It was the same cologne he used back in 2005. "A liberating, feral aroma," is how the bottle described it. He wondered if that's what she could smell. "Yeah, you know me. Old habits."

"Anyway, you smell nice," she said as she gazed at his torso. "And you look very handsome."

"You scrub up pretty well yourself," Roy said. She wore pencil black jeans and taupe merino wool sweater with a white blouse that protruded above the neckline and beneath the sleeves and waistline. She held a charcoal-colored zip-out hooded parka delicately folded over her arm.

"Where are we off to?" Melanie asked excitedly.

"Piazza della Signoria. It's just inside the city. There's a beautiful restaurant there called Zafferano." Roy led her out through the hotel's ornate arched entrance. "It's one of my favorites."

"Sounds lovely—I'm famished."

~~~

After a short drive from Porte Santé, they found Zafferano's and were seated close by the open-plan perimeter. No sooner had they taken their seats than Melanie rolled up her sleeves as if to indicate a significant amount of work was about to commence. "Where do we start?" she asked eagerly.

"As I said, I went to see Catherine St. Ledger," Roy said. "Some place she has there—full of character. Anyway, to cut a long story short, after a little searching, we found two emails that her father had obscured in the nose of this antique canon up on one of the castle's turrets. They basically confirm that Kasinov's passport was acquired fraudulently." Roy pulled out a white manila envelope and reached inside, handing her the two sheets. "Have a look."

Melanie glanced through the first, then the second, then back to the first again. A disbelieving wince appeared on her face. "If this gets out," she said, pausing to look up at Roy, "he's in big trouble."

"Yeah," Roy replied. "But I think that's his business."

"C'mon, Roy," Melanie said impulsively. "I'm not judging, but might I remind you that you've aided and abetted the escape of the world's most famous convict, you're caught up in trying to find Sakharshenko's killer, and now St. Ledger's killer, most probably. The Russians and the British are having a political ego contest that could become intractable. And you, you're just cool and calm and so relaxed!"

Roy could feel her eyes hit him like a laser penetrating the back of his retina. "I can't control what's happening nine hundred miles away, but I can do my very best to influence it," Roy said as he raised his hands in submission. "Anyway, I'm going to find out one way or another who killed Vladimir and St. Ledger."

Melanie just shook her head.

Time to change the subject before she pushes too far, Roy thought. "How's work?"

"Oh, it's all fine." Melanie sighed. "That reminds me, I'll have to call Finlay in the morning and tell them I'm doing some offshore research." She let out a little chuckle.

"I'm sure they won't mind." Roy gazed at her reverently. "From what I hear, you're a bit of a superstar inside UGC."

"Thanks, but I'm just doing my job."

"You'll have to help me with something here," Roy delved inquiringly. "I don't get the logic around the culture of the city. First the stock markets celebrate Kasinov's release as if the prodigal son has returned. Then, the next day, something else happens to him, and the market will probably be selling off in a frenzy, like he's some old nuclear power plant leaking radiation?"

"There's a distinct science around investment logic," Melanie replied profoundly. "The stock market, however . . . I'm afraid it's one big amorphous entity, susceptible to the irrationality of misguided perceptions."

"And where does Zeron Oil lie on that continuum of reality?" Roy asked.

"Sometimes there is no logic to stock market movements," Melanie tried to explain. "In theory, Zeron's earnings could double overnight if they get their hands on Russian oil. There's logic right there. In reality, though, more often than not, it can only be explained by people's perception of the future at any given time, and this may have nothing to do with reality. To be totally honest, a lot of people that operate in this space are greedy, and several of them rather ghastly, I might add."

Roy looked back at her in amazement, trying to fully understand the context and extent of the "ghastly" adjective. "Sounds terrible."

"It's a bit like Kasinov's personality," she said rhetorically. "You know, all over the place."

Roy laughed. "He's a bit special, all right—more than you could imagine."

"What do you mean?"

"I did some research on his handwriting. There's something unique about it. Well . . . not altogether unique."

~~~

Unperturbed by the geopolitical fracas that emerged around him, Kasinov sat before the mirror, motionless and apathetic. The reflection staring back at him was a rather disconsolate-looking figure of a man with paper toweling tucked around the inside of his shirt collar. He looked more like a contemptuous movie star about to go on set than an ex-billionaire and president-elect for the Russian Federation.

The makeup lady buffed his cheeks and then his chin, after which she layered one last coat of foundation on his face. Behind her on either side, two tall men dressed in black jackets, black trousers, and black shirts with black ties watched impassively. Paranoid for his own safety, Kasinov had hired around-the-clock security to be with him every time he left the apartment, as well as having them placed outside the apartment while he was there. He snarled at how his reintegration into society was proving avocational compared with his former status as the super-CEO.

Tonight was the night when everything was going to change.

He smiled.

The makeup lady took one step back and looked at him timidly through the mirror. "There you are, sir. I believe we're all done."

Kasinov rotated his head from side to side as he assessed her work, his appearance visibly burnished from the prettification. He nodded. He approved.

Tonight was a big night for him—perhaps the biggest night of all. Tonight, he planned to reveal to the world his story, the true story.

A young man with a clipboard, floral shirt, bowtie, and shoulder braces approached him. "This way, Mr. Kasinov," he said in a soft voice. Then he piloted his guest into the studio and showed him his seat. "You have a couple minutes, sir."

~~~

Before Roy could answer the question Melanie had carefully planted, he noticed the maître d' holding out the remote control with his arm stretched horizontally. His right index finger compressed the upward volume arrow as a crowd started to gather around the TV. Both Melanie and Roy turned to look as the tumult gained momentum.

"What's going on?" Melanie asked.

At the same time, Roy heard a young voice from the crowd shout out. "It's that guy—the one who says he's going to be the new Russian president."

Roy peered through the crowd to the TV screen. There, he saw a picture of a composed Kasinov adjusting his necktie from what looked like a characteristic studio set. An arrogant smile crossed his face as he sat before the sky blue background, poised as if to deliver a history lecture in entrepreneurial governance.

What the hell is he up to now?

Before Roy could say anything, Melanie's phone rang. Fortunately, Lady Gaga didn't get to make an appearance. Melanie had put it on silent mode earlier. It gave off a purring vibration instead. Roy looked down and saw Natasha's name appear in the caller ID. Melanie grabbed the phone, got up from the table, and moved away from the commotion to take the call.

"Be right back," she said, signaling back to Roy to carry on.

Melanie placed her free hand over one ear and the other hard against the BlackBerry. "Hello!" she cried out.

Roy's gaze was interrupted when the waiter arrived at the table with a bottle in one hand and a heavily starched cotton white napkin over the other. "Red wine?" the waiter enquired in a deep accent.

Distracted by a combination of the commotion on the big screen, the unsolicited wine waiter—a man he recognized, a man he knew was not actually a waiter—and Melanie's flailing hand signals, Roy suddenly felt the click of a safety catch at his head on one side and the pinch of a blade to the other.

He didn't look. He didn't need to. He knew what was there.

Instead, Roy stared up at the impostor waiter querulously. "I know you. You don't work here."

The man dressed as a waiter nodded back at him calmly, and then a distinctly pungent wet cloth surrounded Roy's face.

Then the line on Melanie's phone went dead.

Seconds later, she was unconscious, too.

Seconds later, she was sprawled out in the rear of a white transport vehicle, lying on the floor next to Roy.

The entire restaurant patronage that gawped at the screen missed the concealed exodus of the fashionably dressed couple. Then the official waiter arrived with two orders of pasta. He looked around. He looked down. He looked up. Then he went back to the kitchen and approached the maître d'. "The people at table six have disappeared," he said.

Chapter 36
Histrionics

The director raised one hand, showing his five fingers to signify five seconds to go before the slow, silent countdown began.

Kasinov nodded confidently. *Just remember, I am more powerful than Koshenko.*

Opposite him, Angela Boddington sat in the chair of her Brentford studio in West London and fixed her hair, cleared her throat, and took a last sip of her water. She was young, beautiful, and voluptuous. More importantly, though, according to *Time* magazine, she was the most successful political correspondent they had at Sky News.

She must be apprehensive, Kasinov thought. He knew she had built up enormous credibility in the last year after successfully interviewing several world premiers during a series of scheduled political visits to London. He guessed, though, that she had probably never interviewed anyone like him before. In Britain, she was the quintessential political reporter. That was why he had chosen her. To the rest of the world, though, she was just another good-looking female reporter. *That will probably change after tonight*, he thought.

The final finger showed one second, and the interview of the century was about to begin.

"Tonight, ladies and gentlemen, we have a very special guest in the studio," the young presenter revealed. "In 2002, he was declared the wealthiest man in Russia, ranking twelfth on the Forbes list of billionaires with a net worth of over ten billion US. Although probably not the best known here in London, he is certainly known as the most successful Russian oligarch. He has just spent the last seven years in prison in Siberia, where he authored the book *Siberian Liberty*." The camera angle changed to show both interviewer and interviewee sitting opposite one another at a slightly offset angle. "Mikhail Kasinov, welcome."

"Thank you, Angela, for inviting me to the show," Kasinov replied, looking very relaxed and confident next to the exceptionally attractive interviewer.

"Firstly, I'm pleased to say I've read your book—with great interest, in fact. I must say I had several, 'Wow, did that really happen?' moments." Boddington raised her hands in mock surprise. Since its publication, *Siberian Liberty* had been the subject of many book reviewers' columns, political correspondents' talk shows, and literally thousands, if not millions, of social media conversations. To many, his book was considered as the harbinger of the next Russian generation. To others, it was a load of tripe. "So tell me—what kind of person is the real Mikhail Kasinov. Tell us about the man behind the book."

"I would say I'm a fair and caring person, Angela," Kasinov commenced in a sincere tone. "I'm looking to find a way to create a new Russian democracy for the people—something that has been long overdue." He leaned towards her, his arms folded in front of him on the table. "Do you know that Russia holds the largest gas deposits in the world, with sixteen hundred and eighty trillion cubic feet of gas?" he asked rhetorically. "This is almost twenty percent of the world reserves. In addition, it holds approximately six percent of the total oil reserves with seventy-four billion barrels of oil through its Arctic and sub-Arctic fields. This is the eighth highest in the world." He leaned back again with his arms lifted in animation. "Russia is capable of so much economic growth, but unfortunately, the current political and social hierarchy doesn't want to change. They are stuck in a cycle from which they can't escape."

"Okay," Boddington responded. "Let's talk about some of the underlying economic statistics here for a moment, shall we?"

Kasinov nodded in return.

"What sort of growth do you think Russia can achieve, given the current global outlook?"

Boddington queried, transitioning smoothly from her initial moralistic probe to test the underlying fundamental economics of his plans.

"There is no reason in the wide world why the Russian economy should be lagging behind China's near double digit economic growth." Kasinov raised his right arm into a horizontal position with his palm facing down to signify a measure of depth. "We have more resources at our disposal than they have—significantly more."

"You're saying that you believe Russia's economy should be growing at ten percent plus, then?"

"Damn right it should be," Kasinov exclaimed as he leaned back in his chair. After a brief pause, he surged forward again. "The system is holding it back. Today, I can discern very little difference between so-called *pro-capitalist* and *pro-Communist groups* within the Russian political legislature," he added in a sardonic tone.

"So, Mikhail," the Sky News correspondent said gracefully, "I listened to an interview you did a few weeks ago, not that long after you escaped from prison. In the interview, you said you were going to enter the political arena." She nodded, seeking tacit acceptance.

In response, Kasinov maintained a steely gaze on her.

She glanced back at her notes. "You implied that you may in fact want to become the next president of Russia. Is this really your agenda?"

Crazed by his perpetual affliction for power, Kasinov, on hearing the question, couldn't resist the opportunity. "Yes, I believe I am the special one," he said proudly, his eyes half shut with his head nodding in a self-congratulatory ritual. "I'm the one most qualified and experienced to run the Motherland." A shrewd smile broke across his face. "I'm extremely excited about my new adventure into politics. It's a great time to be entering this arena, into a whole new period in my life. It's like the next chapter for me."

In the media, Kasinov had read some very positive reports, quoting his plans as overtly democratic and resourceful. Expectedly, though, some were more scathing, quoting his tactics as surreptitiously despotic—as if he were striving for some unattainable utopian society, portending much worse things to come.

Boddington eyed him carefully. "And what about the comments we see in some of the editorials that talk about your plans being somewhat, shall I say, ephemeral?"

There was silence. Kasinov remained sternly vacuous. He could see beads of sweat forming on Boddington's forehead, about to roll down her face.

Then she twitched her head briefly. "What do you say about that?" the Sky News reporter added after a brief pause.

"I'm not offended by these comments," Kasinov replied before pursing his lips. "I've seen them written before—a lot more disparaging than that, in fact." He smiled. "Angela, in all my business transactions, I've always thought about the long term, and about sustainability. I've always promoted transparency, and have always strived to eradicate corruption. In the early years, when we developed the KasOil story, it was a turbulent but extremely successful development phase for groups of emerging capitalists. When I transformed KasOil into a global oil and gas major, I did it by changing the fundamental business model." Kasinov spoke with ostensible passion, believing that he was invincibly virtuous. "I put an end to all dubious business practices and promoted a code of ethics that met the demands and moral obligations we subscribe to—and of course practices required by investors on the London Stock Exchange."

In his mind, he may have been the vanguard at the Anti-corruption League table when compared to the peer group comparators against whom he measured himself. In the real world, though, his ranking may have been significantly different. No one had the guts to tell him that—except maybe Koshenko and Popov. They weren't there to tackle him, and Boddington didn't look like she was going to challenge him on the subject.

"I have to ask you this," Boddington queried, moving forward in her seat. "In 1977, you acquired the rights to a number of oil and gas fields throughout Russia. Following this, you were acclaimed as Russia's most successful oligarch. You say in your book that you had to invest two hundred and fifty million US at risk. How can you say that this was really a risk when you subsequently turned around and listed the company here in London on the stock exchange with a market capitalization of twenty billion pounds?"

Kasinov felt like throwing his eyes to heaven, but didn't. He had been asked this same question so many times before. "At that time, I didn't have ten million dollars, let alone two hundred and fifty million. I had to borrow most of the money. It was a big personal risk. I had to sign off the rights to my business, my house, to everything I owned in order to borrow that money. I chose those reserves wisely." Kasinov shrugged. "All the fields I picked were rich in easily accessible hydrocarbon onshore enclosures. I used to be an oil assessor when I was a bit younger, so I knew what I was looking for in the seismographs. Nothing wrong with that—I was just using my trade. It paid off, I think, because I chose the right ones."

Kasinov recalled like it was only yesterday, how under Boris Yeltsin, he watched the new Russia transform from a central planning system to a market-based economy. Although he wasn't going to amplify this live on Sky News, the changes included the establishment of a new banking system, the opportunity to buy and sell property, and the establishment of the ruble as a tradable international currency—all necessary constructs in order to attract international foreign investment to boost the new economy. Like any economy, Russia needed to develop a comparable, if not better, market economy to its international peers, and entrepreneurs like Kasinov needed this to attract international capital.

After some early rounds of posturing, Yeltsin sold the country's oil reserves and assets off to a selected few insiders on valuations significantly less than their inherent value, thus creating an oligarchy of nouveau rich Russian elite. This was the prize Kasinov had had his eye on. In the end, he would walk away with the best prize of the lot: the offshore Arctic and onshore Siberian fields. He may have outfoxed Yeltsin, but so did several others.

"I want to talk for a moment if we can about the period prior to the success of KasOil," Boddington said, interrupting his ruminations. "I read with interest that, after a string of successful private entrepreneurial initiatives, you spent time as the deputy minister of fuel and energy of Russia. So I want to check if I've got this right." Boddington looked up at him after shuffling through her notes. "One minute, you're this budding successful entrepreneur, and the next, you're running around po-faced inside the Kremlin. How does that work?"

Kasinov thought her questions were becoming contentious, bordering vexatious, but she had a show to deliver. So did he. He had remained remarkably stolid for the interview thus far, but suddenly he felt sparked into a more relaxed and fervent interviewee. "I received an opportunity to utilize my degree in chemical engineering within our government, and I took it," he said, smiling. "I can't say it was the most exciting part of my life, but it served its purpose. I made some good friends and contacts, which always helps. When the state asset sale came up, shortly after that, I decided I would make a bid. I won."

"And what do you say about all these charges against you?" Boddington probed. "Particularly the one about you purloining billions of dollars in tax revenues from the Russian government?"

"It's not my fault if they kept changing the tax interpretation rules retrospectively. They just wanted me out. They would have done anything to make that happen. They dreamt up all those charges, but I never believed they would have the audacity to proceed to trial. Maybe I was naive," Kasinov added in surrender. "The government under Koshenko's leadership froze shares in KasOil immediately after my arrest." He raised his hands emotionally. "They took my company away from me."

Kasinov could feel his eyes welling up. Before Boddington could say anything, he jumped upright in his chair. "The State Duma destroyed me, and they destroyed all shareholder value along with it," he said with his finger pointing at some illusory Kremlinite in the studio. "I'm not the one who has stolen anything. The Russian Duma is the one that is capricious. They are a ruthless hierarchy with a web of self-interest."

His planned emotional tirade against the Kremlin was gaining momentum—perhaps too much momentum for TV, if there was such a thing. Boddington had given him the perfect soapbox.

The number one Sky News correspondent took a sip of water and let out a little cough. "So tell me, Mikhail, when and why did you decide you had to escape from prison?"

"I spent my first six years in prison at Fire Island. Believe it or not, that wasn't too bad," Kasinov started modestly. "The problem came around the time I was due to be released, when they invented a whole load of new charges against me. Essentially they were the same charges as before; they just changed a few words around— from 'tax fraud' to 'state asset theft,' and 'embezzlement' to 'money laundering.' "

"Without probation and without a fair trial, I was given an extended custodial sentence for the same fabricated crime. I was going to be locked away without any grounds until 2017. Then, in September 2009, I was transferred to Krasnokamensk prison in Central Siberia. The problem with that place, putting the wastrels and cannibals that resided there to one side, was its location. It's right next to Russia's largest uranium mine, where the risk of radiation poisoning is just about guaranteed for anyone who stayed there long enough. The Kremlin knew that. That's why they put me there." Kasinov's grimace became more indistinct. "I've seen first-hand the misshapen inmates that have been there for several years. That place boasted an average life expectancy around the midforties. I was a dead man unless I did something."

"I know that, during your time in prison, you received a lot of international support, and in certain media circles you earned the moniker, 'the Prisoner of Conscience.' What do you think about that?"

Kasinov chuckled to himself, recalling his research on European and American jurisprudence for the protection of human rights in politically motivated litigation. It was far more liberal. *Means nothing in the Russian world.* Back in jail, he was motivated when he had heard that the European Court of Human Rights summarily found that his arrest and subsequent imprisonment was unlawful. Again, it meant nothing in the Russian world.

"I did indeed," he said, nodding. "Although it never officially delivered anything, it did create enormous international awareness." Kasinov looked out into an imaginary international audience. "This support was amazing, and I am very grateful and deferential to the UK, US, France, and to the European Court of Human

Rights in pursuing restitution for infringements by the Russian government against my human rights."

"And what about you personally, Mikhail? Tell me something about yourself; how did you spend all that money?"

"Before they got their hands on it, I invested almost one hundred million dollars in deserving philanthropic projects, both in Russia and internationally. These were mainly orphanages and skills training centers in remote areas—the kinds of projects where people had little opportunity and deserved a break. Everything I have done, I have looked to build sustainable futures for the people that are not so well off."

"Very caring of you, Mikhail. And now?"

Kasinov looked confused. "Now what?"

"Your money? The billions?"

"Gone," Kasinov said with his arms raised. "All gone. They stole everything."

After a brief pause, Boddington regained her focus. "So what's next for Mikhail Kasinov?"

"Angela, there's no turning back," Kasinov replied assuredly. "There is only one way, and that is forward. I have always said that the trials and sentencing that I went through were politically motivated. The Russian legislature, I'm afraid to say, is antediluvian. Government-led legal nihilism is not only straight-jacketing entrepreneurship, it's killing privatization and making a mockery out of any direct foreign investment. Who will put their money into Russia if the legal system has control to interpret any law in its favor and destroy intellectual and capital investment? I want to share the development of our natural resources with international partners. I'm committed to changing that for Russia, and for the world. When this happens, it will deliver a mammoth consequential shift in global economic activity." Kasinov spoke with a confident glare. "Of this, I am sure."

Boddington eyed Kasinov resolutely for the final time, maintaining the same perseverance she had at the beginning of the interview—right until the very end. "One last question, Mikhail." Her gaze on him became more intense. Kasinov assumed it was to signify that this was not a request, but more a prologue to her final question. "Don't you think all of this adverse chemistry between Russia and the United Kingdom is going to harm relations between the two nations?"

Kasinov looked her straight in the eyes without flinching. "Not at all," he said confidently.

Boddington looked confused. "Surely it will have some negative impact."

"It's impossible to harm something that doesn't exist."

Now Boddington looked dumfounded. Her mouth visibly dropped. Kasinov guessed it wasn't the answer she was expecting.

"Okay. Mikhail Kasinov," Boddington concluded, nodding to Kasinov and then towards the live audience. "Thank you for joining us."

"Thank you, Angela," Kasinov said with a bow.

After the interview, Kasinov was exceptionally pleased with himself. He felt he had cajoled Boddington and delivered his narratives with exceptional panache. He was especially pleased with his self-control in response to those penetrating questions she asked. He believed the Russian public and the world would see him as a true visionary, the forefather for a new Russian democracy. Surely they would embrace his vision for double-digit economic growth in Russia—growth that the rest of the world could share in. His strategy to oust the current hierarchy would probably receive a lot of international patronage, too.

It all sounded like an exciting journey to Kasinov—a journey that he believed had a lot of followers, particularly from the old Communist Party. *They are my backbone,* he thought. He was also convinced that the apostasy of the current political and social communities would follow him. There would, however, be several members of the current regime he would have to win over.

I can do this.

I'm going to do this.

~~~

Unsurprisingly, following the international media's digestion of the Sky interview, Kasinov was acclaimed with an uncharacteristic veneration by most media channels—a modern day economic hero; the savior of the world. His indomitable persona was simply contagious. They loved him.

The world's economy, lumbered by a proliferation of subprime debt, was in free fall. It needed a fillip, a catalyst, and most probably a miracle. Kasinov was that miracle.

The media understood and believed in transparency and eradication of corruption. He had played that card particularly well, and had purposefully set out to slander the Russian government's reputation and engender support for his plan.

Kasinov played a tune the media understood. His story was selling papers and serious news time, not to mention the initial positive reaction the world's stock markets experienced with the promise of an expansive economic outlook.

~~~

Troubled by concerns around British-Russian diplomatic relations over Kasinov's domicile, the stock markets had recently been through a bearish outlook and a subsequent correction in prices. After the prodigious and opportunistic economic outlook for Russia and the world portrayed by Kasinov, as seen on Sky News, Kasinov awoke the next morning to read in London's *Financial Times* that US and Far Eastern markets had rallied behind his vision the previous evening and earlier that morning, respectively—up on average 5 percent across the board. Expectedly, though, not all the media were convinced. He was not benign to his share of cynicism. *The Times* publication followed with a headline: PLUTOCRAT TURNS AUTOCRAT.

He knew his TV appearance had been a classic burlesque performance. The Russians probably hated it. The rest of the world mostly loved it. One man would probably be more upset than anyone else, he thought. *Yuri Koshenko.*

Kasinov guessed his covert emasculation of Koshenko's persona had crossed the Rubicon. There was no turning back now.

Yuri Koshenko—now it's time for you to pay for what you did to me.

Chapter 37
Catmalogion

Almost 1,600 miles away from the Sky News Brentford studio, Koshenko stood impotently inside the Kremlin. Flanked by a Russian ministerial quartet, Koshenko was livid at what he saw on the media feed. His crimson face contorted like a rhinoceros. "How can Great Britain host this miscreant?" he bellowed. "Don't they realize what he has stolen from our country?"

Engulfed with rancorous emotion, Koshenko sincerely believed—albeit naively—that Kasinov had rapaciously purloined from him. Worse, he had derided their entire governance. Now he had pulled the gravest stunt of the lot: directly accusing the Russian Federation's president of mass corruption.

Koshenko stood in thought, his hand across his face, his eyes protruding from their sockets, his attaché retreating out of his immediate reach. "As far as I'm concerned, Kasinov is a dead man!" he cried out. "Best case, he'll have to settle for a life of self-abnegation."

Koshenko stared into the screen. "Both Kasinov and Sky should know that it's forbidden to insult this administration publically. How dare they?" Koshenko pressed his opinion confidentially, and at the same time guilelessly, as he barked at the screen like he was on a direct videoconference with Angela Boddington.

When the Sky feed came to a conclusion, he phoned a private number he had for his British counterpart, Andrew Wood. When Wood answered, Koshenko's cheeks tightened. "Andrew, have you seen the histrionics on Sky News tonight?"

"No, I can't say I have. I just returned from tennis practice."

"I've had enough of Kasinov, and enough of you sheltering him," Koshenko thundered down the line. "His rhetoric is seriously undermining my authority, and similarly proving prejudicial to my entire administration. Either you extradite him by end of business tomorrow or things are going to get very messy."

"What?" Wood cried, trying to interject.

"I'm serious, Andrew. I'm not going to stand by any longer."

"I don't respond very well to threats, Yuri. You know that—especially on a Sunday evening."

"It's not a threat. Call it an advanced warning. The egalitarian policies of your government have been harboring enemies of our state for too long now. Send him back to Russia or feel the wrath of Russia on your doorstep."

"Okay, Yuri. Let me have a look at the situation. I'll get back to you tomorrow morning."

"I'll be waiting." Koshenko slammed the phone down and placed his head into his palms with his elbows anchored on the writing sleeve of his colossal desk. He ran his hands tediously through his creamed silver hair, dislodging a few of the outer strands from his mane.

"More coverage on the CNBC international news channels again, Yuri," Popov exclaimed.

Koshenko scoffed. "I don't want to watch any more of this nonsense."

"But it's that Nobel guy," Popov said encouragingly.

Koshenko rolled his eyes and reluctantly motioned to his prime minister to go ahead. Popov increased the volume on the mega-sized LCD screen. Koshenko stared at the feed contemptuously; his wild eyes opening wider and the outer strands from his mane bouncing from side to side like high frequency bunny antennas. "What the hell?" he cried out.

The tag line on the ticker tape read, *Kasinov challenges Russian presidency*. "In the studio this afternoon is Dr. Peter Holtzhazen, professor of economics at Michigan State University," the anchor Betty-Lou Roberts said. "Professor Holtzhazen sits on the board of governors for

Investment America, and is world renowned for his feats in supporting the development of new emerging economies. He is of course cowinner of the Nobel Peace Prize in 2008. Professor, welcome to the show."

"Thank you," the illustrious professor replied with poise befitting a Nobel laureate.

"Professor Holtzhazen, what is your take on all this anarchical posturing we're seeing from Mikhail Kasinov right now," the reporter asked grippingly. "And how serious should we be reading his claims for Russian presidency?"

The camera focused in closer on Holtzhazen now as he conjured up an intellectual-sounding response. "Kasinov is a brilliant mind. All you have to do is look at his track record," the expert answered in a lucid, accented tone. "To be honest, Betty-Lou, this is a pedigree of entrepreneurship that the world needs right now. The veiled stimulus package that he proposes is endearing; it would provide significant opportunities for emerging markets, too."

Koshenko couldn't believe what he had just heard. *When is this bullshit going to stop?* he thought, shaking his head in disbelief. Then he turned his gaze on Popov. "Just turn that fucken thing off!" he yelled. "I've seen enough."

~~~

A new day dawned as Koshenko awoke the following morning. It was December 1—a new month, and possibly a new world. He had just received a phone call from Popov informing him that Monday morning tensions were approaching new heights outside the Kremlin's expansive urban grid. Thousands of Russian opposition movements and adversaries assembled on the streets of Tverskaya, Novinskiy, and Arbat, apparently to vent their frustration at Koshenko.

This is all Kasinov's doing—I'm going to get that bastard whatever it takes.

Koshenko jumped from his bed as his wife, Aleyna, remained in deep sleep. He threw on a dark paisley silk robe and his sheepskin navy slippers and made his way downstairs. Bypassing the kitchen, he made a beeline for his study room, where he flicked on the television. Moscow's Channel One had several reporters out in the field covering the growing rebellion.

Koshenko watched anxiously as the crowds moved with rising passion in unison towards Red Square. *These people are risking custodial sentencing,* he thought. The risk of arrest for protestation grew exponentially with visibility, where a simple conviction of hooliganism could attract a confinement in gulag for up to ten years if demonstrators were deemed part of an anarchic fracas with police. Even so, from what he could see on the screen, several thousand people had gathered.

He frowned when the reporter claimed the assembly was inspired by Kasinov's proclamations. Then he almost fainted when the same reporter claimed over one hundred thousand demonstrators had collectively assembled to be part of the largest ever anti-Koshenko march. Indeed it was claimed to be the largest demonstration since the formation of the new Russia.

Shaking his head in deep frustration, Koshenko turned to make his way to the kitchen and make tea. He heard the reporter's summary follow him. "It would appear the prevalent dissatisfaction throughout both affluent and deprived expanses in Russia have gained extraordinary momentum."

Koshenko winced. *Kasinov, I'm going to kill you.*

Alarmed with the volume of Internet traffic through party political blogs and social media sites, Koshenko had withdrawn all Internet service provider licenses the previous evening. He thought he had put a stop to the antigovernment thrust, but the damage was done. Before the communication networks were closed down, the stream of messages that made it through helped initiate a tidal wave of support that brought proponents of change out in force.

He had approved the demonstration permit, but he had no idea it would become a free-for-all. In approving the permit, though, he had mandated that any early birds that came to catch the worm be rewarded with arrest for assembling prior to the permit commencement time. It was a technicality that he had used many times before. It was also a technicality that emotionally incited opposition groups even further. He didn't care. He was going to put a stop to this no matter what. He had afforded the Russian militia extended governance authority for this day of action, calling for the detention of any opposition leaders from the primary supporting groups found on parade. His plan had worked. Before the march commenced, several hundred detentions had been made.

Within half an hour, Koshenko had travelled to the Kremlin and made his way to the Senate building. Pacing up and down the room, he furiously watched live media feeds of the event. Within the crowds, he could see a phalanx of commingled flags representing factions of nationalism, Communism, liberalism, and even former realm imperialism impaling the skyline above the procession. He was even more concerned when he learned about the demographics of the assembly. Compared to other recent protests, this one was attended in force by a significant number of Communists. Energized by a socialist revival, he watched several groups frantically displaying a plethora of red ribbons throughout the crowd. What was worse, alongside them were an almost equal number of liberal white ribbons. *They are supposed to be my supporters.*

A rampant energy for change reverberated over the columns of disciplined supporters that proceeded legitimately through to the capital's landmark edifice. On screen, the heavily armed state police were seen releasing invective instructions through their handheld megaphones and struggling to maintain control. Several different camera shots followed seconds apart, showing convoys of protestors converging on Red and Theatre squares. At that point, the masses seemed to have come to a standstill.

Unfazed by reproach, the demonstrators, in addition to the cataclysmic collage of flags, held aloft a selection of handcrafted and well-published posters. Although the props had been omnipresent along the route, now, given the standstill, they were clearly legible: KASINOV FOR PRESIDENT; FREEDOM FOR OUR CHILDREN; KOSHENKO OUT; DEFENDING HUMAN DIGNITY; RUSSIA WITHOUT KOSHENKO. These were just a few of the prevailing sentiments. Koshenko couldn't believe his own eyes.

Some of the authorities started to revile the crowds, only to be drowned out by ecstatic roars and the constant buzz of heckling. Around the crowds, an enormous granite statue of Karl Marx stared down. The symbolic association was powerful. Close behind them, a second wave of protestors spilled over and filled up both Bolotnaya and Revolution squares.

Crazed with desire and passion to witness the historic event, several journalists and TV crews moved adjacent to the convoy of support, and captured the euphoria that evolved as the crowds had both physiologically and psychologically strong-armed the authorities in sheer mass. The media feeds were capturing every minute of it. So, too, was Koshenko.

A tidal wave of pressure had grown amongst several million Russian citizens over the previous months. Roars from the crowds had reached maximum amplitude. The arrival of such a throng of supporters on the doorstep of the Kremlin sent an unequivocal message that Kasinov had a significantly powerful network inside Russia—a network that could operate by stealth amidst the impediments and logjams created and inserted by his competitors. An amalgam of drums from within the crowd let off a fusion of thumping blasts. In support, Klaxon horns bellowed penetrating blasts that usurped the wailing of police cars in the background. By now, the heterogeneous mixture had created a white noise hiss that travelled for miles.

Koshenko didn't need to travel that far to hear. He was only several hundred yards away from the rapturous gathering outside, positioned inside the comfort of his luxurious office. Reluctantly he had gathered his ministers once again. "That bloody Kasinov is fomenting this euphoria, and that moron Andrew Wood is complicit in the cause of it all."

When no one replied, Koshenko cried out for someone to tell him the time.

"It's ten minutes after midday, Yuri," Popov responded.

Koshenko nodded calmly. "Then morning has passed, and that man Wood has insulted my intelligence once again. This is the last time. Now I'm going to punish him."

"Where do you want to start?" Popov enquired.

"Contact the British embassy and tell them that we're immediately withdrawing all diplomatic status for each and every one of their expatriate staff. Tell them that they have twenty-four hours to leave the country or we'll arrest them."

~~~

With perspiration rolling down his forehead, British foreign secretary Charles Browne came running into the prime minister's office. Wood sat pensively with a vacuous stare. He had temporized all morning on the permutations of his call with Koshenko from the night before.

I don't have to make a decision on what to do just yet, he thought, satisfying the preemptive and consequential cognitions brewing in his mind.

"I think we have a situation, Prime Minister."

"What's that, Charles?" Wood responded with his head buried in a thick file.

"The Russians are upping the game."

Wood smiled satirically. "Don't worry, Charles. Things move slower than earth's tectonic plates over there." His gaze returned to the file in front of him.

Browne raised his hands. "Well, they must have found a way to accelerate continental drift, then."

A disbelieving grimace crossed Wood's face as tepid phlegm settled in his throat. He swallowed. "What do you mean?"

"They've withdrawn our diplomatic status in Moscow," Browne announced anxiously.

"Why? What's going on?"

"We simply have one too many escaped Russians in Britain," Browne replied.

"I said I would get back to that bully Koshenko this morning." Wood glanced at his platinum Rolex wristwatch. It was just after 10:00 a.m. "It's not midday yet. He's jumped the gun, the bastard."

"You know Moscow is four hours ahead of Great Britain," Browne replied, trying not to sound derisory.

The prime minister's cheeks turned crimson as he suddenly remembered the time difference with Moscow. It was now 2:00 p.m. there. "Surely Yuri must have known we were using Greenwich time as a benchmark."

Browne shrugged. "I don't know what deal you agreed with him."

"Well, in that case they've left us no alternative but to retaliate. We must protect Britain," Wood announced stridently. "Contact the Russian embassy and tell them we're withdrawing diplomatic status for all Russian nationals. Also, have your foreign service networks issue a travel advisory: Britons should return from Russia immediately. That will soften his cough."

One situation: two different responses.

One agreement: two different interpretations.

One opportunity to remedy: two different retorts—one unscrupulous, one ruinous.

Chapter 38
Lost

Roy awoke with a jump, perspiration rolling down his face and his heart beating faster than a pair of flamenco castanets. The image imprinted on his mind was the photo from Budapest. It was Zolotov, Alexander Zolotov, the dubious wine waiter. It was the same guy he saw when he rescued the hostages from Cuito Cuanavale at the end of the Angolan Civil War.

How the hell did that not come to me before now?

He felt weak as he looked down at his disheveled appearance, a sight that drew him back to his current predicament.

Oh shit.

Roy jumped up and saw Melanie sprawled out on the floor several feet away—motionless. He raced over to her on all fours. She was still out cold, but she was alive. He took off his jacket and delicately placed it under her head.

He had no idea where he was. Inside, it was dark, the floor was damp, and there was a musty smell that oozed from just about everything.

Consumed with contemplations surrounding the relationship now between Kasinov and the former Russian military man in Angola, Roy barely noticed Melanie as she awoke. It wasn't until she let out a painful groan that he saw her.

He winced as he rubbed his hand across the underside of his nose. "Chloroform. You can smell the sickly sweet alcohol and acetone combination. Pretty healthy dose we received, as well."

Melanie twitched her nose a couple of times. "I can smell fresh meat, too."

"Not very pleasant."

Although she was putting on a brave face, Roy could see in her eyes that she was petrified. Like him, she had no idea where they were, what had happened, and worse, what was going to happen next. Roy had been in many situations like this— probably a lot worse, the more he thought about it. He guessed, though, that nothing remotely like this had ever happened to Melanie before. The most trouble she had been in up to now was probably the £50 pounds fine she received a few years ago for not paying a congestion charge.

"Where the hell are we?" she enquired nervously.

Roy examined the limited enclosure. "No idea. Looks like an abandoned warehouse to me."

"It all seemed to happen during that period when Kasinov appeared on television," she said, delicately holding her head. "My head hurts. It's really sore." Then, brushing the hair off her face, she took a deep breath. "The only good thing is that the sweet alcohol smells a bit like tequila."

Together they huddled in near darkness. All Roy could see were small rays of light flowing through from under a doorway opposite. Roy studied his wounds. He looked like he had been dragged through wild thorn bushes—most probably because he had been.

"It must be at least ten hours ago since we were taken at the restaurant, considering the way these scabs have congealed," he commented, glancing at the cuts on her face. "We need to find out about Zolotov. He was at the restaurant last night. He showed up just after you took the call. He's the same guy connected with the Cuban military in Angola when I was there, and now he's partners with Kasinov."

Melanie looked surprised. "Don't you think we might deal with the immediate threat first—like getting the hell out of this place?" she said, her eyes half-closed with her hands propping her head in position. "Then we can look into Mr. Zolotov later."

Roy nodded. He knew he would deal with the matter later—assuming he was still alive, of course.

"Who would want to kidnap us?" Melanie whispered. "Especially here in Florence?"

"I have a good idea," he replied. Outside the warehouse, Roy could hear instructions being transmitted. "But I think we're about to find out."

Roy craned his neck so he could see outside through the smallest of gaps in the building's external cladding. There were three of them—maybe four—he estimated. Roy heard what he assumed to be the leader, a rotund man speaking in Russian. He wore what could best be described as a perma-grin. He checked his watch, dialed a number, and spoke. Roy guessed he was dialing his boss, Zolotov.

"Pervyy pozvolyayet poluchit benzin po sklada," he said in guttural Russian. *"Zatem my sprashivayem ikh, a zatem my budem imet delo s nimi."*

Roy listened attentively, trying to decipher the instructions.

"What are they saying?" Melanie enquired anxiously.

Roy's Russian was limited, but reasonably good. "Sounded like they are going to disperse some gasoline along the wall of this warehouse, and after that, we're going to have a few questions to answer."

"And then what?" Melanie enquired.

From her grimace, Roy guessed that she didn't really want to hear the answer. He knew they were dead if they hung around to answer questions, but he didn't want her plunging into panic mode.

"Apparently depending on how good our answers are, they will decide what to do with us next."

"Well, I suppose it could be worse. At least we get a chance to talk our way out of this."

"I don't think we'll be hanging around for a chat with these guys, Melanie."

"How are we going to get out of here, then?"

Kneeling next to her, Roy placed his hand on her shoulder. He wanted to comfort her, but the more pressing matter was the minor issue of escaping a sealed warehouse and a bunch of Russians with gasoline cans. "I'll see what I can do to get us out of this mess," he said softly but confidently. As he lifted off his knees, he was impeded by a shallow, steel-framed mezzanine ceiling with plasterboard floor inserts. The height was so narrow that it restricted his ability to stand fully upright.

Outside, Roy could hear cans of gasoline being assembled in double file. From what he could make out, two of the four assailants were starting to dump initial drums of fuel along the front of the warehouse. After that, he guessed they would make their way to the side and then to the rear.

Inside, holding hands, Roy and Melanie crouched and moved slowly through the dimly lit warehouse. They were definitely lost. Roy guessed it was liked being stuck in the middle of an IKEA labyrinth, but without the guidance arrows. Across, on the opposite perimeter of the building, Roy noticed a web of structural walls and panels made from reinforced concrete columns with precast wall slabs between. *No way out through there*, he thought. Then he noticed the only thing that wasn't concrete. It was a door positioned to the rear of the building. From what Roy could make out, it looked like it was constructed from carbon steel.

Roy looked out through a gap between the wall panels and saw his abductors. They each sported a magazine-loaded AK-47 that hung from their shoulders, interposed between their arm and side. Roy had seen plenty of them in his excursions throughout Africa, so he knew the damage they could cause. Determined to find an exit before the AK-47s and the gasoline found them, Roy scanned the shelving near the rear door. On the lower tier, tucked right at the back, he saw what looked like a medium-duty electric arc-welding machine.

Roy motioned to Melanie to remain poised. "Just stay here," he whispered. "I need to go over to that door."

Despite his restricted vision and his battered physique, he moved around the warehouse floor adroitly. Down on all fours, he scurried across to the other side of the room like a sand crab racing across the shoreline. He grabbed the welding machine and pulled it out from the lower shelf. Then he dragged it to a point adjacent to the steel door and set it down, inserting the power lead into a nearby electrical outlet.

He flicked the switch and nothing happened.

Outside, he could hear the Russians making progress. He knew it was a matter of seconds, as opposed to minutes, before they would make it around the building. Roy pulled out the plug and tried the socket next to it. This time, he saw a dim yellow light come on. Inspired by two weeks in welding school back at Lohatlha, Roy yanked up the main dial to the maximum current of 550 amps. He donned the darkened welding head shield, groped for the heavy gauge welding rods, and attached one to the end of the electrode. He paused and thought about his task. He glanced over at Melanie. She looked frightened. He nodded, and she smiled back at him. He looked back again with both hands slightly raised, checking his tools.

He had everything he needed.

With a downward swoop of his head, Roy flicked the visor shield closed and struck an arc with the parent metal, creating a micro furnace temperature that approached 10,000 degrees centigrade at the point of contact. Melanie looked away from the explosion, squinting as the electrode combusted into the steel door with a prolonged fizzling echo resounding through the illuminating glow. Roy inserted one electrode after another, cutting through the parent metal like a warm knife through butter.

In less than a minute, Roy had cut out a perfect ring at the base of the door—just wide enough for their bodies to fit through. He stood back, kicked straight into the flange panel, and watched it jettison to the floor on the other side with a clank. Melanie looked on in amazement.

Roy grabbed a nearby can of water and quickly poured it over the rim of his handiwork to create a safe passage through the fabricated egress. He looked over at Melanie, pulled his head to his left, and whispered, "You first. Be careful."

Melanie shuffled over, and Roy helped her through the opening. Roy emerged behind her seconds later. *No Russians,* he thought, looking left and right.

On the far side of the warehouse, through a field of untamed bramble, Roy noticed a large white van. On the side of the vehicle, in bold black and gold stenciling, it said VICTUALLER; MEAT PICKUP AND DELIVERIES. He guessed they had been dragged through the coarse shrubbery from the van. He tapped Melanie on the shoulder, pointing towards the vehicle. "Our arrival limousine," he commented.

"Five-star service." She chuckled. "At least it explains the smell."

"And the cuts and bruises," he added.

Melanie yanked her head to her right. "Now can we please get out of here?"

Together they raced for the boundary wall before the two gasoline decanters had turned the second apex points of the eastern and western extremities of the building. Roy got there first, and looked over to the other side of the embankment. To his amazement, he saw a vast, verdant catchment area that seemed to go on forever.

Chapter 39
New World Order

Bill Peterson sat back in his mahogany-framed black leather chair with the well-acclaimed Resolute Desk behind him. His hands interlocked behind his head as he stared through the enormous sash windows that surrounded the west conservatory wall and looked onto the Truman balcony outside the Oval Office. Eternally concerned with the risk of terrorist attacks, Peterson—the Republican, Texas-born president—mandated the annual expenditure of almost US$1 trillion dollars on military and sovereign security initiatives. It was more money than any other nation—more money than most nations put together. Today, however, Peterson wasn't thinking about money or budgets. Instead, his mind was consumed with Yuri Koshenko and his actions. The diplomatic suspension was just for starters. The latest he had heard was that Koshenko had given the British PM a four-day deadline to have the oligarch returned to Moscow before he took what he termed "definitive and devastating action" against Britain.

Peterson wondered if Andrew Wood was strong enough or foolish enough to underestimate Koshenko's brinkmanship for a second time in a matter of days. Intrigued by Koshenko's irrational political attack on Wood, he cogitated over the preliminary esoteric discussions that concerned a New World Order agenda that had been conceived one year earlier between Great Britain and the US.

Peterson's objective to exert greater influence, regulation, and direction on international regimes, businesses, and the world's press was pioneering, to say the least. However, as a collective strategy, it was still very much in its infancy. Although the respective premiers of both nations had discussed the initiative in principle, they both knew that, to achieve this control, they would need full governance of the central banking system. Acutely aware of the sensitivities around this, Peterson and Wood alike knew that any initiative had to be completely clandestine.

The New World Order plans to effect such change would require the selection and insertion of operating staff into leadership roles inside selected national governments and within selected global industrial players. Peterson had been more assertive in leading this initiative than his British counterpart, and had surreptitiously stepped ahead of his ally. Andrew Wood had preferred a slower approach, one that embraced an enlarged consortium of major powers to participate in. Peterson simply didn't have any time for that. He had to move ahead quickly. Subprime write-offs had crippled the economy, and reelections were fast approaching.

The time for a false flag attack was here.

False flag attacks are commonly referred in national intelligence forums as "covert attacks," or programs initiated by one nation against another completely by stealth. Essentially, it is designed to make it appear that any such attack was created by another nation or nations. They were quite common in places like Eritrea and Kenya, or India and Pakistan. They were not that common in the UK, Russia, or the US.

That was up until now.

Driven by a desire to exert greater control on the world economy, Peterson and Wood shared a new platform for strategic partnering, just like they had done in Iraq years earlier. Both leaders were aligned with this common vision for economic control, providing control of inflation and deflation across the world at the touch of a button. It would exert far greater influence and control over the European Union, United Nations, World Bank, and the International Monetary Fund, providing greater influence on interest rates.

Peterson vividly recalled how this had all started. He wondered if he had made the right choices a year ago, and other choices he had made even before that. As he swiveled around in his chair, he placed his hands on the leather inlay on the Resolute Desk and glanced over at the large beige settee that sat inside the Oval Office. *That's where it all started,* he thought.

Two years earlier, Peterson had sat there perusing a file with several papers, statistics, and charts, when his office door swung open, and Jim Vaughan, his secretary of state, walked in.

"Bill, you look a bit forlorn," Vaughan said after making his way through the double mahogany doors. "Everything okay?"

As secretary of state, Vaughan had worked closely with Peterson to develop foreign affairs policies to guide sustainable relationships with key foreign nations. He was his most trusted ally, and had been since the onset of the election campaign that brought them to power.

Peterson placed some of the paperwork onto the opposite side of the table, motioning for Vaughan to read it, whilst maintaining his grip and gaze on the initial report. "I'm meeting up with Brad Dunkley this evening," he recited, glancing up at Vaughan briefly for inspiration. "I'm trying to get my mind around how to handle him."

"What's he after this time?" Vaughan enquired.

"The usual: control of world energy markets," Peterson responded without shifting his eyes, which were still glued to the array of charts clenched in his hand. There were lots of them: hockey sticks, bubble diagrams, parabolas, pie charts, scatter diagrams, stacked bar charts—all with multiple data points drawing correlated references, and all depicted in brilliant blue, green, orange, grey, and red hues.

"But Zeron has had a lucrative position in the Middle East for some time now—a position we helped establish."

Peterson placed the charts on the table and moved forward in his seat. "The problem is that, ever since setting up Saudi Aramco back in 1941, we believed, naively or otherwise, that we had a special strategic relationship with the Kingdom in Riyadh. For sure, we've helped the Saudis and just about all of the surrounding Arab countries, bar Iran, along with our commercial entities, to explore their vast oil fields."

"Yeah, and in return, we shared our technology and know-how with them! Dunkley can't complain. Several American oil companies, particularly Zeron, have benefitted enormously from access to those precious oil and gas reserves. Ever since the seventies' oil crisis, we've enjoyed greater participation in the development of those resources than anybody else."

"Republican and Democratic predecessors alike have had a common frisson when it comes to the Middle East," Peterson said, reaching over to the table to pull up one of the charts he had just read.

"The problem, I fear, is that we shared too much with them. In the last ten years, but more so recently, the emergent Saudis and their neighbors have developed significant wealth matched with audacity in their aversion for assistance." He handed the chart to his secretary of state. "Have a look at this. They haven't said it straight out, but the hankering is over, Jim. The Arabs have figured out that they don't actually need us anymore. Just look at this year alone and the slate of projects they're planning to develop with their own capital and human resources."

Vaughan studied the stacked bar chart thoroughly.

"US oil company involvement is depicted in red," Peterson explained. "You can see the trend over the last five years. The red bar is continuously reducing in size, except for this year, 2008. It's zero."

Vaughan shook his head vigorously.

"Thirty-two billion dollars of investment planned, and apparently we're not part of one of those projects," Peterson yelped.

"But what about the Peak Oil theory?" Vaughan responded, retracting his eyes from the colorful memo. "Isn't that the control mechanism they use all the time?"

Peterson grinned, showing off a set of pearly white, sparkling teeth. "Jim, we've been leading the way on that spin over the last forty years. Most of the major international oil development companies—not just ours—have created the illusion that we're running out of oil."

Vaughan glanced at his boss, angling his head to one side curiously. "But we'll run out of oil reserves one day. I mean, why else would we be pumping so much into nuclear and all the green stuff?"

"All depends. To this day, there remain vast reserves of untapped oil all over the world—especially in Russia. Given that most of these reserves are currently inaccessible to the large international oil companies, they purposefully ignore them in order to buoy oil prices. This tactic has been employed quite successfully by Zeron for several years. However, with current market sentiment, this price control mechanism is no longer available to Dunkley, something they're suffering over right now."

Vaughan pulled back in surprise. "But I thought Zeron was the darling of Wall Street."

"It is," the president reassured him. "Analysts today, however, have become a lot more circumspect. In their research on oil majors—not just on the NASDAQ, but on global stock markets, also—they're a lot savvier than ever before. They simply don't buy this Peak Oil theory, and have generally discounted it from company valuations."

"So it's about Zeron's stock price valuation, then?" Vaughan hypothesized.

"Ultimately, yes, but he has another agenda."

"You mean his Russian agenda?"

"Yes."

"Look, Bill, even with this reverse Peak Oil theory, the general global uncertainty has surely caused the demise in Zeron's stock valuation," Vaughan recounted as he threw his hands in the air. "You and I both have gone out of our way to covertly mentor Dunkley's plans this last twenty-four months to attain political support to access Russian oil. The lobbying inside our administrative network has been substantial. We've given him every platform available: the State Department, the Treasury secretary, the Senate, the US foreign secretary, and anybody else that would listen to him. What more does he want?"

Peterson shook his head. "Dunkley's objective is clear and simple. He wants to work with the US government to gain our support to somehow get access to Russia's vast resources. In his mind, this means supporting a plan where the current Russian government gets augmented, recalibrated, or even unseated—whichever one, it doesn't matter to Dunkley; he just wants to get access to those Russian oil reserves." He handed a second sheet to Vaughan. "His note to me at the end of this little report he compiled was pretty succinct. Here, look."

Vaughan read the note aloud. "Bill, hope you find all this stuff interesting. Please help me denationalize Russia's oil. Brad."

Peterson sighed, pointing to the array of charts and tables on his desk. "I mean, he's a bit brash, and his candor outlandish, but he believes it's a fair request. I don't think he feels in any way disconcerted. After all, Zeron is the biggest oil company in the world, and the catalyst to our economy—or so he keeps reminding me."

Vaughan studied the note a second time. "He does have a point," the secretary said. "Access to the Russian fields would benefit the US economy and our people. It would also benefit the Russian economy, the Russian people, not to mention the world economy—and Zeron, of course."

Peterson chuckled. "Only one problem: Koshenko seems to have complete abhorrence to sharing anything. I didn't fully realize until Dunkley sent me all this stuff." He pointed to the papers on his desk. "But Russia's oil and gas reserves are immense. They have sixteen hundred and eighty trillion cubic feet of gas—by far the largest in the world, followed by Iran, Turkmenistan, and Qatar. On top of that, they have seventy-four billion barrels of proven oil reserves, and potentially a lot more with the unproven reserves in the vast Arctic Circle. If these reserves are truly understood and assessed, they could usurp Saudi's principal rank at the top."

"I like it," Vaughan said, grinning. "They are our new Saudi Arabia."

"In Dunkley's defense, we've pondered and temporized on this for longer than we should. I mean, we've discussed this subject on numerous occasions. It's like mental masturbation. Things just keep going around in circles. It's no wonder he's being a bit more assertive now." The president sighed. "Jim, you're a smart man, and I trust you implicitly. How the hell can we ever achieve a pro-democracy, pro-US regime in Russia?"

Vaughan paused, holding back a grin. "I guess you should hear what Dunkley has to say. No doubt he has his ideas, which I'm sure will be a lot more innovative than you and I are allowed to think."

~~~

Demented after two years of lobbying and exasperating bureaucratic parleys, Peterson knew how frustrated Brad Dunkley was. Despite all his valiant efforts, Zeron was right back at first base. That same evening, Peterson and Dunkley agreed to meet for dinner in Washington. Peterson chose *Marcello's,* off Wisconsin Avenue, an exclusive, private, and discreet Italian dining establishment he had used for meetings like this on several occasions prior.

Peterson arrived early, and was seated in a private dining room to the rear of the building. Dunkley arrived a few minutes later. Peterson could hear him coming before he saw him. Zeron's long-serving CEO, like Peterson, was a true Texan. Two differences: Dunkley sounded and dressed like one, while Peterson didn't. The PR and fashion police at the White House wouldn't allow it. Permanently attached beneath Dunkley's bespoke designer navy Napoli suit were two leather cowboy boots. If the boots didn't give him away, then Dunkley's distinctive Southern drawl surely would.

Peterson rated Zeron Oil as voraciously Republican, resilient supporters of his administration. This was particularly evident during his last reelection. They were still the largest stock company in the US, and they had been the greatest international success story. Their business model had been the envy of the industry. That was up until now. Now things were not looking very pretty. This was an important dinner for both Peterson and Dunkley—perhaps the most important dinner of their lives.

After the greetings, Dunkley didn't waste any time in cutting straight into the business of the evening. "You read the report?"

"I certainly did," Peterson responded. "I was educated."

Dunkley stared Peterson in the eye. "Good, Bill, because ever since the Saudis have judiciously reduced their dependency on our technology and our capital, our market cap has gone through the floor." Dunkley spurted all this out before the maître d' had a chance to return with the menus. "We were valued at three hundred and twenty billion in 2005, and now we're sitting just under two hundred and fifty billion. I don't need to tell you, but that's not a very pretty outlook for shareholders, not to mention its impact as a leading indicator for this country's economic growth."

"I'm sure it's not pretty, Brad, but there are lots of variables at play here," Peterson said.

Dunkley placed his hands firmly on the table and leaned forward. "Maybe there's another way we can do this Russian deal."

"I'm listening," Peterson replied attentively as he dipped his bread into the vinegar-coated virgin olive oil.

"I think we need a Trojan horse," Dunkley said succinctly.

"A what?" Peterson asked incredulously.

"A Trojan horse. You know; someone on the inside—someone who can be a catalyst in the transformation we need."

"That might work in theory, but how can we get that to work in practice?"

"Better still, imagine if we could covertly control the appointment of a new Russian president. This would solve everything." By now, Dunkley sounded more like a frenzied secondhand car salesman. "It would give us direct access to the largest oil and gas reserves in the world and provide a sustainable energy outlook for everyone, along with greater control on pricing. It would create significant growth opportunities for all American international oil companies, not just us."

"Have you lost your mind, Brad?"

"Think about it," Dunkley exclaimed. "It's such a simple solution."

"Sounds simple," Peterson said satirically. "Where are we going to find a new Russian president?" He moved the tablecloth aside and pretended to glance under the table.

"If you think about it, the answer is staring us in the face."

"Let me guess," Peterson responded with some degree of cynicism. "You have someone in mind."

Dunkley nodded and smiled. "Yes, I do: Mikhail Kasinov."

"Isn't he in jail?"

"Currently, yes. I can think of no better man that has more abhorrence against Yuri Koshenko." Dunkley smugly took a sip of wine. "All we have to do is figure a way to get him out, and he'll do the rest himself."

"How well do you know him?" Peterson enquired.

"We've done a few deals together," Dunkley said awkwardly. "I've usually come out second best. He's a very smart individual, I must say."

The history between Dunkley and Kasinov had been more precipitous than the Houston duo. It was probably more melodramatic. Without doubt, it had been prosperous. Although they had known each other for many years, they wouldn't classify themselves as friends. Their very first meeting was when Natasha had translated for them in London in 2002. Subsequent to this initial meeting, and prior to Kasinov's imprisonment in 2003, Dunkley and Kasinov had done a number of business transactions together—all of which had been tactically rewarding for both companies. Zeron Oil had in fact shown a strategic interest in acquiring KasOil just before his imprisonment, the consequence being a significant largesse to Zeron following Kasinov's subsequent fall from prominence.

~~~

The following day after the Houston old boys' dinner at Marcello's, Peterson called Clay Parker and Jim Vaughan to a meeting in the Situation Room at the Oval Office.

"Clay." Peterson closed the door behind him and commenced before he even reached his seat. "I think we may have just found the solution to our plan. I will need you to personally handle this assignment for me."

When the three had finished their meeting, Peterson summarized quite candidly. "Whatever we do, we must cover our tracks. This must never come back to my office, the office of the State, the office of the NCS, or the office of the CIA. If this somehow gets out of control, I'll expect you to have a contingency in place and do whatever it takes to fix it."

~~~

Two years on, Kasinov was set to become the best Trojan horse the US could ever find to accelerate the process of a New World Order. Admittedly, it was one year before Peterson had engaged with Wood on the subject, but he was well on his way to delivering the first stage of the transformation.

The marches throughout Moscow had been a bonus.

Everything was falling into place.

Chapter 40
Viticulture

Roy looked back, and although there was nobody immediately in his vision, he knew the Russians wouldn't be far behind. They got a head start—two minutes at the most. Whatever they did, they needed to find somewhere more urbanized, somewhere with more people, more places to blend in undetected. Right now, unless they did something ingenious, they were as good as clay pigeons stepping out as targets in a once-off shooting event.

After they emerged from the embankment at the other side of the wall, Roy's eyes scanned the area. He was greeted by a voluminous viticulture of vines that straddled across a boundless series of cultivated pathways. In the distance, he could hear a collection of tractors ploughing away through the vines. The south-facing topography unveiled infinite bunches of nurtured but as yet unharvested vines, and here they had to make their way through them somehow. There was nothing else. They had no choice but to keep going. They couldn't turn back. Roy knew that, once the Russians reached the disgorged access, they would be in fast pursuit, but it didn't stop him from pausing to look.

Roy steered Melanie through the closest row they came upon, frantically brushing aside overhanging lianas as they proceeded through the fertile tunnel. Moving hastily through the extremely dense foliage, Roy thought about how he had always wanted to experience a more hands-on tour of some of Tuscany's finest wineries. That would have to wait for another day.

Together they started to dance over never-ending concentric circles of snakelike irrigation piping that surrounded the inside of the sealing canopy. Melanie stumbled behind him. Roy stopped, pulled back, and grabbed her hand.

"Okay, let's stay on the pipes," he said calmly.

He knew that any imbalance and subsequent fall, Melanie would probably end up in an undecorated morass. It would be like attempting to fish out a piece of embedded parsley from the middle of a fresh bowl of spaghetti. After Roy grabbed her hand, they cautiously tiptoed and danced their way along the top of the tubing, heading south. Roy didn't know how long the tunnel was; it just seemed to go on forever. He knew, though, that if he kept going in that direction, he would be putting distance between them and the Russians. So far, he didn't hear them—instead, all he could hear was the sound of the plastic tubing grumbling back at them as it bounced off the rigid, dewatered floor.

Roy glanced across at her as they ran. "I can't imagine the safety harnesses in the back of that truck were five-star, either," he said.

"I can't recall," Melanie responded as she tried to get her breath. "I was unconscious. So were you."

"We were probably bouncing around all over the back of the van like junkies on speed."

"Probably why my head hurts so much," Melanie said. "I can't believe we were taken through Piazza della Signoria unobserved."

Roy shook his head. "Yeah, and with all the tourists around the Fountain of Neptune."

"Just goes to show: people do enter a different world when they come to Florence."

Roy knew the errors from his youth were coming back to haunt him. "Zolotov and his crew have improved since his days in Angola, I'll give him that." He had had his chance to get rid of Zolotov in Angola, but didn't take it. Now he was regretting it more than ever. "I should have killed him when I had the chance."

After shuffling and dancing their way down the tunnel, the sunlight emerged in front of them as they approached the exit. Exhausted by the run, Melanie stopped, breathing wildly, her head down with her hands on her knees.

Roy moved on ahead and approached the verge of the roadway to see a nearby bus that had just pulled up to alight passengers. He looked back to Melanie. "Can you walk?"

Panting and red-faced, Melanie looked up from her crouched position. "I'll try," she replied in a tense tone as her eyes began to well up.

Roy heard the clunk of the first gear being engaged. "In that case, I'll need you to run. Let's go."

Reenergized by the appearance of the conveyance, and although completely wild and guerrilla-like with their wounds, Melanie and Roy ran frenziedly toward the departing bus. Roy looked ahead to see the bus starting to pull away. Desperately he chased after it, holding onto Melanie, almost dragging her along. Roy reached the roof access ladder at the back of the bus and grabbed it, with Melanie still desperately hanging on to his other hand. With one vigorous swoop, he pulled her forward and she grabbed onto the ladder. Roy jumped on behind her. They were over the first hurdle and on the move, but Roy knew there was a long way to go.

As he gripped tightly to the rear gangway, Roy spotted a road sign that read, SCANDICCI TOWN CENTER 1 KM.

He knew Scandicci was at least seven miles southwest of Florence. *Not good,* he thought. *But at least we're heading in the right direction.*

Roy looked behind. Then he looked back at Melanie. "Too long!" he cried out. "C'mon, let's go."

"Let's go where?" Melanie replied.

Roy nodded upwards. "Up there!" he shouted, pointing at the roof.

With four whitened knuckles clenched to the rear aluminum appendage, they ascended the ladder one tread at a time. Melanie reached the roof first, and almost collapsed backwards when the wind caught her upper body.

Roy grabbed her and pushed her forward gently. "Keep your head down and move slowly," he encouraged.

Together they crawled along the rooftop and reached the skylight window near the front of the bus. Roy looked down through the orange translucent window and saw the driver. He was a middle-aged man who looked content in his job. Roy glanced back at the skylight louver again— more specifically its fastening mechanism. It looked like it was made from some kind of polycarbonate or acrylic material. Whatever the chemical characteristics of the window, it looked hard and brittle, which meant it was toughened and probably shatterproof. With a single sharp movement from his right side, Roy sliced off the top of the louver. With its chemical characteristics, it may have been resistant to several things like ultraviolet rays, thermal contraction, and oxidation degradation, but it wasn't resistant to a wallop from Roy's elbow. Roy and Melanie both leaned back and watched it somersault off into the distance before landing on the roadside.

Inside the bus, a chilled vacuum immediately followed the swooping sound as astonished passengers looked up in fear. They pulled backwards in fright as Roy landed in the middle of the aisle. Several of the passengers were quite elderly and visibly frightened.

Roy gave them a friendly nod. "Just a routine quality inspection," he said in perfect Italian pronounced with a Tuscan dialect. "Nothing to worry about, folks."

The passengers began to settle when confronted by his disarming smile and calmness. That was until a second apparition appeared through the skylight window.

"Gender equality," he followed as Melanie swung to the floor.

Roy grabbed her hand, turned around, and moved towards the driver. "Sorry, pal. Move over," he said, grabbing the wheel. The driver looked incredulously at Roy, looked back out at the road in front of him, and then slid out of the way with his hands raised in mock surrender.

Roy thumbed him to the back with the rest of the passengers. Then he motioned to Melanie to sit in the seat adjacent. He glanced in the rear-view to see a black Suburban in the distance. From what Roy could make out, it had extra-large wheels and privacy glass. Following closely behind was a second Suburban of the same description. Roy didn't waste any time putting some metal to the pedal. Suddenly the speed on the dial went from forty miles per hour to just over seventy. From underneath the bus, Roy could hear a wailing sound. *Probably from the rear suspension leaf springs*, he thought. *I guess I'll be testing them to the brink of their design capacity.* Terrified once again, the passengers braced themselves as the vehicle began to shudder and careen from side to side while Roy navigated his way through the meandering country route. Once he reached a straight section of the road, he opened up the throttle again, and a road sign appeared ahead.

TRAM STATION 1 KM.

He glanced at Melanie. She was as white as a ghost. Her hands tightly gripped a metal divider bar that separated the seats. Roy guessed she had probably never been this scared in her life. *I shouldn't have asked her to come to Florence,* he thought.

Then he raised his eyebrows. "Our stop is up next."

Roy recalled hearing recently that a new tramline now linked Scandicci with Firenze through an integrated Tuscan urban communal framework. Optimistically, he hoped that the Scandicci leg had been commissioned. If it had been, he knew this would take them bang into the center of Florence. If it hadn't, he would need a different plan.

In the rear-view, the black suburban was gaining ground. It was maybe six hundred feet away now. He pulled the bus to a grinding halt outside the tram station entrance as the wheels locked and skidded, until they eventually stopped. Outside, plumes of dust from the braking wheels created a powdered cloud, smothering the bus and surrounding cars throughout the station entranceway. Nearby travellers waiting to board the bus pulled back in surprise as the semiautomatically driven diesel engine let off a series of jittering thuds. "This will have to do us," Roy shouted, launching himself out of the driver's pod and grabbing Melanie's hand.

Moments later, they emerged through the side door of the bus. Apprehensive that the Cossacks would be close on their tail, Roy knew they needed a change. He looked back. Through the dust cloud, he could see them. Now they were only three hundred feet from the station. He looked at Melanie anxiously. She was fading, her face ashen and her pupils starting to dilate.

"We need to make a quick pit stop," he said. "You okay?"

Melanie was cupping her head like a baby. "My head hurts."

Roy grabbed her hand once again and cut a trajectory straight towards a reasonably well-sized clothing retail outlet. Together they ran inside, where Roy made a beeline for the accessories section. He grabbed a red baseball cap and picked out a white one for Melanie. Then he grabbed two cropped jackets. They were zipped and made from cotton. *Light and comfortable*, he thought. One was beige, the other one navy. They were slightly oversized.

Roy pulled the tags from the garments. "Here, put this on," he said, handing Melanie the navy jacket and the white cap. Then he donned his jacket and cap, dropped €100 on the sales assistant's counter, and before she could look up to give him back his change, they were gone.

Concealed somewhat by their sartorial enhancements, Roy and Melanie strode calmly along the pavement after leaving the store. Roy looked up at the signage. They were less than thirty feet from the tram ticket booth. Fortunately, the peripheral pathway that connected the array of shops making up the high street of Scandicci was well populated with late-morning shoppers. No need to run. Roy knew running would attract too much attention. Cognizant that the Russians had most probably enveloped the area, Roy glanced to his right and spotted a large black Suburban about a hundred feet away and racing towards the station. He looked to his left and spotted its twin coming in the opposite direction. Without thinking, he quickly threw his arms around Melanie and kissed her, holding his lips there for a long while. She didn't move away. In the background, Roy could hear whizzing Vespa flywheels pass them by in their dozens. He couldn't hear any Suburbans breaking to a halt. *They will either have gone a hundred feet past or they'll be parked right in front of us*, he thought. He hoped for the former.

Roy pulled away, glancing to his right and then his left. Nothing. Then he left off a sigh of relief. *They must have passed.* Serenely, he gazed back into her eyes. "Sorry. I just needed to do that," he whispered. Roy could see Melanie was weary, fatigued, and disorientated. He guessed it must have been adrenalin that had kept her going this far.

"No problem," Melanie replied, barely getting the words out of her mouth.

Roy could see her eyes were saying something different. He knew she wouldn't be able to get much further. "C'mon, let's go," he said, grabbing her hand.

They walked briskly a little further, arriving at the ticketing window, where Roy approached a young female attendant. "Has the Firenze route opened?" he asked the girl sitting behind the glass screen.

The attendant smiled, revealing a bright set of perfectly manicured teeth. "Just commissioned yesterday."

Roy looked around to see if his abductors had caught their tail. No sign of any Suburbans. No sign of any Cossacks, either. "Two tickets," he said.

~~~

When the tram arrived in the center of Florence, Roy hailed a taxi. The driver, not accustomed to such fares, looked disbelievingly as the couple approached his rear door. Roy pushed Melanie inside and followed straight in behind her.

He eyed the driver. *"Portaci all'Ospedale di Santa Maria Nuova, è in via Sant'Egidio,"* he said in perfect Italian.

Then Melanie collapsed in his arms.

Chapter 41
False Flag

Bill Peterson liked to wander. His leadership style, according to his office staff, was contained within the acronym MBWA (Management by Wandering Around). Today he was wandering around his abode, 1600 Pennsylvania Avenue in Washington, DC. He was on his way to the library on the ground floor. The library was his favorite room when he needed time to think, and today, he had a lot of thinking to do. He nodded confidently to his staff as he passed.

Absorbed with bureaucracy and international cooperation protocols, Peterson was not just a complicit supporter of a New World Order, he was the architect. His accomplices: world, central, international, and private banks within the Federal Reserve System. Peterson knew the US banking regime was deflated after three years of subprime write-offs, and the entire banking hierarchy was about to face another downturn in global economic activity with a subsequent squeeze on development. This would doubtless deflate interest rates once again to a new all-time low.

In the banking world, low interest rates meant low margins. Low margins meant low bonuses. Low bonuses normally meant Toyotas instead of Porsches.

On the other hand, Peterson figured an imminent conflict would induce distress, creating an urgent need for cash from the banking world in support of military and infrastructure repairs. Consequently, this would cause a rapid increase in interest rates. Substantially increased profits and bonuses for the entire banking community would naturally follow.

Inside the library, he meandered his way around old antique furniture pieces randomly placed around the room, poking his head into one of the expansive mahogany bookshelves for inspiration. He wasn't particularly worried about whether he drove a Toyota or a Porsche. He never got to drive anywhere, anyway. He was more interested in the positive influence that an imminent conflict would have on the US economy—an economy that badly needed a catalyst.

There was nothing new about this. Hidden within international intelligence archives around the world over the last one hundred years, an amalgam of conspiracy theories inferring false flag actions resided—all of which were perfect catalysts for conflict. Peterson may not have had security clearance to all of them, but he had enough to go on. In most cases, he found them expertly concealed, with esoteric conjecture subsequent to the action.

Peterson guessed this was pretty standard intelligence protocol. *I'm not doing anything different from my predecessors,* he thought. He was encouraged to read that the Russians themselves had used this tactic to great effect. The KGB was rumored to have conducted a series of bombings throughout Russia in order to justify war against Chechnya and put Vladimir Putin into power. Kennedy also used similar tactics in a plan, code-named *Operation Northwoods,* to blow up American airplanes in the 1960s—ultimately blaming it on the Cubans in order to justify an invasion against them. Peterson was acutely aware of this one, given that the US government documents were already declassified. Even as far back as the 1950s, false flags were flying at full mast on the *TPAJAX Project,* when reportedly CIA-recruited Iranians posing as Communists engaged to stage bombings in Iran in order to turn the country against its prime minister, Mohammad Mossadegh.

The United States government, however, had never attempted anything on the scale of this coups d'état before—especially on Russia. This thought had never crossed Peterson's mind until his lifetime friend Brad Dunkley had suggested it. Mikhail Kasinov was now the point man, and Great Britain, their long-term ally, the sacramonial initiator of the false flag strategy. Peterson, for his own esoteric reasons, had not kept Andrew Wood in the loop on some of the more pertinent details surrounding Kasinov's escape: ergo, it was inspired from the White House.

Peterson, now perched behind a small reading table in the center of the library, was startled from his ruminations when his mobile phone rang. He picked up the receiver and answered it sternly. "Yes."

His assistant, who was sitting two floors up adjacent to the Oval Office, announced, "I've got Clay Parker on the line. Is it okay to put him through to your mobile?"

"Yes," he replied economically.

Peterson paused until he heard Parker's voice. "Thanks for returning my call," the president said. "I know you're pulling your teams together on this. May I strongly suggest you reengage Xenop? You need to get him over here, ASAP."

"Will do, Mr. President," Parker responded reverentially.

Peterson placed the phone on the table. Turning away, he thought about how heads of state around the globe were anxiously holding their breath as the precipice of world chaos unfolded before them.

He smiled. *Everything was falling into place perfectly.*

In the eyes of the world, it looked like the Russians had started it.

They were the false flag.

Chapter 42
Hypothermia

By the time the taxi arrived at the Santa Maria Nuova Hospital, Melanie had lost consciousness and was immediately admitted. Attentive to emergency arrivals, medical staff members were on standby to help as Roy assisted, lifting her from the taxi. "We'll take it from here," an elderly nurse said as she feverishly wheeled her away on a rather primitive-looking gurney that squeaked a lot. Roy followed, pushing the gurney from behind.

As the doors into the infirmary opened, Roy could feel the waft of a healthy blend of carbon, hydrogen, and iodine ingredients that made up the iodoform antiseptic disinfectant for covering the wards and corridors. It radiated an inimitable pungent whiff that was almost nauseating. Unruffled by the aroma, Roy followed the medical staff until they stopped and entered a room marked 3C. He watched the staff transfer her onto the hospital bed and then plug monitors, catheters, and a plethora of other medical gadgets he didn't recognize into as many orifices as were available.

"You should wait outside," the elderly nurse told him.

Roy nodded. "If she wakes up and asks, just let her know I'll be right back. I have to go and make a phone call." He went in search of a quieter zone where he could catch up with the seven missed calls indicated on his phone.

He found it outside the hospital. Six of the missed calls were from Clay Parker, and one from a number he didn't recognize. The messages from Parker were a series of haranguing pleas that crescendoed on the final message:

"Roy, I've been trying to reach you for several hours. Please pick up. You better get over to Washington, ASAP. The Kasinov affair is getting out of control. Your assistance is required urgently. Call me."

The last message was different: "This is Alexei Lugovoy. You paid a visit to my house. We need to meet. Call me."

Roy was addled by this message. With his mind focused on Lugovoy's voicemail, he returned and went straight to 3C. He opened the door and looked inside. Melanie wasn't there.

Through the ward corridors, Roy ran to the nearest nurse's station and approached the female nurse sitting behind a tall, Spartan desk. "Excuse me," he said in an extremely harried manner.

"Yes, may I help you?" the tired-looking nurse asked.

Roy pointed back to the room where he had last seen Melanie. "Where is Melanie Bauer," he asked anxiously. "The girl that was in ward 3C?"

"Doctor Martenelli is looking after her," the young lady answered.

"Where is he?"

"He's in surgery, I'm afraid," the station attendant answered nervously.

"Show me where he is—where she is," Roy exclaimed, turning, his eyes darting over the labyrinth of corridors that emerged from the central area.

"I'm afraid I can't do that. You'll just have to wait, sir."

Roy, unable to penetrate the reception sentinel of Florence's oldest medical establishment, waited pensively. Half an hour later, the young lady who had asked him to wait waved her hand in the direction of the east corridor. "That's him there."

Roy looked over to see a young man in a white coat with dark, creamed-back hair and shiny, pointed shoes walking briskly towards the nurse's station with a chart in his hands. Roy approached him feverishly. "Doctor Martenelli?"

"Yes, I am Doctor Martenelli."

"I'm looking for Melanie Bauer," Roy snapped. "She was in ward 3C. I'm the guy who brought her in."

Martenelli glanced back at his chart. "I'm afraid I'm not permitted to release information to anyone except family members," the young doctor replied in a theatrical tone.

Roy guessed he had recited that line on several occasions. He could feel his mouth drying up inside. "I'm the only family she's got here in Florence, so you better tell me," he croaked authoritatively.

Martenelli eyed Roy up and down. "You were with her when all this occurred?"

"Yes."

"Perhaps you can explain what happened."

"It's complicated," Roy replied. "We were abducted."

"In that case, I need to call the police. It's standard procedure in all cases like this." He turned as if to make his way for the nurse's station.

Roy grabbed his shoulder. "Wait! It's better the police are not involved. If you call them, I'll be stuck here till midnight answering stupid questions, which I have no intention of doing."

"But what about hospital protocols?" the young doctor exclaimed, his arms raised in the air.

Roy had noticed on his way through the hospital reception that construction had halted on what seemed to be an expansion in the left wing. "I see you're doing some development on the west wing," Roy said, pointing in the direction he had seen rusted scaffolding and discolored site signage.

"Yes, we were," Martenelli replied despondently. "We had a whole new pediatric intensive care section planned, including an emergency ward. We were just about to place orders for mechanical ventilators and patient monitoring systems. I even had the résumés of three new unit respiratory therapists short-listed, ready to hire them. But as with everything else in this place, the government ran out of money."

Roy reached behind the nurse's station, helped himself to a pen and paper, and started writing. A minute later, he handed the sheet to Martenelli.

"What is this? A confession?"

"Just read it," Roy said calmly.

"To Whom It May Concern," the doctor read. "I, Roy Young, commit to provide all necessary funds to carry out the completion of the new pediatric west wing of Santa Maria Nuova Hospital." The young doctor's eyes shifted upwards at Roy before fixing them back on the handwritten offer. "This includes all mechanical ventilators, patient monitoring systems, and staff. Signed, Roy Young."

Martenelli looked to the nurse, who had the phone cradled to her ear. "Cancel that call, Nurse."

Roy looked back at Martenelli and nodded. "Now, Doctor, what about Melanie?"

Martenelli paused and looked at the chart again. "Okay," he began, nodding. "She has just finished

MRI and CT scans. I wanted to check for any intracranial bleeding. From what I've seen, I think she'll be okay. But when you brought her in, she was suffering from severe concussion, which turned quite serious. She received a pretty nasty blow to the side of her head. Somewhere along the course of the last twenty-four hours, she also received a substantial dose of chloroform. This unfortunately comes with a few undesirable post-anesthetic effects. Along with the concussion, she had some respiratory problems, and I needed to make sure there were no long-term side effects. I gave her pentobarbital, a barbiturate, to sedate her. It's pretty strong, so you won't see her awake for a couple of hours. She'll need plenty of rest after she wakes. She seems like a pretty strong girl. I'm sure she'll pull through just fine."

Roy swallowed hard. Although mystified with all the jargon the young doctor had rambled off, he felt relieved when he heard the final cadence. He brushed his brow and let out a sigh of relief. "Thanks," he uttered, nodding.

"You look like you need some medical attention yourself," the young doctor pointed out.

"I've taken a couple aspirin. I'll be fine."

"I think you might need some stronger analgesics to arrest the pain," Martenelli said, pulling out a pad from his pocket. "I'll write something up for you."

~~~

Several hours later, under the gazes of fifteenth-century Bernardo Buontalenti frescoes, Melanie awoke. She sat up and stared ahead, trying to figure out where she was. Despite its historical significance, the Hospital of Santa Maria Nuova was pretty utilitarian and efficient. After all, it was the Tuscan city's most historical welfare institution. As Melanie came around, she gazed over Roy's head and off to the side. Roy turned, craning his neck upwards and down along the corridor to see the ceiling details and paraphernalia around the inside of Santa Maria Nuova. It looked more like a metamorphic retrofit of the Sistine Chapel with clothed tables, tourists, and Roman memorabilia replaced with nurse's stations, medical staff, and gurney carriages. *No wonder she looks puzzled*, he thought.

"Hello there, Miss," Roy said softly, his smiling nimbus gaze usurping the ancient artistry as he placed his hand firmly on hers.

Melanie clenched his hand in return. "Hello, Mister," she replied, her voiced strained and husky. "You certainly know how to get yourself into and out of trouble, don't you?"

She may have been unconscious for almost six hours solid, but she hasn't lost her wit, Roy thought, smiling back at her. "I try my best."

"That was a pretty mesmeric performance back there," Melanie added, pushing aside several catheters attached to her arm. "Thank you for saving me."

Roy held his palm against the side of her face.

"Least I could do after inviting you to Florence."

She issued a weak chuckle.

"The phone call you took at dinner last night," Roy said. "I'm pretty sure they took advantage of that distraction to pad us with chloroform. It was Natasha, right?"

"Yes, it was Natasha."

"What did she say?"

Melanie sat upright. "She said that she was in Cyprus and met Kasinov's private banker. Wait for this . . . He managed to siphon out almost nine billion US dollars!"

"Why am I not surprised?" Roy nodded. "Anything else?"

"Yeah. She said everything stacked up with Mikhail's accounts, except for three payments made to some Chechen guy called Pavel Belayev." As she spoke, some color started to restore to her face.

"Anything else?"

"That I should Google his name."

In Roy's opinion, Natasha was an unknown and untested accomplice. Although she had travelled to Cyprus to investigate spurious financial transfers, he wondered if she had her own agenda. "I think she might be trying to set us up. Either that or someone else is pulling her strings."

Melanie frowned. "I think she's the real deal—honestly I do. I trust her."

"Why?" Roy probed.

"She said something about art—that it's not

what you see, but what you make others see." Melanie motioned to the curves of her body. "I guess she used her assets."

"I'm sure she did." Roy laughed. "All of them." Roy wondered when he might get to check out Melanie's assets. *Another time.* He knew he had to get moving—and fast. "Look, Melanie, I'm sorry to spring this on you," he said after a brief pause. "I have to fly to Washington. Since our diversion at dinner last evening, it appears that Britain and Russia have withdrawn diplomatic privileges. Tensions are escalating. Clay Parker from the CIA sent me an urgent message. I need to get there quickly, to be part of a mediation team to try and get some fingers off the self-destruct buttons in this political ego contest."

Melanie looked at him graciously. "After what I've seen, I'm sure your definition of mediation will be slightly different from theirs."

"Probably."

"I wonder if Kasinov's TV exhibition last night has something to do with the standoff."

"I'm pretty sure it has," Roy replied. "Every time he opens his mouth, he seems to upset someone. Anyway, pressure relief valves are going off all over the place. And from what I hear, a few more nations have joined in on the dispute. This thing could explode unless we can put some manners on it." Roy placed his palms on her cheeks. "I've got to go," he said, kissing her firmly on the lips. "I'll be back as soon as I can."

Roy could see her eyes were welling up. He didn't know if it was in disbelief or admiration.

"Okay, take care of yourself," she said. "I'll be fine."

Roy turned and departed down a staircase surrounded by expansive glass casings that overlooked the Cloister of Bones Temple. His mind was in a whirlwind, determined as he was to get to the bottom of the whole mess. The Russian-British diplomatic malaise was about to engulf the world, but Roy's mind wasn't concerned with that—at least not right now. Instead, his thoughts toggled over a cluster of unlikely connected Russians. He knew Kasinov was up to his neck in all of this mess, but he needed to find something that connected Kasinov, Zolotov, and the Chechens.

And how come Lugovoy is making contact now?

Roy passed the administrative hall, exiting the hospital before making his way through Piazza di Santa Maria Nuova and jumping into a taxi. "Aeroporto Galileo!" he cried from the backseat.

Chapter 43
Black Tuesday

Roy awoke with a thud the following morning when the wheels on the Boeing 777 hit the runway, touching down at Dulles International Airport after a seven-hour transatlantic flight. Tired and unkempt after an eventful twenty-four hours in Florence, Roy had slept the whole way. He was still covered in cuts and bruises from the unscheduled expedition to the Scandicci suburb. He had experienced many days when he felt good about how he looked and what he wore. Today was not one of those days.

From the safety deposit box he kept at Galileo, Roy had retrieved one of his extra passports, along with a copy of the information he had received from Nikoletta Lukas. Now, as he joined the US Immigration queue, he pulled out the crispy, fresh passport from inside his pocket. The queue was moving slowly. From his experience, it had moved slower ever since they had inserted the new biometric facial recognition checks to collect and store personal electronic data. Up ahead, everybody approached the dock and placed both their feet on the designated spot, where two yellow foot imprints were situated below the camera line on the floor. Everyone always took great care to make sure their feet aligned perfectly in the yellow imprints. Roy knew that the calibration of the camera taking the photo didn't require such level of accuracy, but most people performed the routine anyway. *Someone must have performed this move once,* he thought, *and now everybody just follows.* When it was Roy's turn, he didn't look at the yellow footprints. He just looked at the camera—click, and he was done. Then the shuffling started again behind him.

Casually he made his way through customs, bypassing a few disbelieving glances, and was met by the contract NCS limousine service outside arrivals. The awaiting driver displayed Roy's name in bold black writing on a white card.

Roy approached the dark-suited chauffeur. "I'm Roy Young."

"You're Roy Young?"

Roy looked at him more deeply this time. "I just said I was Roy Young. You hard of hearing?"

The limousine driver looked him up and down. "Sorry, sir. I was just expecting a government type guy, not a jeans and T-shirt kind of guy."

After an extensive journey that took almost thirteen hours from the time he left Santa Maria

Nuova, Roy eventually arrived at the Langley Hotel just off Sixth Street. His welcoming reception consisted of two early-morning leaf blowers making a roaring racket outside the hotel's frugal entrance. He nodded to the operators as he stopped to check his watch.

It was 6:00 a.m.

After checking in at the Langley, he walked along the corridor to his room. He thought about his 7:00 a.m. pickup and the 7:30 a.m. meeting with Parker and Company. In his room, he whipped off his clothes and jumped into the shower, shaved, and dried himself. He checked his watch again: 6:15 a.m. He put on his slim-fitting white cotton shirt and his Napolise ISAIA 52-long suit, which he had picked up at the Rinascente outlet at Galileo Airport. He did up his tie, put on his shoes, set his alarm for 6:55 a.m., and carefully lay down on the neatly made bed.

Cognizant of the momentum that the political standoff had reached, Roy's emergency trip to Washington to meet with Parker was critically timed. Nobody had anticipated the contagion effect from the Russian-British fracas. The world was heading into chaos. Threats of weapons of mass destruction being prelaunched, armed, and directed at opponent countries were appearing faster than a blackjack card dealer in full flow.

Roy closed his eyes and went to sleep. Forty minutes later, he was awake again. He brushed himself off and left the room, picking up the copy of *The Washington Post* that the staff had kindly suspended from the handle of his door. It was Wednesday morning, the 3rd of December, 2010, and the headline that jumped off the page startled him: BLACK TUESDAY: WHERE DID ALL THE MONEY GO?

Roy paused and read the article. It seemed that havoc had prevailed in the money markets the day before, inspired by the punitive Russian and British diplomatic actions. After the initial volleys of diplomatic withdrawal initiated by the pugnacious Russians, neither side had succumbed to the power struggle, neither magnanimously nor thoughtlessly. Instead, the affray had been amplified through the initiation of a military standoff, with threats of nuclear armament. As a result, the day had been branded "Black Tuesday," with London and world stock markets free-falling on average 25 percent, dumping US$200 billion in market capitalization write-offs in one day alone. Roy shook his head and chuckled. *Kasinov contagion—you see, Melanie? I told you they would hang him out to dry.*

Contracted by the US government, Roy had helped free Kasinov. As part of that agreement, his fee included a six-month observation period to deal with any complications that arose. This was a complication.

More of a major complication, he thought.

Kasinov's escape was the nexus for the distrust and the savage internecine of exchanges that followed between Russia and Great Britain. Overtly exacerbated by the world's media, it had reached a point of no return. It had brought the world to the brink of nuclear action.

Roy arrived at the Pentagon as planned to participate in an emergency military mitigation strategy session. As he alighted the NCS chauffeured vehicle, he wasn't surprised to witness a shroud of TV camera crews and support staff, along with several spectators, engulfing the boundary entrance. The reporters stood a few steps back from their cameras, collectively aligned like a cavalry regiment in procession—each one parlaying their story without any cognizance of their competitors.

Nearest Roy as he arrived was CNN's senior military correspondent, Zach Zoller. Roy stopped and listened.

"After all the years of testing and demonstrations," Zoller said into his camera, "we have finally reached this zenith. If this escalates to the next level, our research suggests that there may be a proliferation of some four thousand nuclear warheads that could be pulled out from warehouses, subsea vessels, and solid steel bunkers from across the globe, and preassembled ready for use. The countries believed to possess nuclear arms include the United States, Russia, the United Kingdom, France, China, Israel, India, Pakistan, North Korea, and South Africa. Those that are set to join the isotope fission and fusion beauty contest have unveiled their menu of atomic cocktails, all designed to deliver enormous mushroom clouds with nowhere to go but into the atmosphere. The technology has advanced so much in the last ten years that modern thermonuclear weaponry can be so easily concealed, physically weighing as little as a ton, but capable of producing an explosive force that can devastate an entire city from the initial blast, the resultant fire, and the contaminant radiation."

Roy shook his head in disbelief. "Definitive and devastating action," the Russians had said. That's pretty clear. No ambiguity. *Okay, let's see if we can put some manners on this*, he thought as he moved towards the security checkpoint.

Resolved to working with the NCS and other international bodies to find a solution, Roy marched through the operating floor of the building after passing security clearance. He could feel the stares from many eyes as he walked. It was like he was on parade, like he was heading into the center of the Coliseum to face a battle for his life. Most diplomatic assignees or military representatives would be shitting themselves. Roy was calm. He knew what had to be done.

For every problem, there is always a solution.

~~~

Melanie approached Martenelli with sincere humility in her eyes. She knew her convalescence would be short-lived. It had to be. "Look, if you really want to help me, Dr. Martenelli, then tell me where I'll find the nearest Internet café."

"Okay, okay. But these Internet cafés appear and disappear with amazing regularity," Martenelli said. "Last time I looked, there was one just around the corner." He gestured a circuitous routing.

"Great. What's the address?"

"If you take a left out of here, and then the second left again, I think it's there on the right-hand side of the street, on Via Fiesolana."

Melanie planted a big kiss onto Martenelli's cheek. "Thanks," she said, releasing a smile as she turned away. All the staff nurses looked on awkwardly. Martenelli blushed. Melanie didn't. Instead, she made for the exit and checked herself out of hospital the day after she awoke, much to Martenelli's discontent. She was persuasive, for she had work to do.

Determined to research each piece of data that had been accumulated, she exited Santa Maria Nuova Hospital and turned left on to Via Sant'Egidio. Passing a mobile phone shop, she went in and picked herself up a pay-as-you-go Italian mobile for €25. Even though her bag and everything else in it was gone, she had some cash and a card tucked inside the pocket of her pencil black jeans. She exited the phone shop and took the second left into Via Fiesolana, following Martenelli's directions meticulously. There, halfway down on the right-hand side was a sign that read INTERNET POINT SKY WAVES

INTERNATIONAL, just like the good doctor had said.

From outside, it resembled a rented shop front—more windows than wall. Unperturbed by its apparent parsimony, Melanie entered. Inside, a bunch of computers were placed randomly on a series of old veneered oak desks. She wasn't concerned. As long as she could get a decent DSL connection, this would do just fine. Around the room, there were three clusters of four desks each, all of which faced each other with small privacy dividers between. The place was empty except for a kid sitting at the rear of the room. Melanie studied him. He had long, unkempt hair, with a baby fluff beard. His ears were adorned in red Dr. Dre Beats headphones. He couldn't have been more than seventeen years old. *He probably has that unique skill held by teens today, being able to partially communicate while listening to some R&B-Rap anthology.*

"How much?" she asked the young attendant.

"It's ten cents per minute or fifteen Euros an hour. Take your pick?" the young attendant said, waving his hand over the array of tables and computers.

Melanie performed several seconds of elementary calculus in her mind. "I'll take it for one hour," she replied succinctly, handing the young man her Barclaycard.

The young man swiped the card. "Screen five. That one over there," he said, pointing to the twenty-two-inch, battered-looking Dell monitor at the corner desk facing the window.

Melanie raced over, sat down, and looked at the Italian keyboards, immediately noticing that some of the letters were displayed differently. She started to type, inserting an extraneous comma or two before figuring out the different symbols. Eventually she launched the web browser, settled into her chair, and started pressing keys faster than the speed of inlet valves opening and closing on a combustion engine.

Alexander Zolotov, Angolan War, she typed.

She scrolled down and selected an article that gave a descript précis on the role, responsibility, and authority vested to Zolotov. After reading the article, she paused, sagaciously assessing what appeared on the screen before her.

Then she followed with *Pavel Belayev.*

The results were quite complimentary:

Pavel Belayev owns Bezopasnost, one of Russia's premiere security firms. The firm has grown tenfold over the last four years.

RusOil awards long-term contract to Bezopasnost for Barents Sea development.

Pavel Belayev, Russia's up-and-coming entrepreneur, awarded honorary degree from Moscow University.

Melanie continued scrolling through onto the third page in the search engine's results and found one article that gave a different view:

Bezopasnost is known by FSB as a hit company, run by a group of former Chechen rebels known to have commercialized their trade. Their owner, Pavel Belayev, is also known as Russia's number one exterminator.

Melanie emerged incredulous from behind the computer, looking like she had just discovered the missing equation to commercialize nuclear fusion. She checked her personal email account and pulled up an email Roy had sent her after they met in London. She groped in her pocket for the phone she had just acquired. Then she called the number.

Chapter 44
Cuban Veracities

Surrounded by several other NCS and CIA agents, international ambassadorial assignees, members of the International Atomic Energy Agency, NATO representatives, and an amalgam of foreign secret service agents from Germany, France, and the UK, Roy sat at a center placing around a colossal walnut-veneered U-shaped boardroom table inside the Pentagon's soundproofed, aptly named War Room. It was an international diplomatic orgy of who's who. Roy estimated there must have been at least fifty people in the room.

Parker came rushing over to Roy, greeting him as soon as he arrived. "You look like shit," Parker said. "What happened?"

"Slipped in the shower," Roy said. "It was nothing."

"Nasty fall! Anyway, thanks for making it over." Parker glanced at his wristwatch. "If you'll excuse me," he said softly. "I better get this meeting started."

Subdued but seemingly resolute, Parker introduced the session, welcoming everyone and thanking those present for their attendance. "Gentlemen, we are at the precipice of the greatest international military challenge this world has ever known. For some reason, Russia has reacted with uncharacteristic perniciousness."

Roy eyed Parker. He knew that the NCS director had embellished some of the facts. The main fact he forgot to mention was that the NCS had implanted Kasinov in the UK. *Minor oversight.*

"It has allowed a domestic oligarchical squabble to blossom into a potential nuclear catastrophe," Parker said. "We as the pillars of the international intelligence community need to find an intelligence solution to a political problem—and fast."

Parker continued without over-amplification of the gravity of the situation. He asked the attendees to be assertive, pragmatic, and decisive, although he came across somewhat derisive as he spoke during his introductions. Roy could see he was visibly under pressure and starting to show it. In Parker's world, pressure was something that followed him wherever he went. In Roy's world, pressure was for tires.

As Parker's prologue continued into its tenth minute, Roy's phone vibrated. He could see it was Melanie. He knew that she was quite adept at connecting the dots between significant financial events that affected stock market trading, and was hopeful that she would unearth something. Roy swung around in his chair, facing away from the meeting. His eyes were wide open with his eyebrows raised. "Hello," he said quietly as he pressed his free hand to his ear to block out the noise of Parker's speech.

"Hi, Roy. It's Melanie. Can you talk?"

"Of course. How are you feeling?" he enquired eagerly.

"I'm fine. Quick recovery." Melanie spoke with great enthusiasm in her voice. "I have a few things here which might be of interest."

"I'm all ears." Roy rose from his seat, threw his backpack over his shoulder, and searched for a quieter passage outside the Pentagon's capacious boardroom. He motioned to Parker to indicate that he would be back after he finished the call.

"Okay," Melanie said. "I looked up Pavel Belayev, and the results were a bit mixed. He owns a company called Bezopasnost. It says he could be anything from the next generation of Mother Teresa to a Russian version of Jason Bourne. This is the company that Kasinov's account made payments to."

Roy placed the phone down on the adjacent table and reached into his backpack, pulling out an A4 manila envelope. He removed a sheet from inside and scrolled through it.

"Roy, are you there?" Melanie queried.

Roy grabbed the phone again. "Sorry, yes. I'm here. Did Natasha tell you the dates of those payments?"

"No, she didn't."

"I'm looking at the file I received from Nikoletta in Budapest. I made a copy before I gave the original and electronic copy to Kasinov." His eyes stopped halfway down the list. He tapped his finger on the sheet several times. "Here it is on Vladimir's list. A payment was made to Bezopasnost in 2001, in January. I see another two payments in 2002, May and September. One million US each time."

"But I thought the Chechens hated the Russians," Melanie enquired.

"They might," Roy answered. "But in international espionage, the power of the dollar trumps everything else, I'm afraid."

"What were the payments for, do you think?"

"I'm not one hundred percent sure, but I've got a pretty good hunch," Roy answered.

"I might have found something else here," Melanie said with renewed enthusiasm. "I spoke with your friend Alistair in Johannesburg, and he helped me get my hands on some old Soviet research expenditure journals from back in the late eighties. Roy, Kasinov's alumni partner, was the bagman in Angola. He was the Soviet financier. He controlled everything."

"Let me guess. Zolotov?"

"You're right. You had seen him before.

Alexander Zolotov was in charge of all Soviet activity there from 1987 to 1990."

"I should have killed that bastard when I had the chance," Roy repeated, shaking his head.

"After having gone through the files that Alistair sent to me, I estimate that the total expenditure for the Soviet military in 1988 was about thirty-three billion US. That was more than half the total annual budget expenditure of sixty-five billion, twelve percent of GDP at two hundred sixty-four billion."

"All sounds very interesting, but what does it mean?" Roy enquired without confrontation.

Despite her obvious excitement, Melanie remained calm as she tried to decipher exactly what might have been going on in Zolotov's mind at that time. "It gets interesting. The real nexus is even more curious. It appears Zolotov purposefully overestimated the costs of the ongoing Soviet activities supporting Cuba's military front in Angola. I found a file claiming that he would need to increase troops by almost fifty percent in 1988, bringing the annual bill up to 7.5 billion. He said it was to guarantee completion and conduct cleanup operations, along with much needed reinforcements in personnel, MiG-23 fighters, T62 tanks, AA missile and radar systems—all that kind of military stuff."

Roy pulled back from the phone with a look of astonishment. "But the war was just about over then."

"Yeah, it should have been—but that's not all," Melanie said decisively. "Zolotov was also involved in several other international Soviet missions in Cuba, the Far East, and Eastern Bloc countries. In all cases, he had purposely overestimated all of the budgets. He was looking for another twelve billion for 1989 alone, against a total Soviet budget of thirty-three billion."

Roy worked out the numbers in his head. "That's a thirty-six percent growth in expenditure. No wonder they shut him down."

"That's not all they shut down, Roy," Melanie exclaimed.

"What do you mean?"

"They couldn't afford any more international expenditure. They had no capital. They couldn't pay thirty-three billion, let alone another twelve billion on top of that. Zolotov was the straw that broke the camel's back. His tempestuous accounting caused the Soviet hierarchy to cull all international expenditure," Melanie continued, exhorting her hypothesis authoritatively. "He caused the withdrawal from the Soviet presence in Angola, and the withdrawal from the Eastern Bloc countries. Roy, he knew what he was doing."

Roy stood in the Pentagon's lengthy corridor, shaking his head incredulously as he listened to her précis. "Incredible," he grunted.

"Incidentally, in case you were wondering, today that same military budget is about forty-eight billion, about eight percent of the total budget of six hundred billion, and about 2.5 percent of the total GDP of 1,920 billion. This bit is for information, not action." Melanie let out a little laugh.

"Thanks!"

"Roy, one other thing," Melanie chirped. "I looked at the current net present value of all the Russian assets sold off after the fall of the Soviet Union. It totals 230 billion dollars. That's how much latent value the oligarchs took out of the economy. State asset valuations were significantly reduced in 1989 based on *ministry assessments*. On average, the oligarchs made a staggering return on investment of about 9900 percent each!"

"Unbelievable! It all makes sense now." Roy exhaled. "Pretty sophisticated covert plan led by those who stood to benefit from the collapse of the Soviet Union. They would benefit from the sale of state assets that followed the collapse in order to keep the new Russia liquid."

"Plus," Melanie added, "Kasinov was an oil assessor in his earlier career. He knew exactly all the right assets to buy. And worse, he was deputy minister of fuel and energy just before the sale."

"Kasinov and Zolotov set the whole thing up," Roy concluded, reflecting on all the pieces. "They were probably both members of the Communist Youth League back at Uni. After they split up, Zolotov campaigned for considerable additional funds to finance the Soviets' ongoing support for Cuba in Angola, and a glut of other pointless international campaigns. Kasinov, as minister for fuel and energy, devalued oil and gas assets belonging to the state, significantly and disproportionately reducing international borrowing capacity. Together they caused the downfall of the Soviet Union, Melanie. Zolotov's signature on one, Kasinov's on the other. You figured it out."

"Thanks! Together they connived to orchestrate the bankruptcy of the Soviet Union, setting up the sale of the century. It was only a matter of time after the capital permutations surrounding these concurrent events that the maths provided no alternative. Between 1988 and the ultimate demise of the Soviet Union in 1991, it was about damage limitation. The whole thing was one big subterfuge—a scam of colossal magnitude. It was meticulously planned and implemented with complete deception."

"How the hell did the Soviet leadership at the time not connect the dots?" Roy queried.

"Maybe they did. Maybe they knew all along."

Roy knew he had been engaged as a Kasinov ally. After all, the Russian was his employer. However, his superficial allegiance was about to transform into agnostic adversary. In Roy's mind, the thought of Kasinov as the quintessential humanitarian was now officially out the window.

I can't be a pawn in your game anymore, Kasinov. Someone's going to have to take you down.

Most people would panic.

He didn't. He knew what he had to do.

He paused and thought about the call. More specifically, he thought about how Melanie was proving to be a lot more astute than some adjunct to his research requirements. She was unfolding the entire conspiracy behind the demise of the former superpower.

He looked at his watch. Forty-eight hours to go.

He had made some notes during the call. He looked down at the pad in front of him. Punctuated between a series of intertwining curved arrows were the names of four capital cities: Washington, Dublin, Moscow, and London.

"Okay, Melanie," Roy said. "I have to go." Then he switched off his phone.

Chapter 45
Dominos

Melanie sat at the edge of her seat. She was glued to the giant Samsung LCD TV inside Roy's Porte Santé Villa. Every news channel was covering the story. Melanie scanned them all, and eventually settled on Sky News. She wanted to hear what Angela Boddington's take on all this was. She respected her.

Boddington appeared on screen holding a miniature radio frequency receiver against her ear. *Probably some producer giving her an update,* Melanie thought. Then Boddington dropped her hand from her ear, nodded, and launched into communication mode. "Several nations have joined the political fight that has been dubbed *The Superego War*," the Sky News reporter said. "Following Great Britain's refusal to extradite escaped prisoner Mikhail Kasinov, Russia has declared a political and possible nuclear war on Great Britain, claiming extensive political interference in its domestic affairs through harboring Russian criminals and oligarchs—and worse, repudiating repatriation after ultimatums from the Kremlin.

"Embassies in both countries have been closed now for two days, and citizens are returning to their home countries on foreign service advisory warnings." The Sky News anchor paused to take a breath. "Russia has issued a very clear threat that unless Mikhail Kasinov is returned to Moscow or its embassy by the end of business today, they will initiate nuclear action on Great Britain. It seems like it's a case of using a mallet to crush an ant. But let me tell you, ladies and gentlemen, this is real, and it's happening right now in front of our very eyes. Our political correspondent in Moscow, Maxim Sterkov, who met with Kremlin officials earlier today, confirmed that Moscow has stated that Kasinov is a serious threat to the stability of the Russian economy, and they cannot tolerate his anti-Russian rhetoric any further. They say that they have persisted now for several weeks to conclude an amicable agreement with Andrew Wood and Charles Browne, but this has not been fruitful. This has become an ego war out of all proportion between these two power mongers, a battle that the Kremlin says it was coerced into after being snubbed by Great Britain. Koshenko's own words this morning were that he was deeply offended, according to Maxim." Boddington delivered the synopsis of the impasse with a look of extreme apprehension.

Melanie sat with her mouth open. *Someone is going to have to bring this ruthless pig to justice.* She couldn't believe what she was hearing. She feared for her safety, and for Roy's safety, too. She picked up her phone and tried to call him. There was no answer. His phone was switched off.

Where are you? she thought.

Melanie placed the phone on the table so she could see and hear if Roy called back. Then she focused back on Boddington.

"The latest we are hearing at Sky," Boddington continued, "is that Iran, China, and North Korea have come out in support of Russia, potentially prelaunching and activating weapons in anticipation of an attack by Russia on Great Britain and the subsequent aftermath of retaliation strikes. The US, France, Israel, and Germany have come out in support of Great Britain in the event of an attack, and likewise have initiated preparations for their weapons for prelaunch checks. This could be a catastrophe out of all proportion."

Shit. Kasinov, give yourself up, you bastard.

Melanie thought how lucky she was to be sitting in Florence and out of the UK. She glanced at her phone again to see if she had received any messages.

Nothing. I wish there was something I could do.

~~~

Inside the Pentagon's weapons of mass destruction surveillance and control center in Washington, Bill Peterson stood with perspiration marks down the inside of his shirt sleeve and all over his back. Standing next to him was Tom Ryan, the WMD director who had operated the center for over four years.

Surrounding Peterson and Ryan were numerous agents, advisers, and staff. More importantly, though, were the twelve enormous wall-mounted reconnaissance satellite heat sensor screens, each of them designed to search and identify active nuclear missiles. The combing nuclear prelaunch detection technology—known simply as FINOS, or Future Intelligent Nuclear Observing Satellite System—registered across twenty-two different satellites. Its primary function: to ensure global primary and latent coverage for every country on Earth. FINOS had the ability to detect magnetic fields in close proximity to any combination of enriched uranium, plutonium, americium, and hydrogen, and was capable of providing intensity parameters on activated nuclear warheads anywhere around the globe.

On the other side of Peterson, Chuck Miller, director of the International Atomic Energy Agency, looked on. Under the mandate of the United Nations, Miller had responsibility to oversee controls on proliferation and testing across all nations. He was also charged with encouraging the development of peaceful applications for nuclear technology. Now was the time to see the accomplishments from his twenty-year career—or alternatively, to discover a breadth of covert nuclear development activity taking place directly under his nose.

Pensively, the three men surveyed the FINOS screens in front of them. Peterson knew that the verity concerning nuclear weapons development only appeared in a situation like this: on activation, ready for deployment. To his astonishment, he could see major continental perimeters and primary oceanic corridors variegated with amphibious permutations of short-range missiles, long-range intercontinental ballistic armaments and submarine-launched ballistic devices, all strategically positioned to attain maximum certainty of success. He shook his head furiously. He didn't like what he saw. The screens were scattered with a plethora of deep yellow dots appearing over Russia, Iran, Israel, Cuba, North Korea, and UK.

The domino effect was building momentum.

So, too, was the tension inside the room.

Peterson shuddered in disbelief. He knew that, in one blink of an eye, the whole world could go up in a ball of smoke. *One domino falls, the whole world falls.* He checked his watch. Twelve hours to go.

"I was assured by every adviser under the sun that Iran does not possess any nuclear weapons," Peterson bellowed, pointing vigorously at the illumination on screen four. "What the hell is that?"

"A few months ago, Tehran doubled Iran's capacity, increasing its stockpile to 91.4 kilograms of uranium enriched to twenty percent purity," Miller recited timidly. "This was at their underground facility near the holy city of Qom. We weren't that concerned initially. Our guess was that it was barely enough for conversion into fuel rods for a research reactor, let alone a full-scale weapon system. We estimated they were at least twelve months away from being able to produce weapons-grade fuel—even longer to make a reliable warhead for a ballistic missile."

Peterson stared at him without saying a word.

Miller raised his hands in submission. "They must have reconfigured their centrifuge machines," the director from the International Atomic Energy Agency added.

Peterson had heard enough of Miller's rhetoric on Iran's nuclear renditions. He shook his head and looked back at the international luminosity challenge, his eyes focused on the screen over the Russian mainland.

Beside him, Ryan yelped. "Holy shit," the Pentagon's WMD director cried out. "Look at the volume of nuclear initiation coming up around Moscow."

Peterson glanced up at screen three on the FINOS system. He could see an enormous illumination decorating Moscow. It was lit up like

Christmas lights. It possessed significantly greater radiance than anything on the other screens. "Are you sure these screens are functioning correctly?" Peterson asked, hoping there might have been some error with their calibration.

"They are functioning just fine, I'm afraid," Miller answered awkwardly. "We received feedback early this morning from our contacts inside FSB that they were planning to activate weapons that we believed had been destroyed previously."

"Destroyed previously? What do you mean?"

"That can only be one thing: the Tsar Bomb," the International Atomic Energy Agency director replied assuredly.

"What the hell is the Tsar Bomb?" Peterson asked, wishing he didn't have to hear the answer.

Miller looked to his feet, shaking his head. "That thing was supposedly destroyed after the fall of the Soviet Union. I saw a video of it being dismantled into hundreds of pieces and destroyed. The bastards must have had a second one."

"Why is the overall illumination so great?"

"It's a one-hundred-megaton device!" Miller replied. "That's why. It operates with an impeded parachute designed to be released at an altitude of about three miles up, allowing the release bomber safe passage. It's the largest nuclear weapon ever constructed or tested. There has never been a design quite like it. It has a lead-impregnated uranium fusion tamper of the tertiary stage to eliminate fast fission by the fusion neutrons, making it the most efficient weapon ever tested."

Peterson raised his hand and watched his finger dart around the screen, pointing in a circular motion. "What about all those other dots scattered around it?"

"That will be their arsenal of Topol SS-25s. They're road-mobile single warhead missiles possessing a six-thousand-five-hundred-mile range with inertial navigation. They're supposed to be the only strategic nuclear delivery system in production in Russia. They have almost four hundred of the buggers in service, last time I checked."

"What's the fallout if they detonate them simultaneously?" Peterson asked.

Miller pulled back and did a quick whistling inhale through his lips. "The effect of that cocktail, at full yield on global fallout, would be gargantuan," Miller said, nodding. "On impact, the Tsar is supposed to release a thermal pulse fireball with an upwards swell to approximately the same height of the release plane. The blast pressure from that old thing is six times the peak pressure experienced at Hiroshima." Miller then turned and pulled out an electronic tablet from his briefcase. "If my calculations are correct," he said, pushing keys on the screen, "the Tsar, together with the single warhead missiles, would wipe out the entire land mass of Great Britain in a matter of seconds."

Peterson looked over at Ryan and pointed to the screen two down from the Russian arsenal. "Pull up Great Britain on screen five, please." The president looked on in disbelief to see four yellow dots appearing on the screen at a point somewhere off the coast of Dover. "Shit, that doesn't look promising," he bellowed, turning to Miller.

"It appears that the British have honored their disarmament covenants." Miller looked almost pleased with himself that someone had stuck to the terms of the comprehensive treaties he had created. "All of their WE177 bombs were removed from service years ago. They're only supposed to have four nuclear weapon systems in service, all on board the trident submarine, HMS *Vengeance*," Miller added before rolling his right hand towards screen four. "And there she is."

"I thought they had more than four," Peterson said, shaking his head as he wrestled to cope with the torrent of revelations coming at him.

"They do," Miller insisted. "They have two hundred operationally available warheads on the trident—fifty warheads per missile."

Peterson grinned. "That sounds better. What's the range on them?"

"They're designed to travel nine thousand miles."

"And empirically, what have they actually achieved?"

"They have actually never been tested, sir."

"Wonderful," Peterson said, rolling his eyes. "And the capacity?"

"They're about five-to-ten kiloton each."

Peterson shook his head. "It looks like a classic David versus Goliath match!"

After a brief pause, Peterson tapped Miller on the shoulder. "Chuck, can we have a private word?" he asked, ushering his International Atomic Energy Agency director to an adjacent office at the rear of the control center.

Peterson eyed Miller after shutting the door behind him. "Chuck, how the hell could this happen?" the president grunted as he wiped beads of sweat from his forehead. "I thought you guys were supposed to be watching this and keeping some regulatory protocols in place."

Miller stood with his arms raised in submission. "This is implausible," he answered, gazing back out through the Plexiglas window and pointing randomly at the FINOS screens. "I know we never got close to complete disarmament, but we put the Partial Test Ban and Nuclear Non-Proliferation treaties in place several years ago— and the Comprehensive Test Ban Treaty back in 1996. We limited and significantly reduced the nuclear arsenal testing, and all of these stockpiles were supposed to have been destroyed. I have no idea where the fuck all these weapons have come from."

Peterson could feel his body cringe. "Fuck!" he shouted. He turned his gaze to the control center, where he watched the group continue with frenetic military intelligence dialogue. He had planned on rousing the Russians into action against Great Britain. He had assumed Koshenko and company would adopt some frosty posturing, some diplomatic and economic sanctions, maybe a mini-Cold War reenactment at worst—whatever it took to shake world capital markets into low interest rate territory. What he hadn't anticipated was this. "Fuck!" he shouted again, shaking his head.

"Bill, I know you probably don't want to hear this," Miller continued. "But the atmospheric contamination from this fallout will destroy the world as we know it. There'll be nothing left."

"Thanks, Chuck. Any more good news?" Peterson said sardonically.

Miller glanced back at him with a puzzled look.

"Now if you'll excuse me, I need to make a phone call. Presidential duty."

Chapter 46
Countdown

Ten hours before the expiry of his own presidential dictate, Koshenko sat at his boardroom table between senior ministers Vasily Popov and Andrey Borodin. Po-faced and disheveled in appearance, Koshenko looked up to see Valentin Sokolov, his minister of security, strolling confidently into the boardroom with a series of rolled charts under his arm. He beamed as he entered. His encouraging expression was not reciprocated by Koshenko or any of his cortege.

"Put them down here," Koshenko roared, pointing at the large, darkened oak veneer table. "Let's have a look."

Sokolov undid the band that held the charts together, holding one end with his hands pressed down against the table. A series of sizeable diagrams and maps unraveled and went flying across the table, stopping just in front of his FSB director counterpart. Then, one by one, Sokolov peeled them off, placing four charts in front of Koshenko, arranged in a seamless symmetrical quadrant. "We've positioned Topols in these defined locations across the western perimeter of Moscow, as shown by the red stars. All access roads in the areas here, here, here, and here have been cut off." Sokolov pointed to the four primary access zones that sealed the gateways to all secondary roads entering and leaving Moscow.

"Excellent," Koshenko exclaimed, breaking out a rare prodigious smile. "Have we everything in place and ready to launch?"

"Yes, sir, Mr. President."

Koshenko craned his neck slightly, extending his gaze up to meet Sokolov's eyes. "What about the big one?"

"We have the refurbished Tupolev intercontinental bomber at Shatalovo air force base, about one hour from here," his security minister confirmed. "As per your request, we have inventively reunited the tests from five decades ago: the Tupolev together with our last remaining Tsar Bomb. The parachute casing has been assembled, attached, and tested. We need about a half hour of preflight routine. You just have to say the word."

"Excellent, Sokolov." Koshenko nodded. "You seem to have redeemed yourself."

~~~

Commander Robert Thomas was on his feet and angled forward, with his hands primed to the control panel desk inside the central control room of HMS *Vengeance*. His submarine officer, officer of the deck, and his operations officer flanked him. "Larry, I want to run down the prelaunch procedure. Do you copy?"

On the other end of the maritime Tannoy was Larry Fluke, his chief military officer. "Yes, sir. Copy that." Fluke was positioned twenty-eight feet below, inside the missile chamber in the basement of the sub.

Thomas commenced the sequence mechanization routine. It was no different from the weekly audit routine they conducted each Friday aboard HMS *Vengeance*—except this time, it wasn't an audit routine. This time, it was for real.

"GPS navigational settings."

"Check."

"Triangulation inertial vanes."

"Check."

"Cluster munitions settings."

"Check."

After the ten-minute procedure was completed and double-checked, Thomas turned to the radioman of the watch on his right-hand side. "Patch me through to the PM's office," the commander said lucidly.

~~~

As he awaited the call from HMS *Vengeance*, Andrew Wood sat behind an antique walnut desk with a dark green leather insert covering most of its surface. Inside the privacy of Number 10

Downing Street, Duncan Nairn, head of MI6, sat directly across from him. Nairn was there to brief him on the Russian arsenal.

Despite his twenty years in the field across three continents, and entrenched as the leader of MI6 for the last five years, Nairn looked like a worried man now. His lobster-red face and rotund, diminutive disposition amplified his anxiety. "Our intelligence is telling us that the Russians are rolling out warheads across the capital's perimeter like fireworks on New Year's Eve," Nairn said with conviction. Although Scottish by birth, Nairn was educated at Henley and then Oxford. His accent, however, sounded more English than Scottish.

Sitting next to Nairn was Nicholas Stone, admiral of the fleet of the British Royal Navy. Stone was a large man, well above six feet, with jet-black hair and a well-manicured goatee with silver strands. He was fully attired in naval standard navy blue and white, with five embroidered insignia on his cuffs and a combination of crowns and swords arranged across his shining epaulettes. His cap was on the desk in front of him, his hands cradled around it and almost covering the gold leaves that protruded its peak.

Wood looked across at Stone with rivulets of perspiration visibly flowing down his face. "Well, Admiral?" he enquired.

Stone glanced at his watch. "We should be

hearing from HMS *Vengeance* any moment now, Prime Minister."

Wood turned his gaze to the head of MI6. "Duncan, while we're waiting—anything positive to report?"

"Yes, our research suggests that most of their weapons are conventional intercontinental missiles."

"What does that mean exactly?" the prime minister enquired.

"It means that, if they're launched, they can still be aborted up to at least five miles before impact."

"Very reassuring," Wood replied sardonically, rolling his eyes upwards. "Thank you for that, Duncan."

Wood's phone rang, and after three rings, he answered. "This is Andrew Wood."

"Prime Minister, this is Commander Robert Thomas aboard HMS *Vengeance*."

"Yes, Commander Thomas," Wood replied. "I'm here with Admiral Stone and Duncan Nairn, head of MI6."

Stone sat up and interjected. "Relay your position and status, Commander Thomas," the colorfully dressed admiral requested.

"We are currently orbiting around 51.1278° N, 1.3156° E off the southeast coast of Dover. I can confirm that all four of the trident nuclear missiles have been tested, calibrated, and are ready for prelaunch routine—each with an individual capacity of fifty warheads. Destination coordinates as instructed, aimed at Moscow, Saint Petersburg, Nizhny Novgorod, and Sochi."

The admiral acquiesced towards Wood with compressed lips, bulging jaws, and a bouncing head movement.

"Thank you, Commander Thomas," Wood replied. "Please stand by for further instructions."

"Yes, Prime Minister."

In the space of a few minutes, Andrew Wood's phone rang out for the second time.

"Andrew, this is Bill. Not sure how much you're aware, but you've got a major situation," the US president professed. "The Russians have everything, including the kitchen sink, ready to send your way."

"Yes, I've just now been briefed on Koshenko's latest premonitions of impudence by my head of MI6," Wood responded diffidently.

"So you know you're in the shit?"

"I'm here with the admiral of our Royal fleet, Nicholas Stone, and we've just got off the phone with Robert Thomas, our captain aboard the HMS Vengeance—our warheads are mobilized and ready to be fired."

"Not sure if your guys at MI6 have told you the whole story or if indeed they have the full picture."

"Go on," Wood urged.

"I've just stepped out from our WMD control center at the Pentagon, where I've been with Tom

Ryan, our director WMD, and Chuck Miller, director from the International Atomic Energy Agency, who you know well, I'm sure," Peterson said. "Andrew, according to FINOS intelligence data the Russians have over four hundred Topol SS-25 road-mobile warhead missiles. Plus, they seem to have unearthed a mysterious Tsar Bomb. That thing has a blast capacity of over a hundred megatons. This strategic and tactical cocktail, if launched, could eliminate the entire conglomeration of your island. Your trident retaliation will look like a kid's air-gun attack in comparison."

"What?" Wood screamed in disbelief, looking at his head of secret intelligence service sitting opposite him.

Nairn sat there with his hands up. "Are you receiving additional intelligence data from the Americans?" he enquired naively.

Wood put his hand palm-up in front of his MI6 leader, drawing his ear closer to the phone.

"Andrew, we all know nuclear deployment is supposed to be a doctrine of deterrence, but this is getting out of hand," Peterson urged. "You've got to give Kasinov back to the Russians."

Wood's resilience was remarkable, even though he knew he was in deep rapids with no rescue plan. "Never." His pusillanimous character flaws were showing, and the citizens of Great Britain were the ones that would suffer. "I'm not going to bend over for Koshenko—not this time."

Chapter 47
Lotusman

Without frenzy or emotion, Roy arrived back in London. He knew he had to find a solution—and fast. Koshenko had promised "definitive and devastating action," and time was running out.

Roy had all the pieces of the puzzle. No one else had. He had relentlessly gathered everything, with Melanie's assistance, over the last number of days, but he knew he still had to weave all the parts together. He tried not to overthink it, but in the back of his mind, he knew the task was enormous and the consequences gargantuan. It was like trying to unlock some secret alchemists' algorithm that would provide eternal life, with just a beaker and a Bunsen burner. Time was of the essence.

Roy checked his watch. Three hours to go before Koshenko pulled the trigger.

Most people wouldn't know what to do. Roy knew what to do.

Although in his midtwenties at the time, Roy knew the collapse of the Soviet Union in 1992 had been probably the single most significant historical economic event of our time, and now the whole underlying assumptions around its demise were in question.

Someone else can rewrite the history books. I've got work to do.

After navigating a sinuous route from Washington, Roy arrived in Covent Garden to find Kasinov in the middle of the living room floor at Natasha's apartment. Natasha had left minutes earlier after receiving a call from Melanie. She had passed her access key to Roy outside before he made his way through a barrage of press that had assembled along the roadside. The Russian looked totally relaxed, deep into his yoga. He was seated in the lotus position, his hands together as if in repentance, his eyes closed in deep meditation. He was emotionless.

It was alpha versus alpha. Someone was going to win and someone was going to lose. Roy had no plans for losing.

"Mikhail, sorry to disturb you."

The Russian didn't move. "I used to do this every day in prison, you know. It kept me sane." Kasinov spoke in a condescending tone, his eyes remaining closed.

"Well, I'm glad you kept up the practice," Roy said. "You're going to need it where you're going."

Kasinov's eyes shot open wide. "What the hell are you talking about? The British will never hand me over," Kasinov snapped back with a growing confidence. "It would be political suicide against the US. After all, Roy, you know it was Peterson and Dunkley who masterminded this mission. In fact, you were employed by them, as well, if I'm not mistaken." He seemed reassured that he was standing on the hallowed moral high ground.

"Of course you're right, Mikhail," Roy replied. "Andrew Wood and Charles Browne wouldn't have the balls to hand you over."

Kasinov smirked back at him arrogantly, shifting his weight towards Roy.

"Unless, of course, you were in the UK illegally." Roy appended his sentence with clarification after watching Kasinov's haughty grin rise.

Kasinov emerged from his lotus, without savasana, to a regular standing position. He took a towel from around his neck and rubbed it against his forehead. "Well, as I'm here legally with a legitimate passport, I feel this conversation is completely perfunctory," the billionaire said dismissively.

He must have gone to a special school to learn such arrogance. I definitely should have left the bastard behind bars.

Roy didn't react. Instead, he eyed him coolly as he took out a letter from his inside pocket and placed it delicately on the table. "I'm afraid there's a problem with your passport, Mikhail. Have a look at this."

Kasinov glanced down at the paper and then back at Roy.

"You see? I went to visit your old friend's castle outside Dublin and found some paperwork surrounding the acquisition of your original passport back in 2001." Roy waited to see the Russian's reaction. There was none. "Unfortunately for you, it appears you bought it. That means you paid a government official for something that you thought you would never need, but liked the idea of having. Regardless, it's illegal." Roy moved suavely and seamlessly from a position of contract operative to one of citizen law enforcer without remorse. "David St. Ledger was the best man to arrange the name change. There's nothing wrong with that bit. That is perfectly legal."

Kasinov moved forward and picked up the paper. "So what's this, then? The proof?" He started waving the letter about like a magic wand. "Well done, Dr. Young. You found the evidence."

"No, it's not proof," Roy replied sharply. "It's better than that. It's a letter from the Irish foreign affairs minister rescinding the authenticity of your passport."

Kasinov's eyes almost popped out of his head.

"I took a little trip to Dublin on my way here," Roy added. "And after I made the minister aware that the passport was acquired illegally, he sat down and wrote the letter. It's amazing how efficient the Irish can be when they have to."

Despite his feigned nonchalance, Roy knew Kasinov was livid. He could sense it. He guessed that Kasinov had held a fictive and misguided belief in the protection that the illegitimate Irish passport had afforded him. Kasinov picked up the letter again and read it this time, shifting his weight from one foot to the other. His head was now tilted and his mouth had turned aquiline as he read its contents. His eyes seemed to protrude from their sockets like a pair of paparazzi zoom lenses.

Judging by the expression Kasinov wore, Roy assumed that he had never calculated the ramifications of his passport being withdrawn. If he had applied, the British would probably have given him political asylum, anyway—but he never applied. *Bad move, Mikhail.* He stared back at Roy with vengeance in his eyes. He looked very much like an injured rat trapped in a corner. Regardless, he remained incorrigible.

"Don't try and confuse me with the facts," Kasinov exclaimed with bemused regard. "You're just trying to test me."

"I'm afraid not, Mikhail. Might I remind you that invincibility isn't a virtue? Just so you're aware, this is a copy of the letter. I dropped the original at the British foreign secretary's office on my way over here. Charles Browne seemed quite pleased when I gave it to him."

"What did Browne say?"

"He said that your time had come to an end. I think he phrased it quite well, saying something about the time coming for the body to reject the organ." Roy shrugged. "I guess that's not good for you, Mikhail."

"Why are you being so vindictive?" the Russian demanded.

"You tried to have me killed, you'll remember. You added me to your list after you killed Vladimir and David St. Ledger. Nothing personal. No hard feelings. I would prefer to live, to be honest. So it's better if I don't have to keep looking over my shoulder the whole time to see your ugly face or one of your Chechen mobsters."

Kasinov pointed at Roy. "You and your clever girlfriend should have kept your noses out of my business."

"Some of your moves were a bit too extravagant to miss." Roy motioned to Kasinov's phone on the adjacent table. "I'm pretty sure if I checked your speed dial for KCU, or should I say 'KasOil Cleanup,' I would get hold of Alexander Zolotov."

"You don't know Alexei from a bar of soap."

"In fact, I do know him. I had a brief run-in with him in Angola in 1989. He masterminded the kidnapping of twelve innocent people, and killed a good friend of mine. Bag man then, hit man now. I should have killed him back then."

Kasinov said nothing.

"You also tried to bullshit me about the investor list. I knew that wasn't Vladimir's investment portfolio. It was a record of your illicit deals, cash in and cash out. I assume that's what Zolotov was looking for in Budapest. That's why you killed Vladimir: he knew the real Mikhail Kasinov. I just don't understand how anyone can kill their so-called best friend."

"He knew too much," Kasinov snorted. "Unfortunately, he had to go. Anyway, we never really got on. He was too confrontational and irreverent. Whenever I wanted to do something new, he would argue with me. He was holding me back."

Roy interjected. "I checked your Cypriot financial records."

The Russian's head pulled back suddenly. He said nothing.

"They show you made three payments, each for a million dollars US to a Chechen security services provider called Bezopasnost. Ironically, the payments were made in the same months of the three murders that your former head of security, Vitaly Kuznetsov, is currently in custody for. In January 2001, Klaus Muller. In May 2002, Olga Corneyeva. And again in September 2002, Vlada Morozov. They held up your oil field expansion plans or looked for more money from you, and you had them terminated. You set Kuznetsov up, didn't you?"

"He was supposed to get those deals done. He didn't. I had to clean up his mess. I'm a perfectionist. He's not. Call it OCD."

"You don't need to worry about OCD and perfection, Mikhail. You're never going to reach it."

Kasinov looked vacantly into space.

Roy didn't budge. "But worst of all, I know the real story about you and Alexander Zolotov and your surreptitious master plan. You were both equally complicit in bringing down the Soviet Union. You undervalued assets significantly to reduce Moscow's capacity to borrow badly needed funds, while Zolotov vastly overstated international military expenditure by almost twelve billion US. Your joint actions significantly dissipated Russia's sovereign wealth. Together, you destroyed the Soviet economy—and the Soviet Union. And for what? So you could buy the rich oil and gas assets at basement prices and turn two hundred fifty million dollars into twenty billion pounds a few years later? Well, I'm sorry, Mikhail, but the game is up."

"It wasn't just me who gained from the downfall of the Soviet Union," Kasinov said with his arms raised in renunciation. "I wasn't the only oligarch in town. There were several of them. They all participated in the purchasing of undervalued assets."

"You're right, of course. How could I be so naive? The only difference is they didn't kill anyone."

Kasinov let out a roar of laughter. "Now you've really lost the plot, Roy."

"I think we've both established that I'm no longer a gold member of the Mikhail Kasinov fan club."

"You never were a member."

"I never applied."

"You think this is a game?"

"No, I don't. It's more of a dare, really. Whoever dares, wins. Unfortunately, you dared and lost. Your time is up, Mr. Oligarch."

The Russian held his hands to his head and started pacing around the room like a madman ready to attack. "I'll give you a billion dollars," the Russian said, beseechingly pointing towards his computer. "I'll transfer it to your account right now, and we can make this whole thing go away."

Roy's expression indicated he was unmoved by the offer. If anything, by this juncture, he thought Kasinov's supplications were embarrassing. "I don't think the juice is worth the squeeze on that one," he said in a humorous tone.

Kasinov stood ashen, perplexed, and speechless.

"There may be a MasterCard solution for everything else in your life," Roy added unashamedly. "But there are some things money can't buy. Times change, Mikhail—values don't.

Thanks for the offer, but to be honest, I would have no idea what to do with that amount of money."

The pantomime continued as Kasinov, no longer sanguine about his freedom, offered an ultimatum. "So what are we going to do now?"

Roy paused and looked at his watch. One hour to go.

He could see the oligarch was about to capitulate. "It's quite simple, Mikhail. You will peacefully make your way with me now up to Number six Kensington Palace Gardens, where you will surrender to your ambassador. You can tell Mr. Pushkin that you have suddenly been overcome with a bout of homesickness. In return, I won't reveal anything of what we have just discussed. If you decide not to take me up on my offer, that's okay." Roy glanced at his watch. "However, if I don't call Melanie Bauer in the next five minutes and tell her that everything is fine," Roy said, glancing behind him, "then the British police, Interpol, and your good friend at Sky News, Angela Boddington, will all be fighting for a space in that lift shaft faster than you can get yourself back into that lotus position." Roy pointed at Kasinov's lilac yoga mat. "Your choice, Mikhail."

"But what about you?" the Russian exclaimed. "You're guilty, just like me. You broke me out."

"I thought you might bring that up," Roy said with a curt nod. "I took a little trip to Moscow

yesterday between coming here and my brief
stopover in Dublin. I went back to see Alexei
Lugovoy. Thank you for the introduction, by the
way. I cut a deal with him. It was very simple: I
deliver you, and they don't prosecute me. They
don't care about me, Mikhail. You're the main
attraction for those boys."

The nonplussed Russian shook his head in
disbelief.

"You are—or were—a fervent catalyst about to
ignite a global nuclear outbreak because you
threatened their presidency," Roy announced.
"Bad move, Mikhail. I mean, did you really think
that you could just supplant the president of
Russia?"

"I never wanted to be president," Kasinov
uttered. "It would be too boring for me."

"Of course."

There was no response from Kasinov, but Roy
could see his jaw tightening.

"Just one question, Mikhail—something that's
puzzled me for a while. Why did you employ me
to find Sakharshenko's killer when it was you who
had him murdered?"

"I was hoping that you would take out the
Russian government—or alternatively, they would
take you out," Kasinov responded arrogantly.
"Either one would have done. It would have been
a win-win for me, whichever way it went."

Roy laughed back at him.

Kasinov looked bewildered, like a long-distance runner who had just finished a marathon and was told that he still had another mile to complete. By this stage, his abrasive personality was starting to ablate, and he knew he and his accomplices were accursed to repentance for their homicidal acts and their destruction of the Soviet Union.

Roy guessed Kasinov had figured out that he was destined for an unsolicited return to Siberia. Roy knew exactly where he was taking the Russian defector.

Chapter 48
Cognitive Dissonance

Roy arrived back in Porte Santé later that same evening. He made his way straight to the villa, wasting no time in briefing Melanie on how he had interrupted Kasinov's yoga routine earlier in the day.

"Where is he now?" Melanie asked anxiously.

"I dropped him off at the embassy," Roy replied. "It was a bit strange over there. All the Russian staff except Pushkin had returned to Moscow. He was in the process of packing up his office and about to head for the airport. Just as well he was there. Otherwise, I would have left Kasinov with the receptionist. The poor girl nearly fell off her chair when we walked in."

"What is it with men? I don't get it?"

"Get what?"

"Why they walk around with their finger on the self-destruct button most of the time," Melanie said irritably. "It's as if they're just looking for some reason to push it."

"Male logic, my dear," Roy replied sarcastically, holding up his hands in simulated submission. "In fact, it's ego before logic, I'm afraid. But thank you for stereotyping us."

"I don't mean all men," she corrected. "Just some."

"Of course," Roy replied with a wink. "I knew what you meant." Then he added, "Anyway, thanks for all your help—couldn't have done this without you."

"You're welcome. I hope all the stuff I gave you helped in some way. It was all a bit circumstantial, though."

"It was great."

"What was it that convinced you he was guilty?"

"His handwriting."

"Huh?"

"We both know his demeanor was pretty erratic. One minute, he was extremely cool, calm, and collected; the next, a rancorous megalomaniac. It was a classic case of schizophrenia-like psychosis. That was enough for me to want to dig a little deeper."

"What has his handwriting got to do with all that?"

"He wrote down a note with some directions to the Arsenal box. I thought nothing of it at the time, but when I saw it again, I did a little research. His writing style suggests that he's got a few issues going on."

"What issues are those?"

"In no particular order, his writing style confirmed that he is delusional, psychopathic, and schizophrenic."

"Oh dear. Not a very appealing combination! What did he say when you put all the facts together in front of him?"

"It was funny, actually. First, he threw a few expected expletives at me, along with denials and threats. Then, when all that failed, there came the blackmail. Attractive, but I earnestly declined. The epilogue was the best, though—he said he never wanted to be the president of Russia!"

"I don't really get that. Why would he say that now?" Melanie asked in a totally confused tone. "I thought that was everything to him—his whole life, the next chapter."

"I don't think he meant it, to be honest," Roy answered. "Ergo, he really did want to be president."

"I know he's a bit of a psychopath, but why do you think he would say something if he didn't mean it?"

"It's a common case of cognitive dissonance."

"Cognitive dissonance?" Melanie queried.

"It has actually been around for more than fifty years. It's like the linkage between a person's attitude on one hand and behavior on the other. The focus of the cognitive dissonance theory is attitude and behavior change. You see, there's an invisible continuum between the two, where a change in one affects the other. It's like an emotional counterbalance to return a person's state of mind to equilibrium—back to their comfort zone. Simply said, some people, when faced with the reality of a situation they feel some discomfort with, tend to say certain things just to make themselves feel better about that situation. People do it all the time, saying things they know aren't really true. But it makes them feel better. That's cognitive dissonance."

"Oh."

~~~

After Roy dropped Kasinov off at the Russia embassy, the former oligarch was arrested and extradited back to Moscow that same day.

Pushkin called Roy later that evening and updated him on events. Roy figured the Russian ambassador was pretty clever, after all. Not only was Pushkin determined to wait until the very last minute before leaving the embassy for Moscow, he also convinced Kasinov to call Zolotov to come to the embassy to meet him. Along with Zolotov came his accomplice, a baby-faced, short, and rotund man by the name of Pavel Karamov. Both were detained for questioning by the police and Interpol in connection with murders in Ireland and Hungary.

Although Roy had operated on both sides of the table, he had brought Kasinov to justice. It was a natural conclusion. Capturing Alexei Zolotov, he felt was a bonus. He had successfully vanquished his nemesis from the Angolan border war. It almost felt like he had done this for Leon.

Chapter 49
Siberia Revisited

Exactly one month to the day, Mikhail Kasinov was back in Central Siberia. This time, though, there was no Mil Mi-14 helicopter to transport him. There was no welcoming committee, no hugs and kisses, and no Airbus. Instead, he sat ashen-faced, completely desegregated in the surrounding snow-laden landscape, perched on the rear bench of a Kamaz armored security vehicle. His hands were cuffed to a central roll bar, his tired body molded to the worn leather seat, and his Herculean anarchism no doubt already etched in posterity into the blueprints of future historical text. Sheepishly, he glanced back from inside the Kamaz truck at an awaiting anthology of media and penitentiary aides.

Destination: Krasnokamensk penitentiary facility.

His story had captured the attention of the world. Why wouldn't it have? He almost brought the world's greatest superpowers to their knees. The media had played their role in creating the uproar, and they knew it. For weeks, they had venerated Kasinov's plan and campaigns. However, after his arrest and subsequent precipitous slide in popularity, there weren't too many media apologists left in the press galleries. Most of them had seamlessly performed a perfect turncoat maneuver. Those that had been disproportionately extreme in their veneration were now unsurprisingly taciturn.

Snow had fallen heavily for two weeks, and the snowflake blanket up ahead was un-trodden by foot or by vehicle. The afternoon air was moist, and several clouds obscured the skyline as the outside temperature had dropped to a low of -47 degrees Fahrenheit. The Kamaz truck pulled away to the supple sounds of tires crunching against the snow, setting off on an epic 550-mile journey to Krasnokamensk. In the audience, there were a few brave photographers that had made it to the final point before Kasinov left for his destiny. Their clicking cameras were the only other sound. There they took their final images of him.

Inside the Kamaz, Kasinov contemplated his future with a forlorn, dilapidated grimace. The only thing he could envision was the life of an ascetic Buddhist monk. After a short while, the vehicle was out of sight, and so, too, was the fallen oligarch.

~~~

Back on Roy's Florence patio, a bright moon appeared above, nestled in amongst a starlit sky as a bottle of Tignanello was uncorked and poured into two large bow-shaped wine glasses.

"How are you feeling?" Melanie enquired with a cheesy grin.

"Well, Mel, it's like the old motto I picked up from working with the US Navy SEALs in Angola: *the only easy day was yesterday.* I can honestly say it's the first time this adage has rung true for me."

Roy's phone rang as he placed the Tignanello back on the table.

"Hello," he answered.

"Hello, Roy. Clay Parker here."

"Yes, Clay."

"I received the email you sent with the encrypted scanned documents attached."

"Okay, good. Then you know the problem."

"We had no idea that Kasinov was a murderer or in any way connected with the downfall of the Soviet Union," Parker claimed. "I assume our confidentiality clause will be upheld."

"Of course, Clay. I won't pass this information to the media."

"Very good. I knew I could trust you from the moment I met you."

"There is one thing, though."

"What's that?"

"I'm not the only one in possession of this information. I had some research assistants on this one. They have everything that you have."

"I trust you can control them."

"It's possible."

Pause. "What do you mean by possible?"

"Back in the Angolan Civil War, you caused the death of a good friend of mine. Not you directly, but your government's continued interference caused the Russian-Cuban consortium to take the war to a different level, prolonging military combat. My friend's name was Leon Chamois. We went to school together. He was an only son. Leon was twenty-four years of age when he died. He had a wife and two young kids. His parents and family still live alone in Knysna, on the Cape. I set up a fund to help the family survive after Leon passed away. He was the breadwinner in the family. To answer your question, yes, I can turn possibility into certainty."

"Are you trying to blackmail me?"

"Absolutely not. Are you trying to silence me?"

"How much are we looking at?"

"Well, let's see, Clay . . . How much is a life worth these days at the National Clandestine Services?"

"We don't have a generic number for that."

"Let me give you one, then: ten million dollars."

"I don't have authority for that sort of expenditure. You've got to be kidding me."

"No problem, Clay. I understand."

"Good."

"I will just deal with someone who does. I'm sure Bill Peterson would be delighted to be doing a deal with me on this."

A heavy sigh rattled through the receiver. "He's a busy man, Roy. He's got a lot on his plate."

"I know about the relationship between Dunkley and Peterson. I'm not a fool."

"Okay, fine. I'll make it five million."

"You know, Clay, you really will have to look at your due diligence procedures in these kinds of things in the future. There seems to be some major holes in your intelligence networks, and most likely leadership. I'm quite surprised that you guys didn't pick up the fact that Kasinov was a bit special."

"Special?"

"Just a minor detail that your boys missed. You know that he's psychopathic, schizophrenic, and delusional? I think I included some information on that in the pack I sent to you. That doesn't even get started on Zeron's interest in this whole mess."

There was a pause on the line. Roy could hear Parker's intense breathing resonating back at him. "Okay, okay, Roy," the National Clandestine Services director submitted. "Ten million it is. And that's it."

"Nice doing business with you, Clay. I'll send you on the bank account details."

Roy pressed the off button on his mobile and smiled quietly to himself.

Retribution at last.

~~~

The following morning, Melanie and Roy awoke early to the beauty of a Florence winter sunrise inviting them to celebrate with a delicate collection of pastries and espresso. All around, smells of freshly brewed coffee engulfed the air. They proceeded to Piazza della Signoria and sat at a café, where they watched an eclectic mix of business professionals, tourists, and shopping enthusiasts pass by.

Bespectacled in dark sunglasses, they gazed at each other and noticed their own reflections in each other's lenses. They smiled, and Melanie let out a sigh of happiness.

She smelt of cherry blossoms.

He still smelt of Chanel.

Roy thought it was a good time to place on the table the folded copy of *The Florence Times* that he had picked up on his way to the café. After they had ordered their food, he opened it up. There on the front page was a photo of Kasinov seated inside the Kamaz truck, gazing back out through the rear window, destitute and vindictive. It was almost as if he was staring right back at the two of them. The headline, embossed across the top of the front page, was unmistakable: MIDDLE OF NOWHERE.

Roy tutted derisively. "Poor Mikhail," he said, shaking his head slowly.

Melanie chuckled. "Lucky Natasha."

"Oh, that reminds me. I need to let her know about a new philanthropic project she's getting involved in."

Melanie's head turned in anticipation. "And what's that?"

"Santa Maria Nuova Hospital."

Acknowledgements

To Bill Greenleaf, for all your literary support throughout the finishing phases of the project. It has been both invaluable, and educational.

To Dr. Liam Casserly, for all your support, aiding my navigation through unfamiliar terrain such as morgues and emergency operating theatres. A medical education!

To Brian Ryan and Colm Doyle, for all your support in military vernacular, especially outlining the key differences between non-commissioned and commissioned ranks! Plus your wisdom and experience in the military hierarchy from across the globe; from battalions and brigades to details and companies.

To David Leahy, for helping me describe some of the world's greatest architecture and scenery, and realize its potential.

To John Kinlough, for all your support throughout the project. Hope you liked your castle!

To Layne Walker at New Friends Publishing for helping get the story out there!

To Fin, for all your help, and your reinforcement, in connecting the dots throughout the story.

Coming later in 2014

Roy Young is back in
The Vatican Deception

After being approached by Sofia Russo, a young and extremely fashionable Italian prosecutor, Roy Young is commandeered from a military training consultation he is about to commence and immersed in the middle of a Vatican centered machination that takes him from his villa in Florence onto a pivoting tour of the most salubrious addresses across the Mediterranean.

Following the death of Sofia's mother—who as a young woman spent several years working as a housekeeper at the Vatican, which included working for his Holiness John Paul 1, during his 33-day tenure—and the revelation of a mysterious secret she held for most of her life, delivered on her death bed—Roy together with Sofia pilot their way through the honchos and deputies of the Vatican Bank, the Jesuits, pharmaceutical majors, and two of Italy's most notorious Mafia groups—*Potente* and *Impavido*—in search of the meaning of the revelation, where it seems everyone holds some esoteric wedge of a more sinister master plan.

Roy and Sofia dodge capture and death more than once after coming head-to-head with Cardinal Alejandro Barros, CEO of the Vatican

Bank and Monaco-based Reiner Hoffmann, Chairman of Hoffmann Enterprises, a global corporation with holdings in several mega pharmaceutical firms. With both organizations sharing an unhealthy relationship through the partnership of StemTech—an emerging and extremely successful medical research company about to make a major innovative breakthrough in Stem Cell implant research—it would appear that it is StemTech's discovery, and its proposition to extend the human life by up to ten years, that binds common interests amongst an assortment of antagonists. But then again, everything is not as it appears as Roy in his quest to help Sofia determine the provenance of her mother's secret, uncovers a series of malicious commercial arrangements materializing beneath the veneer of pioneering advancements in genetic treatment.

About the Author

Jon Paris is a consultant and investor in the oil and gas industry with over 25 years experience. He previously held the position of chief executive of a major energy consulting and services organization. Prior to that he spent a number of years with the one of the world's largest mining corporations. His educational pursuits took him from a university degree in engineering, a master's in business administration and a doctorate in management and behaviour. He lives in the southwest of Ireland with his wife and three sons.

28029320R00344

Made in the USA
Charleston, SC
29 March 2014